To NOHEMI NAISH
Best wishes.
Stay Sa-
[signature]
Rom 8:28

Bishop's Gate

ANDREW G. NELSON

Published by Huntzman Enterprises

Huntzman Enterprises
Edinburg, IL. 62531

First Printing: March 2015

ISBN-10: 0996133410
ISBN-13: 978-0-9961334-1-8

Printed in the United States of America
1 3 5 7 9 10 8 6 4 2

DEDICATION

To my wife Nancy; without your love, support and constant
encouragement this book would never have been possible.
Thank you for always believing in me.

And to God, through whom all things are possible.

Romans 8:28

Other Titles by

Andrew G. Nelson

The future belongs to he who has the bishops.

Siegbert Tarrasch (1862 – 1934)

CHAPTER ONE

Bellevue Hospital, Manhattan, New York City
Thursday, February 14th, 2013 – 4:35 p.m.

Maguire had faced death so many times before that its sting had ceased to hold any real meaning to him. That was until now.

He sat in the darkened room staring at her. The dim lights positioned above the hospital bed casting a cold, bluish hue over her pale skin. As he watched, her chest rose slowly and then fell, her breathing orchestrated by the ventilator that she was presently connected to.

It had been less than twenty-four hours since she had been shot by the terrorist, Bashir Al Karim, whom Maguire had then dispatched to the after-life to search for his seventy-two virgins.

The single bullet that had torn into her had wreaked havoc on her body. It had hit one of her ribs causing the soft lead bullet to fragment, sending tiny shards of metal and bone coursing through her body. She had spent more than ten hours in the operating room as the surgeons repaired the damage to her lung and blood vessels.

Melody Anderson had survived the shooting, but she was not out of the woods just yet.

Maguire leaned back in the chair and rubbed his weary eyes. He had already been awake for over thirty-six hours and he was beginning to feel the effects. It had been much easier for him when everyone was around, but now, as he sat here alone, it became harder to block out the mechanical sounds that signaled just how close he came to losing her.

Earlier in the day the hospital had politely begun to request people to leave. Rich and Mary had put up the biggest argument, but James had reminded him that he still had the Department to run and Mary had the kids to take care of. Besides, it was obvious that she wasn't going anywhere quick and he would need the help over the coming days. Before he left, Rich had contacted the commanding officer of the 13th Precinct and had them assign a fixed post to her room. At the very least she would have around-the-clock police protection.

Maguire's security detail remained behind as well. They'd worked it out amongst themselves to ensure that a team would be with him at all times. The evening shift had just come back on duty and was waiting down the hall, in a room the hospital had set aside for them. It was the least they could do for the girlfriend of the NYPD's 1st deputy police commissioner. It also probably didn't hurt that she was *that* Melody Anderson as well.

He looked up at the clock on the wall. He knew that he would have to leave soon, as well, but for different reasons. There was so much to do and time was not on his side.

Genevieve Gordon was still missing and he couldn't help but think that her disappearance was somehow related to Keith Banning, a person whom they had all previously believed to be dead.

It seemed that even in *death*, he was still playing this twisted game.

Still, the thought of leaving Melody's side troubled him, even though he knew there was nothing more that he could do. She seemed so frail, so weak, as if her hold on this life was tenuous, at best. It was a far cry from the strong, defiant woman he had seen a few hours earlier. He didn't know what he would do if he lost her.

Just then, the door opened slowly and Monsignor Francis O'Connor stepped inside the room.

"Didn't you just leave here?" Maguire asked with a weak smile.

"We have a new cook at the rectory," the priest replied. "The food is much better *here*."

Maguire laughed.

"Besides, the two of you are the neediest sheep in my flock right now."

The man shrugged off the navy blue NYPD overcoat he was wearing, hanging it on the back of the door with his uniform hat and took the seat across from Maguire.

O'Connor was the chief of the NYPD's Chaplain Unit. A group of multi-faith ministers that tended to the spiritual needs of the Department and its officers.

While they were civilians, each held a rank equivalent to an inspector, while O'Connor, as the head of the unit, held a rank equivalent to an assistant chief.

Maguire had always found the priest's Irish brogue to be comforting. It reminded him so much of the conversations he had shared with his own late father.

"By the way, I sent that nice lad from your security detail, Luke Jackson, to get us some coffee."

"Thanks, I can certainly use a cup."

"Besides," O'Connor said, "I didn't really have anything going on tonight and I figured you could use a break from here as well."

"I'm almost too afraid to leave," Maguire replied.

"That's understandable, James. I've spent countless hours with families in your situation and I have yet to hear any of them say 'well, *nothing more I can do here, guess I'll go get something to eat.*'"

"I'd be hard pressed to get anything more than coffee in me right now."

"It was the Madame de Stael who once said '*We understand death for the first time when he puts his hand upon one whom we love.*'"

"You know something," Maguire said. "I've always wondered, do you study obscure quotes or do you just make them up as you go along?"

"James, you should know better than to ask a question like that," O'Connor replied with a smile. "We're Irish."

Maguire was about to reply when there was a knock on the door.

Detective Luke Jackson stepped inside and handed each man a cup of coffee.

"Thank you, Luke," Maguire said.

"No problem, Boss," the man replied. "By the way, Commissioner Stargold called and wanted to tell you there's food waiting for you at his place."

"Thanks, I'll call him back. Have you guys eaten yet?"

"Yeah, the staff here has been great. They brought us up some food before."

"Good, I don't need you guys feeling like me."

"We're fine," Jackson replied. "Let us know if you need anything else."

"I will."

Jackson stepped back out and closed the door behind him.

Maguire removed the lid from the Styrofoam cup and took a sip.

"That's probably a good idea," O'Connor said. "Why don't you get out of here for a while?"

Maguire cradled the container in his hand and stared out the window. He knew the priest was right. Despite what he wanted to believe, he knew he wasn't doing anyone any good sitting here in the room.

Dr. Julius Rothman, Chair of the Department of Surgery, had stopped in earlier in the day to bring him up to speed on what the surgeons had done. The surgery had gone well, but she would be kept sedated as long as she was on the ventilator. They would monitor her and begin to reassess her condition tomorrow.

O'Connor could see he was having a hard time with it all.

"Go, James," he said. "I promise you, I won't leave her side. If anything changes I will call you immediately."

Maguire took a deep breath, exhaling slowly, and stood up.

"Thank you," James said.

"Don't mention it," O'Connor replied. "Besides, I just got one of those new-fangled e-book readers and downloaded a book on Father Francis P. Duffy. I'm working on material for my second career as a *seanchaí*."

"You? A story-teller?" Maguire said, as he put on his coat. "What a novel idea."

"Go ahead and scoff," O'Connor said. "At least Melody won't complain."

Maguire looked down at the man.

"There's nothing to say, James. Go get some food and allow yourself to relax a bit. She'll be fine."

Maguire nodded as he stepped out into the hallway. He made his way down to where Jackson and Detective Peter May were camped out and peeked into the room.

"You need something, Boss?" May asked, setting his newspaper down on the table.

"I've decided to take the commissioner up on his offer," Maguire replied.

"Thank God," Jackson replied. "I don't think I could have listened to another sports show telling me how bad the Knicks are doing."

"Eh, they'll probably win just enough games to make the playoffs and then break your heart," Maguire said.

"I'm used to it," Jackson said, turning off the television. "I'm a Mets fan as well."

"I can't help you with that," Maguire replied. "You're on your own."

"That's what Pete keeps telling me," Jackson said as he put on his coat.

"He needs to come to the dark side and become a Yankee's fan," May replied.

"I need to find the two of you some productive hobbies."

The three men made their way out of the hospital and toward the waiting Suburban. Once in the back, Maguire removed his cell phone and called Rich.

"Is everything okay?" Stargold asked.

"Yeah, I'm on my way over to you," Maguire replied.

"I'll let Mary know," Rich said. "The food is still hot."

"Thanks."

"How is she doing?"

"Doc said we'll know more tomorrow."

"Who's with her now?" Rich asked.

"Monsignor O'Connor," James said. "Have you heard from Gregor?"

"They have the car locked down and are going over it. He sent me a scan of the package that was left behind in the car. I'll show you when you get here."

"I should be there in about fifteen minutes."

"Okay, I'll see you then."

Maguire ended the call and dialed Gregor Ritter.

"Hello," the man answered.

Maguire could hear the weariness in the man's voice, even through his German accent.

"Did you find anything?"

"*Nein*," Gregor replied. "The car was clean. The only thing that should not have been in there was the package."

"Rich said you sent him a scan. Did you open it?"

"Yes, we checked it for any explosive residue first, but it was clean. There is a note inside from Banning, addressed to you, along with a pair of women's panties."

Maguire leaned back against the seat, he felt drained. This was getting more surreal with each passing moment.

He had spent months tracking down Banning, only to watch the clues evaporate as quickly as they had come. He had always believed that it was all part of some grandiose chess game that the man was playing in his mind. Each move engineered to wear Maguire down until he slipped up and Banning could force him into checkmate. Unlike the game, this conclusion would be final.

At least it was, up until he'd been notified by the state police that Banning had died in a car accident, along with Lena Marx, somewhere in the mountains of northwest Maine.

The package that was left behind, after Gen had been kidnapped, would seem to indicate that the rumors of Keith Banning's death had been greatly exaggerated.

But they matched the DNA, he thought.

"What does the note say?" Maguire asked.

"Jimmy, it was good seeing you up at the cabin last October. It has been awhile, so I just wanted to let you know that we have some unfinished business we need to settle. In case you forgot, I'm sending along a trinket to remind you that you still have something to lose. I'll be in touch, Keith."

"I swear I'm going to skull fuck this prick when I get my hands on him."

"But if he's dead...." Gregor said.

"I know," Maguire replied. "How does a dead man send a package? I'm still working on that part. Did you find out anything on Gen's phone?"

"The last signal was from a tower outside Greenfield, Massachusetts. Then it went dead."

James had to force himself not to laugh. There was nothing inherently funny about what Gregor had said, but rather the way he said it. His heavy accent reminded Maguire of the former governor of California.

"Well, I doubt that the battery just died," Maguire said. "Which means that he's just toying with us."

"I'll keep checking to see if it pings off any other towers," Ritter replied. "How is Melody?"

"No change," James replied. "Probably won't know anything more until tomorrow. I'm just heading over to Rich's to get something to eat."

"Do you want me to come in?"

"No," Maguire said. "I appreciate it, but there's no point. I'm not doing any good here either. Melody's in the best hands at the hospital and right now we need to focus on finding Gen. Just keep digging on your end and I will call you back."

"Okay, James, I will talk to you later."

Maguire ended the call just as they came out of the Battery Park Underpass and headed up West Street. It then made a left onto Thames, navigating the back streets to the apartment building. The Suburban pulled into the underground parking lot, and took up a spot next to Rich's vehicle.

Melody had given her companies apartment, in Battery Park City, to Rich and Mary, after he'd been offered the police commissioners slot, by the newly elected mayor, Alan McMasters.

"If you guys want to go and grab some coffee or something I'll be fine," Maguire said.

"Are you sure?" Jackson asked.

"Yeah, I'll be here for a while," he replied. "I'll call you and give you a heads-up when I'm getting ready to leave."

"Okay, Boss."

Maguire got out of the truck and made his way to the elevator, riding it up to the penthouse apartment on the twenty-second floor. When the doors opened he stepped out into the foyer, where a small desk had been set up for Rich's security detail.

"Evening, Commissioner," said the detective sitting at the desk. "I didn't get a chance to tell you earlier how sorry we all are about what happened to Ms. Anderson."

"Thanks, Joe," Maguire replied. "I appreciate that."

Maguire walked up to the door, keying in the security code for the electronic lock, and entered the apartment.

Mary Stargold was the first to greet him.

"Come here," she said, wrapping her arms tightly around him. "How's she doing?"

"She's a fighter," Maguire replied. "Thank God."

She released her hold on him and took a step back, looking into his eyes.

"How are *you* doing?" she asked.

"Ask me after she comes out of it."

Mary frowned.

"Come with me," she said. "You need something to eat or you're not going to be any use to her."

She took his hand and led him toward the dining room.

"Sit down and I'll get your plate."

Maguire removed his jacket, hanging it on the back of the chair and sat down. A moment later, Mary reappeared carrying a plate and a glass, which she sat down in front of him.

"Rich is upstairs, talking to the girls," she explained. "This has hit them pretty hard. They've both come to love Mel."

"I know," he said. "She loves them too."

"We haven't even told them about Gen," Mary said. "How's Gregor doing?"

"He's a professional. He's holding it together."

Just then they heard Rich's footsteps coming down the staircase from the 2nd floor.

"I'll let you two guys talk," Mary said. "If there is anything you need, just let me know."

"Actually, I am going to need you to cover for me at the hospital soon."

"Do I even want to know?" she asked.

"Probably not," Rich replied, as he took a seat at the table.

"Make him eat," Mary said, as she got up. "And *don't* let him do anything stupid."

"Cause I have had such good luck with that in the past," Rich replied sarcastically.

"You two realize that I can hear you," Maguire said, as he took a bite of food.

"I'm going upstairs," Mary said. "Say goodbye before you leave."

"I will."

After she left, Maguire looked over at Rich.

"You have that scan Gregor sent you?"

"Yeah," he replied, removing the folded paper from his shirt pocket and handed it to James.

Maguire pushed the half eaten plate off to the side, opened the paper and stared at the image. It was a scan of a small manila envelope. In the upper left hand corner was a return address with the name K. Banning. They would have to track down the address, but Maguire already knew it would be fictitious. He stared at the delivery address with his name on it. Banning was making a statement with this. There was nothing *veiled* here, just a clear reminder to Maguire that their *game* was not over yet.

"So what are you planning on doing now?"

Maguire looked up from the paper, staring at Rich for a moment.

"This has got to end," he said. "Until I see the life drain out of that bastard with my own eyes, I cannot rest."

"I understand that," Rich replied. "But Melody needs you right now."

It was the first time that Maguire had been faced with a dilemma like this. He didn't want to leave Melody's side, but Gen was in the hands of that maniacal bastard and he didn't want to imagine what she was going through. Melody had the best medical care available right now and that left only one real choice for him to make.

"You and I both know that as long as Banning remains free, everyone is still in danger," Maguire said. "And now the clock is ticking on Gen's life."

"We've got a ton of resources available to us, surely we can find them."

"What did all those resources do for the task force? Banning was tracked throughout the entire northeast, for the better part of nine months, and every time they came up short. Then, out of the blue, they said he was dead, had the body and everything. That didn't work out very well either. Then again, perhaps I'm being too cynical, maybe Gen was kidnapped by a friggin' ghost."

"You don't actually believe that, do you?"

"At this point it's about as plausible an idea as anything else," Maguire said. "Christ, Rich, I don't know what to believe anymore. All I know is that Melody is lying in a hospital bed and that *sonofabitch* has Gen."

"You want a drink?" Rich asked.

"God knows I could use one."

Rich headed into the kitchen to get the drinks, while Maguire got up from the table and made his way into the living room. He stared out the large, panoramic window, which overlooked the Hudson River, toward the Statue of Liberty, that sat in the middle of the harbor.

"Here you go," Rich said, handing a glass to James.

"Thanks," he replied.

"Let's go sit down and weigh out our options."

James followed Rich through the sliding glass doors, which led out onto an enclosed patio, and took a seat in one of the lounge chairs.

"So what are you going to do?" Rich asked.

Maguire took a sip of whiskey and set the glass down on the small table in front of him. It was a question that he had been wrestling with for the better part of the day.

It was only six weeks into this administration and they had already been through so much, a baptism by fire, figuratively as well as literally. He didn't want to, but he knew what he had to do.

Maguire reached into his pocket, removing the small, black leather case that contained his police shield and ID card. He laid it on the table in front of Rich.

"I need to take a leave of absence," Maguire said.

Rich stared down at the leather case lying on the table. He reached over and grudgingly picking it up.

"You don't have to do this," Rich said. "Not this way."

"Yes I do, buddy," James replied. "We both know how this ends."

"No, we don't," Stargold replied.

"You can tell yourself that all you want, Rich, but the truth is, this is a one way ticket for either him or me. He won't surrender and I have no intention of *arresting* him."

"Do you know what you're saying, James?" Rich asked.

"I do," he replied, picking up his glass and taking another sip.

"Banning's not your common criminal, Rich, and you know that. To him this is a game, something that he enjoys. He gets a thrill out of it, the way someone else watches a baseball or football game on television. Arresting him won't do anything more than prolonging the inevitable. Besides, I don't believe that he will even allow himself to be taken in."

"What makes you say that?"

"He has too much invested in this to go off quietly to prison. He knows the charges he is facing and the thought of not being able to see this through, to its final conclusion, would be too much for him to stand. No, trust me on this, at the end of this game one of us will lose."

"Why not turn it over to the locals?" Rich asked. "Tell the task force he's alive and to reopen the case."

"What locals? For all we know he could be anywhere from New York to Canada. Hell, for shits and giggles, he could have made a left at Yonkers and is now living in Chicago enjoying some *deep dish* pizza."

"You sure I can't change your mind?"

"No, and you know I'm right about this."

Rich leaned over and handed the shield case back to Maguire.

"Put that back in your pocket, First Dep, that's an order."

Maguire stared down at the black leather case.

"Rich, if this doesn't end well you're going to need plausible deniability. At least you can say that I was on a leave of absence and acting outside the scope of my employment. That should at least keep the wolves in the media off your ass, can't make any guarantees about the sharks in city hall."

"James, I have known you for the better part of a dozen years. In that time, not only have I known you as a great cop, but you're my best friend. Hell, you're the brother I never had, for that matter. Not only would I trust you with my life, but I'd trust you with the lives of my family. I guess what I am trying to say is, if I have to choose between my job and you, there really is no choice. Besides, I make a habit of not worrying about shit storms until they actually happen."

"I don't know what to say," James replied, as he accepted the shield case back.

"There's nothing to say, James. I just wish I could go hunting with you, but someone's got to be the responsible adult and put things back together here at home."

"Uh huh," Maguire said with a laugh, handing his glass to Rich. "Go get me a refill, Mr. *Responsible*."

"There is something to be said about having designated drivers."

As Rich headed off to the kitchen, Maguire withdrew the folded paper from his pocket. He examined it again, looking for some kind of clue. Nothing about it seemed unusual, just your typical piece of mail.

A moment later Rich returned, handing James his glass, and sat down.

"Do you want me to call Crime Scene and have them go out? They can dust it for prints?"

"What's the point?" James replied. "I know who sent it."

"True, but we might be able to get an idea where it's been."

Maguire continued to stare at the image. Something was wrong with what he was seeing.

"Fuck me," he said softly.

"What?" Rich asked.

"It's so friggin' obvious."

"What are you talking about?"

"The package," James said. "He left it in the car, but the damn thing has a postmark on it, from Belkin, New Hampshire."

"Let me see that."

Maguire handed Rich the paper as he removed his cell phone and placed a call.

"Hey there, *Mister First Deputy Commissioner*," a female voice said on the other end. "I thought you didn't have time for *your old partner anymore.*"

"Alex, I need you to do me a favor and I need it done ASAP," Maguire replied.

Four hundred miles away, James' old partner, Alex Taylor, sat up on the couch. She sensed the urgency in his voice.

"Whatever you need, James, just name it."

CHAPTER TWO

Belkin, New Hampshire
Friday, February 15th, 2013 – 8:13 a.m.

Alex Taylor pulled the black, unmarked Dodge Charger into the parking spot in front of the U.S. Postal Service office in downtown Belkin.

She cracked open the car's window and pulled a pack of cigarettes from her pocket, lighting one up.

In her mind, she replayed the conversation she had with Maguire the night before. At first she had thought that he was playing a joke on her. She had heard about the attack in the city, but a kidnapping? It was all too hard to process, even now.

Back when the two of them had been partners in the Seven-Three Precinct they used to refer to cops, who had an especially bad run of luck, as *black clouds*. They would cringe when one of these officers would show up on a job as back-up, knowing that things would only get worse. Maguire, it seemed, was now experiencing a run of *black cloud 2.0*.

One thing was for certain, whoever this Keith Banning was; he had a major league hard-on for Maguire, one that apparently extended from the grave itself.

From the seat next to her, she picked up the photo he had e-mailed her the night before and looked it over. The image showed a small manila envelope with the postmark from the post office in front of her. She rolled it up and slid it into the interior pocket of her jacket.

Alex took a final drag off the cigarette and then flipped it out the window.

"Show time," she said and got out of the car.

As she walked through the front door, a small bell, attached to the frame, rang, alerting the employees that there was a customer.

"Be right there," a voice called out from the back.

Alex walked up to the counter and took a look around. The interior of the post office looked as if it had been suspended in time, caught in some eerie time warp that kept it trapped in the 50's.

A moment later, a slightly overweight, elderly woman emerged from the back room and slowly made her way to the counter. Her silver hair was pulled up in a bun and she had pudgy little red cheeks that gave her the quintessential look of a benevolent grandma.

"How can I help you, young lady?"

Alex reached into the back pocket of her jeans, withdrawing the case containing her badge and showed it to the woman.

"I'm Chief Alex Taylor, from the Penobscot Police Department," she said. "I need to ask you a few questions."

"Oh my," the woman said, clearly startled. "I'm sorry officer, is there anything wrong?"

"I'm following up on a request made by the police down in New York City," she said. "I need to ask you about a package that came in here about two weeks ago."

"I'll try to help in any way I can, officer," the woman replied, "but I do get a lot of packages in here each day."

Alex reached into the jacket, removing the photo, and laid it down on the counter.

"What can you tell me about this package?"

Alex watched as the woman looked down at the image in front of her and then slowly back up at Alex. The eyes told her everything she needed to know.

"I,.. Uhm,....I don't know..." the woman replied.

Alex knew what the woman was thinking. She recognized the package and she knew that she hadn't handled it properly.

"Ma'am, we have no interest in whether or not it was processed correctly. What I need to know is what you remember about the man who sent this."

"Man?" the woman replied. "Oh no, it wasn't a man. It was a young woman, about your age."

"A woman? Are you sure?"

"Oh, I'm positive," the woman said. "She was a sweet thing, very upset."

"Tell me everything that you can remember," Alex said. "Nothing is unimportant."

"Well, she came in to send that package. She paid for the postage, then, before I could put it in the outgoing mail bin, she broke down and asked for it back."

"Did she say anything about why she wanted it back?"

"Well, at first she said that she was breaking up with her fiancé and then it seemed as if she had a change of heart. I felt so sorry for her. I knew it was wrong, but I couldn't have that on my conscience."

"Then what happened?"

"After I gave it back she thanked me and left."

"Do you remember what she looked like?"

"Oh, I'd say she looked a bit like you," the woman replied. "She had blonde hair and was about your height and weight. Don't remember the eyes, but they were very pretty."

"She had blonde hair?"

"Yes, she wore it in a ponytail."

Alex took out a notepad and began making notes on the woman's description.

"Do you recall what she was wearing?"

"Not really," she replied. "I don't recall it being anything fancy, just your normal clothing for around here."

"Is there anything else that you can remember?" Alex asked. "Maybe there was a vehicle that she got in?"

"No, as I recall it was the first thing in the morning and that's when it is the busiest around here. I have to sort all the mail that has come in and put it in the post office boxes. Once she left I went back to doing that."

"How long have you been working here?"

"This summer will be thirty-five years," the woman replied.

"So, if she was from this area, you would most likely know her?"

"Oh I would think so. At some point everyone in this community has come through my door. I would have recognized her."

"Well, I appreciate your time, Mrs.?"

"Thompson, Beatrice Thompson. But everyone just calls me Bea. I'm the postmaster here."

"Thank you for speaking with me, Mrs. Thompson."

"This investigation won't have to go to the postal inspectors will it?"

"No ma'am, like I said we're more interested in the sender than the package."

"Thank you," the woman replied. "I know I shouldn't have done it, but she really did seem upset. I just didn't want to cause any problems for her."

"Don't worry," Alex said. "Everything will be fine."

Alex turned around and left the building. She got back in the car and started it up. She remembered seeing a coffee shop as she entered the town. She needed a cup and another cigarette before she called Maguire with the information she had obtained.

A half hour later she sat in the parking lot of the shop. Alex took a sip of coffee and then finished off her cigarette, flicking it out the half open car window. She then picked up the cell phone and dialed his number.

"What do you have for me?" Maguire asked.

"Your mystery just got more mysterious," she replied. "It wasn't a guy that brought the package in, it was a woman."

"A woman?" Maguire repeated. "Are they sure?"

"She was positive. She said the woman came in to send the package and was really upset, something about breaking up with her fiancé. Then she asked for it back, after she'd paid for it."

"What about a physical description?"

Alex pulled out the pad and began going through her notes.

"Female, blonde hair, about 5'7" and around one hundred thirty to one hundred forty pounds. She said she was in her late thirties; maybe her early forties. No real clothing description, just that whatever she was wearing was unremarkable."

"Did she see a vehicle?" he asked.

"No," Alex replied. "But she did say that she didn't recognize her as being from around here."

There was silence on the line as Maguire tried to process this latest round of information. Nothing seemed to make sense.

"You need me to do anything else?" she asked.

"No, you've done enough already, Alex. I really appreciate the help."

"I don't know what you're doing, James, but I know you're planning something. Don't shut your old partner out."

"I'm not going to ask you to risk your newly resurrected career on something that might not end up going down well."

"Bullshit," she replied angrily. "I wouldn't have a *newly resurrected* career without you and I sure as hell don't give a rat's ass about any fallout. We didn't operate that way back in Brooklyn North and we sure as hell aren't going to start now. Or do I need to come down there and kick your ass?"

Maguire laughed.

"Easy there, tiger," he said. "I get your point. I'll keep you in the loop. I promise."

"You'd damn well better," she replied. "That being said, where do you look now?"

"That's a good question, Alex. To be honest with you I'm not sure. Right now I feel like that kid's toy where I'm being stretched in two different directions. I just hope I can bounce back. I know I need to direct all my energy at finding Genevieve, but I can't get my mind off Melody."

She could hear the stress in his voice. It was something that was completely foreign to her. He'd always been a rock, always knew exactly what needed to be done under any given situation and did it. Now the voice reminded her of some old boxing champ who'd taken one too many body shots and was just trying to make it out of the round so he could get his wits about him.

"Do what you always told me," she said. "Go after the bigger problem. I know you feel the need to be with Melody right now, I get that. But you're no doctor, James, you're a cop. You can either sit in that hospital room, with your thumb up your ass, or you can do what you're good at and go after whoever did this."

"How'd you get so smart?" he asked.

"Me?" she replied. "Remember, I trained you, rookie. I figure you're the one that got smart hanging around me. Too bad you didn't get my good looks too."

"Okay, I've gotta go. It's starting to get a little *deep* here."

"Call me when you know something more."

"I will, Alex. Thanks again."

"Anytime," she said and ended the call.

She took a sip of coffee, replacing it back in the cup holder and lit another cigarette.

He wasn't thinking right and she knew it. He was too involved. He was having difficulty separating what needed to be done and what could wait. That's why it was important to have a partner in things, someone who could think clearly when you couldn't.

Alex looked over at the clock, it was a little after nine. She'd make it back to the office by noon, just in time to check back in and then pack a bag. With any luck she'd be back in New York City by around nine that evening.

They were partners. He'd always been there for her, and she was sure as hell going to be there for him.

CHAPTER THREE

Northern Maine
Friday, February 15th, 2013 – 5:31 p.m.

Genevieve sat on the edge of the bed; her ankle handcuffed to the metal frame, and wondered how long she had been there.

Time had quickly ceased to mean anything within the small confines of the windowless room. Actually, it wasn't even a room, but more like the inside of a shipping container, from what she could tell.

The woman had brought food in some time ago, but it was a sandwich and coffee. It didn't give her any indication of whether it was day or night. In fact, she had been sleeping when it happened, so she hadn't even had a chance to get a good look at anything.

She had tried to listen, to see if she could hear something that would give her a clue as to where she was, or who might be involved, but that didn't get her very far. Occasionally she would hear what sounded like things being moved about, just beyond the door, but it wouldn't last for long.

Gen had thought about screaming out, but abandoned that idea. Judging from the overall silence she doubted that her voice would carry very far. Instead she tried to focus on her environment and what she might be able to use to get herself free. Unfortunately, that plan had so far proven to be unsuccessful.

It was clear that the room had been designed with one purpose in mind, to hold someone captive. It contained only the barest of essentials. The bed she was on, a toilet, small sink and a chair. All of which were firmly bolted to the floor. Even the recessed light bulb in the ceiling, which illuminated the room, was housed behind a security covering. It was like the rooms you see in prison photos. Everything was stainless steel and utilitarian.

She had scrounged around the room, looking for anything loose, but there was nothing. Nor were there any nooks or crannies to hide anything. Gen was just about to lie back down on the bed when she heard the sound of approaching footsteps.

The small metal slot in the door opened and she could see someone looking inside. A moment later she heard the sound of a bolt slide and the door opened up. She looked beyond the woman, into the room on the other side of the door. It appeared to be the same type of construction and there were some boxes on the floor.

"How are you doing, gorgeous?" Tatiana asked as she stepped into the room, holding a tray that held a plastic cup and bowl.

"Not too good," Gen replied. "I think I have a fever. Why don't you come a bit closer and feel my head?"

Tatiana laughed.

"You're a funny lady," she replied. "Trust me; there'll be time enough for you and me to get to know each other better."

She set the tray down on the floor, pushing it forward to a place that Tatiana knew she could get to it. For a moment she wondered if that was how she had look, when she was the one who wore the chain around her ankle.

"I can't wait," said Gen. "I'm especially looking forward to the part where I stomp your fucking head into the floor."

"You do have a pair of balls," Tatiana replied. "I'll give you that. But you might as well get comfortable, darling. You and I are going to be together for a little while longer."

"Then you don't know the friends I have," Gen replied.

"I'm afraid you put too much faith in them."

"Well, we'll just have to wait and see now, won't we?"

"If it's any consolation, you weren't my intended target. I just decided to make the most of a bad situation."

"If I wasn't your target, that leaves only one other person," Gen said. "And if that's the case, then you're not only crazy, but you're fucking stupid as well."

"You know, you're adorable when you get fired up."

"So why don't you uncuff me and then you can see just how much fun I can really be?"

"All in due time, my love," Tatiana said. "Enjoy your food."

She turned and headed toward the door, pausing for a moment.

"Oh, I almost forgot. I thought you'd be a little bored so I brought you something to read. It's a classic."

Tatiana reached into her back pocket, removing the paperback book and slid it across the floor toward Gen.

She continued out the door, bolting it behind her.

Inside the room, Gen waited until she could no longer hear the footsteps and then got up, picking up the tray and bringing it back to the bed.

She examined the contents. This time it was some type of beef stew and black coffee. Gen slowly began to eat; she knew that she needed to keep her energy up. Keeping her wits about her might be the only difference between surviving this ordeal and becoming another victim.

If only she could have found something to help her remove the cuff that kept her chained to the bed. She'd love to get close to the door when it opened and get a shot at that crazy bitch.

She looked down at the book lying on the floor and picked it up. It was an old book, and it had an image of the *Arc de Triomphe* with a target scope in the center. She read the title.

The Day of the Jackal, a novel by Frederick Forsyth.

CHAPTER FOUR

Bellevue Hospital, Manhattan, New York City
Friday, February 15th, 2013 – 8:47 p.m.

Maguire looked down at his cell phone and read the text message from Alex.

Where are you? Thought I would check in and see how you are doing.

At the hospital, leaving soon. I'll call you. He typed back.

It was getting to be about that time. The hospital staff had been very gracious in allowing him to stay past normal hours. He'd gone out of his way to make sure that he and the other visitors had not abused it. Still, it was always tough for him to leave.

It was tougher still to go back *home*.

James hadn't managed to do that yet, opting instead to go back to his boat. But even there the memories chased him.

From out in the hallway he heard a commotion.

"I'm sorry, ma'am, but I cannot let you go in if you're not on the list."

"Then you'd better find someone to put me on that list real quick, junior."

It took only a second for him to recognize the voice. He got up and opened the door. He found her standing in the hallway, the uniformed cop blocking her path.

"Surprise!" Alex said, when she saw him appear in the doorway.

"What the hell are you doing here?" he replied, before stepping out in the hallway and hugging her.

"You and I both know you *weren't* going to call me," she whispered in his ear, holding him tight. "So I figured I'd save myself the wait and just come straight here to kick your ass."

Maguire released her and looked down at his old partner. She'd changed, for the better, he noted. Apparently the great north agreed with her.

"You're impossible," he said.

"Damn straight," Alex said. "Now will you inform *Dudley Do-Right* here to put me on his damn *list*?"

"Is everything alright, Boss?" Luke Jackson said, as he came down the hall.

"Yes, everything is fine," Maguire replied. "This is my old partner. She's a cantankerous old sergeant too, so be careful."

"Old my ass," Alex muttered under her breath. "And that's chief to you, rookie."

Maguire laughed and turned to the cop.

"Go ahead and put her on the authorized visitors list," he said. "Her name is Alex Taylor."

He turned around, opening the door for her, "After you, partner."

Alex walked into the room and saw the woman lying in the bed, surrounded by medical equipment. She suddenly felt a wave of guilt wash over her. She'd never met her before, just heard James talk about her, and she was jealous of their relationship.

Alex had always had feelings for him, but she'd never acted on them. When the opportunity to tell him had finally presented itself, she had let it slip away. Now, as she stared at the woman lying in the bed, she felt ashamed.

"Oh, James," Alex said. "I'm so sorry."

"It's okay, really. The doctors say that she is making progress. They did a spontaneous breathing test today. It wasn't a pretty sight, but they assured me she was not in pain and that she did rather well. They plan on removing her from the ventilator tomorrow."

"I can't imagine how hard this has been on you."

"Under normal circumstances I'd make a joke, but I'm kind of at the end of my rope here."

"There's nothing more you can do here, James," Alex said. "Let's go somewhere quiet and have a chat."

"Still bossy as ever, aren't you?"

"I prefer to think of it as being *consistent*," she said. "Besides, I think you owe me a dinner for all my hard work today."

"Okay, just give me a minute and we'll head out."

"I'll meet you out back, I need a cigarette."

"Old habits, huh?"

"Where's the fun in being perfect," she said with a smile.

Alex made her way outside, back to where her car was parked alongside the suburban, and lit up a cigarette. The wind was blowing hard off the East River and she adjusted the collar on her jacket, pulling it up to ward off the cold. She took a drag on the cigarette and stared out across the water. Immediately she was hit with the realization that she was standing in the same place she had been, almost three years to the day.

Alex remembered the phone call telling her that Maguire had been shot and racing to the hospital. She had been working a day tour and got caught up in a search for a missing person. The ensuing overtime had caused her to get stuck in hellacious traffic on the way home. By the time she had gotten the call she hadn't had the time to hit the bottle as hard as she had originally intended. This was a very fortunate thing for her, along with the other drivers on the road, as she raced back into Manhattan at break-neck speed.

"Penny for your thoughts."

She turned to see him approaching her, accompanied by his security detail.

"For *these* thoughts it's going to be at least seventy-five cents," she replied.

"I didn't think you could formulate such high quality thoughts."

"I've grown," she replied. "I'm maximizing my potential."

"You do appear to be more *mature*," Maguire said.

"Kiss my ass," she replied, knowing he was making an age joke.

"I guess it's a *work in progress*. Where do you want to eat?"

"Why don't you be a nice boss and give the twins the rest of the night off?" she asked. "This way we don't have to embarrass them with our *war stories*."

"Might not be a bad idea," Maguire said. "Besides, I think the statute of limitations may not have expired on a few of them."

"Ya think?"

"You guys can take off, Maguire said to the two men. "You deserve an early night after what I have put you through lately."

"Are you sure, Boss?" Jackson asked cautiously.

Maguire could tell what the man was thinking. It was not an easy thing for a security detail to be cut loose, especially when the *protectee* was going out on their own.

"I'm positive," Maguire replied.

Luke eyed the woman suspiciously. Even former cops weren't above the scrutiny of a good security detail.

"Besides, if she was going to get me killed she would have done it back in Brownsville."

"We could follow you," Jackson said. "Make sure you get home okay."

"Honestly, I'll be fine, Luke. You and Pete get an early start on the weekend and enjoy it. I'll let you know if anything comes up."

"Yes, Sir," Jackson replied.

Maguire watched as the two men made their way to the Suburban and got in.

"Aw," Alex said, as she opened the car door. "It's so cute how they dote over you."

"They remind me a lot of you," Maguire said, as he got into the passenger seat.

"I wasn't doting over you, rookie. I was *babysitting* you."

"Yeah, yeah, whatever helps you sleep at night," he said. "What do you want to eat?"

"Anything, but Chinese food," she replied. "I've kinda had my fill of take-out."

"How do you feel about leftovers?"

"You're cooking?" she asked with a quizzical look.

"Hell no," he replied.

"Then I'm game," Alex said.

"You do know that I cook better then you?" he asked.

"That's like saying the XO on the Titanic was the better captain *after* it hit the iceberg."

"God I've missed you, Alex," James said.

"I know," she said, as she pulled the car out of the hospital parking lot and made her way toward the Queens-Midtown Tunnel.

The ride east was spent doing what cops do best, catching up and reliving old times. It was who they were, what they had lived through. They talked about people they used to work with and those who had passed away.

Shortly after the attack on September 11th, the government had gone to great lengths to reassure the public that the air was safe. It wasn't. The attack had claimed many lives that day, but now, over a decade later, the deaths from sickness attributed to the attack had more than doubled the number lost that day and the growing list of those who were ill was staggering.

Traffic never seems to move as quickly as when you are ignoring it, even on the Long Island Expressway. Before either of them realized they were on Sunrise Highway and Alex was just about to get off at exit 65S.

"I'm not at the marina anymore," he said. "Keep going."

"Don't tell me you actually got a place on *terra firma*?" she asked.

"Yes and no," he answered. "After the attack last summer at Melody's place, I floated over the bay to be a bit closer."

"How chivalrous," Alex said with a snicker. "I'm sure that it was really tough on you."

"Play nice," Maguire said.

"*Moi*? Always."

"Don't you mean *rarely*?" he asked.

"I was just meaning that *your* Melody is a very attractive woman, so it couldn't have been too rough on you to get *closer* to her."

"Alexandria Marie," he replied tersely.

"Ah, see I am right," she said. "You only use my full name when I've hit a nerve."

"I'm gonna hit a nerve in a minute," Maguire said sarcastically. "Now pay attention. You're going to turn right onto Tuckahoe Lane coming up here."

"So things are pretty serious with you two, huh?"

"We're really going to have this conversation?"

"We could wait until I start drinking, but we both know that probably wouldn't end very well."

"Yes, it is serious," he replied. "I've never known anyone like her before."

Alex knew the words weren't meant to hurt her, but they still did. It wasn't fair to him, he had no idea.

She had long ago locked away her feelings for Maguire. When they had been partners it was a subject that she had been afraid to broach. They worked so well together, were such an effective team, and she wouldn't do anything to jeopardize that. When he had gotten transferred to the Street Crime Unit she had decided to tell him about her feelings for him. She reasoned that, even if he had said no, she would have at least known that she had taken the chance. The night of his going away party she was the last to leave, waiting for the right moment. Unfortunately for her, that moment came and went, after she passed out from drinking too much. The moment was lost and she never tried again.

"Well, I'm happy for you, James," she lied. "Everyone deserves to have that special someone."

"What about you?" he asked. "Is there anyone interesting in Penobscot?"

"Oh, you know me," she said. "My dance cards always filled."

"Turn here," Maguire said with a laugh.

They meandered through the back roads of Southampton before finally reaching Meadow Lane.

"Make a right," he said.

Alex looked around at the multi-million dollar homes as they made their way west along the two lane road.

"Damn, James, you did well," she said. "My entire annual salary couldn't pay the real estate taxes on an undeveloped lot out here."

"Don't start," he said. "I still have my houseboat."

"Why?" Alex said with a laugh.

"I guess I still like the *illusion* of my autonomy."

"You always were a little thick headed."

"Slow down, it's coming up here on the left."

A moment later she pulled the car off the road and up to an ornate security fence. Just off to the side was a security access panel.

"The code is 2416," he said.

Alex opened the window and entered the code, then watched as the gates slowly opened.

"Impressive," she said.

"It is," he said. "I'll give you that."

As they drove up the driveway they were met by a two man security patrol that stopped the car, approaching it slowly, their automatic weapons held at the ready.

Maguire lowered the window as they drew nearer.

"Sorry, Mr. Maguire," the man nearest to him said, as they lowered their weapons. "We didn't recognize the car."

"It's okay, Thomas," he replied. "I should have called ahead. This is my old partner; she's going to be staying for a few days."

"I'll let control know that, sir. Have a good evening."

The two men stepped off to the side of the road as Alex drove through the gatehouse up ahead and into the interior courtyard.

"Pull up to that door," James said.

Alex got out of the car and gazed up at the massive structure. It was like being in the courtyard of some medieval castle.

"Beats Brownsville, doesn't it?" Maguire asked.

"This beats any *ville*," Alex said. "Are we even still in New York?"

Maguire laughed. "Grab your stuff and come inside."

"James, if this is too weird I can just get a motel room," she said.

"Oh, and me visiting you in a motel isn't going to be weird?"

"Well, now that you put it *that* way."

"Just get your stuff, goofy. There are so many spare bedrooms in this place that, if you're not careful, you can find yourself lost."

Alex grabbed the bag from the trunk and followed Maguire inside. She felt like one of those tourists that walked around Manhattan with their mouths hanging open. He led her into the salon.

"Want a drink?" he asked.

"Yeah," she replied, as she stared at the bank of windows that looked out over the Atlantic Ocean. "Red wine if you have it."

"Wine, when the hell did that happen?"

"A few months back," she said, dropping the bag on the ground. "I decided that whiskey hangovers just weren't worth the *fun* anymore."

"Good for you," he replied.

Maguire poured a glass of wine for her and a whiskey for himself, then headed over to where she was standing, giving her the glass.

"*Sláinte*," he said, raising his glass to hers.

"Up yours," she replied and took a drink.

"Where can I smoke?" she asked. "I feel like I'm in a museum."

"Follow me," he said, "but you better button up."

Maguire led her to the door, which opened out onto the back deck, and stepped outside. The wind was blowing hard off the ocean and he could taste the saltiness in the air.

Alex pulled the collar on her jacket up and turned her back as she lit the cigarette. She took in a deep drag and exhaled, watching as the wind grabbed the smoke, scattering it quickly.

"You know those things will kill you," he said.

"Something has to," she said. "So it might as well be something I enjoy."

Maguire just shook his head. Arguing with her was pointless; she dragged you down to her level and knocked the shit out of you with experience. He leaned his arms on the railing and stared out into the blackness of the sea.

"I know that look," she said, joining him at the railing. "The question is; what nefarious shit are you thinking about?"

"That I need to find Gen quickly," Maguire replied. "That, along with the fact that I need to put an end to this game once and for all."

"Well, fortunately for you, your *cavalry* has arrived," she replied.

CHAPTER FIVE

Southampton, Suffolk County, N.Y.
Saturday, February 16th, 2013 – 8:23 a.m.

Alex made her way down the staircase, following the voices, where she found Maguire and another man standing in the dining room. They were looking down at stacks of papers and maps that were spread out across the length of the table.

Maguire glanced up as she walked into the room.

"Morning," he said. "I didn't know that the *cavalry* kept bankers hours."

"For your information, I've been up since five o'clock," she replied. "I've just been lost on the second floor. I was just about ready to dial 911 and ask them to send a rescue party."

"When you're done making excuses, the coffee's over on the side table," Maguire said. "Or do you need a guide to find that as well?"

Alex headed over to where the coffee pot was, silently mouthing a response as she walked by. Maguire just smiled, turning back toward the map he and Gregor had been examining. When Alex returned with her coffee cup, he introduced them.

"Alex, this is Gregor Ritter. Gregor, Alex Taylor, my old partner from Brooklyn."

Gregor extended his hand to Alex.

"Pleasure to meet you," he said.

"Wow, you're not from around here are you?" she replied, shaking the man's hand.

"No, I'm from *Kali-forn-yah*," Gregor replied.

"I knew I recognized that accent," Alex said with a laugh.

"Gregor used to be with the German federal police anti-terrorism team," Maguire said. "He and I were just going over what we know about Banning, which still isn't a whole helluva lot."

"Whatcha looking at?" Alex asked.

"These are all the locations that Banning has been spotted at. The green dots are confirmed and red are alleged sightings."

"What's the black one?" Alex asked taking a sip of coffee.

"That is where he *supposedly* bought the farm," Maguire replied.

"Is that really confirmed?"

"According to the Maine State Police Lab it is. I reached out to my contact in the New York State Police, who headed up the original task force. I asked him to get back in touch with them and see if they will rerun the tests."

"Will they?" Alex asked.

"Probably, although grudgingly."

"NYSP going to reactivate the task force?"

"Doubtful, unless we come up with something that proves Banning is still alive. If that second DNA test comes back as a match, they'll never waste the manpower."

"Maybe we're focusing on the wrong person," Gregor said.

Maguire and Alex looked over at the man, who was reading the notes from Alex's interview with the postmaster.

"What do you mean?" James asked.

"Well, there is so much we don't know about Banning," Gregor said, gesturing to the paperwork on the table. "For every piece of paper here, there seems to be an even greater imaginary pile of what we don't know. Perhaps we should stop looking at him and begin focusing on the other person in all this, the blonde woman from Alex's interview."

Alex took a sip of coffee, and set the cup on the table. "You think he might actually be working with someone?"

"It's not common, but it wouldn't be the first time," Maguire said. "I remember a man and woman team back in the late seventies. They were tagged with around ten murders out in California. Hell, there were two sisters in Mexico that racked up nearly a hundred homicides during the fifties and sixties."

"Lovely," Alex replied. "So we back off Banning and start looking at this phantom woman?"

"Well, at least we go back to what we do know," Gregor said.

Maguire walked over to a large dry erase board, which was propped up on a serving table, and picked up one of the markers.

"We know Banning allegedly died, along with Lena Marx, on the evening of February 6th," he said, writing the information on the board. "Alex, you spoke to the postmaster and she said the blonde woman came in on the morning of February 1st. That is the same day that Lena was allegedly abducted."

"So whoever it was, they were working together before the abduction," Gregor said.

44

"Then we have an, as yet, unknown person putting the package into the car on the 14th when Genevieve was abducted," Alex replied, taking notice of the pained looked on Ritter's face when she said it.

"You think that Banning's sidekick went solo after his death?" Maguire asked.

"Well, someone abducted Gen," Alex replied. "So, if the corpse, up on the metal table in Maine, really is Banning, then I think we have to run with that theory and see where it leads us."

"The question is; who could it be?" Gregor asked.

"Well, we know who it's not, and that's Lena," Maguire said. "She has the blonde hair, but her abduction came after the woman was spotted in Belkin. Besides, it would have to be someone Banning trusted. Problem is we know so little about him. Hell, for all we know it could be his twin sister."

"Here's the thing that I don't get," Alex said. "Why go through all the nonsense of making it look like you're sending a package, only to back out at the last minute?"

"Maybe the woman changed her mind," Gregor said.

"And defied Banning?" Alex asked. "That kinda blows that whole *trusted* notion out of the water."

"Maybe it's just another one of his twisted tricks," Gregor replied. "Make us look for him in a place that he really wasn't."

"That would make sense if the package had been sent through the mail, but *hand delivering*, so to speak, says something different, something much more pre-meditated and a lot more *personal*."

Maguire had been standing there listening to the two of them, taking in what they were saying.

"What does it say to you, Alex?" Maguire asked.

"It seems to me that someone was sending you a message, James. Obviously they're keeping the game going, even after Banning's death."

Maguire picked up his coffee cup and refilled it, taking a sip.

"You know what it sounds like to me?" he asked. "It sounds like a double cross."

"Double cross?" asked Gregor. "What is that?"

"When one person agrees to do something," Alex said, "and then does the exact opposite."

"But why?"

"Because they have a different plan," Maguire replied. "We've been focusing on the wrong person, people. I think Banning was being played by someone else."

"So you think Banning was, for lack of a better word, the *victim* here?" Alex asked.

"Hear me out," Maguire said. "We know Banning and the woman were working together as late as February 1st. That's when she's spotted and Lena is abducted. Obviously there was a plan in place, so we can assume that this little *union* had to predate that. If it was Banning's plan to deliver the package, then he would have done just that. Keith planned every move he made, nothing was left to chance. So clearly he had one idea, something which she altered at the last minute. The question is why?"

"Disagreement in how things should be done?" Gregor said.

"Yeah, maybe she thought it would bring unwanted attention to them," Maguire said.

Alex reached into her pocket, pulled out the pack of cigarettes and lit one.

"Hey partner, you want to take that out onto the deck?" Maguire said.

"Hush, rookie," she replied, as she leaned over the table and examined the map. "I do my best thinking when I'm smoking."

Gregor looked over at James, who just shrugged his shoulders.

"You asked why she would alter the plan at the last minute. I'll tell you why," Alex said, pointing to the black dot on the map. "Because she knew Banning wasn't going to be around to put up much of an argument."

"You think she killed him?" Gregor asked.

"If they were such a team," Alex asked, "then where is *her* body?"

"*Sonofabitch*," Maguire replied.

"Where exactly did they find the vehicle?" Alex asked.

Maguire picked up a report from one of the piles and began reading it.

"Say's here that it was off County 17, about a half hour east of Rangeley."

"No witnesses?" she asked.

"Apparently it's a seldom used mountain road. The only witness came along well after the crash."

"You have a computer handy?"

"I have a laptop," Gregor said, reaching down and removing it from the bag next to the table.

A moment later he had it opened and powered up on the table.

"Go to Google Maps and get an image of exactly what we are dealing with here," she said.

They watched as Gregor keyed in the location and zoomed in to the isolated stretch of mountain road. A dense forest filled the screen in a massive display of green trees.

"Pull up the street view," Alex said, taking a drag on the cigarette. "I want to see the roadway."

A moment later the screen image of the desolate road appeared. On the left side of the road was a massive granite wall, the remains of the mountain through which the road had been carved out of. On the right was a picturesque view of a valley, complete with a sparkling lake off in the distance.

"Zip around the road, Gregor. Show me what the rest of it looks like."

Gregor advanced the image forward for a mile and then altered his course and went back a mile. All that was displayed was much of the same.

"There's nothing to see," he said.

"And no place to hide a getaway car," Alex said. "This means that if my theory holds true, and our mystery woman did kill Banning, we need to start our search in this area."

"Okay," Maguire said. "Give me your assumptions as to what we might be dealing with."

"Out of the gate, female on foot, at night, middle of winter," Alex said. "Under optimal conditions a person can do three maybe four miles an hour on foot. But this isn't optimal so I'd knock that in half."

"Most likely there was snow on the ground," Gregor said, "so we cannot exclude a snowmobile or skis. That might improve their mobility."

"Let's err on the side of caution and call it eight miles," Maguire said. "I'd rather investigate more and be right, then less and be wrong."

He checked the legend on the map and, using the black dot as a starting point, drew a circle reaching out eight miles.

"That's our perimeter," he said. "Now we need to see how many houses are inside it."

"How do you propose we do that?" Gregor asked. "These maps are good, but with all the trees we will never know if we missed anything."

"I was thinking of something a little bit more *advanced*," Maguire replied. "I have to go make a phone call."

"Gregor, how would you like to show me around the property?" Alex asked. "This way I don't have to worry about getting lost anymore."

"Of course," he replied. "It would be my pleasure."

When they had walked outside, Maguire reached into his pocket, removing the cell phone and dialed the number, listening to it ring.

"Two calls in as many weeks, you're making me proud."

"Don't get too excited, Mother, you haven't heard what I need yet."

"That sounds curiously ominous."

"I need a real time, night satellite pass with thermal imagery."

"Most of my misguided tadpoles ask for a place to crash or bail money, I'm glad you're not asking for something *difficult*."

"If it was just difficult, Mother, I would have done it already."

"Should I ask why you need this?"

Maguire filled him in on what had happened since the two men had spoken last, along with the working theory that had brought him to this extravagant request.

"Honestly, this might just be one of the many wild goose chases I have been on with this prick, but it's the only thing that makes sense right now. If time wasn't of the essence, I'd have figured out a different option. I figure that with the weather conditions up there right now, every place is going to have a heat signature registering. If I can identify the houses, I might be able to bring this to an end."

"E-mail me the coordinates," he said. "I'll see what I can do."

"I appreciate it, Mother."

"I'm sorry to hear about Melody, Paddy," Mother replied. "If there is anything you need, you let me know. We take care of our own."

"Thanks, and I will."

CHAPTER SIX

Dulles International Airport, Sterling, Virginia
Saturday, February 16th, 2013 – 3:23 p.m.

The man stepped off the Austrian Airlines, Boeing 767-300, adjusting the shoulder strap of his carry-on bag, and made his way up the ramp into the terminal building. It took him a moment to orient himself with his surroundings, before he observed the sign indicating the direction for baggage claim.

All around him, people hurried about, either making a mad dash to leave the airport or an equally frantic dash to make a departing flight. He had been through countless airports in his life and it never ceased to amaze him just how chaotic they were. Sometimes he would arrive early, or even sit down after a flight, and just people watch. Unfortunately, he had things to do today, so he grudgingly made his way toward the baggage claim area.

He walked through the maze of carousels, casually observing the bedlam as passengers jockeyed for position in order to quickly claim their items. In the background, shrill alarms sounded the alert that a carousel was about to start-up.

None of that really mattered to him as he always traveled light, ensuring that everything he needed was always in the bag he carried.

Just ahead of him, where a genuinely disinterested security guard half-heartedly checked the baggage tickets of departing passengers, stood a throng of people waiting for friends and relatives. He scanned the crowd and saw who he was looking for.

The man stood off to the side with the other livery drivers. He was dressed in a tired looking black suit with matching tie and held up a rectangular piece of white cardboard with the name

Charles Morgan printed on it. He approached the man and nodded, handing him the carry-on bag, then followed him out of the terminal to the waiting Lincoln Town Car.

It wasn't a particularly cold day, Vienna had been colder when he left, but the bitter wind here made it feel much worse than it was. He adjusted the collar of his overcoat as he walked toward the vehicle. He got into the back seat as the driver held the door open. Once he was settled in, Charles Morgan stretched out his long legs, enjoying the comfort of the American luxury sedan. It was something he rarely had a chance to do in the cars back home.

After securing the carry-on bag in the trunk, the driver got in and pulled away from the curb. The professional livery man made his way skillfully through the meandering roadways of the airport until he pulled the car onto Route 267 and proceeded eastbound.

"How was your trip, sir?" the man asked.

"Long," he replied, as he stared out the window.

Outside, a blanket of snow covered the center median and shoulders of the roadway. The ominous, dark sky served as a warning that more could soon follow. If everything went as planned he wouldn't be here long enough to see it.

And just how often do things ever go as they are planned? he wondered.

A half hour later the car turned onto the Theodore Roosevelt Memorial Bridge as it made its way over the Potomac River and into Washington, D.C. As the driver continued east, along Constitution Avenue NW, Morgan stared out the window at the Mall. Off to his right was the Lincoln Memorial. Even in the middle of winter there were still tourists milling about.

A moment later he looked over to his left as they passed by the White House. In the distance he could make out the four large pillars of the south portico.

So close, he thought. *Maybe one day.*

At 7th Street SW, the car made a right turn and headed south. A few minutes later it arrived at its destination, The River Inn.

The driver pulled the car up to the covered front entrance and got out. He opened the door for his passenger and retrieved the carry-on from the trunk.

"Have a good day," the man said, handing Morgan the bag.

Morgan handed the man a tip and made his way into the hotel.

As he walked into the main lobby, a man standing at the front desk looked up at him from a computer screen.

"Good evening, sir. May I help you?"

"I have a reservation, the name is Charles Morgan."

The man tapped a few buttons on the keyboard and found the entry.

"Yes, sir," The man replied. "I have you in room 214, paid up until February 20th. I just need to see some ID."

Morgan reached into his jacket pocket, removing the passport and handed it to the man.

The man tapped a few more keys and then slid an electronic keycard through a machine. He then handed it to the man, along with the passport.

"You're all set, sir," he said. "Elevators are straight ahead of you. Once you get off on the second floor, make a right and it will be just down the hall on your right."

"I'm expecting a package," Morgan said. "Can you check to see if it has arrived?"

"Certainly, sir."

The man went into the back, returning a moment later carrying a small cardboard box that he handed to Morgan.

"Thank you," Morgan said and headed toward the elevator.

He made his way up to the second floor room, turning the light on as he closed the door behind him. It was a fairly modest room, by Washington, D.C. standards, but it would have been quite opulent in his native country. He laid the box on the small writing desk and then placed his bag on the bed.

He wished he had something to drink. He should have told the driver to stop along the way, but he was tired and just wanted his traveling to be over for the day.

He pulled the drapes back and opened the sliding glass door, which led out to a small patio. He stepped outside, walking over to railing and leaned on it. He glanced out at the boats anchored in the marina below him.

Such wealth, he thought. *Squandered by rich idiots*.

Everywhere he turned, he was confronted with the extravagant excesses of the nation. From the room he currently occupied to the method of transportation that had brought him here.

How did one country deserve so much? he wondered. *Yet, less than a day's journey by plane, children died in squalid conditions.*

It was times like this that steeled his heart to the things he did. It was hard to feel empathy for your enemy when they looked down upon you from their gilded perch, tossing crumbs, while they dined on a feast.

The sun had almost set, and with the encroaching darkness the wind seemed that much colder. He stepped back inside and closed the door.

He had noticed a restaurant when he had first arrived. Surely they would have something to drink there. He decided to grab a hot shower and then go down to have dinner.

He might have disliked the extravagance of his current surroundings, but he also wasn't above enjoying them while the opportunity presented itself. It would be absurd to suffer, just for the sake of suffering. Only a fool would turn down a seat at the feast because he found the host objectionable.

CHAPTER SEVEN

Bellevue Hospital, Manhattan, New York City
Sunday, February 17th, 2013 – 11:43 a.m.

Maguire sat in the leather chair, watching the news show on the television screen and reading the closed-captioning. He'd turned off the volume so as not to wake Melody.

They'd successfully removed her from the ventilator and, according to the endless stream of doctors that came and went, she was doing remarkably well. He knew that he should be doing more, but he felt that he needed to be here until he knew with certainty that she was out of the woods. It was one thing to hear it from the doctors; it was an entirely different thing to see it with your own eyes.

Besides, it wasn't as if everything had come to a halt in his absence. Alex and Gregor were back at the house working on the tactical and logistical issues. Outside of his former SEAL teammates, there wasn't anyone else he trusted more.

He took a sip of coffee, and set the Styrofoam container down on the small table next to his chair.

The world was still in a perpetual state of insanity according to the panel on the news program. A suicide bomber had struck at the United States Embassy in Turkey, North Korea was claiming to have detonated a nuke, civil war raged in Syria, and the Pope had just announced that he was resigning.

Just how bad do things have to be in the world for the Pope to resign? he wondered.

He leaned back in the chair and closed his eyes.

"Hey, cowboy," a raspy voice said from the bed next to him.

Maguire opened his eyes with a start, and looked over at Melody.

"Angel," he said, leaning forward in the chair and taking her hand in his. "How do you feel?"

"Like I just drank two pitchers of Gen's *piña colada* mix."

"I bet," Maguire replied, trying not to let anything show on his face.

"Is it over?" she asked.

"Yes, angel, it's over."

Melody smiled and closed her eyes, lightly squeezing Maguire's hand.

"You had me worried there for a bit," he said.

"Eh, I thought you were getting a bit too comfortable," she said. "I figured I should mix things up."

"Yeah, you might want to re-think that in the future."

"God, I feel so tired," she said.

"You need to take it easy, babe," James said. "You've been through a lot, even if you haven't been awake for it. Besides, once the nurses find out that you're up they're never going to let you rest. They seem to delight in making you move around."

"How long have I been out?"

"Several days," he replied. "The doctors thought it was best to keep you sedated while your body healed."

"If this is how I feel after a few days," Melody said weakly, "can you ask them to put me back under for a few more?"

Maguire laughed, raising her hand up to his lips and kissing it.

"No, and I can tell you from experience that this is when the *real fun* is going to begin."

"Why don't we pretend that I'm still asleep," Melody replied.

Just then the door opened and Mary stepped inside.

"Oh my God, you're awake," Mary exclaimed.

"Too late, cat's out of the bag now, angel."

Melody looked up at her and smiled.

"Barely," she said, "but it beats the alternative."

Maguire could hear her voice becoming hoarser.

"Ok, that's enough talking, gorgeous," he said standing up. "You really do need to rest and I've got to go down to headquarters for a little bit, the paperwork never ends. Mary is going to babysit you for a while, but I will be back later."

Melody smiled and nodded. "I love you."

"I love you too, angel," Maguire said, leaning over and kissing her. "Get some rest."

As he turned to leave he motioned at Mary to follow him and the two of them stepped out into the hallway.

"Does she know about Gen?"

"No, and I don't want her to. She is still too weak."

"I agree, but she is going to ask."

"If she does, tell her she had to go out of town on business and that she'll be back soon."

"But what if...," Mary began, letting her words drift off.

"She'll be back soon," Maguire said. "I'll make sure of that."

"I know," she replied. "Is there anything you need me to do while I'm here?"

"Just try to make her rest, if that doesn't work, Monsignor O'Connor will be up later this afternoon. If memory serves me correctly, I never had any problems falling asleep when he used to visit me."

Mary smiled and then hugged him; pulling him close and holding on to him tightly.

"I don't know what you're planning, but please be careful, James," she whispered into his ear.

"Always, Mary," Maguire replied.

As he made his way back to Southampton, it dawned on him just how odd it was to be driving his own car. He hadn't realized how acclimated he had gotten to being chauffeured to and from. Normally it made sense, as he was able to get a lot done during the commute, with someone else behind the wheel. Now, as he maneuvered the Mustang in and out of traffic, it felt good to be in control.

Maguire didn't want to leave the hospital, but he knew that he had to. He'd scheduled a meeting with Gregor and Alex at two o'clock to finalize their plans. They needed to ensure that they had everything ready, just in case they had to go at a moment's notice. Maguire knew they'd find Gen, he just hoped that they would be in time to make a difference.

The ringing of the cell phone brought him out of his thoughts. He reached down; picking it up from the seat next to him, before he realized it wasn't the one that was ringing. He removed the *other* cell phone from his jacket pocket and answered it.

"Mother?"

"Got that information you asked for. It's patiently waiting for you as we speak."

"I appreciate it. I hope it didn't cause you too much trouble."

"No," Mother replied. "Actually, it was no trouble at all. That is unless your girlfriend wants to send me a bill for hijacking her satellite."

"Huh? What are you talking about?"

"You have no idea what toys she has access to, do you?"

"Obviously not," Maguire said. "How about you give me a refresher course?"

"How many times do I have to tell you tadpoles to *pay attention, you're going to see this shit again*?"

Maguire grimaced.

"You are aware that you're little lady owns one of the largest military contractors there is?" Mother asked. "If it shoots, flies, or can otherwise ruin someone's perfectly good day, they have it. More importantly they have the ability to watch it all unfold from sixty-five thousand feet above *terra firma*. So I figured why bother the fine folks over at the NRO, for something I can do on my own."

"So no one knows about your little sneak and peak?"

"I doubt the people over at Global Defense Logistics even know we took their toy out for a quick spin."

"I thought you didn't like civilian hardware."

"The way the military budgets are getting beat up under this administration, we might all be going to war via American Airlines soon, with connecting stops in Atlanta and London," Mother replied sarcastically. "That, and the fact that we are now having to make our way to space aboard some half-assed, third world rocket ship, equipped with massaging bead seats and floral pattern, pink velour cockpits, is making me appreciate *our* civilian military contractors a lot more these days.

"Any luck with the cell phone number I gave you?"

"I've tried everything, from *Happyfoot* to *Squeaky Dolphin,* not a peep."

Maguire had often tried to envision the person tasked with assigning program code names. He pictured someone sitting in a windowless cubicle, an espresso machine set to strong, sitting on one side of the desk, along with an anagram generator and a perpetual frazzled look on their face. One thing was certain; the government loved their code words.

"That phone is as dead as the proverbial door nail," Mother continued. "Then again, I'm limited in what I can do. I don't think you want me setting off any bells and whistles, by going through *official* channels. Besides, the scuttlebutt is that it is in everyone's best interests these days to steer a wide berth around the folks over at Fort Meade."

"That sounds nefarious."

"Sometimes the folks doing all the watching forget that they are not the only ones with eyes."

"Do I even want to know?"

"Even if you did, it's way above your pay grade, my son."

"Well, I guess I owe you two dinners now, huh?"

"And all the drinks are from the bottles on the top shelf."

"Thanks, Mother."

"Anytime, Paddy," the man said. "Happy hunting."

"Hooyah," Maguire replied before ending the call.

He wondered what Mother had meant about the scuttlebutt. Fort Meade was home to the National Security Agency, affectionately known in intel circles as *No Such Agency*. It was tasked with the production and collection of SIGINT, or signals intelligence, as well as the surveillance of targeted individuals. If it beeped or breathed, the NSA knew about.

Oh well, they're certainly big enough to weather any storm, he thought.

It was just before two o'clock when he pulled up to the houseboat. He needed to make a pit stop and see what Mother had sent him. The computer he used had been built by a SEAL-*nerd*. As a result, he didn't have to worry about the aforementioned NSA. At least that's what his *froggy* friend had led him to believe. Still, there had been no *o'dark thirty* raids on the boat by black ninjas, so he had to believe the *security measures* were still working.

Maguire went through the customary steps to ensure that, in his absence, no one had paid an unannounced visit to the boat. When he was sure everything was secure, he sat down at the desk and booted up the computer. It only took a minute to access the email program and find the message in the saved drafts folder.

All the members of his team had an account in the event that they needed to communicate with each other securely. The messages were saved in drafts, which kept them from being effectively 'sent' across the internet. He opened the thermal images and printed them out on the laser printer, before shutting everything down and heading over to the main house.

Inside the house, he found Gregor and Alex in the dining room, looking over the topography maps of the area that they had identified as the crash site.

"Hot off the presses," he said, waving the photos in the air.

Maguire laid the stack of photos on the table.

"How is Melody?" Gregor asked.

"She finally woke up," he replied. "Still very weak, but it felt good to finally see her awake. Mary is there with her now. I told her I'd be back later."

He picked up one of the mugs and poured himself a cup of coffee.

"Did she ask about Gen?" Gregor asked.

"No, she got weak pretty fast. I told Mary if she brought it up to tell her that Gen had to go out of town on GDL stuff. I figured that would ease her mind. But knowing Mel, we won't have much time before she's trying to find a phone to call her."

"More importantly, time is not our friend in finding Gen," Alex said. "So I hope those photos give us something to go on. That being said, I need a cigarette and some fresh air."

"Alex, do you realize how absurd that sounds?" Gregor asked.

"Don't be such a *sour kraut*, Gregor," she replied, as she stood up and headed toward the patio door.

"She's cranky," Gregor said, when the patio door closed.

"Nah, she was born that way," Maguire replied. "If she's idle, she's dangerous."

"Well then let's find her something to do."

"We need a bigger space," Maguire said, picking up the photos.

He walked over to the wall and removed a painting that hung there. Maguire then began to tape the photos onto the wall, arranging them according to the longitude and latitude coordinates. After a few minutes they had a bird's eye view of the entire area. The thing they had going for them was that the temps in the area were very low and it was heavily wooded. This provided good contrast between the thermal heat signatures of the isolated homes and the surrounding forest.

Gregor unrolled one of the topographical maps and they began making notation on where houses were located.

A moment later they were rejoined by Alex.

"Feel better?" Maguire asked.

"I think the sea agrees with me," She replied. "How many potential targets?"

"Twenty-six," Gregor said. "The question is how do we check them all out, without setting off any, how do you say, bells and whistles?"

"Fortunately for us," Maguire said, "I still have some rather *intrusive* software that allows me access to most state records. What we need to do now is get the identity of the physical addresses of these locations. Then we can start looking into the owners."

"I love technology," Alex said. "Unless it gets into the wrong hands."

"There is always *that* problem," Gregor replied.

"Time to fire up the computers people," Maguire replied. "We've got some electronic eavesdropping to do."

CHAPTER EIGHT

Northern Maine
Sunday, February 17th, 2013 – 8:11 p.m.

Genevieve sat on the edge of the bed listening to the sounds coming from just beyond the doorway. She could hear the feint sounds of scraping, as if heavy things were being dragged along the floor. Then there would be silence and a short time later the process would start back up again.

She struggled with her surroundings, trying to come to terms with what was happening to her. The environment was beginning to get to her, physically and emotionally. The lack of windows removed all point of reference, making her completely dependent on the environment around her. The only problem was that it was being artificially manipulated. The woman had taken to randomly turning the lights on and off. When the lights were out the room was pitch black. With nothing else to do she would try to sleep, only to have the lights come back on a short time later. How long she had slept was anyone's guess. An hour? Eight? More?

Even something as simple as meals had gone out the window. She tried to keep track of things that way, but the woman had even begun to manipulate that, serving small portions of random things. For all she knew she was getting macaroni and cheese at two o'clock in the morning.

Gen had already given up on trying to figure out what day it was. She knew that she had been taken on Thursday night, but could only fathom a guess as to what the current day actually was.

You'll go crazy before they find you, she thought.

She leaned back against the wall, picking up the book next to the bed, and began reading. Gen knew that she needed to do something, to keep her mind occupied. James and Gregor were out there looking for her, she knew that, and she had to keep her mind sharp for the time when that rescue came.

She had just finished the first page when the door opened and the woman stepped inside carrying two mugs, steam rising from the top of them.

"I thought you could use something to drink," she said.

Tatiana put the mug on the floor and slid it over toward the bed.

"Plus I figured we should get to know one another."

"Sure," Gen said with a smile, as she reached over and picked up the mug. She patted the bed next to her. "Come right on over and make yourself at home."

"I'd love to, but not right now, maybe later. First, I think you and I need to get a few things straight."

"Well, lucky for you, you have a *captive* audience," Gen replied sarcastically, raising her cuffed leg for added emphasis.

"I want you to know that this is nothing personal. Like I told you before, it wasn't you that I was after."

"That's so reassuring. I'll be sure and let the police know it was all a big mistake, as they cart your lifeless body away."

"They always said redheads were a fiery bunch," Tatiana said with a laugh. "But seriously, things will go a lot easier if we can just establish a few rules."

"This should be fun," Gen replied, as she took a sip of the coffee.

"Like I said, this isn't personal. You weren't my intended target, but you learn to make do. That whole 'when life gives you lemons' bullshit. You're probably thinking that they are out there looking for you, and you might actually be right. The only problem is that between where you are and where they are is a whole lot of *nothing*. I went to great lengths to make sure you *disappeared*."

"Clearly you don't know the people I do," Gen replied.

"Oh, I wouldn't be so sure of that, sweetheart," Tatiana said. "The bottom line is this: You can dig your heels in if you want. You can keep your attitude and pray that they find you real soon, but the odds are they won't. Or you can be smart, just accept your current situation and make the best of it with me. Either way, I can be a much bigger bitch to you, than you can be a pain in the ass to me."

"Why the sudden turnaround?"

"No turnaround," Tatiana replied, taking a sip from her mug. "You see, the truth is, the bad thing about living out in the middle of nowhere is that there simply isn't anyone else to talk to. Don't get me wrong, I love the solitude that the wilderness offers. However, there comes a point when you long to hear another human being's voice."

"You know, I'm curious," Gen said, as she finished the coffee and set the mug down. "When does Keith Banning make his grand appearance?"

"Keith?" Tatiana asked. "Oh, he's otherwise *preoccupied* right now. Would you like some more coffee?"

"Sure," Gen replied, holding out the mug. "Maybe next time we can have cookies."

"You certainly are a card," Tatiana said, as she carefully refilled the mug.

"Yeah, that's me, the life of the party," Gen said, taking a sip of coffee. "So, what is it exactly that you would like out of this new found friendship between you and me?"

"Well, realistically I don't think either of us believes we are going to form our own little sisterhood here. But I wouldn't mind having someone to talk to on a regular basis, and, for that luxury, I'm willing to play a better host. I'm sure that by this point you have no idea whether it is one o'clock in the morning or one in the afternoon. I imagine it is becoming harder for you to rationalize the time. The odd assortment of meals, coupled with the inconsistent times the lights have been on and off, certainly don't help. The reality is that you've only been here for a few days. I'm willing to make some changes, if you are."

"Let me get this straight. You drug me, kidnap me, and lock me away in some God forsaken hellhole. Now you want to have slumber parties and movie nights with me?" Gen asked incredulously. "You are a psychotic little bitch."

Gen was vaguely aware of the fact that the last part of that came out slightly slurred. She felt a bit weird, as if things had begun to suddenly move at a much slower speed. The edges of her vision began to narrow, fading out a bit. She heard the muffled sound of glass shattering, than realized she was no longer holding the mug in her hand. Before she could react, darkness began to fill the room.

"Oh, you have no idea just how psychotic I can be," Tatiana said.

The last thing Gen saw, before everything faded to black, was the woman standing up and walking toward her.

CHAPTER NINE

Washington, D.C.
Monday, February 18th, 2013 – 6:48 a.m.

Charles Morgan slid his legs over the side of the bed and sat up. He had forgotten to close the drapes the night before and now the sun was shining brightly into the bedroom. Outside, he could hear the loud squawking of a seagull.

It wasn't exactly the way he would have preferred to wake up, but his comfort was a secondary matter.

He made his way to the bathroom, stopping to turn on the coffee pot along the way. Morgan knew that he needed to get moving. Today was an important day. The instructions he had been given called for this part to be accomplished *before* noon. If he screwed it up he could not tell how long he would have to remain in the city. The people that he worked for were not in the habit of shrugging off mistakes lightly.

A half hour later he emerged from the hotel and began walking north along 7th Street SW. This section of the city was filled with residential homes, apartment buildings and recreational parks. That would all change in a matter of minutes when he crossed over the Southwest Freeway I-395 overpass.

The freeway was like a dividing line, separating this residential section from the city proper. The Monday morning rush hour was still going strong, and the roadway was packed with motorists trying to get to their government jobs. It was a far cry from the veritable ghost town, to which he had arrived, two days earlier.

On the other side of the freeway, the city took on a completely different look. The first example one encountered was the Robert C.

Weaver Federal Building, the headquarters for the Department of Housing and Urban Development. It was a prime example of the *Brutalist* style architecture, which was so popular with governmental buildings, from the fifties through the seventies. As the man continued north, he was amazed at the examples of excess that he encountered in the massive structures that surrounded him.

They have a department for everything, he thought, as he read the agency names on each of the building exteriors.

As he crossed the Mall, he stopped, glancing over to his right at the Capitol complex, its dome extending up into the dark grey morning sky. The weather report, on the morning news program, had predicted another snow storm for later today. He adjusted the collar on his jacket as he continued his trek. He needed to be cautious, but he also wanted this part to be finished. He didn't handle the cold well.

At Constitution Avenue NW, he turned left, making his way toward the White House. A block later he found a taxi, idling just outside the Andrew W. Mellon Auditorium, and got in.

"16th Street and Blagden Northwest," he said to the driver.

The driver pulled away from the curb, making a right turn onto 15th Street, navigating his way around the White House grounds, before making his way to 16th and heading north. It was a surprisingly easy drive and they arrived about fifteen minutes later.

Morgan paid the man and got out of the cab, looking around to get his bearings. He was relying on memory at this point, based on photos he had spent countless hours examining. He didn't have the luxury of a *cheat sheet*. In a game like this, there was no room for error.

He crossed 16th Street and headed north. The houses in this area were much different from the ones where he had started off from. You could tell that money lived here. Every house was different. Some had large front porches with ornate fluted columns, while others looked as if they had been transplanted from some small town in Germany, with their timber framing and terracotta tiled roofs. Many of the front lawns were edged with stone walls, giving the impression of some medieval boundary line.

When he reached Colorado he turned left and headed south. At 18th Street he turned left again, and headed back over to Blagden. He followed the road until it turned into Rock Creek Park, then headed north on Beach Drive listening to the melodic sounds of the small creek off to his right.

He practically had the park to himself.

Every now and then a bicyclist, braving the morning chill, would pass him; along with the occasional car. No one seemed to pay him any mind. To the average observer he was just another one of those *odd* nature lovers, out for a morning stroll. It would have been perfect, save for the time of year. Morgan imagined that this place must look like a lush oasis in the summer.

A short way up the road there was a small rest area, just large enough for a car to pull off in. Along the edge of the curb were wooden posts, sunk into the ground, presumably to keep errant motorists from pulling too far off the road and plunging into the creek.

Just beyond the rest stop, and across the road, was a large rocky outcropping. The man looked around, ensuring that there was no one in the area, and crossed quickly. He reached into his pocket and removed an oversized piece of chalk. As he walked by, he marked the largest stone facing the roadway.

In tradecraft it was called a *dead drop*. It was a discrete method of communication, between two parties, which did not involve either of them having to meet one another, face-to-face. The chalk mark would send a message indicating that he had arrived and that everything was on schedule.

Morgan then turned and quickly proceeded across the road, heading back in the direction that he had just come from. Now that he had left his mark, his counterpart could initiate their dead drop."

CHAPTER TEN

"Charles Paine," Maguire called out as he scrolled through the listing. "1157 North 625 West Road."

Across the table from him, Alex entered the information into the Maine Department of Motor Vehicle database and waited for a response. At the same time, Gregor marked the name on full size map which they had mounted to the wall. So far they had managed to identify twenty-three of the twenty-six residences shown in the photos.

Checking, and cross-checking, the various databases had proven to be much more time intensive than they had originally thought. Some proved hard to access, while others were available for the asking. In the end they had sorted through real estate, county taxes, water, power, and phone records. The only two left were motor vehicle and criminal information.

"Charles Paine, male white, date of birth, March 11th, 1965," Alex called out. "Two vehicles currently registered at the address. A 1997 Ford Explorer, gold in color, and a 2006 Chevy Silverado, blue in color. I have seven old records dating back to 1987 at the location. Before that, I show one vehicle with an address in Skowhegan, which was first listed in 1983."

Maguire ran the name through the Maine Criminal History Record Information database.

"Two priors," he said, when the record appeared. "Illegal consumption in 1986 and a driving suspended in 1987. I've got nothing else since then."

"So now we are down to two," Gregor said.

Alex stood up and stretched. "Union rules, coffee and cigarette break."

Maguire looked down at his watch. They'd need to get moving soon. The helicopter was already sitting on the helipad awaiting them. It would take them directly to Rangley Municipal Airport where Maguire had two vehicles rented and waiting.

Earlier in the day Maguire had gone to the hospital to see Melody. He couldn't believe how much improvement there had been since she had first woken up. Her voice was almost back to normal and she was already moving around.

Doctor Rothman had stopped in to say that, if she continued to improve the way she was, they expected her to be released before the end of the week. Of course she would still have private care, but the doctor believed that the quicker they could get her out, the less likely that she would be exposed to infection.

Now that she had her wits about her again, it was even more imperative that they find Gen. She had again asked about her *missing* friend and Maguire had lied, saying that she had called while Melody was asleep. He said that she was out in the field doing some testing on the ground vehicle for Dragon's Breath and that the cell signal had been very poor. He told her that Gen had promised to call back as soon as she could get better reception.

Maguire had broke the news to Melody that he would also be gone for a few days, explaining that he needed to appear before a Congressional oversight committee. He said that they were looking into how the terror cell, which had target New York City, had managed to slip quietly under every federal radar. That part actually elicited a laugh from Melody.

He hated lying to her, but he also didn't want anything to hamper her recovery.

Maguire stood up and walked over to the coffee pot. He poured a fresh cup and returned back to the table.

"How are we looking from an equipment standpoint?" he asked Gregor.

"I put Ernst on it," Gregor replied. "I explained the situation and the terrain. He understands the conditions; he used to work at the Cobra unit in Innsbruck. He assured me that everything has been loaded up in the helicopter already, along with backups for all that we might need."

"I really appreciate everyone's help," James said.

"They would much rather be going with us," Gregor replied.

"I expected as much, no one at that level likes to be kept on the bench when the game is at stake," Maguire said. "But the three of us flying in won't set off alarms the way a full loaded team would. Maybe if we had more time to get there covertly, but time is not our friend right now."

"It would have been nice if we could have gotten a surveillance team up on these two places," Gregor said, pointing at the map.

"In a perfect world, we would have," Maguire said. "I just pray to God that one of them is the right place."

"We'll find her," Gregor said.

"Miss me?" Alex asked as she returned.

"Just discussing where we go from here," Maguire answered.

"Well, since we are down to only two possibilities, you've got a fifty / fifty chance of being right on one of them," she replied.

Maguire looked at the map, taking in the roads and the layout of the homes they had identified.

"Banning's not a fool," he said. "Throughout this entire game the one thing that has come through loud and clear is his propensity to plan ahead. It makes sense that he would be completely off the grid. Not having anything running into your place, like electricity or water, means that there is no reason for anyone to come to check things out, when they break.

"What's your gut telling you?" Alex asked.

"Banning's father was Soviet military," Maguire replied. "That means he would have taught him based on that. If you are planning for a battle, you always want to have the high ground. If I were him, I'd be right here."

James pointed at one of the two *unknown* locations on the map.

"Look at the topography. You have one way in and out, with a critical choke point, right here," he said, motioning to the switchback in the road. "You control the high ground with a 360 degree view. Anyone trying to make an assault would be chopped up like hamburger meat."

"That's encouraging," Gregor said. "Maybe we *should* bring more people."

"Nah, we have something better."

"What's that?" Gregor asked.

"We have *her*," Maguire replied, looking over at Alex.

"Well, on that note, I guess it's time to suit up and go make the fat lady sing," Alex replied.

CHAPTER ELEVEN

Washington, D.C.
Tuesday, February 19th, 2013 – 8:42 a.m.

The vice grip, in which winter had held the city, had loosened just a bit. While the temperature was still cold, the clouds had lifted and the sun now shone brilliantly in the sky above. Mentally, at least, it made the temps seem much more palatable.

Morgan walked out of the hotel and put on a pair of sunglasses. He took a moment to scan the scene, watching the cars and people busily moving about. To his left, several taxis sat idling, their drivers chatting amongst themselves.

He made his way in that direction, but turned to the left at the last moment, circling around the building and walking down to the promenade, that lined this stretch of the Potomac River. As he made his away along the water's edge, he passed row after row of docks. While, there were a handful of few ships still berthed at the marina, the majority would not return for a few more months.

Toward the end of the promenade, just past the tennis stadium where the Washington *Kastles* played, he turned right and made his way back up to Water Street and waited. Less than ten minutes later he flagged down a passing taxi.

"Georgetown Mall," he said to the driver.

Fifteen minutes later the taxi pulled up across from the location. Morgan paid the driver and got out, making his way across Wisconsin Street NW where he headed into the mall.

Georgetown Park, as it was formally known, was a shopping mall and condominium complex in the historic Georgetown district of Washington, D.C. At various times in its life, the building had served as a stable, for the horse drawn streetcars of the old Washington and Georgetown Railroad, a machine shop for cable cars, and even as an annex building for the Defense Communications Agency. At one time the mall had been home to a number of high end stores, but difficult financial times had left it a shell of its former self. Not that any of that mattered to Morgan, because his reason for being there wasn't to shop, but to access the small pathway that ran parallel, between the foundation wall of the old building and the Chesapeake and Ohio Canal.

He slowly made his way along the snow covered path looking for the mark. He had walked about a hundred yards when he spotted it, a small white chalk mark, on the stone wall to his right. He paused, reaching into his pocket to remove the pack of cigarettes, and lit one. He walked to edge of the path and casually examined the waterway. It took him a moment, but then he spotted the thin black nylon cord bobbing on the surface. He glanced around to see if anyone else was walking along the path. When he was sure that he was alone he reached down, grabbing the cord, and pulled it. He felt some brief resistance, but then the spike slid out of the mud and popped up out of the water.

Morgan quickly put the small metal tube into his jacket pocket and zipped it up. He then took a drag on the cigarette and flicked it in a perfect arch, hearing it sizzle as the ember hit the water. Then he turned around and headed back in the direction he had just come from.

Once he had made his way back up to the street, he turned left and headed a block north, over to M Street. He found a small coffee shop and stepped inside, ordering a large black coffee. He took a seat near the front window and watched the people pass by.

This was always the hardest part, when you had the item in your possession and you waited for *them* to come snatch you up. It had never happened to him before, but he knew that day would eventually come. You could only be good so many times before your luck finally ran out. There were very few *old* spies.

Will I see it? he wondered. *Will I be sitting in some coffee shop, like I am now, watching and see them coming for me?*

He chased away the thoughts. He was a professional and he knew what he had to do. He had chosen this life and enjoyed the perks that came along with it. At the end of the day you could only do what you were trained to, and hope the other guys were not as good.

When he was satisfied that the street was moving in a *natural* rhythm, he stood up and made his way toward the front door. Outside he stepped into the throng of pedestrians and allowed himself to be swept further away from the scene.

This section of the city was filled with a myriad of small shops and boutiques. Even though he hadn't sensed any threats, there was always the need to practice ones *tradecraft*. From time to time he would stop, peering into the window of the stores. He'd scan the reflections in the glass to see if anyone stopped to see what he was doing. If the team doing surveillance was good, he'd never see them, but that didn't mean you stopped trying. Every once in a while you'd catch one who would slip up.

He paused for a moment, glancing at his reflection in the window. There were places in the world where a black man would stand out like a sore thumb, but not here. It was one of the reasons he liked coming to America, it truly was a melting pot. It was a place where he could walk around with total anonymity.

Midway through the block he spotted a liquor store and stepped inside. It gave him the opportunity to get warm and observe the street again. He scanned the doorways on the other side to see if anyone else had ducked inside to await his next move.

"Can I help you?"

Morgan turned around to see a small, white haired Pakistani man appear from behind a counter.

"Yes, I hope so," Morgan said. "I need some whiskey, but I'm looking for something different. Perhaps something flavored?"

"I think I have something that will do the trick," the man said.

He led Morgan over to a back wall and picked up a bottle from the shelf.

"Fireball," he said. "It has a cinnamon taste. It is very smooth and very popular. I have a hard time keeping it in stock."

"Sounds wonderful, I'll take it."

When he had paid for his purchase, he walked outside and turned back in the direction he came. Half way up the block he spotted a taxi approaching. He stepped out into the street and waved it down.

"River Inn, 7th Street SW," he said, as he shut the door.

Morgan leaned back in the seat and stared out the window, watching as the people passed by. They were like sheep, going about their day, oblivious to what was actually going on in the world. They thought they knew. Most of them even believed what the talking heads in the *idiot box* told them.

It wasn't really their fault. They were just too preoccupied with their own lives. They worried about their finances and family. How they would love to quit their jobs; because their boss was a complete asshole to them. How their spouse frivolously spent their money and the way their children always seemed to demand more and more. They had too much *clutter* going on in their minds to think clearly. When it came time to vote, they had no clue. They elected the person who lied best to them and who promised to give them the most. The fact that all of those promises were actually paid for by their collective taxes, was lost on them.

That being said, it was hard to be sympathetic toward them. For their part, they were clueless when it came to real suffering. They lived in a country that was rich with resources. They lacked for nothing, yet took everything for granted. Worse yet, they wasted with ignorance. The closest any of them had ever come to true hardship was when the power went out for a few days and you would think that the end of the world was at hand. He thought back to the aftermath of Hurricane Katrina and how they had so quickly turned on one another. Even the politicians had joined in, quickly pointing fingers and blaming the other side, even as they lined their own pockets with money that had been promised to the victims. There was no responsibility on the part of anyone.

They deserved their fate, he thought. *They deserved to live the way people in other countries did.*

Maybe the item zipped up in his pocket would facilitate that change.

Morgan reached into the brown paper bag and opened the bottle and took a drink. He tasted the warmth of the cinnamon as it passed over his tongue, and then felt the hot burn, as the liquid went down his throat. He needed something to take the edge off. He knew what was coming next and he needed to be relaxed.

Ten minutes later he was safely back in his hotel room. He laid the jacket on the bed and poured himself another glass of whiskey, before lighting a cigarette. He opened the patio door and stepped outside. The sun felt good on his face and the drink warmed his stomach. He stared out over the Potomac, watching as the sunlight danced on the surface of the water, like a field of sparkling diamonds. He took a drag on the cigarette, as he took in all the little details, creating a mental picture for himself. It was a beautiful view.

One that he was certain he would most likely never see again.

Morgan took one last drag before flipping the cigarette off the balcony. He had delayed this process long enough and knew he needed to get it over with. He stepped back into the room, closing the door behind him and shut the curtains.

He reached over and turned on the desk lamp, then he walked over to the closet where he removed the cardboard box from the shelf. He walked back to the desk, setting the box down, and removed the spike from his jacket. He took it over to the bathroom sink, rinsing it off, and then dried it thoroughly. He brought it back over to the desk and placed it off to the side as he began unpacking the contents of the box.

Inside the box was a sealed package which held a sterilized syringe, with a large bore, stainless steel injector needle. He then removed a pair of latex gloves, gauze pads, tweezers, a package of swab sticks, a small container of aspirin and surgical tape. There were also two bottles, one containing isopropyl alcohol and the other iodine. He laid each of the items neatly on the desk, then cut two long strips of the surgical tape and stuck them to the edge of the desk.

The last item in the box was the most critical. He picked up the sealed bag containing the cell phone and tossed it on the bed. He would need that later.

Morgan then picked up the spike and carefully unscrewed the top, retrieving the foam insert which held the small glass microchip. He slipped the microchip from its cocoon, holding it up to the light, and examined it.

It was elongated, about twice as large as a grain of rice. In many ways it bore a resemblance to a traditional radio-frequency identification tag, more commonly referred to as an RFID. Those devices were used for the wireless, non-contact, use of radio-frequency electromagnetic fields to transfer data.

These first gained popularity in non-commercial use when they were implanted in animals. They were used to reunite lost pets with their owners. Despite the controversy regarding human applications, the so called *Mark of the Beast* in some religious circles, human beings soon began to enjoy the benefits. By implanting them sub-dermally, they could link them to a variety of items, granting them secure access to vehicles, computers, and electronic doors. For the most part, it was a limited use novelty.

However, in this case, appearance was the only thing that this device had in common with a normal RFID. The small microchip was not limited in the way an RFID was. Traditional RFID's had only two kilobytes of data capacity, while very high end expensive ones had one megabyte. This particular device held nearly twenty gigabytes and came equipped with military grade encryption. More importantly, to him, the device was undetectable by airport security metal detectors or hand scanners.

He laid it on the desk and got up, retrieving a drinking glass and a hand towel from the bathroom. He laid the towel down on the desk and then opened the bottle of alcohol, pouring it into the glass. He carefully placed the chip into the glass, along with the tweezers, submerging the ends into the clear liquid. When he was done he poured himself another drink for courage, drinking it quickly.

Morgan kicked off his shoes and unzipped his pants, laying them on the bed. He then went to the bathroom, thoroughly washing his hands with soap and hot water. When he was done, he went back to the desk and sat down.

The initial step was to disinfect the insertion area. He opened the bottle of iodine and dipped one of the sticks into it. He then began to swab the skin on the interior of his right thigh. While the iodine began to work, he began prepping everything else.

First he put on the latex gloves and then opened one of the gauze pads. Next he opened the syringe, laying the tip on the gauze pad. Then he picked-up the tweezers and removed the chip from the glass, slipping it carefully inside the tip of the needle. He picked the syringe up and depressed the plunger until he could just see the tip of the chip.

He picked up the towel, folding it over, and put it in his mouth, clenching down on it. With his left hand he reached down and grabbed the skin of his inner thigh. He pinched it, pulling it up slightly like a small tent, and pressed the tip of the needle into the skin.

He felt the pain as the needles sharp tip penetrated the skin. As it made its incision, he released the skin, continuing to press the needle in further. Once he was sure that he had achieved the desired depth, he depressed the plunger, pushing the chip out and under the skin. He felt an intense burning sensation from the alcohol that remained on the chip. When it was done, he reached up and grabbed a gauze pad, pressing it against the skin. Morgan slowly withdrew the needle, leaving the chip imbedded between the dermis and fascia of the skin.

He reached up, removing one of the pieces of tape and then placed it over his thigh to hold the gauze in place. He then removed the second, laying it diagonally to the other, creating a large X pattern.

Morgan leaned back in the chair and closed his eyes. He suddenly felt weak, as if something had just physically drained out of him. It wasn't the worst pain he had ever felt, not even close. He'd suffered through a number of brutal beatings in the past. Yet, the fact that he had to do it to himself, seemed to make it so much more difficult. Mentally, it was much easier to have a stranger hurt you.

He reached over, picking up the pack of cigarettes and lit one. He took a long, deep breath, hearing the ember sizzle. It seemed to calm him down and allow him to concentrate on something other than what he had just done. Morgan opened the aspirin bottle and removed several of the pills. He then picked up the whiskey glass and took another drink, washing the medicine down.

He would have the remainder of today to rest, but then it would be time to move on. By this time Wednesday he would be back home and his part in all of this would be complete. Then it would be up to someone else to put the data contained in the microchip to good use.

CHAPTER TWELVE

Northern Maine
Tuesday, February 19th, 2013 – 1:17 p.m.

Maguire checked the map, then pulled the Ford Explorer off the road and headed up the crushed gravel driveway. This was the last *unknown* house before the one at the end of the road, the one that he believed to be Banning's.

Earlier in the morning, long before sunrise, they had devised a plan to keep the *primary* location under surveillance while Maguire conducted the interview of the secondary location.

Gregor and Alex had gone out to set up an observation post, on the other side of the valley, across from the house that they believed was Banning's. The location they'd chosen was on state owned land, so they didn't need to worry about being *found* by some irate landowner.

While Gregor conducted the actual observation, Alex manned one of the vehicles, parked discretely back on a seldom used access road. If Gregor spotted a vehicle attempting to leave, he could alert her quickly enough that she could intercept it on the main road. That left Maguire free to do the actual interviews.

Prior to hitting this location, Maguire had done some interviews of several of the other locations, just to insure that they had been correct in ruling them out. He'd met initial resistance from several of the residents that he interviewed. Clearly they didn't get many *unsolicited* visitors up here and, more importantly, it seemed that they preferred to keep it that way. While they seemed to be more receptive when they heard why he was bothering them, a fabricated *tear-jerker* story about a fatherless child who needed a bone marrow transplant, they still didn't have any tangible information which could help him positively identify the location as belonging to Keith Banning.

As Maguire pulled up to the old, weathered cabin, he saw a man step out onto the porch, eyeing him suspiciously, a shotgun held down at his side.

Great, he thought. *Here we go again. Isn't anyone up here the least bit happy?*

Maguire got out of the car and slowly made his way toward the man.

"Morning, sir," Maguire said.

"I'm not buying anything," the man replied tersely. "So get back in your car and get the hell off my property."

"I'm not selling anything," Maguire replied.

"I don't give a damn either way," the man said, raising the shotgun up. "You need to leave my property, unless you have a badge. And if you do have a badge, you'd better have yourself a warrant."

Maguire raised his hands up and took a step back.

"All I'm trying to do is locate a man about a dying girl."

The man stepped off the porch and into the front lawn.

"If you don't leave my property, someone's going to be looking to notify your next of kin that *you've* gone and died."

Maguire stared at the man, who was now less than twenty feet away from him. He was an older man, probably in his seventies, with a well-established pot-belly protruding from the bib overalls he was wearing. He wore a baseball cap on his head that depicted a large angry bee that was holding a machine gun in one hand, along with a hammer and wrench in the others. Despite the slovenly appearance, Maguire could see the hardness in the man. First appearances could not only be deceiving, but deadly.

"Were you a Seabee?" Maguire asked, as he continued to back up toward his car.

"That's right. Is there a reason you're still talking and not driving yet?"

"Just an observation, I was in the Navy as well."

The man stopped his advance, lowering the shotgun slightly.

"Oh yeah?" he said, "What was your rating?"

"Gunner's Mate," Maguire replied. "I was in SEAL Team Four."

"Every half-assed *wannabe* claims to have been a SEAL nowadays."

"True, but I'm going to say the vast majority of those half-assed wannabes would have pissed themselves the minute you raised that Mossberg up," Maguire replied. He looked down at the front of his pants. "I'm still good."

The man laughed. "Most of the SEAL's I've known are pretty hard-charging, knuckle-draggers. What did you do in the teams? And don't give me that 'it's classified' bullshit."

"Mostly we drank beer, chased base bunnies and liberated beer money from *dirt* sailors."

"Well, you've got a smart mouth like most of the SEAL's I've known, I'll give you that."

"That's what my senior chief would tell me."

"Sounds like a smart man. What was your rate?"

"I got out as an E-5 back in '95, what about you?"

"I retired as an E-8, probably before you were born."

"Vietnam?"

"Yeah, I spent several *wonderful* years in Southeast Asia," the man replied. "You want a beer?"

"It's five o'clock somewhere," Maguire replied.

The man lowered the shotgun and headed back to the house with Maguire in tow. Once inside, he hung the shotgun in a rack above the door.

"Grab a chair," he said, motioning Maguire toward one of the chairs in the living room, as he walked over to the refrigerator where he removed two beers.

Maguire walked into the living room and looked up at the wooden display case hanging on the wall. In the center of the case were several rows of medals, the top two spots held the Bronze Star, with a 'V' device, indicating that it was awarded for combat, and the Purple Heart.

"Dong Xoai, June 1965," the man said, as he walked into the room and handed Maguire a beer. "I was in Team 1104. The compound came under attack by a Vietcong regiment. I started that day off as a snot nose kid and ended it covered in the blood of some of my best friends. You ever been in combat, son?"

"Yeah, I have," Maguire replied somberly.

"Well, may God have mercy on us," the man said, raising his beer can in a mocking salute. "To another fine Navy day!"

Maguire took a drink and set the can down on the coffee table in front of him.

"So what's your name frog?"

"Maguire, James Maguire. But everyone calls me Paddy."

"Mike Ryan, but you can call me Chief," the man said with a smile.

"Hooyah, Chief" Maguire replied.

"So what's the real reason you're up here, Paddy? Gimme a real no-shitter and save that charity story for the chaplains."

"I'm hunting someone who supposedly lives in these parts. He might be a neighbor of yours."

"Neighbors in this neck of the woods tend to be, more often than not, a bit *reclusive*. I've been up here for damn near forty years and I could probably count on one hand the number of times any neighbor has stopped by here."

"Well, I'm thinking that nothing say's 'unwelcome' like the business end of a shotgun."

"It's a universal language," Ryan said, as he took a drink. "So who's this fella you're looking for?"

"Name is supposedly Keith Banning, but that might not mean anything to you. He's a tall guy, about six feet. He'd be in his early forties with close cropped blonde hair. I have a hunch he might live in the house up the road."

"Name doesn't ring a bell," he replied. "I usually judge people by whether they are a nuisance or not. I can't recall ever seeing or hearing anyone from that part of the hill. In my book, that's a *good* neighbor. Occasionally I'll hear someone shooting or riding a snow machine, but those sounds are as common as traffic in the big city."

"Judging from how far up from the road you are, I guess you don't see many vehicles heading to or from there."

"I get out about once a week to head into town. Every two weeks in the winter. Other than that, I rarely make it beyond the end of the driveway."

"I was afraid you might say that," Maguire replied. "I've been hitting a brick wall at every turn with this guy. Some days I wonder if I'm not chasing a ghost."

"Wish I could have helped you out more, son."

"So do I, Chief," Maguire said, as he finished the last of the beer. "Well, I'm sorry to have taken up your time."

"Not at all," Ryan said. "At least I didn't have to shoot you."

"Yeah, who wants to do all that paperwork," Maguire said with a laugh.

"Paperwork my ass, the grounds so hard I'd have had to wait till May before I could have buried you."

"Point taken," Maguire replied.

He stepped out onto the porch, making his way down the steps, before he headed toward the car.

"Fair winds and following seas, Chief," he called back to the man.

"You too," Ryan called out. "Happy hunting."

Maguire was just about to get into the truck when he saw Ryan turn around and start walking back toward him.

"Hey, Paddy," he called out.

"Yeah, Chief?"

"I do remember something, not your man, but a car."

"What about it?"

"I was heading into town one day and was just about to pull onto the road when this vehicle came whipping around the bend. Another second quicker and he would have t-boned me."

"Okay," Maguire said hesitantly, unsure where the man was going with all of this.

"Anyway, the car was coming from the direction of where you think your guy lives. That was odd enough, but he was driving the same car that you have. That's actually what reminded me of the incident."

"He was driving a Ford Explorer?"

"Yep," Ryan replied.

Maguire leaned into the car and pulled out a folder, thumbing through the pages until he found the Maine State Police report. He searched through until he found the vehicle description of the car that Banning had crashed: Ford Explorer.

"Bingo!" Maguire said.

"You gotta pay attention," Ryan said, as he turned to walk back to the house. "You never know when you're going to see this shit again."

"God bless Navy chiefs," he muttered, as he climbed back into the vehicle.

Maguire removed the cell phone from his pocket and called Gregor.

"It's him," he said, when Gregor answered.

"There's movement inside the house," Gregor replied. "But I can't get a positive ID."

"Where's Alex?"

"She's down on the access road, in the event that anyone tried to leave."

"Ok, it's time for plan 'B'," James replied. "You continue to keep it under observation and let me know immediately if anything happens. I'll let you know when we are ready to begin."

"*Ja wohl*," Gregor replied.

In times of stress you reverted back to what you knew, including your native tongue. Gregor couldn't think of anything more stressful then sitting on a ridge and looking at a cabin through a sniper scope, all while wondering if his girlfriend was alive or dead inside.

On the other side of the mountain, James ended the call and immediately reached out to Alex.

"Where are you at?"

"Fuck if I know," Alex said, taking a drag on her cigarette and exhaling. "But it beats the livin' shit out of Brownsville, I can tell you that."

Maguire laughed.

"Well it's show time for you, tiger," he replied.

"I thought you'd never ask," Alex said. "Where do you want to meet up?"

"Come over to me," Maguire explained. "Once you turn off onto route 23 come down about two miles. You'll spot some utility lines, there's an access road about a hundred feet up on the right. I'll meet you there."

"Roger, roger."

Maguire ended the call. He drove down the driveway and made a right, heading back toward the main road. About a half mile later, he turned off onto the access road and waited for her to arrive.

It was about five minutes till he saw the late model, Ford Econoline van pull in and head up to where he was parked. Alex got out, quickly making her way over to the passenger side of the Explorer, and climbed in.

"Fuck, it's cold up here," she exclaimed. "And that POS you got me has two temperature settings, arctic breezes and cold as a witch's tit."

"You done bitching?" he asked.

"And the cigarette lighter doesn't work," Alex said. "There, I'm done now."

"Are you ready for this?" he asked.

"*Me*?" Alex replied. "I was born ready, rookie."

She was dressed in a faded blue denim shirt with navy blue cargo pants. The shirt had large red initials on the left breast, which read RDS, and a little speeding truck underneath. Affixed to either side of the van, and on the rear door, were large magnetic placards that read RDS / Rapid Delivery Systems. If anyone checked they would find an online presence for the company, which of course was a dummy. It was not an in-depth cover, but it didn't need to be. If anyone called to verify, they would get put on a 'your call is very important to us' call-waiting limbo.

"Don't be a hero, Alex," Maguire said. "This fucker is the real deal. He's a USDA, Grade 'A', certifiable lunatic. I've seen what this asshole can do. Just draw him out and let Gregor take the shot."

"That's if *he* is there," Alex said. "But that crispy critter in the morgue just might be him. In that case, we need to know who we are dealing with now, but I promise that I won't do anything stupid."

Maguire reached into the back seat and picked up a box, which he then handed to her.

"Reginald Bertrand," Maguire said. "It's one of the alias' we discovered for Banning early on in the investigation."

"What's in the package?"

"A tee shirt and invoice from McP's Irish Pub in Coronado."

"I take it that's an *inside* joke."

"Just run with the script," Maguire said. "See what you can, deliver the package, and get the hell out of there."

"I love it when you get so protective," Alex replied. "Trust me, James; at the first sign of a potential problem I'll personally put the bullet in that fucker's head. Now, if you don't mind, I need to go deliver a package."

"Then I guess that it is show time," he replied.

Alex got out of the truck and headed back toward the van.

Maguire picked up the phone and called Gregor.

"She's going in," he said.

"Everything's quiet, no movement."

"If there's any sign…"

"He won't get close to her, James," Gregor replied. "I promise."

CHAPTER THIRTEEN

Northern Maine
Tuesday, February 19th, 2013 – 2:43 p.m.

Tatiana stared through the small window at Genevieve, who was asleep on the bed. Try as she might, it was becoming more and more difficult to resist the urges she was feeling. When Keith was here, she could at least count on the fact that he could never go very long without needing to be with her. Now that she was alone, she was becoming more restless with each passing moment.

No, that wasn't true, she thought. *The fact was, she wasn't alone and that was what made this so hard.*

Two nights ago she had let the opportunity pass. She'd only been trying to prove a point and hadn't actually used enough of the drug. After the woman had passed out, she had allowed herself to have a *peek*, not realizing that this act would only make it harder on her.

It was like having chocolate in the house, you never wanted it until it was actually there for the taking.

There was a part of her that hoped she might be able to *bond* with the woman, to make her see things from her perspective. Still, it was very early in this game. She needed to accept that, even with her and Keith, it had taken quite some time for her to come around.

Not that this understanding made it any easier for her *physically*. Tatiana slid her hand down the front of her jeans and pressed her fingers against herself. She could feel the wetness through the thin material of her panties. She bit down on her bottom lip to keep herself from moaning. She ached inside and desperately needed release. Now the question was could she wait? Even more important, did she want to?

She still had the prescription drugs, which she had taken from the medicine cabinet back at her old apartment. She could use them, but what would that get her? An unconscious victim? Banning could do it, because he just needed a warm, wet hole to fill. She needed something more, she need a *willing* participant.

At least for now, she would just have to rely on the trusty vibrator in the nightstand to take the edge off.

Tatiana closed the door on the viewing slot and headed back upstairs. The pills reminded her that she still had an unsettled score to take care of with Lena's former girlfriend. Unlike the little redhead downstairs, Tatiana could care less if Susan Hadley was a *willing* participant or not. Actually, she kind of hoped that Susan would put up a fight. It would make the end so much more rewarding.

She had just closed the trap door to the basement when she heard the sound of a car door slam shut outside. She turned and made her way to the living room, where she knelt down on the couch, and peered out the window.

A white van was parked outside and she could see the rear door open in the back.

"Who the fuck is this?" she wondered out loud.

Keith had never mentioned anything to her. In fact, in all the time they had been there, she couldn't recall anyone coming to the cabin. Then again, it had only been recently that she had been given free run of the place.

As Tatiana continued to watch, she saw the door of the van close and a woman, with blonde hair, emerged from around the back of the vehicle. She was wearing a blue uniform and carried a package in her hands. As she made her way toward the front door, Tatiana lost sight of her.

"Fuck!"

She stood up, her heart beating quickly.

What do I do? she wondered.

This was nothing she had ever expected, let alone prepared for.

Should she answer the door? *Should she just ignore it*?

The thoughts whipped around her mind to fast for answers, and then she heard a knock at the door. Tatiana tucked her shirt back into her jeans, and ran her hands through her hair.

Look normal, she told herself.

She made her way through the kitchen and toward the front door, peering out the window at the woman standing outside. She looked around, but didn't see anyone else, and opened the door cautiously.

"Can I help you?" Tatiana asked.

"Yes, I have a package for Reginald Bertrand," Alex said.

"Who?" Tatiana replied.

The name sounded vaguely familiar to her, and she struggled to remember where she had seen it, without looking like an idiot to the woman.

"Reginald Bertrand," Alex repeated.

Suddenly Tatiana remembered seeing the name on a fake license see had found during the search of the bunker. With that realization, Tatiana felt herself calm down, her breathing returning to normal.

"Oh, I'm sorry, Reggie's not here right now," she replied.

"Great," Alex replied. "It requires his signature. Do you have any idea when he'll be back?"

"I wish I could," Tatiana said. "It could be five minutes, five hours or five days. Reggie has a tendency of being *unpredictable*."

Tatiana looked at the woman, taking in the details. She was a bit smaller than she was, but she certainly filled out the uniform she was wearing quite well. The top button of her shirt seemed to be barely containing what was underneath, and the cargo pants that she was wearing hugged the curves of her body, as if they had been painted on.

"Can't I just sign his name?" she asked.

"I'm sure you're a very nice lady," Alex said. "But I did that shit once, when I worked down in Augusta. Turns out I delivered the girlfriend's anniversary gift to the wife. Which is why I work up *here* now, trying to deliver packages to people with bad attitudes and shotguns."

"Well, I certainly don't want you to get in trouble," Tatiana replied.

"I had a hard enough time finding this place; I was hoping that I would get lucky the first time."

"That's funny," Tatiana said, "I was thinking the same thing."

"Huh?" Alex replied, taking in what the woman had just said.

"Uhm, I just meant,...."

"Oh, I get it," Alex said with a smile.

"You do?"

"Uh huh," she said, as she looked around furtively.

Tatiana seized the moment.

"Would you like to come in?"

"I don't know," Alex replied. "My boss is so far up my ass, I can't even take a cigarette break without him busting my chops. They even went and put GPS unit's in the trucks, so they can track our every movement."

"So," Tatiana replied, taking a step backward. "Just tell him that you had to go to the bathroom."

Alex glanced at the truck and then back at Tatiana.

"Fuck it," Alex said. "Do you have any coffee?"

"I've got anything your little heart desires, gorgeous."

Alex followed her into the cabin, closing the door behind her.

"Nice place you have here...," Alex said, as she laid the box on the table.

"Tatiana," she replied. "And you?"

"Wow, that's an exotic name. I like it, I'm Alex."

"I'm very pleased to meet you, Alex."

"This is a lot nicer than most of the places I stop at."

"Thanks," Tatiana replied, as she poured two cups of coffee. "You want anything else in this? Milk, sugar, whiskey?"

"If it was four hours from now, Tatiana, I'd say all of the above, but black is fine, for now."

Tatiana laughed as she walked toward Alex, handing her the mug. "You sound like my kind of girl, Alex. Follow me."

Tatiana led her into the living room and took a seat in the chair. She didn't want to come on too strong, so she thought it was better to give her some space and see how things progressed.

Alex sat down on the couch, taking a sip of coffee.

"Thanks, I really needed this. My ass has been dragging like it's a Monday."

"You're welcome," Tatiana replied.

Alex noticed the cigarettes and ashtray on the coffee table.

"You mind," she asked.

"No, not at all," Tatiana replied. "As a matter of fact I could use one myself."

Alex removed the cigarette pack from her pocket and lit one, then leaned over to light Tatiana's.

"Thanks," she replied. "So do you get around this area often?"

"Around here?" Alex asked. "Probably once a week. I try to save everything up so I can do all my deliveries in this area on one day, although that could certainly change."

"Really, and what would it take to make you alter a system that seems to be working out so well."

Alex smiled, picking up the coffee cup and taking a drink.

"Finding a place that serves hot coffee is a good start."

Tatiana squirmed in her seat. The wetness she felt before paled in comparison to what she was feeling now. The ache inside her had grown stronger every minute since the woman had come inside. It took everything in her to contain her desire and not pounce on the woman. She took a drag on her cigarette, exhaling slowly.

"I'll make sure to keep a fresh pot on," she said. "Just in case you decide to make more frequent stops in this area."

"So let me be honest, Tatiana. This Reggie, is he going to get pissed off if he sees me stopping in for *coffee* on a regular basis?"

"Reggie," Tatiana laughed. "No, Reggie won't be pissed. In fact, the truth is that he's hardly ever around. I doubt that you'd even cross paths with him, Alex."

"That's a relief," Alex said. "I don't need no jealous *others* calling my boss. If they ship me any further north, I'll be delivering frozen moose balls to Canadians and, to be honest, my French really sucks."

"Then we'll have to make sure that nothing happens to take you off this route," Tatiana replied.

"Fuck me, the route," Alex said, looking down at her watch. "If I don't get the rest of those packages delivered, they'll pull my tracking log and bust my balls over why I was here so long."

"They don't track your *off* time do they?"

"Not yet," Alex replied. "At least I don't think so."

"Well, in that case, why don't you go finish delivering your packages? When you get off, come back and I'll make us dinner?"

"Good coffee, good looks and a potentially good dinner, what girl could say no to that offer?" Alex said, as she stood up, crushing the cigarette out in the ashtray.

"I was hoping you'd say that," Tatiana replied.

"If you don't mind, can I use your bathroom? The shocks on that van are killing me."

"Be my guest," Tatiana replied. "Just down the hallway there."

"Thanks."

Tatiana watched as she walked down the hall. The girl definitely had one helluva body on her. She couldn't wait to see what it looked like when she peeled her out of those pants. A few moments later, Alex emerged from the bathroom.

"So what time do you think you'll be here?" Tatiana asked.

"I get off at five, figure about forty-five minutes to get back here, an hour tops if the dickhead at the desk has anything to gripe about. The question is, do you want me to stop home first and change or will you take me as I am?"

Tatiana bit her lip as she felt her face flush. This had been an unexpected turn and something she was completely unused to. She was certainly unabashed and open about her feelings. Tatiana was about ready to beg her not to leave; she wanted her now, not five hours from now.

Calm down you fucking idiot, she thought. *You're acting like a teenager.*

Tatiana took a deep breath and composed herself.

"That's totally up to you, Alex, but for the record, you look absolutely perfect the way you are right now."

"I was hoping you'd say that, I'd rather come straight here after work. Should I bring anything with me?"

"Nope, all I need is you."

The two women walked toward the front door and Alex grabbed the box as she passed the table. As Tatiana reached down for the doorknob, Alex reached out with her free hand and stopped her. Tatiana turned to look at her and suddenly felt Alex's lips on hers.

It was a short, passionate kiss, and it left Tatiana standing there, wide-eyed, mouth open and speechless.

"Just a little something to keep that fire going, till I get back," Alex said.

Tatiana watched as Alex walked out the door and headed off toward the van. She watched as she climbed inside, and waved as she drove off.

She closed the door, locking it behind her. Her legs were a bit wobbly and she felt slightly lightheaded. She needed to lie down, so she headed off to the bedroom. She had a big night ahead of her and she would need to be well rested.

Maybe I don't need you after all, she thought as she walked past the trap door.

CHAPTER FOURTEEN

Northern Maine
Tuesday, February 19th, 2013 – 2:51 p.m.

"What the fuck do you mean she went into the house?"

"She just went inside," Gregor replied, as he continued to stare through the scope at the front door.

"Fuck!" Maguire exclaimed. "What the hell does she think she's doing?"

"I don't know, but I didn't witness any threatening gestures. She turned, looked around, and I think she smiled."

"Could you see who answered the door?"

"No, they stood inside, it was too dark."

Maguire's mind was racing. She said that she would be careful, and here she was being her usual reckless self.

"Keep watching," Maguire said. "Tell me anything that goes on."

"There's movement inside the living room," Gregor said. "But I can't see clearly."

The minutes ticked slowly by as Maguire waited. He struggled with what he should do. Alex was street smart, probably one of the best, and she could handle herself better than most. But he also knew what Banning could do, and until he knew for certain that the man was dead, he couldn't rule anything out.

Still, could he risk rushing inside now? The wrong move, one misstep and there would be two hostages, not just one.

Maguire looked down at his watch.

Five minutes, he thought. *Five minutes and you take the door.*

He watched as the second hand began its march around the dial. Suddenly, he heard Gregor's voice over the phone.

"Movement!"

"What do you see?"

"She just walked out; she's back in the van."

Maguire closed his eyes, feeling a wave of relief wash over him. He was just grateful that she was okay, this way he could kill her himself, once she got back here.

"Okay, keep watching and I will let you know what's going on as soon as I talk to her."

"Will do," Gregor replied.

Maguire ended the call, placing the phone back into his pocket. He waited impatiently until he saw the van pull back up the access road, then jumped out of the explorer.

Alex came to a stop and put the van into park, then rolled down the window.

"Are you fucking crazy?" he screamed. "Do you have any idea just how incredibly fucking stupid that was?"

She reached into her pocket, removing the pack of cigarettes and lit one up, as she continued to stare out the window listening to him.

"What did I say, Alex? Stick to the fucking script, don't do anything stupid, so what do you do, fucking go inside the place.

Go inside! Did you fucking listen? Did you even hear anything I said? Are you out of you fucking goddamn mind?"

Maguire stopped, and stared at her. The only sound was the wind blowing through the pine trees.

"Are you done?" Alex asked.

Maguire opened his mouth and began to speak, then stopped.

"Yeah," he said a moment later. "I'm done."

"Has anyone ever told you that when you get mad, you look like one of those monkeys on a chain; their mouths yapping away in four quarter time?"

Maguire closed his eyes and fought the urge to laugh.

"Please tell me there was a good fucking reason for what you just did?"

"Of course there was," Alex replied. "Now are you going to get in the van and let me explain why, or are you going to stand out there like a *schmuck* and make me waste all this heat."

Maguire walked over and got in the van.

"So what was this good reason?"

"Well, first a blonde haired woman answered the door, not Banning. I'm guessing it's the same one from the Post Office. I figured if what you told me about Banning was right; if he were there, he'd have answered. I got the impression that our *Reggie Bertrand* isn't around and the odds are he won't be coming back."

"What makes you say that?"

"Just the way that she acted; her mannerisms. I don't think Banning is there."

"So why did you go inside?"

"Because we needed a look and the opportunity presented itself. Remember, the *ghost* doesn't ask the *undercover* why they do certain things; they're just there to protect them. Likewise, the *undercover* does certain things because they know the *ghost* is there to protect them. I knew you guys had my back, and I was willing to take the chance."

"Damnit, Alex, do you know how worried I was?"

"Easy, rookie, you know that I'm hard to kill. Besides, if she tried anything, I'd have put her lights out."

"What else did you find?"

"Well, it's the right place. The dumb bitch gave me a cup of coffee in a sheriff's office mug. The interior is fairly large. Three rooms from what I could see. The front door leads directly into the kitchen with a living room off to the right. There's a short hallway that leads down to a bedroom and the bathroom is off of it. I did spy a closet, with what appeared to be a crease in the rug. It's probably a trap door, but I didn't want to risk getting caught taking a look without some backup. I figured I could do that later."

"What do you mean?" Maguire asked.

"I got dinner plans tonight," Alex replied with a smile.

"Are you fucking kidding me?"

"You know what they say, rookie. If you go *bi*, you double your chances for a date on Friday night."

"You're insane," Maguire said.

"Eh, what could it hurt? I've been in a slump lately."

"What's your plan?"

"I come back under the pretense of my date. I figure she'll be off-guard at that point. You guys give me fifteen minutes to let things settle down. By that time you'll be able to come up undetected and stage outside. I'll make an excuse of needing to use the bathroom. When you see the light go on you hit the door. Once I hear you breach, I'll go to where I saw the trap door and gain access to whatever is below."

"Oh, is that all?" Maguire asked.

"Hey, you asked me what my plan was; you didn't ask if it was a good one."

"Nope," Maguire said, shaking his head. "No possible way that any of this can go wrong,"

"You only live once, Mr. *Happy*. Don't go getting soft on me now."

CHAPTER FIFTEEN

Washington, D.C.
Tuesday, February 19th, 2013 – 5:31 p.m.

Morgan sat on the edge of the bed nursing his drink. His leg ached and the medicine wasn't doing anything to take the edge off. The bottle of whiskey that he had picked up was nearly empty.

I should have gotten the bigger one, he scolded himself.

He would have to get up and make his way down to the restaurant for dinner. He needed to eat something, and he was certainly going to need more to drink.

Morgan picked up the package containing the cell phone and opened it, removing the phone and its battery. He opened the back cover and installed the battery, then powered it up.

When the screen appeared, he opened the contacts folder and selected the number that was pre-entered into it. He waited as the call was connected. A moment later a female voice answered.

"Hello?"

"Hi, my class is getting out early and I don't have a ride. Can you have someone pick me up?"

"Yes, your brother will come get you and bring you home, be outside."

"Thank you," Morgan said and ended the call.

He removed the back of the phone and took the battery out. This, and the number he had just called, were both disposable phones. Before dinner, he would take a walk down by the marina and dispose of the phone in the river. He imagined that the one on the other end was already destroyed.

The call was a ruse, a simple method to notify his contact that he had completed this part of the task and that he was ready to continue. Everything had been prearranged well in advance. He looked down at his watch. He had a little more than fourteen hours remaining, before his ride got here.

Morgan got up and walked over to the edge of the bed. He picked up the pants and put them on. It was too bad that they didn't have room service here. He'd much rather spend the evening in his room, as opposed to the noise of the restaurant and bar downstairs.

Oh well, one more day and, God willing, he would be on his way back home for some much needed rest.

CHAPTER SIXTEEN

Northern Maine
Tuesday, February 19th, 2013 – 5:39 p.m.

"Are you sure that this is the way you want to play this?" Maguire asked.

"Can you think of a better way?" Alex replied.

Maguire took a deep breath, exhaling slowly, and looked over at Gregor, who sat next to him in the van. Gregor shook his head, unable to give him a better idea.

Knowing that Alex was right didn't make accepting the decision any easier.

"Get in that bathroom as quickly as you can," he replied.

"I know how to do this, James," Alex scolded him, as she took a drag on the cigarette. "Give me fifteen minutes. Let the dust settle before you come up and wait for my signal."

"Fifteen minutes," Maguire.

"*Wait* for my signal," she said, as she got out of the van, crushing the cigarette out under her foot, and headed toward the Explorer.

Alex turned the interior light on in the car and adjusted the rearview mirror. She applied some lipstick and tugged at some errant strands of hair. Then popped a piece of gum in her mouth and turned the light off. She pulled down the access road and headed up to the house.

A couple of minutes later she pulled up to the front door and got out of the truck. She was just about to knock when the door opened.

"Hey," Tatiana said. "I was getting worried you might not come?"

Alex smiled and stepped through the door, closing it behind her.

"Really?" she asked. "And why didn't you think I'd show?"

"I don't know," Tatiana said. "I guess I was just being silly."

"I'd have been here sooner, but the dickhead who signs my checks decided that he hadn't chewed my ass out enough this month," Alex said with a laugh, as she turned around playfully.

"Do I still have an ass left?" she asked. "He did a pretty good job."

Tatiana reached down and ran her hand playfully along the material of the faded jeans that Alex wore.

"Oh yeah, baby," Tatiana said, the words coming out low and seductive, "and what a fine ass it is!"

Alex turned back around to face the woman.

"I'm glad you approve," she said playfully. "So, have you been thinking about me?"

"Maybe a little," Tatiana said with a smile.

"I really could use that drink now," Alex said.

"Go into the living room and I'll bring it to you. Dinner will be ready in about a half hour."

Alex walked into the room and sat down on the couch, waiting for Tatiana. A moment later she came in, carrying two glasses of whiskey on the rocks, and handed one to Alex.

"To new friends," Alex said, tapping her glass against hers.

"New friends," Tatiana said and took a sip.

She sat down in the seat across from Alex. She'd wanted to sit next to her, but thought it would be too forward. So far she liked what she saw in the woman and didn't want to ruin anything.

Would it last? she wondered. *Did it matter*?

Suddenly, the image of Lena kneeling in the back of the truck, flashed in her mind. The look of fear in her eyes as she had pulled the trigger and ended her life.

Was that the way to have a relationship? she thought. *Use them, discard them, and find a new one*?

It certainly did have its merits. It would always be new and exciting, like it was now.

How would the night end? she wondered.

Suddenly, a vision of the two of them in bed flashed through her mind.

"Earth to Tatiana," Alex said. "Are you with me, Tatiana?"

Tatiana shook her head, chasing the thoughts away and felt her face turn hot.

"Wow, did you just zone out," Alex said with a laugh.

"I'm so sorry," Tatiana said and took a sip.

"No need to be, what were you thinking about?"

"Honestly?" she asked. "You, I was thinking about you."

Alex put her drink on the table and got up. She walked over to where Tatiana was, straddled her legs, and sat down on her lap, wrapping her arms over the woman's shoulders.

"And pray tell, what exactly were you thinking about me?"

Tatiana was at a loss. This woman was unlike anything, or anyone, she had ever known before. Her will was so strong, so straightforward, that for a moment, Tatiana felt nervous.

"I was thinking about you, and me, and eating....."

"Mmmm, doesn't that sound yummy," Alex said with a smile.

"Oh shit," Tatiana exclaimed. "The food!"

Alex hopped off the woman's lap and sat back down on the couch, as she watched Tatiana jump up and run toward the kitchen.

"Don't sweat it, baby," Alex called out. "Anything can be fixed with more alcohol."

"It's okay," Tatiana called out. "I saved it."

Alex reached over and picked up the glass, downing the rest of her drink. She got off the couch and headed into the kitchen. Tatiana was standing over the stove, stirring something and she walked up behind her, wrapping her arms around the woman's waist.

"Can I have a refill when you're done," she whispered, then kissed her neck.

"You can have *anything* you want, baby," Tatiana replied.

"Be careful," Alex said. "You don't have any idea just how much I may want."

Tatiana moaned softly.

"Hold that thought," Alex said. "I'm going to go to the bathroom. I'll be right back."

Alex released her arms, and playfully slapped Tatiana's ass as she headed toward the bathroom.

Tatiana covered the pot and reached up into the cabinet, removing the whiskey bottle. She removed the top and poured the remainder into Alex's glass, filling it halfway.

"Fuck," she said. "Really?"

She put the empty bottle on the counter and grabbed her coat, pulling the hood over her head. Then she headed out to the shed where Keith kept the rest of his stash.

Alex walked into the bathroom and closed the door behind her, leaning back against it and took a deep breath. Across from her was the sink and she looked at her reflection in the mirror just above it.

"You, my dear, are one twisted little bitch."

She took a deep breath and reached down, removing the snub nose, Smith and Wesson .38 caliber revolver from the ankle holster, and waited.

• • •

Outside, Maguire and Gregor watched as the light came on where Alex had indicated the bathroom was.

"Okay," James said, "Let's go."

Just as they got ready to move they saw the front door open and a hooded figure emerge.

"Hold!" James said.

As they watched, the figure headed over to a small wooden shed and slipped inside.

This wasn't part of the plan, Maguire thought.

"What do we do?" Gregor asked.

"Fuck it, let's go," James said.

The two men raced out of the tree line, approaching the cabin with their guns drawn. As they drew near to the house James pointed toward the cabin door. Gregor veered off and rushed toward the front door as James continued in the direction of the shed.

As the figure emerged, it turned suddenly and immediately fled in the opposite direction, racing at full speed toward the tree line. James pursued, but his unfamiliarity with the terrain, coupled with the darkness that had enveloped everything, slowed him down, allowing the fleeing figure to maintain a slight distance between them.

He could feel the ground under him begin to slope as they made their way down the backside of the mountain. He reached into his pocket, removing the flashlight, and shined it ahead of him. As he continued the pursuit, he caught glimpses of the figure weaving in and out of the massive pine trees.

The pursuer always had the harder job. Not only did you not know where you were being led, but you had to be prepared for the unexpected. Like the person that you were chasing, doubling back and ambushing you. They had probably gone about a quarter of a mile when he watched the figure slip inside a dilapidated wooden shack. Off in the distance, he could hear the loud roar of rushing water.

He approached the shack cautiously, at an angle, scanning to make sure the person didn't come out the back. He turned the light off, pausing a moment to allow his eyes to adjust to the darkness. Slowly he approached, positioning himself near a wall that had no windows, as he made his way toward the doorway.

There is no easy way to enter a room, especially not alone. In the end it all came down to three things: *Surprise, Speed, and Violence of Action*. Unfortunately, one was out the window, two was highly questionable, and three was yet to be determined, given the fact that the person inside might still be their only link to finding Genevieve alive.

He positioned the flashlight in his left hand, and then brought the gun in his right hand down on top of it.

It was showtime.

Maguire slid through the doorway, turning quickly to his left, scanning the room for threats as he moved quickly along the wall. fifteen feet away, standing in the corner of the room, with their back toward him, was his quarry.

"Don't move," Maguire cried out. "Put your hands on your head."

As he watched, the figure's arms rose up slowly, and then placed their hands on top of their head.

"Turn around, *slowly*."

Maguire watched as they began to move, shifting slowly until they came into view. He hit the button on the flashlight, lighting up the figure and stared into the eyes of Patricia Browning.

"Hi, James," she said. "It's been a long time, hasn't it?"

"What the fuck?"

"It's weird, I know."

"Tricia, what's going on?"

"Are you really going to shoot me, James?" she asked as she slowly lowered her hands to her sides.

"Where's Banning?" he asked, allowing the barrel of the gun to dip down slightly.

"Keith? Keith's dead, James. I would have thought you'd have known that by now."

"How do you know he's dead?" Maguire asked.

"Because I killed him," she replied matter-of-factly.

"You? They said he died in a crash."

"But you really didn't believe that, James, did you?"

Nothing about Banning's death had made any sense to him. The thought of the man skidding off the road to his demise had seemed too perfect, too convenient. As if all the stars had aligned in some cosmic, billion-to-one, death *Powerball*.

"What about Lena?" James asked.

"Sad, but unavoidable," the woman replied. "Although, truth be told, she had a willing hand in her own demise. You can't use people up and then discard them. There are no *innocent* victims, James. Even if it means they were just in the wrong place at the wrong time, they chose to be to there. You understand what I mean, don't you?"

"No one would have blamed you for killing Banning, Tricia. You could have ended it all and went back to your life."

"Really? And what life would you have wanted me to go back to, James? The one with the abusive *husband,* who blackmailed his *wife* into marrying him? Or the one who took perverse pleasure in fucking *his* lesbian wife? I never even told Lena about all the things he did, because I was too afraid that, if she knew, she wouldn't even want me. What the fuck do you know about my life, my reality? You left me and you never even bothered to look back."

"I came back, as soon as I heard what happened," James said. "I looked for you."

"Wow," she said, with an exaggerated look of shock. "I guess I should be honored that the *great* James Maguire deigned himself to look for little old me. It must have been such a hardship. Tell me, did you actually spend a whole day looking for me before you traipsed back to your girlfriend's little castle? You know, if she was a guy, I'd wonder if she was overcompensating for something. Know what I mean? Don't get me wrong, she's a knock-out. I had intended that it would be her that I had gotten to know, in my little cabin in the woods, but you know what they say, shit happens."

Maguire's head was reeling. The face of the woman standing in front of him was familiar, but the words that came out of her mouth made her seem like a complete stranger. It was as if he had stepped out of reality and into a nightmare.

"It's over, Tricia," he said. "You need to come with me."

Even the words were painful to say.

"Oh, James, If only that were true," she said with a hint of sadness. "If only I could just *go with you.* We could escape this place and relive our lives. Sadly, that cannot happen and therefore, I cannot just come with you."

"You don't have a choice, Tricia."

"Don't I?" she replied, holding up her hand.

Maguire could make out the small, rectangular device she held. It was a transmitter. Instinctively, he raised the gun back up, lining the sights up in the center of the face of the woman he had once loved.

"Always have a plan 'B', James," she replied. "I imagine that right about now, that devilishly good looking bitch you sent in, is trying to figure out how to get *Red* out of her little prison cell. Unfortunately, for her, she has no clue the world is about to blow up around her. It seems that Keith really had this thing for explosives. I guess this is the point where I should tell you about something called a *dead man's switch*? Oops, my bad."

"Don't do this, Tricia."

"James, Tricia's dead. She died a slow, agonizing, death at the hands of others. You, Lena, Paul, Keith........." she said, letting her voice trail off. "You all had a hand in it, intentionally or otherwise. But when she died, something else emerged. Call it my *phoenix* moment. I'm a new woman now, James, and my name is Tatiana."

Maguire stared at her, and it was like reliving a nightmare. The matter-of-fact attitude, the detachment, instinctively he knew she was right. Tricia *had* died. The woman in front of him was no longer the same woman he had once known.

He watched as she walked toward him; slowly, seductively.

"Tsk, Tsk, Tsk," she said, her lower lip protruding in a sulky pout, "poor James is in a quandary. If you kill me, your little friends die too."

Tatiana let out a sigh.

"Decisions, decisions, James. We all have to make them."

The words cut into his soul. Everything inside him told him to shoot, to end this, and yet, he knew he couldn't. He knew what would happen in the confines of the small cabin. The image of his friends, being ripped apart in the explosion, played out in his mind like some bad horror movie.

Tatiana reached up, placing her hand on the barrel of the gun, and lowered it.

"I loved you once, James. I might not have said it, but I did. Maybe I was scared; maybe it was just lust that I felt for Lena and lied to myself. Over the years I came to accept that I actually did love you. So, out of respect for that I'm going to let you go save your friends."

She leaned forward and kissed him, then stepped back, and held up the transmitter. When she spoke next, the words were cold and devoid of any emotion.

"You've only got fifteen minutes, James," she replied. "So I would suggest that you hurry."

Maguire stared at the woman, the battle raging inside of him. It was as if she could sense the quandary.

"Tick, Tock," Tatiana said.

Maguire turned and headed out the door, leaving the woman behind. He raced back up the hill that he had just come down, desperately trying to beat the clock that was counting down in his head.

What would he find when he got there? Would they be able to get Gen out in time? If they couldn't, would any of them be willing to leave?

A few moments later, Maguire reached the edge of the tree line. The cabin, silhouetted by the rising moon, was about twenty-five yards directly in front of him. As he passed the last of the pine trees, he was blinded by a sudden flash of brilliant light and immediately knocked backward by the concussive force of the blast which, a split second earlier, had reduced the cabin to a pile of rubble.

CHAPTER SEVENTEEN

Bellevue Hospital, Manhattan, New York City
Tuesday, February 19th, 2013 – 5:42 p.m.

"Hey, girlfriend," Mary said, as she walked into Melody's hospital room. "How are you feeling?"

"A lot better than I was," Melody replied.

"She's actually doing quite remarkable," Dr. Rothman said, as finished making an entry into the computer terminal next to Melody's bed.

"Don't listen to him; he just wants to get rid of me."

"I do," Rothman replied. "Hospitals will make you sick."

"What are you thinking about doing, Doctor?" Mary asked.

"Honestly, if her condition continues to improve, I'd like to send her home tomorrow," he replied. "She can rest just as easily at home, and probably have better nursing care there as well. Besides, I wasn't joking about hospitals making you sick."

"How do we set something like that up?" Melody

"I'll have the patient advocate stop by, they can let you know what you'll need going forward," Rothman replied. "Basically it will be just primary nursing care to monitor your vitals and conditions, but I don't see any major issues going forward. The key is to just take it easy and not rush back into your normal routine. I'll come out and see you in about ten days."

"The head of the Department of Surgery is going to make a house call?"

"I'd like to say how magnanimous I am, but my sister lives out in Water Mill and I am going to be out there for my niece's birthday party."

"Your secret's safe with me," Melody said.

"Like I said, your patient advocate will stop by shortly to go over what you'll need," Rothman said, as he gathered up his computer terminal and headed toward the door.

"It was good to see you again, Dr. Rothman," Mary said.

"Always a pleasure, Mrs. Stargold," the man replied and walked out of the room.

"You know," Mary said, as she turned back to look at Melody. "You could move in with us."

"Thank you, but I think Rothman is right. It will be nice to be back home. Besides, you don't need to babysit me, I'll be fine."

"Between you and Gen, I'm not sure who will be babysitting whom."

Mary closed her eyes, trying to will the words back into her mouth. For a moment there was silence in the room and she hoped that her misspoken comment had been lost on Melody.

"Why would Gen need babysitting, Mary," Melody asked.

"No, I just meant that Gen...."

"Stop," Melody said. "You are a terrible liar, Mary."

"I don't know what you mean?"

"Really? Where is Gen?"

"Working?"

"Yeah, that's what everyone keeps telling me," Melody said. "The only problem is that the gates of hell wouldn't have stopped Gen from being here, I know this because, if the roles were reversed, they certainly wouldn't keep me from being at Gen's side. Which brings me back to my previous question, where is Gen?"

Mary squirmed in her seat, wishing she was anywhere but there right now. She looked over at Melody who stared back at her with steely blue eyes.

"Where is Gen, Mary?"

"James thought it would be best if you didn't have the added stress."

"I love you, Mary, I really do," Melody said. "So I'm begging you, don't make me come over there and beat you senseless with this IV pole. What exactly did my darling boyfriend ask you to lie about?"

"Gen has been kidnapped," Mary blurted out.

"Excuse me?"

"The night of the shooting, she was kidnapped on the way home from the party. James has been searching for her ever since."

"He's not in D.C.?"

"No, he and Gregor are out looking for her."

Melody's eyes darkened and Mary could see the muscles in her jaw clench as the woman reached over, picking up the cell phone off the table, and hit the speed dial number.

"Don't be angry, Melody," Mary said. "He was so worried about you."

Melody held up a finger; as she listened to the call go directly to voicemail.

"I swear to God, you call me the minute you get this or I promise that as soon as I am out of this hospital I'll serve your nuts, up on a stick, to the dogs that patrol the grounds."

She hit the end button and tossed the phone onto the table.

"Everything, Mary," Melody said. "I want it all, from the beginning, now."

Mary looked at Melody, seeing the rage behind her blue eyes. She understood her anger. Even though James thought he was doing the right thing, the truth was that Melody deserved to know what had happened to her best-friend. Lying about it, even if he was only trying to protect her, was still a lie. She'd felt uncomfortable about it all along. She hated sitting here with her friend and lying about what had happened to Gen.

Mary took a deep breath and spilled her guts.

CHAPTER EIGHTEEN

Northern Maine
Tuesday, February 19th, 2013 – 6:49 p.m.

Maguire struggled to his feet, staring out at the pile of burning debris that littered the landscape, where the cabin had stood mere seconds earlier.

He made his way over to what remained of the structure, trying to process it all. Some of the back wall remained intact, along with a portion of the east facing side wall. The explosive must have been some type of shaped charge, because it had blown out both of the other two walls.

Maguire began frantically sorting through the debris, discarding pieces as he tried to make his way down into the heart of the rubble. It was a monumental task and one that he knew he was on the losing end of.

Fleeting seconds turned into desperate minutes, as he tried to claw his way closer to his friends. In the back of his mind, he held onto the belief that there might still be time, even though he knew the shockwave from the explosion would have been physically devastating to them at such close range.

While he continued to dig, the memory of what had just transpired with Tricia played out in his mind, like some horrible movie.

What the hell had happened to her? he wondered. *Maybe that was it. Maybe she had spent too long in hell, first with Browning, then with Banning.*

She'd changed. He had not seen any trace of the girl he had once known. It was as if something had invaded Tricia's body, killing her from the inside. What remained was someone cold, someone who was detached and devoid of any empathy.

Maguire had seen it so many times back in Brownsville. He had seen it in the faces of........

Of what? he thought. *Stone-cold killers?*

He stood amongst the rubble of the cabin and looked around.

She had said that he had fifteen minutes. It had taken him less than a few minutes to sprint back up that hill, and yet the cabin had exploded before he was able to get to it. The thought was as chilling to him as it was clear.

She had intended to kill them.

The realization left him feeling as if he had been sucker punched. The woman, whom he had once loved, had become the very thing he had spent a large part of his life hunting down.

As hard as it was to admit, he knew that he should have killed her when the opportunity had presented itself. He had committed a fatal error, allowing his emotions to interfere with his good judgment. Now she was gone, and so were his friends.

The enormity of the conclusion left him feeling numb inside and he collapsed onto the rubble. Despite the pain that coursed through his body, his friends were buried below and he couldn't stop, not now.

His mind raced back to September 11th, the same images of debris and fires flooding his memory. Just as he had done that day, he steeled his mind to the task at hand and resumed digging through the ruble for his friends.

Suddenly, he heard a sound behind him and looked back, in the direction of an old run down barn. One of the doors swung open and he watched as Alex and Gregor emerged, holding onto Genevieve. Maguire rushed over as the three of them collapsed to the ground. Gregor immediately began examining Gen for any injuries.

"Holy shit, I thought you guys were gone."

"I told you I was hard to kill," Alex exclaimed as she reached into her pocket, removing the pack of cigarettes and lighting one up.

"What the hell happened?" Maguire asked.

"I have no idea," she replied. "One minute we were in some fucking bunker and then the world exploded. The next thing I know *Captain Commando* over here is dragging us through the *wormhole*."

Gregor looked back over at James.

"It's a German thing," Gregor said. "The first rule of having a bunker is to make sure you always have a way out. You always need an escape route, just in case."

"How's Gen?" Maguire asked.

"Gen's fine," Gen said. "And so is her hearing. Thanks for asking."

"Your mouth still works too, I see," Maguire said with a laugh.

"So where is the crazy bitch?" Alex asked.

"She got away," he said. "I chased her through the woods and turned back when I heard the explosion."

"Oh Goodie," she said sarcastically, taking a long drag on the cigarette. "I can't fucking wait to see what happens on our *second date*."

"Gregor, get Gen out of here. You don't need the aggravation of having to answer questions as a foreigner and she's in no condition to talk. Take her back to the motel and let her relax. We'll wait until the cavalry arrives. Once we're done answering their questions, we'll meet up with you. Call Bob Miller and arrange to have him fly-in to pick us up."

"Okay," Gregor replied.

Gregor helped Genevieve up and began leading her over to where the van was parked.

Gen stopped when she got to Maguire. She reached out, wrapping her arms around him and kissing his cheek.

"Thank you for coming for me, James," she whispered in his ear. "I knew you would find me. I love you."

"Love you too, Gen," he replied.

He watched them walk away, getting into the van and driving off. Then he turned around and looked over at Alex, who was still sitting on the ground.

"Malingerer," he said.

"Fuckin' A," she replied, taking a drag on her cigarette. "Work smarter, not harder."

"Where was she?"

"She was locked up in some *shit hole* shipping container buried under the cabin. Ironically, it was probably what saved us when the bomb went off."

"How'd you get in?"

"*Master key*," she replied, tapping the holster on her ankle. "So you wanna tell me how that crazy cunt *really* got away?"

"I caught her in an old shack down the side of the mountain over there," he said, pointing in the direction of the tree line. "Had her corned, nowhere to go. Then she showed me the transmitter in her hand. I had to choose between taking her out and saving you guys."

"Cause that worked out so well," Alex said, as she blew a smoke ring.

"Well, I thought it was the right thing to do at the time."

"That girl could definitely benefit from some fucking professional help," Alex replied.

"It's Trisha Browning," he said. "The one Banning kidnapped."

"Your old girlfriend?" Alex asked.

"Yep," Maguire replied. "One in the same."

"Bet that was quite the little reunion."

"One for the ages," he replied.

"You think she snapped?"

"Like a hollow tree in a hurricane," Maguire said. "You remember Ceelo?"

"Yeah, the guy we collared for popping Heavy D's family over in the Marcus Garvey Projects."

"Yeah, well she's crazy like that now. It was Tricia that killed Banning *and* Lena Marx."

"In that case, I guess I should be glad we never made it to second base," Alex replied.

"Do I really want to know?"

"The things I do for the job," Alex said with a laugh. "In all seriousness, James, you need to be careful. She may have taken up permanent residence in the penthouse suite of the asylum, but she's not dumb."

"Trust me, I know," Maguire replied.

"You probably should have taken the shot, rookie."

"Then we would, most likely, not be here having this charming conversation."

"I told you, I'm hard to kill."

"Does that go for the people around you as well?"

"You're still alive aren't you?"

Maguire shook his head and took out his cell phone. He scrolled though the contacts and selected a number, then waited for it to connect.

"We got her," he said when Rich answered the phone. "We'll be flying home tonight."

"Thank God," Rich said. "I'll let Mary know when we get off the phone. She's over at the hospital with Melody."

"How's Melody doing?"

"She's doing well, James," Rich replied. "Really well. In fact, so well that the last I heard she was talking about how she's going to cut your nuts off and feed them to some dogs at the house."

"What?"

"Yeah, listen *somehow* she found out from *someone* about what happened and where you are...."

"*Jesus H. Christ!*"

"Oh, I don't think that He's even going to be able to save you, buddy. Although if she doesn't calm down, there is a distinct chance you might be meeting Him soon."

"I don't believe this," Maguire said.

"I'd double your security detail, but I doubt that it would make a difference. That never seemed to help Clinton."

In the distance, he heard the wail of a siren.

"I gotta go, Rich. I'll call you when we land."

"Is everything all right?" Alex asked.

"Melody found out," he said. "She's on the warpath."

"I need an evening shift supervisor in Penobscot," Alex said with a smile. "Pay sucks, but I have a couch you can use."

"Thanks, that was almost funny."

A fire truck pulled up the driveway followed by a state police patrol car.

"Gotta love the response time out here," Maguire said. "Glad it wasn't anything *serious*."

"Play nice, rookie. We're going to need a ride back to town," Alex said, pointing toward the charred remains of the Explorer. "You did take out insurance, didn't you?"

CHAPTER NINETEEN

Washington, D.C.
Wednesday, February 20th, 2013 – 7:03 a.m.

Morgan walked out of the hotel and got into the waiting car. His leg still hurt a bit, but he felt much better than he did yesterday.

"Good morning, sir," the driver said.

"Yes it is," Morgan replied, taking a sip of coffee from the travel container he'd bought at the restaurant.

Morgan took a last look at the hotel as the car pulled away. It always seemed to leave him feeling a bit melancholy, knowing he would never see a place again. This hotel had been especially nice. He had enjoyed the view of the water from his window. It was a simple thing to most people, but something that always seemed to be in short supply where he lived.

Oh well, he thought. *You couldn't live in the past, no matter how appealing it was.*

The car made its way up 7th Street, bypassing the highway, which was jammed with commuters, and continued through the back roads as they headed into Maryland via New York Avenue. He leaned back in the seat, watching as the landscape changed from grand architecture, to a poor urban neighborhood and then finally into the rural countryside. In Maryland, the car made its way to I295 and began the trek northbound to its final destination, New York City.

The planned trip should have taken only four hours, but nothing on the east coast ever really went as planned. So it was nearly two o'clock when the car finally pulled up in front of the building on New York City's Upper East Side.

"Thank you," Morgan said to the driver.

He got out of the vehicle, walking up the steps of the well-appointed brownstone building, and passed the bronze sign on the exterior wall that read: *Consulate of the Republic of Sudan*.

CHAPTER TWENTY

Bellevue Hospital, Manhattan, New York City
Wednesday, February 20th, 2013 – 2:43 p.m.

Alex leaned against the wall, opposite Melody's hospital room door, listening to the muffled *discussion* going on inside. Luke Jackson stood next to her looking very agitated.

"Do you think we should go in?" he asked.

Alex looked at the man and rolled her eyes.

"You've got a lot to learn, junior. You might save him now, but that'll only piss her off more. Let her get it out of her system, while there are witnesses around."

"You women are evil," he replied.

"You don't know the half of it," Alex said with a laugh.

Inside the room, Maguire wished that he was back up on the mountain. He was pretty sure that it was infinitely *safer* there as opposed to his present location.

"And when exactly were you going to fill me in on what was happening, James?"

Inside he cringed. It was actually their first real fight, and he was wondering how he was going to talk his way out of it.

"You'd just been shot, angel. I didn't think it was the right time."

"Yes, and it didn't kill me, so exactly what was it that you were *saving* me from?"

"I'm not going to win, am I?"

"Of course you're not going to win, you idiot. You left me here thinking everything was fine. *'Gen's in Wyoming, I'm going to D.C.........'* You lied!"

"Would it have been better off if I told you when you woke up, *'oh by the way, Gen's been kidnapped and we have no idea where she is?'*"

"Yes," Melody said. "Finally you're getting it. At least I would have known. You ever think for a moment how it would have been if Monsignor O'Connor had to come in here and tell me that you died trying to rescue her? Wouldn't that have been a fine *how-do-you-do*?"

"With everything else going on, I didn't think it was the right time."

"That's the problem, you didn't think. Either I'm strong enough to handle this shit, or I'm not. I'm not a friggin' mushroom, James. So don't feed me bullshit and keep me in the dark."

He knew that she was right. This was the brutal business side of her, the one he had never really seen before. Melody hadn't gotten to where she was today by being a sugar-coating kind of girl.

"What do you want me to say?"

Melody looked at him, her eyes wide in amazement.

"Seriously? You have to ask that? I want you to grab my bag and I want you to shut up."

Melody got up from the bed and opened the door. Outside, a nurse stood waiting with a wheelchair and Melody sat down.

"Take me home, Luke."

"Yes, ma'am," he replied.

As they made their way down the hallway, and got on the elevator, Alex leaned over and whispered in his ear.

"And here I thought Brooklyn North was brutal."

"Shut the fuck up, Alex."

Taylor just smiled as the elevator doors closed shut.

Peter May was waiting with the Suburban when they walked outside. Luke Jackson opened the rear passenger door and waited for Melody to get in.

"Are you sure you can't stay another day, Alex?" Melody asked as she stood up out of the wheelchair. "Lord knows we have the room."

"I wish that I could, but if I'm gone any longer, there's no telling what kind of trouble my misfit cops will get themselves into."

"Boy, doesn't that sound vaguely familiar?" Melody replied, throwing a look over at Maguire. "Thanks again for keeping him safe."

"Everyone has their cross to bear," Alex said, and gave her a hug. "Tag, you're it."

"I'll do my best," she said with a laugh. "You'll have to come down for a long weekend when the weather gets better."

"Come to think of it, Gen did mention something about making some piña coladas."

Melody got into the truck and looked back over at Alex.

"Yeah, call me. We'll talk about *those* later. Stays safe, Alex."

"You too."

Jackson closed the back door.

"Go ahead and climb in Luke," Maguire said. "I'll only be a minute."

"Yes, sir," the man replied and got into the front seat of the truck.

"You gonna be okay?" Maguire asked Alex.

"Me?" she asked. "It's not *my* ass you should be worried about."

"Thank you again," he said. "We couldn't have done it without you."

"I know, but that's what partners are for, right?"

"For life," Maguire replied.

"You be careful, James," she said, wrapping her arms around him. "I've kinda grown fond of having you in my life."

"I will, and the same goes for you. Call me as soon as you get back to Penobscot."

"You got it."

Maguire gave her a kiss on the cheek, then watched as she got in her car and drove away. He climbed into the back of the Suburban.

"Take the lady home, Peter."

Melody reached over, taking his hand in hers, and laid her head on his shoulder. *Home* sounded so wonderful right now.

CHAPTER TWENTY-ONE

Sudanese Consulate, Upper East Side, New York City
Wednesday, February 20th, 2013 – 7:23 p.m.

Morgan was escorted into the small office and shook hands with the consulate's security officer, Mansour Yousif Wansi.

"*Assalam alaikum*," Morgan said.

"*Wa alaikum assalam*," the security man replied. "How was your journey, my friend?"

"Long," Morgan replied. "But I have had much worse."

"Please, have a seat," Wansi said.

Morgan sat down in the leather chair across from the man's desk. He watched as Wansi sat back down in his chair and opened the center drawer of his desk. He removed an envelope and then slid it across to Morgan.

"There is your diplomatic passport and a first class ticket home. Your plane leaves at eleven o'clock out of Kennedy. The car should be here any minute to take you to the airport.

"*Shukran*," Morgan replied. "Thank you."

"When you land in Khartoum, a car will be waiting to pick you up on the tarmac and take you over to a private jet. From there it will take you to Port Sudan."

"It will be good to finally be back home," Morgan replied. "It has been much too long."

"It has been two years for me," Wansi said. "I have another year until I will be reassigned. But it is not a hardship for me; there are some benefits to working in this city."

"If I could be in one place, I think I would agree with you. But it has been quite some time since *they* have kept me in one place."

"Maybe after this assignment you will get a permanent posting."

"You, my friend, are an optimist," Morgan said with a laugh. "Unfortunately, I am an eternal pessimist."

There was a knock at the door.

"Come," the security man called out.

The door opened and a young woman walked in.

"The car is here, sir," she replied.

"Thank you, Ms. Karti," Wansi said, as he stood up. "Have a good flight home."

"Thank you," Morgan said, and followed the woman out the door.

Outside, a light rain had started to fall. The street lights reflected off the wet surfaces, like diamonds glistening on the black asphalt. He pulled the collar of his jacket up, and then walked toward the black Lincoln Town Car parked outside the consulate.

"Evening," the driver said, as he held the back door open. "Kennedy Airport?"

"Yes," Morgan replied, as he slid inside the back seat.

As the car pulled away, he opened the envelope Wansi had given him and examined the contents. He had a first class ticket aboard Saudi Arabian Airlines. It wasn't an easy flight as there was no direct service to the Sudan. He'd have a stop in Jeddah, Saudi Arabia, and from there fly into Khartoum.

He examined the red diplomatic passport, opening the cover and looked at the photo. It was him, only now he was Ibrahim Abboud.

Do you even remember your own name anymore? he wondered. *How long had it been since he'd used it?*

It seemed as if his entire adult life had been one big lie. Everywhere he went he was someone different. He had been Henri Shaddad in the UK, Abdullah al-Azhari in Yemen, Mustapha Yasin in Austria, and Amed Hamad in Uganda. The identities he'd had over the years were now too numerous to count anymore. Some nights he would have a nightmare that he'd been stopped by security agents in a foreign country and could no longer remember what name he was using. The last thing he would see was them dragging his flailing body off to some *dark place* before he would wake up in a cold sweat.

He had no illusions that he would leave this world earlier, rather than later. There were lots of old politicians, lawyers and doctors, but there were very few old *spies*.

"There's a bad accident on the Long Island Expressway," the driver said. "We'll have to take the Belt Parkway."

He had no idea what the driver was talking about, nor did he particularly care. He just wanted to get to the airport as quickly as possible and get a drink. He placed the documents onto the seat next to him.

"That's fine," Morgan replied.

The car made its way south, down the FDR drive, looped around the tip of Manhattan, and headed through the Brooklyn Battery Tunnel. On the Brooklyn side, it passed through the toll plaza and got on the Gowanus Expressway.

Morgan stared out the window at the rows of drab, commercial buildings. In between them he caught glimpses of the Hudson River and the Statue of Liberty, which sat in the middle of New York Harbor. The car changed lanes, moving to the right, and Morgan looked up to see the green highway sign, indicating the exit for the Belt Parkway.

Up ahead he could see the lights of the Verrazano-Narrows Bridge, spanning across the entrance to the harbor and beyond that the darkness of the Atlantic Ocean. As the car continued south, Morgan leaned back in the soft leather seat and closed his eyes.

He'd only been asleep for less than a minute when the car was suddenly rocked violently. The sound of screeching metal penetrated the interior of the vehicle, jarring the man awake.

"What the...."

"Fuck!" yelled the driver. "You stupid cocksucker!"

Morgan looked around, catching the sight of a white van slowing down behind them, its hazard lights flashing.

"What happened?" Morgan asked.

"That crazy fuck tried to change lanes and never looked over," the man explained.

The limo driver turned on his own hazard lights, and then began to slow down as he pulled off to the side of the road.

"I'm going to have to pull over and check the damage, sir. If it's bad I'll have them send a new car for you."

"Make it quick," Morgan said, as he rubbed his eyes wearily.

Great, he thought. *Just what I need.*

If he had to wait for another car he wasn't sure if he would get to the airport in time for the flight, let alone a drink.

The car pulled off into a parking area at the base of the bridge.

"I'll just be a minute," the man replied as he got out of the car.

Morgan could hear loud talking behind him. He looked out the rear window and could see the driver arguing with another man whom he presumed to be the driver of the van, which had pulled in behind the Town Car.

Like I really need this?

Suddenly, the passenger door swung open and he was violently pulled from the back of the car. Morgan struggled to get his footing as he was dragged from behind by two men, toward the waiting van.

His mind was racing, as he struggled to fend off his attackers. As they neared the van he swung his arm down and out, managing to strike the leg of one of the men. The man lost his footing on the wet asphalt and the three of them fell to the ground hard. As they hit the pavement, Morgan broke free, leaping to his feet and raced past the van.

"Get him!" one of the men said, as he scrambled to his feet.

The two drivers gave up their pretense of *arguing* and pursued the man as he ran along the highway.

Morgan looked to his left; there was nothing but the river. Across the highway he could see a park and beyond that the lights from houses overlooking the highway. It was his only out and he had to take it.

He watched the on-coming traffic, gauging the flow. When he saw a break, he turned and headed into it. He heard the sound of screeching tires which were immediately followed by the sound of twisting metal as several cars careened off one another in their effort to avoid hitting him. He raced into the on-coming lanes of traffic, as the men continued to chase him, slaloming in and out of the wrecked vehicles.

Morgan approached the center divider, glancing over his right shoulder. The left lane was clear and he vaulted the concrete *jersey wall* that separated the two sides. He ran along the wall, looking back over his shoulder at the traffic that was now heading toward him. A car was approaching in the left lane, but he could see that the next lane over was empty, through the darkness of the on-coming vehicle's rear window. He waited for the car to pass and then he broke right, racing for the safety of the park on the other side of the road.

The driver of the late model, black Grand Am didn't know that his front right headlight was out. He had just dropped a college buddy off at his house in Bay Ridge and was heading home, when out of the corner of his eye he saw a dark figure rush out into the roadway. He tried to react, but it was already too late. The car hit the man, sending him flying into the air.

The force of the impact carried Morgan's body over the hood of the car and into the next lane of traffic. The injury that he sustained, while serious, was actually quite survivable. Unfortunately, the injuries he sustained, as the result of the *second* car striking him, were not.

Traffic on the Belt Parkway came to a complete stop as motorists began to exit their cars and rushed toward where the dying man lay. The men, who had been pursing Morgan, quickly turned and headed back to their vehicles before fleeing the scene.

Several of the witnesses to the accident called 911 and within minutes several patrol cars from the Six-Eight Precinct had responded to the accident, along with an FDNY ambulance. The roadway was immediately shut down for an accident investigation. Officers began directing motorists off the highway and onto 4th Avenue, creating a nightmarish traffic condition.

Once the EMT's pronounced Morgan dead, the patrol supervisor and precinct detectives, along with the Highway Patrol's, Accident Investigation Squad, were requested to respond to the scene for the fatality.

The patrol supervisor, Sergeant Terrance Shea, was the first to arrive.

"What do we have?" Shea asked Police Officer Paul Fisher, who's sector was assigned to the original call.

"Fifty-Three with a fatality, Sarge," Fisher said. "He was hit twice. Driver of the first car is over there getting checked out by EMS. I spoke with him and he said the guy just ran out in front of him. My partner is interviewing some of the other witnesses now."

"We have any ID on the victim?" Shea asked.

"I haven't touched him," the officer replied. "I wanted to wait for you to get here."

The two men walked over to where Morgan's body lay under a yellow, waterproof tarp. Fisher donned a pair of latex gloves and removed a portion of the tarp. He began rummaging through the man's pockets, but found nothing.

"Clean, boss," Fisher said, "no wallet or anything."

"*Sonofabitch*," Shea exclaimed.

Just what he needed, a dead *John Doe*.

At that moment Fisher's partner, Police Officer Anthony Napolitano approached them.

"Hey, Boss," Napolitano said. "We've got a problem."

"What now?" Shea asked.

"Our *vic* wasn't out for an evening jog; several of the witnesses say that at least three, maybe four, guys chased him into traffic."

"Are you shitting me?" Shea asked. "You have any other good news for me?"

"Yeah," Napolitano said. "They said the guys chasing him were all white."

Shea grabbed the radio from his belt and keyed the mic. "Six-Eight Sergeant to Central."

"Go ahead, Sarge," a voice replied.

"Central, have the duty captain respond to my location."

"10-4, Sarge. I'll notify him to respond."

Shea put the radio back on his belt and looked back down at the body. He had been less than a few hours from the start of a three day swing and had planned on leaving early in the morning to head up to Windham Mountain Ski Resort.

So much for that dream, he thought.

CHAPTER TWENTY-TWO

Southampton, Suffolk County, N.Y.
Wednesday, February 20th, 2013 – 10:19 p.m.

"How are you feeling?" Maguire said to Melody, as he walked into the bedroom.

"Better," Melody said, laying the papers she had been reading on the bed. "I'm glad to be home. I was starting to go stir crazy in the hospital room."

"You still mad?" he asked.

"Yes," Melody replied. "Did you think I wouldn't be?"

"I was hoping," he said with a half-hearted laugh.

"I'm more annoyed that you didn't think I could handle it," Melody said. "That you didn't give me enough credit for being stronger."

"I know, I know," he said, raising his hands in *mock* surrender. "I should have told you, I get it."

"You ever do that again, and it will be the only thing you *get* for a long time," she said with a smile.

"Yes, ma'am," he replied.

Melody patted the bed next to her. "Sit down, cowboy."

Maguire sat down next to her, and brushed some stray strands of hair from her face.

"I almost lost you," he said.

"But you didn't," she replied, "so stop dwelling on what *didn't* happen."

He started to speak, and then stopped.

"Who says men can't be taught," Melody said with a smile. "How's Gen?"

"Gen's fine," he replied. "She's ornery as ever. Not making light of what she went through, but I think if we hadn't found her, she would have gotten sent back to us by the end of the week."

"That's my girl," Melody said. "How's Gregor doing?"

"Glued to her side. Peter gave him a thirty day leave of absence from work. She's staying with him today over at his place. He had some paperwork he needed to get caught up on before he went on leave and didn't want her home alone. She'll be back in the morning, she sends her love."

"Yeah, we were texting back and forth a while ago."

"Oh I'm sure it won't be long before the two of you are knocking back piña colada's and exchanging war stories."

Suddenly Maguire's cell phone began ringing.

"No rest for the wicked," Melody said.

"It's Rich," he said.

"What's up, buddy?" he said, answering the phone.

"I hate bothering you," Stargold said. "But I figured you'd want to know what was going on."

"What happened?"

"Operations just notified me that we had a traffic fatality over in the six-eight. Guy sprinted across the Belt Parkway and got nailed just before the finish line."

"Tragic, but that doesn't seem to be something we needed to know tonight."

"It is when the runner is black and he was being chased by several white males."

"Fuck me," Maguire said. "Please tell me this is a joke."

"I wish I could," Rich replied. "I'm heading over to the command now. I told Ops that I would notify you and let you know what was going on."

"I'll head in."

"No, you stay with Melody. Tony Ameche is on his way. He can hold my hand for one night. I just wanted to give you a heads up, so you didn't walk blithely into the shit storm tomorrow morning."

"Are you sure?"

"Absolutely," Rich said. "If it looks like it is about to start spiraling out of control I will call you back."

"Ok, thanks, Rich," James replied and ended the call.

"What's wrong?" Melody asked.

"A guy got run over on the Belt Parkway; looks like it might have been racially motivated."

"Are you serious?"

"Unfortunately, yeah."

"Do you have to go?"

"No, Rich and Tony Ameche are going to handle it. It seems as if you're stuck with me."

"Good, I didn't want my first night back home spent alone."

"Hey, I thought you were mad at me?" Maguire asked.

"You're starting to grow on me again," Melody said. "Don't push your luck."

Maguire leaned over and kissed her. "God, I've missed you."

"Turn out the light and get in bed, cowboy."

"I thought you were supposed to be convalescing, angel?"

"I was shot, I'm not dead, but what I really need you to do now is to just hold me close."

"That I can do," he said, as he reached over and turned off the light."

CHAPTER TWENTY-THREE

1 Police Plaza, Manhattan, N.Y.
Thursday, February 21st, 2013 – 6:49 a.m.

"What do we know, people?" Maguire said, as he walked into the office.

"A storm is already brewing, Commissioner," Police Officer Lisa Adams replied. "The *Right Reverend* Archibald Jennings has hijacked every news reporter with a microphone and is sowing the seeds of discontent. We are already getting reports of sporadic violence in parts of Manhattan, Brooklyn and the Bronx."

"Notify Ops to put the Task Forces on alert. We're not going to get caught with our pants down like we did in Crown Heights."

"Yes, sir," Adams replied. "I also have copies of everything that has been done so far on your desk."

"You're the best, Lisa." Maguire said, as he headed to his office. "When Inspector Martin comes in, tell him I need to speak with him."

"Will do, sir."

Maguire sat down at his desk and began to shuffle through the paperwork till he found the Unusual Report prepared by the duty chief who had responded. He began scanning the report. What struck him as odd was that they still knew almost nothing about the victim. Besides the clothes he was wearing, the victim had no ID or jewelry on him that would aid in the investigation. There was no reason for him to have been there. The cops had conducted a search of the vehicles in the parking lot, but all of their owners were identified and accounted for. Most were just young lovers watching the *submarine races* under the bridge.

There were also no easily accessible houses that he could have come from.

Even more peculiar was the fact that, despite several witnesses noting the exact license plate number of the van that fled the scene, there was no record of it on file.

Who puts on fictitious plates to do a hate crime? he wondered.

The body had been removed to the morgue and would be fingerprinted. Hopefully that would put a name to the victim, but for now, he was just another John Doe, on a cold steel tray, in the basement of the city morgue, over on First Avenue.

Who are you and where did you come from? he thought as he stared down at a crime scene photo of the body.

"Morning, Commissioner."

Maguire looked up to see Inspector Liam Martin standing in his doorway.

"Morning, Liam. Grab a cup of coffee and come in," Maguire said.

A few minutes after the man returned and sat down.

"I hear our friend Rev. Archie is up to his old tricks," Martin said.

"I often wonder exactly where he got his *theology degree* from," Maguire replied.

"That's easy," Martin replied. "He was ordained by the prestigious *Glory Hallelujah University of Schuck and Jive*."

Maguire laughed, but the truth was that Jennings' credentials were actually far less stellar.

Archibald Jennings had been born and raised in the Fort Greene section of Brooklyn. His father had left the family when he was only four and his mother had moved them into the New York City Housing Authorities, Fort Greene Houses. After managing to *eke* out a high school education, he got introduced to Elijah Chapman, a prominent local politician who championed radical causes. Chapman took him under his wing and began steering him from one issue to another.

Chapman liked the young man's fiery exuberance and had gotten him a side gig as a *guest* preacher at a store front church in Bed-Stuy. This ultimately led to his *ordination* by the church elders. The Rev. Archie was Chapman's lap dog, used to incite the masses over *racially sensitive* issues. Once Jennings had whipped people up into frenzy, Chapman would come in and play the moderate, seeking to *heal* the wounds of racial injustice. No one ever really seemed to put two and two together and figure out that it was really Chapman, through his surrogate, Rev. Archie, who was actually creating the racial tension in the first place.

"It would be nice if someone would pass a law prohibiting charlatans," Maguire said.

"What fun would there be in that," Liam said with a laugh.

"I don't envision a whole lot of fun in our future," Maguire replied. "McMasters hasn't exactly been accommodating to their bullshit. I think they are going to see this as an opportunity to exact a pound of flesh from him. Jennings has already started his not-for-prime-time tirade; so I'd expect to see unrest in all the usual areas. I had them put the Task Force on stand-by. If it even hints like it is going to blow, cancel all leave and recall everyone. I don't want our people getting hurt unnecessarily because we weren't prepared."

"Yes, sir," Martin replied.

There was a knock at the door. Maguire looked up to see Detective Mike Torres from his security detail standing in the doorway.

"It's starting, Boss," Mike said. "Rev. Archie just said he's marching on City Hall this morning."

"Thanks, Mike," James said, as he picked up the phone and called Rich.

"Did you hear?"

"About the march?" Stargold replied. "Yeah, Ops just called. What do we do?"

"Bring in the Task Force and head them off. If he gets to the Manhattan side it will be a mess. Let's get on top of this early."

"Okay, I'll take care of Rev. Archie," Rich said. "I want you to take the lead on the investigation of the victim. I have a news conference scheduled at City Hall at one o'clock."

"What's on your mind?" Maguire asked.

"I don't know, James. I'm just not getting the warm fuzzies. Something about this whole thing just doesn't feel right."

"I know what you mean," Maguire replied. "I have the same feeling."

"Good to know. I was beginning to think I was letting this job get the better of me."

"Soon as I hear something I will let you know."

"Thanks," Rich replied and hung up the phone.

"Liam, reach out to the Chief of D's, find out who has been assigned the investigation. I want to speak to the C.O. forthwith."

"Yes, sir," Martin said, as he stood up and headed for the door.

Fifteen minutes later, Maguire was on the phone with Captain Ann Johnson, C.O. of the Major Case Squad.

"What can you tell me, Captain Johnson?" Maguire asked.

"We're working with the Hate Crime Task Force on this, Commissioner," she replied. "But until we get a lead on who our victim is, we won't know if this is an actual hate crime or something else."

"What theories do you have floating around?"

"Everything from a drug deal gone badly to a possible love triangle."

Maguire thought about that for a moment. Both were actually plausible working theories. The area was frequented by a variety of different people at that time of the night. The vic could have been going to meet his lover, but ended up meeting the ex and his friends instead.

"Where are we at with the ID?"

"We have a guy over at the morgue right now rolling his prints. As soon as I have something I will call you back, sir."

"Thanks, Captain. I don't have to remind you that time is *not* our friend," Maguire said.

"It never is, sir."

Maguire hung up the phone, then reached down and picked up his cell and placed another call.

After a few rings a gruff voice answered.

"Monahan."

"You're in early, Dennis," Maguire said.

"I've been in since two this morning," the man replied. "Lover's quarrel with a chain saw resolution."

"Ouch! That's a little extreme."

"Cheaper than an attorney."

"True," Maguire said. "Hey, I don't want to hold you up, but I just wanted to make sure you got that paperwork from Maine."

"Yeah, I'm still kinda shocked over the whole thing with Tricia," Monahan replied. "Guess you really never do know what's going on inside another person's head."

"Amen to that. So is the state going to do anything with it?"

"Just keep it as an FYI. We notified the locals to be on alert, but since our case with Banning is now officially closed, the powers that be feel it is all in Maine's lap now."

"Oh well, can't say as I blame them," Maguire replied. "If you do hear anything more, let me know."

"Will do."

"Talk to you later, Dennis. Stay safe."

"You too."

Maguire ended the call and began going through the paperwork in his in-basket.

"Commissioner?"

Maguire looked up to see Torres standing in the door way.

"Yeah, Mike?"

"Ops just called to notify us that they are getting multiple 10-85's over the air in the Eight-Four and Eight-Eight Precincts. Parts of the protest are breaking off and they are smashing windows and looting along Flatbush Avenue."

"And so it begins," Maguire said sarcastically. "Never let a good protest prevent you from committing a crime."

He looked up at the clock on the wall; it was just after seven-thirty. It was going to be a very long day, and an even longer night.

He got up and went to get a cup of coffee.

CHAPTER TWENTY-FOUR

Office of the Medical Examiner, Manhattan, N.Y.
Thursday, February 21st, 2013 – 7:31 a.m.

"Morning, Carlos," Detective Bill Hennessey said, as he walked up to the security officer at the New York City Morgue.

"Morning, Bill," the man replied. "You're up awfully early."

"No rest for the weary, my man," Hennessey said. "Besides, I'm leaving early today. Going down to Atlantic City this afternoon, won't be back till Sunday. That is of course unless I win big."

"Who's better than you," Carlos replied.

"Hey, you see the Giant's signed McElroy from Houston?"

"Great, just what they need. Another overpaid safety who's three years past his prime. If they want to piss their money away, they can just give it to me. I can miss tackles just as easy as he can."

"Yeah, but you won't make it look as good on prime time."

"I can't make it look as bad."

"True," Hennessey said. "Hey, check your records and let me know where the stiff from the Belt Parkway is."

The security officer began punching keys on the computer terminal in front of him. Once he found the screen he was looking for he scrolled through the entries till he located the deceased.

"Here he is," the man replied. "John Doe. He hasn't been cut up yet, should be on table four."

"Thanks, I need to print him so we can find the next of kin."

"Please do that," the man replied. "It's been so fucking cold that they can't dig graves over at Hart Island. We're starting to run out of room here."

"Look at it this way, at least no one is going to be complaining." Hennessey replied and made his way down the hall toward the autopsy room. He located the body bag and unzipped it.

Fingerprinting dead people had become a mundane task for the man. Actually, it was a lot easier than fingerprinting the living. Dead people didn't try to *help* you. One of the actual challenges in obtaining prints from the deceased, was when rigor set in, stiffening the body, or mummified fingers from someone who had been dead for a long time.

Hennessey opened the case he was carrying and removed a container of black fingerprint powder along with a camel hair brush. He then removed a roll of clear tape and cut off ten individual strips. He set a print card on the table next to him and began the task at hand.

He removed one of the man's hands and began to apply the powder to the fingers. He brushed off the excess, then pressed one of the pieces of tape firmly against the finger, starting in the center and worked outward. When he was done he removed the tape and placed it on a fingerprint card. When he was done he repeated the steps for each finger.

Since the prints where not in the same orientation as standard prints, he made a notation that it needed to be reversed before entry was made into the identification systems.

After he completed the printing, he packaged everything up and made his way back outside.

"Done already?" Carlos asked.

"Yeah, I could do these in my sleep."

"Bet that thought helps your wife sleep soundly at night," the man replied.

"It's the cold hands that get to her," he said with a laugh. "Hey do me a favor, put a bug in their ear that they need a rush on this one."

"Will do," the man replied.

"I've got to run these prints downtown, Carlos. I'll see you when I get back."

Hennessy turned and headed back out the door into the cold.

A short time later he arrived at 1 Police Plaza, where the fingerprints ultimately made their way into the Integrated Automated Fingerprint Identification System, also known as *IAFIS*. The program is an identification and criminal history system maintained by the FBI. *IAFIS* provides automated search capabilities and is the largest biometric database in the world. It houses the fingerprints and criminal histories of seventy million subjects as well as thirty million civil prints. It also contains more than seventy thousand fingerprints of known or suspected terrorists.

In addition, the system also housed fingerprints obtained through the *United States Visitor and Immigrant Status Indicator Technology*, commonly known as *US-VISIT*. This system is managed by the U.S. Customs and Border Protection and is used to track individuals deemed by the United States to be either terrorists or criminals, as well as illegal immigrants. Biometric information, in the form of digital fingerprints and photographs, are collected from all non-U.S. citizens between the ages of fourteen and seventy-nine when they apply for visas or arrive at major U.S. ports of entry.

While the fingerprint submission was sent with a request for the search to be expedited, due to the nature of the investigation, it would still take several hours before the call was received at Major Case confirming the hit.

At just before noon, Mike Torres knocked on Maguire's door.

"Boss, Captain Johnson is on line two for you."

"Thanks, Mike," Maguire said and answered the phone. "What do you have for me, Captain?"

"This is an odd one, sir," she replied. "Prints came back to a Charles Pierre Morgan; residence is listed in Baltimore, Maryland."

"What's odd about that, Captain?"

"Well, the hit seems to have originated from CBP records on a passport entry. It looks like he flew into Dulles International on February 16th from Vienna, Austria and was scheduled to fly out of there again, at 10:40 this morning."

Maguire leaned back in his chair and rubbed his eyes. He didn't need a mystery, not today.

"An American living abroad, maybe a businessman?" he asked.

"I guess anything is possible."

"Check with Baltimore PD, see if they have anything. Maybe they can knock on some doors and find a next of kin."

"I'll have my people reach out to them and get back to you." she said.

"Thanks," Maguire said and ended the call.

Maguire picked up the DD5's, the reports prepared by the detectives, and began reading through the witness interviews. There were some minor inconsistencies, which was to be expected. Most people think that they see things clearly, but time of day, lighting, and the stress of an incident can all negatively impact a person's recollection. However, the majority of those with a clear view all said the same thing. They observed the man being chased, until he got hit by the car. Several witnesses said they then saw the men flee from the scene. None, however, had observed the men approach the injured man.

Why didn't he have any ID on him? Maybe they got it before he ran into traffic, Maguire thought.

It was always a possibility that he could have been ripped off at the scene, but under these conditions he thought that was highly unlikely. If he'd died on some street in Brooklyn North he could see that happening, but none of the witnesses to this incident seemed the type to go rifling through a dying man's pockets nor had they recalled seeing anyone touching the body. Among them were an accountant and his wife, a professor of Anthropology, a psychiatrist, and a host of other middle class folks. Even the kid, who had initially hit him, was a student that was on his way home from a night course at Kingsborough Community College. It was hardly a rogue's gallery of potential thieves.

Nothing was making sense to him. It seemed as if, for every new answer, there were two more new questions.

Why is someone, who is scheduled to fly out of the country in the morning, heading out toward Long Island, the night before his flight? he wondered.

There were so many things that just weren't adding up. He's here in New York, but he has a U.S. Passport, with a Baltimore address. Yet he arrived from, and was returning to, Austria.

Perhaps he really was a businessman, he thought.

Hopefully Baltimore P.D. would give them some better news.

CHAPTER TWENTY-FIVE

Southampton, Suffolk County, N.Y.
Thursday, February 21st, 2013 – 10:59 p.m.

"How are you feeling?"

Gen looked up to see Melody peering in through the office door.

"Oh my God," Gen squealed, as she jumped up from the desk and rushed toward Melody. "I didn't want to wake you."

She wrapped her arms gingerly around Melody, hugging her close.

"I've missed you so much," she said.

"Missed you too, chicky," Melody replied. "It looks like we've both got one helluva story to tell."

Gen released her hold on Melody and stood back, taking in her friend's condition. She had to admit that she looked a lot better than she had imagined. Despite what everyone had told her that Melody was fine, she had still been anxious to see her for the first time.

"You're the one with the story," she replied. "I just had to babysit some psychotic bitch for a few days."

"And here I thought I was the only psychotic bitch you had to take care of."

"Speaking of psychotic, what are you doing up?"

"Oh, don't believe all the doom and gloom bullshit, I'm fine," Melody said. "Besides, I have to get up and move around; doctor's orders. I just can't overdo it."

"Ok, well humor me and come sit down," Gen said.

Melody walked over and sat down.

"Coffee?" Gen asked.

"God yes," Melody replied. "I wish I could just get it mainlined into me. It might help me to feel a bit more energetic."

"I might be going out on a limb here, but I'm going to guess that they probably don't want people, who are recovering from a gunshot wound, to be bouncing off the walls."

Melody waved her hand dismissively.

"So where is your *shadow*?"

"Gregor?" Gen asked. "He went over to pick-up some of his stuff; he's moving in to *take care* of me."

"How are you doing?"

"*Moi*? I'm okay. I'm still feeling a bit *icky*. I haven't been able to completely shake whatever bug I came down with before the party, you know the one you thought I was *lying* about."

"You're not done beating that dead horse yet?"

"Not a chance," Gen replied.

"Well, the medical staff is getting set-up as we speak. Once they are up and running why don't you go check in with them. Maybe they can get you started on something."

"I will, as soon as I have a free minute."

"Good," Melody said, taking a sip of coffee. "So, are you doing okay with everything that happened?"

"Surprisingly, yeah, I am," Gen said. "It might seem kind of funny, but I never had any doubt that they would find me. I just kept myself mentally busy, thinking about what I could do to help when the time came."

"Still, that had to be scary at times."

"Oh, I probably should have been. I mean that woman definitely has a hardware stores worth of loose screws in her head, but I think I was too angry to be scared. In fact, I don't think that I was ever really scared until I saw Gregor come through the door with that woman, Alex. I guess my melodramatic, horror movie mind went into overdrive and I was waiting for the psycho bitch to show up with a carving knife."

"You, melodramatic? Perish the thought!" Melody said with a laugh.

"So, did you get a chance to meet Ms. Taylor?" Gen said.

"Oh yes, I did."

"And?"

"She seems very nice, but I did get the feeling that she has certainly got an *edginess* to her," Melody replied.

"Well, she was James' partner," Gen said. "I guess she would have to be tough."

"That is very true."

"So, you're okay with her?"

"She's a tough, intelligent and *very* attractive woman," Melody replied. "I plan on making sure that I keep her close to me."

"That's exactly what I thought," Gen said with a smirk.

"I didn't get to where I am by being stupid or naïve."

"Well, now that I know your mind is as sharp as ever, how is your body doing?"

"Still a bit sore," Melody said, "but I certainly feel a lot better than I did."

She drank the last of the coffee and set the cup down on the table in front of her.

"I imagine I'll have a horrible scar from all of this. So I guess that strapless dresses are probably a thing of the past."

Gen rolled her eyes at her friends comment.

"Only you would consider how *unfashionable* getting shot is," Gen replied. "What are the doctors saying going forward?"

"Just to take it easy for a bit, let my strength return slowly, but I should recover completely."

"That had to be scary as hell, Mel."

"I think it happened so fast that I didn't have time to be really scared. All I remember was trying to take care of Tippi Fisher. Then, the next thing I knew, James and the other cops were storming into the room. Everything after that is a bit hazy, until I woke up in the hospital room."

"Yeah, Gregor told me about what happened to her," Gen said. "I can't even imagine what you went through. All I had to contend with was being cooped up in a tiny room, fed shitty food and drinking bad coffee."

"Actually, that pretty much sums up my hospital stay as well."

"Sans the bullet to the back, of course."

"Well, there is that," Melody said with a smile. "So what are you doing at your desk this morning?"

"Oh, just trying to get caught up," Gen said.

"You're working? Already?"

"Not really working, *per se*. I'm just kind of organizing my papers, before I begin working."

"I guess I shouldn't point fingers, I started going through all my paperwork last night. Honestly, it feels good to be back in my element."

"Trust me, I know what you mean," Gen said. "Don't get me wrong, I like having Gregor around, but what I really needed was to be doing something productive again."

"Did someone mention my name?"

Both women turned toward the door where Gregor was standing.

"Hi, Gregor," Melody said, as he walked into the room and gave her a hug.

"How are you feeling, Melody?"

"Better," she replied. "A lot better now that I know everyone is safe at home"

"And how is my little *mouse*?" he said, turning toward Gen.

"I'm fine, dear," she replied. "I love you, but please don't be buggy."

"The two of you under one roof is going to be trouble, I think," he replied.

"If you think we're trouble now, wait until she starts making piña coladas," Melody said.

Gregor closed his eyes and slowly shook his head.

"Well, on that note, I think I will leave you two love birds alone," Melody said, as she stood up. "Don't forget to see the nurse later and get checked out. Let them put you on something to get rid of whatever *heebee-geebee* thing you've got going on."

"Yes, ma'am," Gen said with a mock salute. "Now get out of here and go rest."

"I'll check back later," Melody said, as she walked out the door.

"What is a *heebee-geebee*?" Gregor asked.

"Oh, nothing," Gen said dismissively. "I probably just have a case of the flu and need to get a shot."

"Well, then we should do it."

"I will, later," Gen said. "Right now I have a lot to catch up on. So be a dear, and scroll through the gazillion cable channels we have and find a soccer match to watch."

"You're very bossy," he said, as he sat down on the couch, at the far end of the room and picked up the remote.

"That's funny," she replied with a grin. "You didn't seem to mind that last night."

CHAPTER TWENTY-SIX

Office of the Medical Examiner, Manhattan, N.Y.
Thursday, February 21st, 2013 – 12:31 p.m.

Dr. Joanna Miller stood in the cold, harshly lit, autopsy room, and donned a pair of gloves. To the first time visitor, the room was a mélange of smells that fought to overpower the senses. Death had its own distinct smell. It was something that permeated everything including a person's hair, clothing, and hands. The smells ranged from the heavy aroma of formaldehyde, to the strong, antiseptic, scents of cleaners; such as bleach and ammonia.

It often overwhelmed people, the first few times they were there, leaving them feeling nauseous and with a severe headache. To those that worked there, it just became part of their world.

After she put the first pair of gloves on, she slipped on a second set, which seemed to help keep her hands from smelling afterward. There was nothing like going out to eat and having to smell your last victim, while you tried to eat your *Spaghetti Marinara*.

When she was done, she walked over to one of the eight metal tables and pulled the sheet off the body. She began her initial physical assessment, speaking into a microphone that would record the audio portion of the autopsy.

"Dr. Joanna Miller, case #13-1521, body of a male black, identified as Charles Morgan. Victim appears to be in his early thirties, approximately five feet, ten inches tall. Victim was apparently struck by an automobile on the Belt Parkway on February 20th."

Miller walked around the body, examining the man's extremities.

"Multiple contusions and lacerations are evident. There is significant trauma to the head, torso, abdominal area, as well as the legs. The left humerus is fractured, with a portion of the bone visible through the epidermis. In addition to the most recent injuries, there are also numerous indications of past trauma with heavy scarring on both the upper and lower portions of the body."

When she was done with the physical assessment, she began performing the actual autopsy.

It was an archaic, and often brutal, process. One that remained relatively unchanged since the procedure was first standardized by the 19th Century German doctor, Rudolph Virchow. The tools of the trade were varied and included Tupperware containers, used to store vital organs, soup ladles, which aided in the removal of liquids from the chest cavity, and hedge clippers that were used to cut ribs.

The internal examination began with a 'Y' incision. The dissection technique used to gain access to the internal organs of the torso. She made the cut from each shoulder to the sternum and then straight down to the groin. Once the incision was made, the man's skin was pulled back and the ribs were then cut along the sides. She then removed the rib *plate,* exposing the organs. Each was removed, weighed, and photographed. They would be dissected to look for abnormalities that might have aided in the death of the deceased. Just because he had been hit by a car, didn't mean that there wasn't another *perpetrator* lurking beneath the man's own skin.

When she was done with the chest exam, she began cutting the scalp around the back of the head, exposing a majority of the cranium. Once this was done, a bone saw was then used to cut through the skull to allow access to the brain. She carefully sliced open the dura, a thin white film, which most closely resembled an opaque colored saran wrap, and removed the brain for further examination. It was not an overly lengthy process, but it was about four-thirty when she was finally finished.

As she prepared to put the body into one of the lockers, she noticed the discolored wound on the man's thigh. She had originally dismissed it as a by-product of the accident, but as she examined it closer, she noticed that there appeared to be something hard under the skin. Miller retrieved a scalpel and made an incision and discovered the small microchip.

"Damn techno-geeks," she muttered. "One day they are going to go too far in their *body modification* bullshit. We're human beings, not damn garage door openers."

She placed the chip into a plastic evidence bag and finished securing the body. When she was done, she scrubbed up and changed into her civilian clothes. Before she left, she sat down at her desk and picked up the phone. She dialed a number and waited. After a few rings it went to voice mail.

"Hi, Mike this is Doctor Miller. I'm finished with your autopsy from the Belt Parkway fatality. I'm sending you an email with the preliminary report, but at face value it looks like the cause of death was blunt trauma caused by the accident. Oh, by the way, I did find something a bit odd, a microchip. The vic was probably one of those *techies*, who used it to open his door or turn on the lights. Anyway, I've got it secured and I'll put it into the evidence locker. I'm going out of town for a few days, so if you have any questions they'll have to wait until Monday."

She hung up the phone, grabbed her car keys and headed for the door, dropping the plastic bag off into evidence before she left.

CHAPTER TWENTY-SEVEN

1 Police Plaza, Manhattan, N.Y.
Thursday, February 21st, 2013 – 9:33 p.m.

Maguire sat at the desk watching the live video feed from multiple scenes, including both City Hall, on the Manhattan side of the Brooklyn Bridge, as well as the Flatbush Avenue side over in Brooklyn.

Despite their best efforts, the protest march had succeeded in making its way to the gates of City Hall before being pushed back. The problem arose in getting the necessary uniformed resources there in time. At the initial stages the precinct personnel couldn't contain them and they forced their way onto the bridge, bringing the normally brutal morning traffic to a complete standstill. This radiated outward to all the connecting arterial highways and major roadways, further hampering the response.

While traffic was being diverted off the bridge, the Rev. Archie Jennings seized the moment to go into an epic tirade about the supposed state of racial equality in the City of New York. All to the fervent cheers of his supporters, as well as the throng of media cameras that had descended onto the event.

In between his inflammatory outbursts, he would stop and whip the crowd into a frenzy, giving the media their evening news sound bites.

"What do we want?" Rev. Archie would yell.

"Justice," the crowd would reply.

"When do we want it?"

"Now!"

It was his *shtick* and it had nothing to do with justice. In fact, Jennings could care less about the victim. The reality was that the Reverend Archie only did this for himself, for his brand. A segment of society lauded him with praise and titles. He was called the 'Champion of Justice' or 'God's Community Activist' by the media who fawned over him, but it was a thinly veiled disguise.

Jennings didn't actually care about the community. In fact, he didn't even reside in the community that he supposedly served. When the sun went down, he would slink back over the George Washington Bridge to his palatial home in Englewood Cliffs, New Jersey. If there was one thing about the Reverend Archie Jennings, he was a shrewd businessman.

His corporation, *The Horns of Jericho Ministry*, was, for all intents and purposes, a front. It was a 501(c)(3) tax exempt religious organization, meaning that the Reverend Jennings didn't own anything. Not the car he drove, the house he lived in, or the clothes he wore. Everything was bought by the company and paid for by his congregation, who, in most cases, lived hand to mouth themselves.

But Archie Jennings was the consummate performer. Whether he was strutting on the altar or on the public stage he told people what they wanted to hear. It wasn't them, it was the system, and it was inherently racist. When the system is against you, then the rules go out the window. How can you be expected to follow laws that are founded on racism? Archie never concerned himself about facts; just how he could parlay something into more media attention, which would generate more donations into the coffers of his company.

It wasn't just the government that he vilified. In fact, they were becoming less interesting to him then the private sector. Archie had come to realize that it was there, in the canyons or Wall Street, or the Hollywood Hills, where the real power and money was. Companies were now terrified to get on his bad side, fearing that he would call for one of his boycotts. They seemed even more willing to placate him, for fear of losing profit share.

After giving him his moment in the camera lights, Rich gave the order to use the Task Force to push the protestors back over the bridge. The only problem was that, once they were dispersed on the other side, they began breaking into smaller groups that continued the damage and looting that had preceded the protest march. The majority of the Task Force units were patrolling in Brooklyn North now, trying to restore some semblance of order and quash the smaller disturbances before they spiraled out of control.

Maguire glanced down at the cell phone on the desk as it vibrated. He picked it up and looked at the incoming message from Melody.

You okay?

He picked up the phone and called her, it would be easier than trying to type it all out.

"Hey, angel," he said. "Yeah, I'm okay, just drained. It has really been one of those days."

"We seem to be having a lot of them lately."

"I could remind you that you were the one who talked me into taking this job," he said.

"I don't recall that I had to twist your arm too much," she replied.

"I see you're feeling better."

"Nice way to change the subject," Melody said.

"Go easy on me," Maguire said. "I'm not thinking straight."

"Have you made any progress on the investigation?"

"If you define progress as something other than hitting brick walls at every turn, then no."

"I'm so sorry, James," Melody said. "I wish I could help."

"I know," he replied. "Hey how's everything going there? Did you and Gen have a chance to talk?"

"Everything's fine here and yes, Gen and I talked several times today as I went on my strolls. I can't believe what she went through. That woman is insane."

"I know," he replied. "Lord only knows what Banning did to break her, but she went head first off the deep end, that's for sure."

"You think they will find her?" Melody asked.

"I have no idea, angel. She spent months with Banning, no telling what he taught her or what others safe houses or supply caches he has out there. Banning was a very resourceful person."

"I didn't think I would ever say this, but I'm happy to have the *men in black* back at the house."

"Get used to it," Maguire said. "They're going to be there for a while. Speaking of which, how are the other new house guests working out?"

"The nurses?" Melody asked. "They're okay. I know they are only here for a limited time, so that's much easier to deal with. Plus I'm glad to have them here to watch over Gen too. She's gone through so much, and yet she was already trying to take care of me. I told her that I wanted her to get checked out as well."

"That was a smart move. What about Gregor?"

"He actually moved in this morning. He spent the day fine tuning the security. Made me feel better knowing he was on top of it."

"I'm glad," Maguire replied. "With me stuck here I feel a lot better knowing he is there as well. So what did Gen have to tell you?"

"Oh, nothing much really, just your usual chick talk. Besides, you have enough on your plate without having to deal with the ranting of a madwoman."

"Wonderful," he replied.

"I assume you are staying over?"

"Yeah, we are sitting on a tinder box here. The only thing keeping this from exploding is the cold. If this was August, Brooklyn North would be burning."

"Please be careful, cowboy," Melody said.

"Careful?" he exclaimed. "I'm cooped up here in *Puzzle Palace*. I'd be safer on the streets."

"Well, I for one am glad you are there. I don't need you going around leading some half-assed charge through the streets of Brooklyn."

A cop tentatively approached Maguire, who waved him over.

"Sorry, Commissioner, the P.C. is on the phone for you," the cop said.

"Thank you," Maguire replied. "Hey, babe, Rich is on the other line. I've got to call you back."

"Don't worry about it, cowboy. I'm tired; I'm going to go to bed. I'll see you tomorrow."

"Ok, angel. I'll see you then. Love ya."

"Love you too, be careful."

"I will. Goodnight."

Maguire hung up the cell phone and picked up the desk phone.

"Hey, Rich, what's going on?"

"I'm trying to figure out what I ever did to you, that you would have recommended me to take this job."

"Must be something in the air, I just had this very same conversation with Melody. I didn't win that argument and I'm not holding out much hope for you."

"Thanks," Rich replied. "I appreciate the support."

"Hey, if you're looking for an uplifting sermon, track down Rev. Archie."

"That prick needs to be in cuff's," Rich replied. "I can't believe they fall for that charlatan."

"He's a snake oil salesman with a clerical collar."

"That's putting it mildly. What are you seeing from Command and Control?"

"Starting to get quiet, the cold is helping us," Maguire said. "Some isolated pockets of stuff over in Brooklyn, but even that's beginning to subside. Tomorrow will be a different story. The shit will hit the fan when all the store owners start calling City Hall. Probably call for your head on a pike as well."

"Well aren't you just the bearer of wonderful news?"

"You didn't hire me to piss on your leg and tell you it's raining."

"Well, can you check your crystal ball and let me know if I survive the storm?"

"Oh, you'll survive. Everyone in the media pays lip service to that fat bastard, but the ones that matter know what he is all about. We just need to make sure this thing doesn't flare back up tomorrow."

"What do you suggest?"

"We need to hold the platoons over. Cancel days off and put everyone on standby, at least through the weekend. I'd rather pay the overtime and avoid any problems. There's nothing like turning on the television and watching the live feed of the city burning."

"Any other suggestions?" Rich asked.

"Start praying for snow."

CHAPTER TWENTY-EIGHT

Office of the Medical Examiner, Manhattan, N.Y.
Thursday, February 21st, 2013 – 10:12 p.m.

Damien Baptiste watched the four men come through the back door and approach the desk. They were wearing suits and clearly had the look of law enforcement officials.

"Can I help you?" Baptiste asked.

"Yes, we're here to pick-up a body," one of the men said, as the other three milled around behind him. "A Charles Morgan, male, black. He came in last night. He was the victim of a vehicle accident on the Belt Parkway."

"And you are?" Baptiste said, looking the man over cautiously.

He was tall, over six feet, with blonde hair and blue eyes. He had, what could best be described as a California surfer look mixed with a corporate CEO. He exuded confidence and a sense of purpose. From the deferential treatment of the other men, it was clear he was in charge.

"I'm Dean Oliver, U.S. State Department, Diplomatic Security Service. I'm the Special Agent in Charge of the New York Office."

"Sorry, sir," Baptiste replied. "I'd like to help you, but I can only release a body to a licensed funeral director. If you want to make arrangements to have one come over, I'll be happy to help you out."

"Yeah, well, rules are made to be broken," Oliver replied. "We, the U.S. government, have received a formal request from the man's next of kin and I have every intention of fulfilling it."

"But the law says...."

Oliver held up his hand dismissively.

"What's your name?" he asked.

"Baptiste, Damien Baptiste," the man replied.

"Mr. Baptiste, I don't think I made myself clear," Oliver said, flashing a gregarious smile. "You see, this is a United States Government matter, and we *will* be taking the body with us. Now, if you would like to assist us in this matter, I will be pleased to write a letter to your supervisor and explain how your cooperation in this *delicate* matter reflected greatly on the professionalism of the New York City Medical Examiner's Office."

He paused for a moment, letting that sink-in. When he continued, the smile had vanished and his tone became much more ominous.

"However, if you insist on continuing to interfere with my mission, Mr. Baptiste, I will retrieve Mr. Morgan's body without your help, and I will have my men remove you from the premises. The federal system is vast and far reaching. Sometimes people get lost for days, weeks, months....."

He let the words trail off.

Baptiste swallowed hard as he realized that the other three men had closed ranks around their boss. They were now looking at him, their faces cold and impenetrable, and he felt a cold chill run down his spine.

"Well, let's just say that I hope you have people that will put as much effort into finding you, as we have done for Mr. Morgan's family," Oliver said. "Do I make myself perfectly clear?"

The man swallowed hard as the thinly veiled threat played out in his head.

"Since it is the federal government, I'm sure that an *exception* can be made," Baptiste said nervously.

"See, this is what I mean, gentlemen," Oliver said to the men standing around him. "If everyone else could work in cooperation like Mr. Baptiste and I just did, the world would be a much better place."

The men around him simply nodded their heads in agreement without saying a word.

Baptiste looked down at the computer keyboard and began typing information. When he was done, he searched until he found what he was looking for.

"If you gentlemen will just follow me," he said.

"Please," Oliver said, gesturing to the man, "lead the way."

Baptiste led them down the hallway and into the storage room. He located the locker where Charles Morgan was being stored and opened it, pulling the tray out.

One of the DSS agents pushed a gurney over and laid a body bag on top of it, unzipping it. Two of the men donned gloves and then picked the body up. They transferred it to the bag and sealed it up.

"See how easy that was?" Oliver asked.

He extended his hand out to the man as the three agents led the gurney away.

Baptiste reluctantly extended his hand and shook Oliver's, wincing as he felt it close on his like a vise grip.

"You've done your country a great service, Mr. Baptiste," Oliver said, pulling the man closer to him. "I won't forget you."

Dean Oliver turned and walked back down the hallway whistling, leaving Baptiste standing there terrified.

CHAPTER TWENTY-NINE

1 Police Plaza, Manhattan, N.Y.
Friday, February 22nd, 2013 – 7:33 a.m.

"This is a joke, right?"

"I wish it was, Commissioner," Captain Johnson said. "The body was removed last night by the State Department. One of the detectives from the ME's squad called me this morning. He said that the ME had left him a message. When he went over, he found out that the body had been released."

"The State Department?" Maguire asked incredulously. "How the hell did they get involved in this?"

"According to the report I received, four men came into the morgue around ten o'clock last night. They ID'd themselves as being with the State Department. Said that they were acting on a *humanitarian request* from the family and they took possession of the body. Since the victim had been ID'd, and the autopsy was complete, there was no reason not to release it."

Maguire rubbed his eyes, and then let his fingers trail down his jaw line, feeling the roughness of the stumble against his skin. He desperately needed a shave, coffee, and sleep.

"Anything else?" he asked.

"That's it for now," she replied. "As soon as I know something more I will let you know."

"Do me a favor; does it say who exactly the body was released to."

He could hear her shuffling papers on the other side of the phone.

"It doesn't say here, just a notation that it was U.S. State Department."

"Find out for me," Maguire asked. "I'm going to have to go brief the P.C. on this now and, being a former fed, he is going to want to know. If I'm not here, give the information to Inspector Martin."

"Will do, sir. I'll call you back as soon as I find out."

"Thanks," Maguire said and hung up the phone.

Maguire got up and walked out of the office.

"Amanda, I'm going to see the P.C.," he said. "Call me if you need anything."

"You got it, boss," the detective replied.

As he left, he stopped by Liam Martin's office.

"Hey, Liam, I'm going down the hall to talk to the boss," Maguire said. "If I get a call from Captain Johnson, get the information and call me."

"Yes, sir," Martin replied.

A few moments later Maguire walked into Rich's office, grabbed a cup of coffee from the pot on the credenza, and sat down.

"Damn, you look like shit," Stargold said.

"What can I say? Making you look good is a tough job," Maguire replied sarcastically.

"That's funny," Rich replied. "To what do I owe the pleasure of your cheerful countenance this fine morning?"

"Have you ever seen the movie *'Invasion of the Body Snatchers'*?"

"Is this *movie trivia Friday*?"

"You're going to wish it was," Maguire replied. "I just got off the horn with Captain Johnson at Major Case; our victim is in the wind."

"Why are you fucking with me this early in the morning?" Stargold said.

"See, I told you that you were going to wish it was movie trivia Friday," Maguire said. "This isn't a joke. According to the good captain, our friends over at the State Department showed up last night and absconded with Morgan's body."

"I don't fucking believe this. Why would State be involved?"

"It certainly is becoming a bit bizarre, isn't it?" Maguire replied. "Supposedly they took the body at the request of the family."

"I thought we had an address going back to Baltimore?"

"We did, Baltimore PD went to the location. Place turned out to be an abandoned lot. According to the cops, it's been that way for well over a decade. Before that, it was a sporting goods store."

Rich tossed the pen, that he had been holding, onto the desk and leaned back in his chair.

"*Outfrigginstanding*," he replied. "Do we even know if Charles Morgan is actually his real name?"

"I wouldn't bet the farm on it," Maguire replied.

"What's your instinct tell you on this?" Rich asked.

"Honestly, I'm puzzled by all of it, Rich. I just get the impression we are missing something important."

"Have you called State yet to find out why they took the body?

"Not yet," Maguire said. "I don't want to play cards I haven't been dealt."

"What do you want to do?"

"I think it's time to think outside the box," Maguire said. "I can call someone who can peel back the layers and take a peek at the stuff that we're not being allowed to look at."

"You think that we are dealing with something like that?"

"I do," Maguire replied solemnly.

"I hate calling in favors for something that might turn into nothing."

Maguire's cell phone began to ring. He reached into his pocket and removed it.

"Hold that thought," he said, as he answered the phone. "Yes, Liam?"

Maguire listened for a few moments as the man on the other end spoke to him.

"Ok, thanks," Maguire replied and hung up the phone.

"According to Captain Johnson, the person signing the body out of the morgue was none other than Special Agent in Charge, Dean Oliver of the Diplomatic Security Service."

"Wait a minute," Rich said. "Are you telling me that the same guy who whisked our terrorist friend out of an interrogation room is the same guy who stole a body out of the morgue?"

"Apparently," Maguire replied. "I liked them better when they just did protection."

"You know what, buddy?" Rich replied. "I'm getting tired of being treated like a mushroom and fed bullshit at every turn. Make the call."

"I'll let you know whatever I find out," Maguire said. "On a side note, speaking of bullshit, where do we stand with the Reverend Archie and his posse?"

"Please, that fucker is on my last nerve," Rich said. "Now McMasters is in a panic and wants me to meet with him. Jennings is being quoted as saying that he is doing everything humanly possible to keep the lid on this, but unless the powers that be sit down and talk with him, well you never know what might happen."

"Self-aggrandizing prick," Maguire replied. "Someone needs to throw his ass in jail."

"That's a nice dream to have, but it will never happen. He knows too many people, has way too much juice for that."

"So what are you going to do?"

"I don't know," Stargold replied. "The thought of sitting down with that scam artist turns my stomach. But I just don't know how I can't. It's like he is standing at the door to the movie theater with a can of gas and a match, daring us to do something. We both know that we are damned if we do, damned if we don't. No one will blame him for anything, but us, they'll crucify us in City Hall Park."

"Have the Deputy Commissioner of Community Affairs reach out to his people, tell them we'd like to invite them to headquarters on Monday morning to discuss how we can begin to *heal* things," Maguire said. "That we expect that they will, as a show of good faith, maintain the peace until we can talk. Then, if anything happens, we can push back. We can say that we had a meeting set-up and he failed to keep his side of the agreement."

"You think that'll work?"

"Are you kidding me?" Maguire asked. "The thought of him being able to parade up to the front door of this place, and be greeted with a sense of legitimacy, will be too much for him to take. He'll blow his load imagining the throng of reporters who will be there to cover him."

"I hope you're right," Rich said.

"It'll buy us a few days to see what we can dig up. At the very least it gets us through the weekend."

"Let me know what you find out."

"I will," Maguire said.

When he got back to his office he closed the door and sat down at his desk, removing the other cell phone from his jacket pocket. He placed the call and listened to it ring.

"You do realize that I still work for a living, don't you?" Mother said when he answered the phone.

"I figured I would just keep adding to my tab and take you to Olive Garden when I make my way into town."

"At the rate you're tab is building, the only olive garden I'm going to be eating in is the one in Momma Francesca's backyard, in the hills of Tuscany."

"I should get a discount on the last one," Maguire said. "After all, you only hijacked a civilian satellite."

"You pay for the ends, Paddy; not the means."

"Then I guess I'm going to owe you a bit more. I need help and this is definitely one that belongs in your wheelhouse. Do you remember our little foreign friend, who got the taxi ride from the kind hearted folks over at State not too long ago?"

"I do indeed. Still makes my blood boil just thinking about it."

"Well, then," Maguire said, "do I have a story for you."

"I'm all ears," Mother replied.

"You might have heard that I had a DOA on one of the highways here the other night. Black victim being chased by several white makes."

"Yes, I did hear. I also heard some of the locals are beating the old racism drum."

"Yeah, it's a one hit wonder that they drag out every time they need a song for the cameras," Maguire replied. "Anyway, it's an odd story. Guy flies into Dulles from Vienna, and was supposed to fly back out yesterday morning. The only problem is, the night before he is supposed to leave; he is two hundred and fifty miles away with no ID, running for his life in my city."

"Stranger things happen, my son."

"Oh, I didn't get to the strange part yet. After he is hauled to the morgue, we print him and they come back to a U.S. citizen from Baltimore. We ask the P.D. down there to look into it and try to round up some relatives for us. When they get to the location that is listed as his residence, it's a lot that has been vacant for a decade. Before that, it was a sporting goods store."

"Okay, now it is starting to sound like a bit of an enigma," Mother said.

"Now is where it gets better," Maguire replied. "Last night, before the ink was even dry on the toe tag, the morgue gets a visit from a few suits. They claim that they have received a humanitarian request to retrieve the body and return it to the family."

"And these fine upstanding individuals work for the same agency as the ones who provided the government funded taxi ride to our friend Jihadi Joe?"

"Not just the same agency, Mother, the same fucking suit."

"Are you positive?" the man asked.

Maguire could hear the change in the man's voice. The levity was gone and there was now an edge to it. For those who've served, the oath of enlistment is sacred. The part that says 'I will support and defend the Constitution of the United States against all enemies, foreign and domestic,' is not taken lightly. The idea that someone employed by the government might be working against its best interests was unsettling, to say the least.

"Same name," Maguire said. "Dean Oliver, he's the SAIC for the New York Field Office."

"So how the hell did he know?" Mother asked.

"That's the million dollar question that I'm trying to answer."

"I take it that you haven't reached out to State?"

"Nope," Maguire said. "Not until I know exactly what team they are really playing for."

"Smart man," Mother replied. "I need you to send me the alleged pedigree information you have on your vic, including scans of the prints. I'll see what I can pull up for you."

"You'll have them by this afternoon and I'll get the engines all revved up for your Italian adventure."

"If this one involves a rogue, Paddy, it's on the house. I'll even use my own bullet when the time comes."

"Hooyah," Maguire replied and ended the call.

CHAPTER THIRTY

Far Rockaway, Queens, N.Y.
Friday, February 22nd, 2013 – 11:53 p.m.

"One-Oh-One Adam on the air?" a female voice said over the radio.

"One Adam, go Central."

"One Adam, we're getting a report of a 10-59, car fire, in the vicinity of Beach 37th Street and the Boardwalk. Motorist said he saw flames as he was driving east on Edgemere Avenue."

"One Adam, 10-4. We'll check and advise."

"*Sonofabitch*," Police Officer Lisa Reid said, as she tossed the radio up on the dashboard. "I can't even get a friggin' hot cup of coffee before they start this shit?"

"Look at the bright side," her partner, Police Officer Darren Jones, said. "The flames should at least keep us warm."

"Yeah, the *bright side*," Reid said. "Till F.D. shows up and hoses everything down. Then we're left standing in a goddamn slush puddle, out in the freezing cold, trying to read the friggin' VIN plate."

"You know something, Lisa?" Jones asked "You need to get laid more often. You're turning into a very frustrated and angry woman."

"Been there, done that, got the divorce papers. I'll stick to my little lithium-ion powered, bunny vibrator. It doesn't bitch about my work schedule and doesn't screw my *ex*-best friend."

As the radio car turned off Seagirt Boulevard, and headed west along Edgemere, they could see the flames rising up in the distance. Jones made a left on Beach 37th and headed toward the fire, pulling off to the side of the road when they got close.

"One Adam to Central."

"One Adam, go with your message."

"Central, be advised it's a confirmed 10-59, two vehicles, fully engulfed. Is F.D. en route?"

"Affirmative, I show them notified and responding."

"Copy," Reid said.

"They were probably already in their bunks sleeping," Jones replied. "It must be nice to come to work and sleep."

"I don't know," Reid said. "I'd rather chase a shit head with a gun before I run into some house fire."

Jones opened his window and lit a cigarette.

"You know what the problem with that theory is?" he asked. "You might not like it, but if you get the call, you'll still run into a burning building. I don't imagine any of them would be dropping their hoses to run after a man with a gun."

"True," Lisa said. "Then again, they'll just say we're *haters*."

Jones laughed.

They heard the wail of sirens behind them and turned to see a fire engine approaching them.

"It's show time," Jones said.

Twenty minutes later, the shells of the two burned out vehicles sat smoldering. Reid stood over one of the cars with her flashlight, trying to read find a VIN number.

"I ain't got shit, D," she said.

"Me neither," he said. "No tags and it looks like the VIN plates have been popped."

"I don't have time for mysteries," she said and removed the radio from the holder on her belt. "One Adam to Central"

"One Adam, go with your message."

"Central, be advised we're going to need two tows at this location. One is for a Chevy van, the other is for a Lincoln Town Car. No plates or vins on either."

"One Adam, did you say a Chevy van and a Lincoln Town Car?"

"That's affirmative Central."

"One Adam, stand-by. One Sergeant on the air? One-Oh-One Sergeant?"

"One Sergeant."

"Sarge, can you 10-85 One Adam, Beach 37th and the Boardwalk, reference a possible vehicle from 10-53 fatality on the Belt Parkway in the confines of the Six-Eight."

"10-4, show me responding."

"Oh that's great," Reid said. "That's just *mother-fucking-great*. These cars are from that bag of shit? At the rate I'm going I'm never going to get a cup of coffee tonight."

CHAPTER THIRTY-ONE

Southampton, Suffolk County, N.Y.
Saturday, February 23rd, 2013 – 11:57 a.m.

"Maguire," James said, as he answered the cell phone.

"Commissioner, this is Officer Sanchez from Operations," the man said. "Captain Johnson from Major Case is requesting that you contact her regarding the fatal accident in Brooklyn."

"Okay, do you have a number for her?"

"I do," he said and read the cell number to Maguire.

"Thanks," Maguire said and ended the call, then dialed the one he had been given.

"Captain Johnson," the woman said.

"Hey Ann, it's Commissioner Maguire. You wanted to speak with me?"

"Yes, Commissioner," she said. "We've confirmed that the two vehicles used in the accident were the ones recovered in Far Rockaway last night."

"Great, we have any leads on them?"

"Not really," she said. "Both were reported stolen. The van was taken Tuesday evening from a storage lot in the Four-Eight. The Town Car was a livery. It was taken late Wednesday afternoon from Midtown North. According to the complaint report that patrol did, the driver told them that he had gone in to get a cup of coffee at a diner on 10th Avenue. He said he left the car running because it was cold and when he came out it was gone."

"I guess if it weren't for dead-ends, we wouldn't have anything to go on."

"It certainly does feel that way," she said.

"Okay, well thanks for keeping me updated."

"No problem, sir. If anything else comes up I'll let you know."

Maguire ended the call and set the phone down on the coffee table, turning his attention back to the paperwork he had been going through. The investigation seemed to be more of an exercise in futility at this point. Nothing made sense.

No, that wasn't true, he thought. *It already did make sense to someone; it was just that he hadn't figured it out yet*.

All crime was essentially the same. Something was done to someone, or something, and you just had to figure out the reason why. Sometimes you got lucky and there was a connection, sometimes there wasn't. But it was all just a matter of trying to assemble the pieces that you had and figure out how they were interconnected. You just needed that one lynchpin to connect the disparate pieces.

Charles Morgan's death wasn't the issue. That was just an accident. The real question was who exactly was chasing him and why. Obviously this was a planned operation and not a random act, no matter what the Reverend Archie claimed. Was it a meeting that went bad? Did he arrive in one of the cars?

There was something much bigger at play here, but what that was remained elusive. It could potentially involve anything, from sex to money, and everything in between. They just needed to catch a break.

The phone in his pocket began to vibrate.

"I hope you have something for me," Maguire said when he answered the phone.

"You've stirred up one helluva shit storm, tadpole," Mother replied. "I got three 'why are you asking' callbacks before the system developed an apparent *glitch* and the entry was unfortunately *lost*."

"But you wouldn't be calling to tell me that if you didn't happen to see the entry *before* it was lost."

"Smart boy," Mother said. "First of all, your dead man isn't Charles Pierre Morgan, although by the end of this call you're going to wish that he was and that this was all something as mundane as a random hate crime."

"That sounds ominous," Maguire replied.

"It should, because it is. Your road kill isn't an innocent victim. His name is Yusif Tahir Dawai and he's from the Sudan, more specifically the Mahamid clan which is a part of the larger Sudanese-Arab Rizeigat tribe in Northern Darfur."

"Lovely," Maguire said sarcastically.

"Oh, it gets better," Mother replied. "Junior's old man was Abdullah Muhammed Dawai, who, besides being one helluva camel herder, had a side gig as a Janjaweed Brigadier. I say *was*, because he was *tragically* killed in 2005. Unfortunately, his demise came a bit too late. Between August 2003 and April 2004, he was responsible for Janjaweed activities in the Terbeba-Arara-Bayda triangle where 460 civilians were killed."

"We're talking father of the year material here," Maguire replied.

"Yeah, he would have had a lock on the psychotic sub-category, but fear not, we have an heir apparent. His uncle is

Musa Ali Dawai, whose official title is tribal leader, but who the State Department also suspects of being the *defacto* head of the Janjaweed. If that wasn't enough, he is also the chief advisor of the Ministry of Federal Affairs. His position allows Uncle Musa to coordinate military relations with regional leaders surrounding Darfur, as well as with other tribal groups. This political clout gives him a lot of leeway when it comes to the Janjaweed, especially in Khartoum."

"Is this the same Musa Dawai that the State Department and United Nations named as a suspected criminal in the genocide going on in the Sudan?" Maguire asked.

"You're getting good at this connecting-the-dots thing," Mother said. "There's been some *faux* outrage and every once in a while there will be a renewed push to turn him over to international authorities, but the bottom line is that he holds enough information about the current government to pose a serious threat, should it ever decide to turn against him."

"While I appreciate the history lesson and the family lineage, how does this impact on my victim? I mean it doesn't make much sense that the State Department would want to help the family, considering they labeled the uncle a bad guy."

"You'd think," Mother said. "But that's not the end. You see, thanks to Uncle Musa, your *victim* was also a member of the Sudanese National Intelligence and Security Services."

Maguire knew all about the National Intelligence and Security Services, or NISS. It was an incredibly powerful body and its agents had immunity from prosecution for *all* crimes committed in the course of their work. Of course, this left a lot open to interpretation as far as what constituted their *work*. The NISS was known to ruthlessly suppress any activities that could be even remotely considered as anti-government. They had a long history of human rights violations, including secret detention and torture sites that created a climate of fear in the Sudan. Their targets included human rights defenders, political dissidents, students, the press and members of ethnic minorities, who were arbitrarily arrested and detained.

"How big of a player?" Maguire asked.

"Oh, I'd say he's a big fish. Word is that he was an integral part of the ring that brought down Salah Gosh."

Maguire exhaled deeply.

Salah Gosh was an odd bird. He was a Major General who had served as the director of the NISS from 2004 through 2009, when he was promoted to the position of national security advisor to the Sudanese President, Omar Hassan al-Bashir. Prior to that, he had been the personal government *minder* for Osama bin Laden when bin Laden lived in the Sudan between 1990 and 1996.

To the outside world he seemed to be a staunch supporter of al-Bashir's policies. After he had been promoted to director of NISS, he had been accused by many monitoring organizations of having failed to take any substantive action to identify, neutralize, or disarm the Janjaweed. This was on top of condoning the arbitrary detention, harassment, and torture of dissidents of the state.

Just recently however, Gosh had been arrested by the NISS and charged with plotting against the president. Either the man liked to play both sides of the fence, or someone was playing *fuck-fuck*.

"Supposedly, the kid got his position because of the uncle's connection with Gosh," Mother continued. "He moved up pretty quickly in the ranks, where he gained a reputation as a ruthless and cunning adversary."

"Could this have been some sort of retribution hit?" Maguire asked.

"I've thought about that possibility, but I'm not overly convinced," Mother replied. "I'm sure there are some back home who are celebrating his premature demise, but something just doesn't feel right about this. As fast as those *diplo-dweebs* at State slammed the door in my face, something about this doesn't ring true. I think it's safe to say that they know more than they are letting on. You need to keep digging, Paddy. Go back and rethink everything, because I can tell you one thing, he wasn't here arranging his summer social calendar. Don't under-estimate anything and don't overlook the potential terrorism connection. Despite the Sudan government allegedly showing them the door in 1996, Al Qaeda in Sudan is very much alive and well. They even have a student wing at the university in Khartoum."

"Will do," Maguire replied. "Thanks again for sticking your neck out for me."

"Just for the record, I'm expecting a *very* nice Christmas present this year."

"I'll personally wrap it," Maguire said with a laugh. "Talk to you later."

He ended the call and put the phone back in his pocket.

Spies, he thought. *No wonder this investigation has been so fucked up.*

CHAPTER THIRTY-TWO

Southampton, Suffolk County, N.Y.
Saturday, February 23rd, 2013 – 1:43 p.m.

"Hey, chicky," Gen said, as her and Gregor walked into the salon. "Where's James?"

"He had to go back into the city," Melody replied, looking up from the paper she was reading.

"That accident?"

"Yeah," Melody said. "Despite the supposed *truce*, they are still having some issues with sporadic violence throughout the city. I guess not everyone received the reverend's memo. He's having a meeting with all the borough commanders to address the manpower issues and to set-up contingency plans, if things should begin to spiral out of control."

"Lovely," Gen replied, as she took a seat on the couch across from Melody.

"I'm going to bring these bags upstairs and get them unpacked," Gregor said.

"I'll be up in a minute," Gen said. "I think I need to take a nap."

"Still under-the-weather?" Melody asked.

"I was starting to feel better, but then I crashed when we were over at Peter's, packing up the last of Gregor's stuff."

"Did you see the nurse like I told you?"

"No, mother," Gen replied with a frown. "Like I said, I started feeling better so I didn't think it was an issue."

"Until you get on something, you're just going to be on this roller-coaster," Melody said. "I know you too well. The minute you start feeling better you think you're superwoman and over-do it, then you crash. Let them start you on an antibiotic and be done with this."

Gen stuck out her tongue and made a face.

"Listen, we're going to have a lot of work coming up soon, and I need you on top of your game. You're going to be less than worthless if you don't take care of yourself."

"I will," Gen replied. "I promise, I'll check in with the nurse as soon as I get upstairs."

"Good. You have any plans for tonight?"

"Nope, just dinner and a quiet night at home," Gen said. "Monday will be here soon enough, then it's back to the proverbially grind."

"Well, go relax and I'll see you at dinner."

"Okay," Gen said, as she stood up. "Let me know if you need me to do anything."

"Thanks, but I'll be fine."

Gen made her way up to her bedroom suite on the second floor and found Gregor unpacking the last of his bags.

"All settled in?" she asked, as she took a seat on the edge of the bed.

"Yes, but I dread the thought of having to repack it all again when the time comes."

"Well, we'll just have to cross that bridge when we get there, but for now I like the thought of waking up beside you."

Gregor closed to door to the closet and sat down next to Gen.

"You do, mouse?" he asked as he wrapped his arm around her shoulder.

Genevieve snuggled against his body, feeling his hand pulling her closer to him.

"Yes, silly, of course I do," she replied. "It's kind of strange, because I was a bit worried about what it would be like, but it just feels so natural."

"I'm glad," he replied. "I like being with you also."

"You do?"

"Of course," Gregor replied. "A man would have to be crazy to not want to spend his time with the most beautiful woman in the world."

"You *are* crazy," Gen said. "I am *not* the most beautiful woman in the world."

Gregor turned slightly and peered down into Gen's green eyes.

"You are to me, mouse," he said softly and lowered his lips to hers.

Suddenly, Gen recoiled, a look of fear gripping her face.

"Oh, God," she cried and leapt from the bed, racing across the room toward the en suite bathroom.

"*Maus*?!" Gregor exclaimed, as he jumped up and began to follow her until the door slammed in his face.

"Are you alright?" he asked, but from the sound coming from the bathroom he knew that she wasn't.

This was a first for him. During his time in the GSG-9 he had dealt with any number of injuries, from broken bones to gunshot wounds, but he had never had to deal with a sick woman.

"Mouse?" he asked softly. "Should I come in?"

"No!"

He was simultaneously both relived and worried. He looked around the room, as if he might find an answer to her problem. The knock on the bedroom door startled him.

Gregor moved to the door and opened it cautiously.

"Yes?" he asked the woman standing on the other side.

"I'm Lauren Schneider," she replied. "I'm the night shift nurse. Ms. Anderson told me that I needed to check on Ms. Gordon."

"Oh yes, please come in," Gregor said sounding very relieved. "She's in the bathroom."

"Is she okay?" the woman asked.

"I don't know," Gregor replied. "She hasn't been feeling well for the last two weeks, some type of flu bug she says."

The nurse walked over to the door and knocked gently.

"Ms. Gordon, it's the nurse, are you okay."

"Yes, I'll be right out."

A moment later Gen emerged from the bathroom looking pale.

"Please sit down on the bed," said the nurse.

Gregor took Gen by the arm and guided her over toward the bed.

"Has this been happening a lot?" Schneider asked.

"No, not really," Gen replied. "I thought I was getting better, but I think that I may have just over done it."

"Well, let's check your vitals first," the woman said.

After she had completed her examination, she pulled a chair over and sat down in front of Gen.

"Well, everything looks normal," the woman replied. "When did the symptoms first come on?"

"Maybe two weeks ago," Gen said. "I'd been doing a lot of traveling for work, so I just figured my resistance was down and I picked up a bug along the way."

"You're probably right," Schneider replied.

"Can I take anything?"

"Unfortunately, no," the woman replied. "If it's a viral infection it just has to run its course. Have you been running any fevers, sore throat, aches, fatigue?"

"No, not really," Gen said. "I mean I'm tired, but I've been running around a lot."

"Is this your husband?" the nurse asked.

"No, he's my boyfriend," she replied with an impish grin.

"Have you noticed anything unusual?"

"No, I haven't," Gregor replied. "Today was the first time I have seen her get sick like that."

"Hold on for a minute," Schneider said. "I'll be right back."

Gregor sat down next to Gen and took her hand in his, squeezing it tightly.

"Are you okay, mouse?"

She could hear the concern in his voice.

"Yeah, I am," she replied. "I think I'm just worn out, to be honest. I probably just need to admit defeat and stay off my feet for a few days."

"Well, if you let me, I will take care of you," he said.

"You are so sweet," Gen said. "I'll be fine, but if you really want to take care of me, who am I to complain."

"I will always take care of you, mouse," Gregor said with a smile.

"Ms. Gordon," Schneider said, as she walked back into the room. "I need you to do me a favor."

Gen looked up at the woman and then down at her hand.

"Oh, you have got to be kidding me," she said.

CHAPTER THIRTY-THREE

Lake George, New York State
Saturday, February 23rd, 2013 – 6:23 p.m.

Joanna Miller pulled the Nissan Pathfinder out of the Holiday Inn Parking lot and turned left onto Route 9N.

"It's about a mile up the road," the man sitting next to her said. "I hope you like seafood."

"Anything is fine, my love," Miller replied, taking the man's hand in hers. "Too bad they don't have take-out."

"You need to pace yourself, Jo. We still have another twenty-four hours left."

"Don't say that, Roger, it's a depressing thought," she replied. "I don't want to think about that now, especially not before we eat."

To the rest of the world they would appear to be like any other normal couple, out for an evening dinner, but they weren't.

Each of them had put their regular lives on hiatus for the weekend. Miller was supposed to be attending a forensic odontology training course, while Roger Aaron was scheduled to attend a planning board meeting to discuss the architectural issues for a new resort and conference center, which was being built overlooking scenic Lake George. However, none of it was true.

"Well, maybe we can bring our dessert back to the hotel room with us," he said.

"Oh really," she replied with a sultry smile, "and here I thought that *I* was going to be your dessert."

"Maybe we should just get our dinner to go," Roger replied.

"No, you're right. We do need to take a break. Besides, I want to enjoy something *normal* with you."

"You don't think what we are doing is normal?" he asked.

"Not that many times in one day," she said with a laugh. "Remember, I'm older than you, I need to pace myself."

"You didn't act old last night when you were doing…"

Miller leaned over and covered the man's mouth with her hand.

"Hush you!" she replied. "You're going to make me miss our turn talking like that."

"Yes, ma'am," he said, as she removed her hand from his mouth. "It's right up here on the bend."

The Pathfinder slowed as Miller approached the turnoff. The nice thing about being here in the winter was that you didn't have to contend with the high volume of tourists that the summer months attract.

They'd met here several times over the last year. It was neutral ground for them, with less chance of them running into someone they might know. Besides, it was also the midway point they both had to travel.

Miller pulled the vehicle into one of the vacant spots near the front of the restaurant.

"Okay," she said. "Do you think that we can order and eat in under a half hour?"

"Depends," he replied.

"On what?"

"On what exactly you're offering me for dessert?"

Miller turned to face him, then hiked her skirt up showing that she wasn't wearing anything underneath.

"You're such a bad girl," he replied.

"I know," she replied with a smile, "and you know you love it, Roger."

She opened the door and stepped outside. A cold wind was blowing hard off the lake and, at that moment, she regretted having not worn long pants. She pulled the collar of her jacket up and lowered her head before quickly heading off in the direction of the restaurant.

"Hold on," the man replied. "My shoes untied."

"Screw your shoe," Miller replied, the wind howling loudly in her ears. "My hot box is freezing."

The man looked up, opening his mouth to call out another sexual innuendo laced response, just in time to watch as the black SUV slammed into the woman from behind.

Joanna Miller's body was no match for the massive vehicle, with its heavy gauge, tubular steel push bumper. The force of the collision caused her body to lurch forward ever so briefly, before the vehicle caught up with her and pulled her underneath. He heard the sickening thud as the vehicles front right tire rode over her body, crushing it unmercifully under its weight, only to be repeated a fraction of a second later when the rear tire finished the job.

Before he could get to her, the vehicle had reached the end of the road and spun around, roaring out of the parking lot. Even if he'd had his wits about him, and thought about trying to get a license plate number, it wouldn't have done any good. The plates on this vehicle had already been removed.

Roger looked down at her lifeless form. Blood streamed from her nose and mouth, as well as from several deep lacerations in her scalp.

"Joanna! Joanna!" the man cried out, tears streaming down his face. "Baby, look at me!"

Despite his desperate pleas, no response came. Death had come almost instantaneously to the woman. As the man cradled her limp body in his arms, rocking her gently, people began streaming out of the restaurant.

Aaron glanced up from his lover's body to the throng of people gathering around them. He looked at them, as if searching their faces for an answer that would somehow make sense of this carnage. Several of them began dialing 911 on their cell phones to report the hit-and-run accident.

Then, in a moment of clarity, the shock of what had just happened was ripped away, and all Roger Aaron could think of was how he was going to explain why he was here and what he was doing with *her*.

CHAPTER THIRTY-FOUR

Office of the Medical Examiner, Manhattan, N.Y.
Sunday, February 24th, 2013 – 11:13 a.m.

"Good Morning, Shari," Bill Hennessey said to the woman sitting behind the desk at the M.E.'s office.

"Hey, Bill," the woman said, looking up from the crossword puzzle she was doing. "Did you hear about Dr. Miller?"

"No," Hennessey replied. "I've been away. What did she do now?"

"She's dead," the woman said.

"Dead?" the man replied, a shocked look registering on his face. "Are you sure?"

"Yeah, the office was notified last night by the Lake George Police. She was killed in a hit and run accident."

"No shit?" Hennessey said. "Wow. What the hell was she doing in Lake George?"

"That's the million dollar question. Word is she wasn't alone and she *wasn't* with her husband."

Hennessey let out a long, slow whistle.

"*One never knows, do one*?" he said conspiratorially. "She had kids right?"

"Two," Shari replied. "I think the oldest one is in high school."

"Sad," Hennessey said, rapping his hand on the top of the desk, "but that's life in the big city, isn't it? One day you're working on the stiff laying on the tray, next day you *are* the stiff in the tray."

"That would make a nice Hallmark card," Shari replied. "You obviously missed your calling."

Hennessey laughed.

"Maybe when I retire," he said. "For now, I better go and earn the paycheck they give me. Stay out of trouble, Shari."

"You too, Bill," the woman replied and went back to the crossword puzzle.

Hennessey walked down the hallway and made his way to his office. He hung up his jacket and set his bag down on the desk. He then went and made a fresh pot of coffee. When it was done brewing, he poured himself a cup and sat down at his desk, where he began to sort through the papers in his in-box.

He picked up the photocopy of the receipt for the body of Charles Morgan and examined it. He hadn't expected it to be claimed that quickly.

"State Department?" he said. "Why the hell did the State Department claim his body?"

Hennessey laid the paper on the desk and looked over at the growing number of case folders in his 'active' bin.

Don't look gift horses in the mouth, he thought. *It's not your problem anymore.*

After he had caught up with the paperwork, he turned on his computer. As he waited for it to load up, he picked up the phone and hit the button to retrieve his messages.

There was the usual array of questions from family, along with several from detectives with active cases. Then he heard a familiar voice come through the phone.

"Hi, Mike this is Doctor Miller. I'm finished with your autopsy from the Belt Parkway fatality," he heard the voice in the recording say.

Wow, he thought. *That's just eerie.*

Hennessey had genuinely liked Miller. She'd been at the Medical Examiner's Office for a little over a decade, a couple of years longer than he had been assigned there. She was a very attractive woman, something that had always struck him as a bit odd, considering the job she did. There had been any number of rumors about her. If she'd heard them, she never let on. He didn't put too much credence into them. Hennessey thought that is was all about petty jealousy, because of how good looking she was.

He had come to think of ME's as typically being old, slightly ghoulish, men; not someone who looked as if she'd just walked off a fashion shoot. If someone had to be the one to have their hands on him after he died, she would have been the one he'd hoped for.

With your luck, you'll get Dr. Von Graffe, he thought, as he felt a shiver run through his body.

Dr. Von Graffe made Lon Chaney's *Phantom of the Opera* character look positively charming.

"......Oh, I did find something odd, a microchip. Probably one of those *techies*, who used it to open his door or turn on the lights. Anyway, I've got it secured and I'll put it into the evidence locker."

Microchip? That got his attention.

Hennessey got up and made his way down the hall to the evidence room. He located the locker and opened it; retrieving the plastic security envelope and examined it. Inside he could see a small microchip.

First the State Department and now this, he thought. *This case keeps getting stranger by the minute.*

He double checked to make sure it was her name, and that it indicated that the item had been removed from the Belt Parkway victim. He signed it out in the evidence log and brought it back to his desk.

He picked up the phone and placed a call.

"Hey, Captain," he said. "It's Detective Hennessey over at the ME's Squad. You said you wanted to be notified if anything odd happened."

"Yeah, Bill, what do you have?" Johnson replied.

"I just got back from my days off," he said. "Did you know that the State Department claimed the vic's body?"

"Yeah, actually I did," she answered. "They picked it up Thursday night with some BS story."

"Okay, just wanted to make sure you knew," Hennessey replied. "I guess you know about the microchip as well?"

"What was that?" Johnson asked, sitting up in her chair.

"The microchip, that Dr. Miller pulled from our vic's body."

"No, this is the first I'm hearing about it," she replied. "Are you sure?"

"I'm looking at the ugly little thing right now," he said. "There's something else."

"What is it?"

"Dr. Miller, the one who did the autopsy on our vic. She's dead," Hennessey replied.

"What? How?"

"She was killed in a hit and run accident last night up by Lake George."

Ann Johnson stared out her living room window. It had just started snowing outside and she watched as the wind made the powder on the window ledge swirl rapidly around, the same exact way the thoughts inside her head were swirling around at the moment.

She felt a cold chill run through her body. Nothing about this case made any sense and the news of the M.E.'s death made the hair on the back of her neck stand up.

"Bill, listen to me. I want you to meet me down at headquarters, forthwith," she said. "I'm on my way. Bring that evidence bag with you and don't tell anyone what you have or where you are going."

"Yes, ma'am" Hennessey replied and hung up the phone.

He put on his jacket, stuffing the plastic bag into his pocket and headed for the door.

CHAPTER THIRTY-FIVE

Southampton, Suffolk County, N.Y.
Sunday, February 24th, 2013 – 11:57 a.m.

"Pregnant?" Maguire said, looking at Gen, then over at Melody. "How'd that happen?"

"Really?" Gen said. "No one explained that to you growing up?"

"I know *how* it happens, you idiot," he replied. "I'm just…. Wow, I'm just in shock. I don't know what to say."

"Congratulations would be a start," Gen replied.

"Of course, congratulations!" he replied, "to both of you."

He got up from the couch and walked over, hugging Gen first and then shaking hands with Gregor.

"Please forgive me," he said. "This getting no sleep stuff was much easier when I was younger. I don't rebound as quickly as I used to. God, I am so thrilled for you guys."

"I kept telling *miss-know-it-all* that I wasn't feeling good," Gen said, sticking her tongue out at Melody.

"Nice!" Melody said with a laugh. "I hope you mature over these next few months. I don't need *two* children running around here."

Maguire looked over at Gregor, who rolled his eyes.

"Welcome to my world, buddy," James said, "where the inmates run the asylum. Nice to know I'll have someone to keep me company."

"I think maybe we need to go on holiday," Gregor said. "Maybe somewhere quiet, like Afghanistan. I have an old friend from the GSG-9 who is now a member of ASSIK, the Close Protection Team guarding the German Ambassador in Kabul. Surely it will be safer for us there, not to mention much quieter."

Maguire laughed at the thought as the two women continued to trade verbal jabs. He was about to seriously consider the offer when his cell phone began ringing.

"Ok you two," he said, reaching for the phone. "Take a break."

Across from him, Gen wrinkled her nose and stuck her tongue out at Melody again.

"Maguire," he said, shaking his head.

"Commissioner, its Ann Johnson. Sorry to disturb you on your day off, but something's come up. We may have a bigger problem on our hands."

"Don't worry, Captain," he said, standing up and walking over to the window overlooking the ocean. "To be honest, I could use the break. What do you have?"

"I'm at headquarters with Detective Bill Hennessey," she said. "Bill is with the Medical Examiner's Squad. He returned back to work today and had a voice mail from the M.E. handling the case. She said that she found a microchip implanted in our victim. He has it here now."

"What does the report say?"

"It hasn't been completed," Johnson said.

"How about reaching out to the M.E. for more information?"

"That's the problem, the doctor was killed in a *hit and run* accident this weekend up in Lake George. It might be nothing, and her death might just be a coincidence, but I'm getting a weird feeling about it."

Maguire stared out the window at the sea just beyond, taking in what she had just said. Neither his time in Seal Team Four, nor the years spent on patrol in Brooklyn North, had made him a big fan of coincidences.

"Let's err on the side of caution," he said. "Stay put and I will call you back in a few minutes."

"Yes, sir," Johnson said.

Maguire ended the call and then selected a number from his contacts, listening as the phone rang.

"Silverman," the voice on the other end said.

"Kurt, it's James Maguire, you got a minute?"

"Sure, Commissioner," the man said. "I take it this isn't a social call?"

"I wish it were," Maguire said. "I need a big favor."

Special Agent Kurt Silverman was the head of the FBI's New York City Field Office, Joint Terrorism Task Force. He had first met Maguire a few weeks earlier during the hunt for the terror cell. Despite the relatively *frosty* relationship he had shared with the previous NYPD administration, he'd found Maguire to be a complete gentleman. The man had even gone out of his way to personally call the FBI Director to commend the JTTF's participation in the raids, even though it was the FBI SWAT team that had missed out on capturing Bashir Al Karim.

"Name it," Silverman said.

"How hard would it be to get a microchip analyzed?"

"Not hard," the man replied. "We can send it down to the Regional Computer Forensic Lab over in the Newark Field Office, but you guys have your own Computer Crimes Squad that can handle that."

"Yeah," Maguire replied, "but this might have some potential national security implications. For now, I need it done in-house, on a strictly need-to-know basis and really quick."

"I see," Silverman said. "I take it that there is more to this story?"

"You hear about the hit and run on the Belt Parkway?"

"Yeah, some guy ran across the highway and came up a lane short."

"That's the one," Maguire said. "The microchip got pulled from his body by the M.E., right before our *friend* from the State Department took possession of the body."

"That obnoxious little prick who stole our prisoner?"

"One in the same," Maguire replied.

"How'd he manage to pull that one off?"

"He claimed to have been acting on a BS humanitarian request from the family. To top it off, I have reason to believe that the victim might actually have been a foreign agent and the M.E. that handled the autopsy just turned up dead in Lake George, victim of a hit and run."

"Are you fucking kidding me?"

"I wish I was. This might turn into nothing more than some idiot with a weird taste in body modification, but then again."

"How quickly can you get it to me?

"I've got a detective at 1PP waiting for the word to hand deliver it."

"Give me an hour to call my resident hacker and have him meet me at the office. Soon as I know something, I'll call."

"Thanks, Kurt. I owe you."

Maguire ended the call and dialed Ann Johnson's number.

"You need to meet Special Agent Kurt Silverman from the JTTF over at 26 Fed in an hour," he said when the woman answered. "He's going to have one of his people check to see what's on the chip."

"Ok, Commissioner," Johnson replied. "Should we stay with the chip?"

"Yeah, until we know what we are dealing with I don't want you to let it out of your sight."

"Will do, sir. I'll call you as soon as we know something."

Maguire ended the call and went back to the couch, sitting down next to Melody.

"Is everything alright, cowboy?" she asked.

"Just another mystery to solve," he replied. "This investigation seems to have a knack for delivering twists and turns."

"What is it now?"

"The medical examiner found a microchip implanted in our dead guy," Maguire said.

"I'd say that certainly qualifies as a *twist*. Do you know what it does?"

"I have them taking it over to the FBI now," Maguire replied. "Hopefully they will be able to tell us more. Did I miss anything?"

"We were just trying to figure out where to build Gen and Gregor's new *love shack*," she replied. "Going to have an architect come out this week and look at an addition."

"I've got a lovely little house boat," he replied. "It's hardly ever used these days."

Maguire shot a look Melody's way, which she returned dismissively with an upheld hand and a roll of her eyes.

"Thanks, but no thanks," Gen chimed in. "One Popeye in the family is quite enough. My child is going to have a normal upbringing."

Maguire looked over at Gregor, watching as a smile appeared on his face. One thing was for certain, between the influences of the two of them, 'normal' was going to be anything but.

230

CHAPTER THIRTY-SIX

1 Police Plaza, Manhattan, N.Y.
Monday, February 25th, 2013 – 6:41 a.m.

Rich stared across the desk, trying to digest everything Maguire had just laid out for him.

"So you're telling me our dead guy is a fucking spy?"

"In so many words, yes," Maguire replied. "So I don't think that I am going out on a limb here, when I say there is more to this, than meets the eye."

"Do we know what's on the microchip?"

"Not yet," Maguire replied. "They've been working on it since yesterday. The encryption is military grade stuff. One thing is for certain, whatever it is; it does a helluva lot more than open garage doors or turn on lights."

"What do we do about our meeting this morning?"

"With Archie?" Maguire asked. "Oh, I think it's time that the *Reverend* Jennings gets a long overdue wakeup call. He's been the big kid, in the little sandlot, for much too long."

"So you want to play good cop, bad cop?" Rich asked.

"I was thinking more like bad cop, worse cop."

"If he runs crying to McMasters, he won't be happy."

"If we do it right, he'll be curled up in the corner too scared to crawl, let alone run anywhere."

"Fuck it," Rich replied. "I say let's have some fun. I've lasted eight weeks longer than I thought I would."

"That's the spirit," Maguire said, as he stood up. "I'll meet you down at Command and Control at ten. You bring Archie. I'll have everything ready and waiting."

"Ok, this is your show."

"I'll let you know if I hear anything else."

Maguire walked out of the office and headed down the hall.

"Commissioner," a voice called out behind him.

Maguire turned around to see Inspector Nikki Ryan approaching him.

"Hey, Nikki, how are they treating you at Counter Terrorism?"

"It's going well," she replied. "I really like it."

"I'm glad to hear that," Maguire replied.

"Sorry to hear about your girlfriend. How is she doing?"

"Ornery as ever," he said with a laugh. "She went from knocking on deaths door, to kicking the damn thing in."

"Sounds like you have your hands full."

"You don't know the half of it," Maguire said.

Ryan laughed.

"It was good seeing you again, sir," she replied. "I'll let you go."

"Actually, do you have a minute?" he asked.

"Sure, what do you need?"

"Come with me," Maguire replied.

He led her down the hallway toward his office and closed the door once she had stepped inside.

"Coffee?"

"Please," Ryan replied as she took a seat across from the desk. "Black is fine."

Maguire poured two cups, handing her one as he walked toward his chair.

"Thanks," she said, taking a sip.

"So, Nikki, tell me what you know about the state of affairs in the Sudan?"

"Well, since it became an independent country in the mid 1950's it has been gripped with almost non-stop ethnic and militia fighting," she said. "It was the largest of the African countries, until South Sudan broke away a few years back. It has been plagued by internal conflicts, famine, as well as civil wars. On top of that, it is rated as one of the most corrupt governments in the world. It is rife with human rights violations, turning a blind eye to forced labor, child conscription and sex slave trade. Other than that, I guess you could just call it a veritable cluster fuck."

"Actually, that does pretty much sum it up," he replied. "I want you to do me a favor, start looking into the Sudanese National Intelligence and Security Service. See if there is any chatter going on about them, beyond the usual civilian harassment stuff."

"Should I be on the lookout for anyone in particular?" she said, taking out a pad and jotting down notes.

"Yeah, anything regarding a guy named Yusif Tahir Dawai," Maguire replied. "Although, I think that's only one of many names. However, that one should be his primary. Hit up all your contacts, even the foreign ones. I want to know what he has been involved in, what he is linked to. See if anything else surfaces in connection with his movements."

"Just how aggressive do you want me to be?" Nikki asked, taking a sip of coffee.

"Ring the bells," Maguire replied. "See what kind of pushback you get."

"You think someone may be covering for him?"

"Let's just say that I think that there should be records, the question is will they still be there when you make the inquiry."

"Copy that," she said. "Thanks for the coffee, sir. I'll get on this right away and let you know what I find out."

"Thanks, Nikki. Call me if you need anything."

"I will," Ryan replied and headed for the door.

Maguire picked up the folder on his desk and began to go through the contents. There were several crime scene photos of the man they knew as Charles Morgan, and a grainy black and white one that Mother had sent to him the night before. This one was a surveillance photo, taken by the French DCRI, the Central Directorate of Interior Intelligence. It showed the man they knew as Morgan, identified in the report by French authorities as André Renaud, and an unidentified man, in the port city of Marseille. A note with the photo indicated that they had been looking into Renaud on suspicions of trafficking in illegal arms.

Marseille was being rocked by an upsurge in riots and violent drug crime, so much so that it had earned the nickname '*Chicago of the south*'. The idyllic French city, once recognized as a 'cultural capital of Europe', was now sinking rapidly into third world country status.

Nearly forty percent of the current population was Muslim. They had seized entire neighborhoods, which the French government benignly referred to as *zone's urbaine sensible*, and were imposing their own 'checkpoints' manned by gang members. Even the police and fire services had given up trying to enter these no-go zones. The occupants there were intent on reproducing not only the *conditions* found in their home countries, but apparently the law as well, with demands growing for Sharia law to be implemented.

To make matters worse, unemployment among the youth was as high as forty percent, so many turned to selling drugs. While their newly chosen *career path* led to easy money, it was not without peril. Violent turf wars soon erupted, and they took up arms to protect their trade. Soon AK-47's settled scores and enforced territorial disputes.

Marseille had become a city under siege, where the police were overwhelmed, outnumbered and outgunned. Demands for military intervention grew louder, with each passing day.

The DCRI investigation had subsequently identified Renaud as the primary supplier for arms in the area and they were in the process of building an international terrorism case against him. Unfortunately, as was typical, the left hand hadn't told the right what it was doing. The local police in Marseille, looking to gain a foothold in the escalating drug violence, had conducted an early morning raid on a waterfront warehouse being used as the distribution site for the weapons. While they succeeded in getting *that* shipment of guns off the street, Renaud had slipped away before DCRI could tighten the noose.

Fortunately, the justice he had eluded in Marseille, caught up with him on a rain soaked roadway in Brooklyn.

Not that it made his job any easier at the moment.

Maguire picked up the phone on the desk and dialed a number, listening as it rang.

"Criminal Investigations, Special Agent Baxter," the voice on the other end said.

"Bubbles!"

"Paddy, you old goat fucker, how the hell are you?"

"Livin' the dream," Maguire replied, "or at least so they tell me."

Special Agent Charles 'Bubbles' Baxter laughed at the comment. Baxter had been a member of Maguire's SEAL platoon. No matter how bad their situation had been, their platoon leader had always told them to quit complaining, because they were all 'livin' the dream'.

Baxter was an ex-submariner before coming to the teams, hence the call sign. The fact that he was 6'5", bald, and built like a friggin' battleship just added to the overall irony. Baxter had always reminded Maguire of the character in the movie *The Green Mile*. When the dents and dings of their global follies began taking longer to heal, he'd hung up his flippers and went to work for the Criminal Investigations Division of the Internal Revenue Service.

"I hear you went legit, say it isn't so."

"Hate to say it, but I did," Maguire said. "Got myself a steady girlfriend and a nine to five that pays the bills."

"Bullshit," Baxter replied. "The way I hear it, sounds more like you got yourself a sugar mama along with a gig that lets you lean out the window and make that *woo-woo* noise as you cut through traffic."

"Got no time for haters, Bubbles."

"So what do I owe the displeasure?" Baxter said.

"I need a favor," Maguire replied.

"I'm shocked, and here I thought this was a social call."

"What can you tell me about the *Reverend* Archibald Jennings?"

Maguire could almost *see* Baxter become agitated. He'd emphasized the title, knowing it would push the right buttons.

"For starters, he isn't any damn *reverend*," Baxter fumed. "He's just another one of those race-baiting, narcissists, who stir up trouble and then shield themselves behind the Lord. There's gonna be a lot of hand wringing and gnashing of teeth come judgment day, I tell you."

Baxter had been born in dirt poor, rural Georgia and he had been raised by a God fearing, Bible reading, Southern Baptist grandma. He knew his way around the Bible better than ninety percent of the *tele-evangelists* and was known to go on a rant of epic proportions at the very mention of one of their names. In fact, it had been a toss-up as to whether he should be known as 'Bubbles' or 'Preacher'.

"I need a peak into his recent banking activity."

"What are you looking for?"

"Deposits," Maguire replied. "Big ones. I need to know if someone is paying him to fan the flames of unrest."

"When do you need to know?"

Maguire glanced up at the clock.

"Within the next two hours?"

"I'll call you back on your cell," Baxter said.

"You the man, Bubbles," Maguire replied. "I don't care what Mother says."

Maguire barely caught the beginnings of a loud reply before he hung up the phone with a smile.

"Mike?" Maguire called out.

"Yeah, Boss?" Torres said leaning into the office.

"I need you to run this down to C&C for me," Maguire said, holding up a USB drive. "Tell them I need it ready to go in the conference room at ten o'clock."

"Will do," Torres said, taking the drive. "Oh, Special Agent Silverman is waiting outside for you."

"Send him in," Maguire replied.

A moment later Kurt Silverman walked into the office, looking more than a little worse for wear.

"Jesus, Kurt don't you look like something the cat dragged in."

"You mind if I close this?" Silverman said, nodding to the door.

"No, go ahead. Coffee?"

"Yeah, please."

Maguire got up and walked over to the coffee pot, refilling his mug and pouring a cup for Silverman.

"I take it you found something?"

"That's one way of putting it," Silverman said, taking the mug Maguire handed him.

"How bad?"

"Fuck," Silverman said, "this shits way above *my* pay grade."

"Can you talk to me about it?" Maguire asked.

"Honestly, Commissioner, I have no idea, but I do know your background so I'm trusting in that."

"What did you find?"

Silverman took a drink and leaned back in the leather chair, closing his eyes as he chose his words.

"First of all, that wasn't your typical microchip," Silverman replied. "As you are probably aware, these things are all the rage these days among the techies. Mostly their ability is limited to novelty stuff, turning on a light, opening a door, or locating your long lost pet, and that's it. This thing, this is something out of a sci-fi book."

"How so?" Maguire asked.

"The majority of these things are wide open, maybe some basic encryption. This thing was full blown military grade encryption. I have never seen my computer geek look so positively ebullient. Then when he finally cracked it, the reason became obvious. Every page is marked Top Secret. Have you ever heard of something called *Dragon's Breath*?"

Maguire stared at Silverman for a moment and then nodded slowly.

"It's a program that Global Defense Logistics is working on for the Department of Defense."

"That's your girlfriend's company isn't it?"

"Yeah, it is."

"Commissioner, I'm not going to be able to sit on this. This really is national security stuff. I'm going to have to kick this down to Washington."

"I know, Kurt. I don't expect you to hold off on this."

Silverman reached into his pocket and withdrew a piece of paper.

"This is a copy of the cover sheet," Silverman said, sliding the paper across the desk to Maguire. "Judging from the coding on it, I assume it can be traced to a particular user. At least it will allow your girlfriend a jump on locking down any leak."

"I appreciate that, Kurt."

"Clearly there is more to your victim than meets the eye."

Maguire looked down at the folder on his desk, and opened it, sliding the photo across to Silverman, who picked it up.

"Yusif Tahir Dawai, a.k.a. Charles Pierre Morgan, a.k.a. André Renaud, a.k.a. *who-the-fuck-knows-who-else*," Maguire said. "He's a card carrying member of the Sudanese National Intelligence and Security Service. So in answer to your question, yes, there is a lot more to the story than meets the eye."

"Fuck," Silverman said, as he looked at the surveillance photo. "I didn't see that one coming."

"Now the question is how did he come into possession of a microchip containing a top secret military program?"

"That's going to require old fashioned police work."

Maguire's cell phone began to ring. He looked down, seeing the caller ID.

"I've got to take this," he said.

He reached down and picked up the phone.

"What do you have for me?"

"Lot's," replied Baxter. "Do you have the time?"

"Good or bad?" Maguire asked.

"Depends on whose shoes you're wearing at the time. You're going to like it. On the other hand it's gonna suck to be Archie Jennings."

"Are there any transactions from overseas?"

"One recently," Baxter said. "Let me find it."

Maguire could hear the man shuffling through papers on the other end.

"Here it is, from a bank in Khartoum. Does that help you out?"

"You free right now?"

"You gonna buy me lunch?"

"I'll buy you lunch, Bubbles," Maguire said. "Just get your ass to 1PP by ten o'clock."

"Real lunch this time, Paddy," Baxter replied, "with plates, silverware and cloth napkins. I'm serious, man. None of that happy meal bullshit you pulled last time."

Maguire chuckled at the memory of Baxter opening the bag to find a box of chicken nuggets and a Little Mermaid figure inside.

"Fine, but bring you're 'A' game," Maguire said. "I'll tell them to expect you in the garage."

"See you then," Baxter said, ending the call.

Maguire laid the phone on the desk and looked over at Silverman.

"How'd you like lunch?" he asked.

"Who are you planning on ambushing?" Silverman asked.

"Does the name Archie Jennings ring a bell?" Maguire asked.

"You mean to tell me that I get lunch *and* I get to watch Jennings squeal like a stuck pig?"

"That's my plan," Maguire said.

"Traffic's brutal," Silverman replied. "Washington's not going anywhere."

"That's the spirit," Maguire said with a smile.

CHAPTER THIRTY-SEVEN

Southampton, Suffolk County, N.Y.
Monday, February 25th, 2013 – 9:17 a.m.

"*Dragon's Breath*?" Melody said. "How is that possible?"

"Well, that's the *sixty-four thousand dollar* question isn't it," Maguire said.

Melody stared out the window in her office and gazed out at the rough surf that was battering the shoreline below. Her mind was reeling as she tried to come to terms with what Maguire had just told her.

Dragon's Breath was the top-secret military targeting program that GDL was scheduled to begin live trials on next month, at the Navy's Point Mugu, Sea Test Range in California.

How would this impact the testing? she wondered.

"James, there are very few people that have full access to that program. The majority of those working on it are limited to compartmented information."

"Check your email. I sent you a scan of the cover sheet that was extracted. Hopefully you can figure out whose copy it was that got leaked."

"I'll have Gen jump on that and get back to you. What is going to happen now?"

"Silverman is going to have to notify Washington about what they discovered. There's going to have to be an investigation into how the information was leaked."

"What do you want me to do when I find out whose file it is?"

"Nothing, don't say anything to anyone," Maguire replied. "Just give me the information and I will pass it along to Silverman. You and Gen just cooperate with the investigators when they reach out to you."

"Ok, as soon as I know something I will let you know," Melody said.

"Don't worry, angel. Everything is going to be fine."

"I hope you're right, cowboy. Talk to you later."

Melody ended the call and pulled up the email, printing out the cover sheet that was attached to it. Then she picked up the phone and called Gen.

"Get up here, chicky. We have a really big problem."

CHAPTER THIRTY-EIGHT

1 Police Plaza, Manhattan, N.Y.
Monday, February 25th, 2013 – 9:43 a.m.

The Right Reverend Archie Jennings strolled along the brick thoroughfare, which led from the New York City Municipal Building to 1 Police Plaza, with his entourage in tow and an assortment of reporters, still photographers and news cameras leading the way.

In some perverse way he looked like a modern day General Douglas MacArthur wadding onto the shores of the Philippines. That would be if MacArthur were prone to wear his hair slicked back in an exaggerated pompadour, and clothed his portly body in haute couture fashion. Today's ensemble featured a 3XL *Gucci* suit, *Ermenegildo Zegna* shoes, along with an ivory walking stick that had a gold handle with precious stones set in the cap.

Clearly the *Little Sisters of the Poor* had missed out on the memo that religion pays, and does so very well.

"Reverend Jennings, what is it that you expect to get from this meeting with Commissioner Stargold?" one of the reporters asked.

Jennings stopped, leaned his head back slightly, and stared up into the clear morning sky, as if contemplating the question posed to him.

"That's a very good question, Bob," Jennings replied, as he once again began his stroll down the walkway. "It's not what I expect to get from the police commissioner, but what I intend to give him. For too long the minority community in this city has been treated like second class citizens. This city has been built on the backs of the poor and I am here to say *enough*. We will not allow the one percents of this society to look down their noses at us any longer."

Shouts of "amen" began emanating from the throng of people following him.

"I'm here to serve notice that we will not stand by idly, as our innocent young men are chased down in the streets and left to die, with no more dignity than that afforded to a wild animal. The good Lord has made me his voice in the wilderness and I am here to say that we will be heard."

More shouts of *amen* could be heard along with a growing chant of "no justice, no peace."

"This city must learn to place more value on the life of its most impoverished residents. If they won't do it willingly, then they will do it when the people force them to. The people of this city trust in me to be their voice, their champion, and I will not let them down. I will not let Charles Morgan's death be forgotten, nor will I let it go unpunished."

With the practiced, perfect timing of an actor, Jennings finished his walking monologue as he entered the security booth just outside the main building. Much to the chagrin of the large group following him, the majority were turned back by the officers stationed at the checkpoint. Only Jennings and those individuals identified as his closest *advisors* were allowed to proceed into the main building.

As Jennings continued toward the main doors, the chorus of "no justice, no peace" continued to grow louder in the background. As he stepped inside the building he paused, looking back toward the throng gathered just beyond the wrought iron security gate and smiled, waving at his supporters.

The truth was that it could be very difficult at times to be the *iconic* community activist. He had nothing in common with those staring back at him through the gate. At times, he found it mentally draining to play the part that they demanded from him, but he loved the attention and accolades. More importantly, he loved the money.

Jennings embraced the mantra of 'never let a good crisis go to waste.' He was a lightning rod for controversy. Revered as a hero by those who he claimed to champion, and reviled by those who saw him as nothing more than a race-baiting charlatan. He embraced both with equal appreciation, noting that there was no such thing as *bad* publicity. As long as his name was being spoken, he was being kept relevant and on the front page of the news.

Now he was even being courted for a cable talk show, and had recently been invited to the White House to speak on the topic of race relations in America. He had certainly come a long way from his humble roots in Fort Greene.

As they entered the main building they were met by an officer from the Deputy Commissioner of Public Information and escorted through the security checkpoint. From there they took the elevator up to the 8th floor where they proceeded to the Command and Control Center. Outside the doorway, Detective Mike Torres stood watch next to another detective from Rich Stargold's detail. He held up his hand, bringing the group of people to an abrupt stop.

"I'm sorry," Torres said. "Only Reverend Jennings can go inside. The rest of you will have to wait here."

Torres motioned toward a row of hard plastic chairs against the wall. The group of people accompanying Jennings began to complain, but Jennings held up his hand.

"These folks are my most trusted confidants," Jennings said. "I value their counsel."

"Sorry, Reverend," Torres said. "I have my orders. You'll have to talk to the commissioner."

Torres held the door open.

"I'll straighten this out," Jennings said and walked inside.

The Command and Control Center was a massive room. More than a dozen tables and chairs were setup in a quasi-horseshoe pattern in the center. Television screens lined the walls above, allowing those in the room to monitor any events occurring throughout the city. Several smaller rooms where situated along the back wall which allowed executive staff to slip inside for conversation, away from the hustle and bustle that was prevalent when the room was activated.

Stargold and Maguire sat in their usual seats, while Kurt Silverman and Charles Baxter sat off to the side.

"Reverend Jennings," Rich said with a smile, as he rose up from his chair and walked over to the man. "So glad you could make it."

The two men shook hands and Rich directed the man toward Maguire.

"I don't know if you have ever met my second in command, First Deputy Commissioner James Maguire?"

"No I haven't," Jennings replied.

Maguire reached out and took Jennings hand in his, shaking it firmly.

"There seems to be some misunderstanding, Commissioner Stargold. My people are being kept outside. I'm sure you can appreciate the need to have the people closest to you at hand."

"Unfortunately, some of the issues we are going to discuss today have some security implications," Rich replied. "If and when the time comes, we can ask them to join us. Please, have a seat."

"Security implications?" Jennings asked, taking a seat across from Stargold. "I thought we were here to discuss the murder of Charles Morgan."

"Oh we are," Rich replied. "It's just that things are not always so cut and dry."

Jennings looked uncomfortable. This wasn't going exactly how he had planned. Still, this wasn't his first rodeo with politicians and he had always gotten what he wanted in the end.

"Let's cut to the chase, shall we?" Rich said. "What is it that you're looking for exactly?"

Jennings leaned back in his chair, slightly taken aback. It was the first time that someone had been so blunt with him. He knew that Stargold had come from the federal service, maybe it was a good sign. Instead of talking in circles all morning, feeling each other out, maybe they could just get down to brass tacks and he could get a jump on the afternoon traffic.

"Commissioner Stargold, I know you're new here and that you might not have a deep appreciation for what the African-American community has had to endure under prior administrations," Jennings said. "Charles Morgan's murder is just another example of how little value this city places on its minority communities. I've been asked to represent Mr. Morgan's family in bringing to light this reprehensible hate crime and insuring that it does not happen again."

"So, you're representing Charles Morgan's family?" Rich asked.

"Yes, certain members of the family reached out to me because they were aware of my involvement in seeking racial justice for abuses directed against members of the African-American community. They want to insure justice for Charles and to make sure something like this never happens again."

"I'd love to meet with them," Rich said. "So that I could share with them my condolences, for their loss."

"Well, that is certainly very kind of you. As you can imagine, they are grieving at their loss and wish to remain out of the public eye for the time being."

"Well, when the time comes, please extend my offer," Rich replied. "Speaking on behalf of the Mayor, we would like to avoid any further *disturbances* in the city. I'm sure you have seen the reports of rampant vandalism, assaults, and other crimes that were committed in the wake of Mr. Morgan's death. There simply is no need for these criminal acts to continue to take place. They only serve to bring dishonor to the community and diminish the tragedy of Mr. Morgan's death. Wouldn't you agree?"

Jennings shifted in his seat slightly as he considered his reply.

"Of course I agree, but we also must recognize the anger and despair that is being felt in the community. For too long this city has looked down its collective nose at the less fortunate. You can't expect them to just *forget* what has happened. This city is a powder keg waiting to explode and I believe the good Lord has dispatched me to keep the stray embers of racial acrimony from setting it off. Sadly, I am but one man."

Jennings leaned back in his chair, smiling at his host. He looked over at Maguire who stared back at him. There was no smile, just a *hardness* in the man's face that Jennings hadn't noticed before. He'd always had a knack for being able to read people, knowing exactly when to push forward or tactically withdraw. This man was different; there was nothing in his cold eyes, no emotion. He couldn't get a read on him and that made Jennings suddenly feel very uncomfortable. He turned his gaze back toward Stargold.

"But you are, after all, one man who speaks for many," Rich replied. "I'm sure a man of the cloth, such as yourself, could easily turn down the rhetoric and restore calm to the community."

"Yes, but even doing God's work comes at a cost, Commissioner Stargold," Jennings replied.

"And what exactly would that cost entail?"

"I think the community would see it as a sign of good faith if the Mayor would consider appointing a *new* commissioner for the Department of Youth and Community Development."

"Mayor McMasters just filled that position a few weeks ago," Rich replied. "Why would he appoint someone new?"

"With all due respect to the honorable Commissioner Liebowitz, he isn't exactly someone who is going to resonate with *inner city* youth. He has a Park Avenue address and a trust fund that makes him appealing to other politicians, but not to the people that work for him. What the minority community needs is someone who would be an honest advocate for the people in City Hall. Someone they know and respect."

"Someone like you perhaps, Reverend Jennings?" Rich asked.

"Well, I have never sought any political office before, believing my path was in the performance of the Lord's work," Jennings said. "However, in recent years I have come to realize that the two need not be mutually exclusive. Should the Mayor seek out my service, I would feel honored to serve the people of this great city."

"What exactly would the return for us be?" Rich asked.

"Why peace and order would be returned to the streets. You have to understand, this is just the physical manifestation of their frustration. If the people knew that they had one of their own representing them in City Hall, there would be no need to engage in any further acts of civil disobedience."

"Then you get to reward your people, who helped orchestrate the current dilemma, by giving them spots in your new administration."

"*Quid pro quo*," Jennings replied. "We all have people who do the work which we sometimes find *disdainful*. When the opportunity arises to repay them, you take it."

He looked over at Maguire and was again met with that icy, impenetrable gaze. He quickly averted his eyes back at Stargold.

"Surely *you* understand what I mean, Commissioner."

"No, *Reverend* Jennings, I do not," Rich replied, as he stood up. "However, I have been unexpectedly summoned to an emergency meeting and so I will turn this over to Commissioner Maguire. I am sure that he will be able to convey to you the seriousness to which the Department takes this matter. Good day."

Rich turned and walked out of the room, leaving Jennings to stare after him with his mouth open. When he turned back toward Maguire, he saw the other two men walk over and join him at the table. Jennings felt a cold chill run down the back of his neck.

Maguire opened the folder sitting in front of him.

"You've been a very busy man, Reverend Jennings," Maguire said, as he shuffled through the papers. "In 1991 you led a protest at Junior's Clothes Emporium that led to the death of an employee, which you were subsequently found liable for in a civil wrongful death suit. Then in 1993 you led a protest against *alleged* racial discrimination in fire department testing. In 1995 you organized a boycott against a major league basketball team for *lack of racial diversity* in their front office staff, a cause you also championed in 1996 when you protested against CUNY for failing to have adequate minority representation among tenured professors. That however led to a riot which caused nearly $250,000 in damage."

Jennings squirmed in his seat as he listened to Maguire rattle off the information he was reading in the papers.

"In 1999, you filed for bankruptcy protection, which was convenient when, in 2001, you received a million dollar book advance for your epic tome 'Organizing America – How Grassroots Efforts Can Affect Public Opinion'. In 2003 your *Horns of Jericho* ministry was investigated for failing to make proper financial reports, as required for non-profits, not to mention the allegations that companies were making 'donations' just to keep from being boycotted. Then, in 2006, both NYS and NYC filed liens for back taxes. In 2009 you hit the big league and the IRS filed a lien against your ministry for nearly one million dollars for failure to pay back taxes. Don't you think you should have realized that your little activities were going to eventually catch up with you, Archie?"

"I always knew the NYPD kept a *secret* file on me," Jennings bellowed.

The man had managed to regain his composure and sat looking indignant. "All you are doing is regurgitating the same drivel that has been spewed countless times by agents and minions of the United States Government seeking to pursue a political agenda against someone who is a voice for the people, something they fear."

"Indulge me a bit further," Maguire said. "In 2011 you led a highly publicized boycott of a cable news network. Obviously it worked, because in 2012 network execs engaged you in meetings to host a show on the same network which is scheduled to debut in the spring of 2013. And here we are, with you leading protests regarding the death of Charles Morgan."

"What are you trying to imply?"

"Sort of fortuitous, isn't it?" Maguire said, laying the folder on the desk in front of him. "A highly publicized event, right before your show airs; which you have now turned into a national issue?"

"I've never shied away from pursuing justice," Jennings said. "Even when it meant that I would have to risk my own personal safety and freedom. These issues are bigger than one's own interests."

"Wow, that is really magnanimous," Maguire replied. "Did you come up with that just now or have you been practicing that since you turned informant on Elijah Chapman?"

As Maguire watched, the man's eyes went wide in fear and the color drained from his face. His mouth opened, as if to speak, but the words came out mumbled and incoherent. For a moment Maguire wondered if the man had suffered a stroke. It took a few moments, but he was finally able to formulate a response.

"I don't know what you are talking about," Jennings replied, looking around the room, then back over his shoulder, conspiratorially. "Elijah and I are the dearest of friends. He is my mentor and a cherished confidant."

"Sure he is," Maguire replied. "The only problem is that he should have found a more trustworthy person, besides you, to confide in. You've been feeding the feds information on Chapman since what? 2009? 2010? What did they do, run the old 'we got Gotti on tax evasion' story on you? Guess it is true what they say; there really is no honor among thieves? Probably a good choice, your sorry ass wouldn't have lasted thirty days in federal prison."

Maguire made a motion with his hand and a voice began playing over the sound system.

"Elijah will kill me if he knew I was speaking to you," the voice of Archie Jennings said.

"No will ever know," a male voice replied. "You'll have a confidential number that the Bureau will supply you with and a special telephone number you will call. You'll just give your number and any information you have. Your handler will reach out to you if necessary."

Maguire motioned again and the speakers went silent.

"This is a set-up," Jennings cried out. "You're trying to railroad me for being the advocate for Charles Morgan! A man without a voice, killed for the color of his skin."

"Please spare me the theatrics," Maguire replied. "Your affinity for Charles Morgan has less to do with the color of his skin and more to do with the color of his money, or should I say his family's money?"

"What are you alleging?" Jennings said indignantly.

"*Alleging*? Nothing," Maguire said. "I'm stating a *fact,* that you accepted money from Morgan's family."

"Charles' family simply provided me with funding to take his case to the people," Jennings said smugly.

"So you admit that you accepted money from his family?" Maguire asked.

"I'm a poor community activist," Jennings replied. "The funds given to me provided me with the opportunity to give aid to his cause."

Maguire turned to look at Silverman and Baxter, then back at Jennings.

"That's an interesting way of putting it," Maguire said.

He reached over and lifted the phone up, pressing a number.

"Did you get all that?" Maguire asked to the person who answered. "Thank you; please replay that last part in here."

Over the speakers in the room, Jennings heard a slightly tinny, but very clear recording of his voice play.

"*The funds given to me provided me with the opportunity to give aid to his cause.*"

"Reverend Jennings, for the record I would like to introduce you to Special Agent Charles Baxter, of the Criminal Investigations Division of the Internal Revenue Service. To Agent Baxter's right is Special Agent Kurt Silverman of the Federal Bureau of Investigations, Joint Terrorism Task Force. I have asked them to join me here today because of their expertise."

"I don't understand," Jennings replied. "What's going on?"

"The man you have been publicly defending is not Charles Morgan," Maguire explained. "He's real name is Yusif Tahir Dawai, and he was a spy employed by the Sudanese Government. Mr. Dawai's real reason for being in the United States was to engage in acts of espionage against the United States in order to potentially render material aid to a terrorist organization."

Jennings once again began stammering, trying to speak and failing miserably. This time, Maguire didn't give him the opportunity to regain his composure.

"As you said, you accepted money to provide *material aid* to his cause. Agent Baxter here was able to back trace the deposit to a bank in Khartoum. An investigation determined that it is a shell account run by the Sudanese Intelligence Service."

"I don't know anything about a shell account," Jennings stammered.

"I'm sure you don't," Maguire nodded compassionately. "Still, it doesn't really look good for you now, does it? First you get caught up in tax scandals, and then you turn informant on your best friend. Now you're linked monetarily to a dead spy who was in possession of top secret military information."

"I think I need to speak with my attorney," Jennings said, as he stood up.

"Sit down, Archie," Maguire replied. "That train left the station a long time ago."

Jennings sat back down.

"Here is how this is going to play out. You have a couple of doors in front of you right now. Door one is you walk out of here and say you are convinced that the NYPD is doing everything they can in this matter, handling it with the utmost sensitivity and respect. The protests and rioting end now. Agent Baxter goes back to his job and, if you're lucky, you figure out how to repay all the money you currently owe and get to move on with your life."

"And the other door?" Jennings asked hopefully.

Maguire frowned and nodded somberly.

"Door two is a bit bleaker. By your own admission you accepted money to provide aid to a spy who was most likely engaged in supplying top secret information to terrorists. That means Agent Silverman will take you into custody and you will be immediately transported from here to McGuire Air Force Base in New Jersey. Kind of ironic isn't it? From there you will board a military transport and be taken to Camp Seven in Guantanamo Bay, Cuba. Camp Seven is also known as *Camp No*, as in: *No, it doesn't exist*. It's not a really nice place, Archie. Over a period of time you will be *interviewed* at length to determine exactly what you know. I'm sure that, in the end, you'll be cleared of any wrongdoing, but the *experience* will change you. You will never be the same again. Unfortunately, for you, there is no door three."

Jennings sat staring at Maguire, then at Baxter and Silverman. None of the men betrayed any hint of emotion. There was no one to encourage him, no one to clap him on the back and tell him how smart he was, or how no one could keep up with his keen intellect. He was alone, and he began to feel the weight of Maguire's words.

"I don't want to go to jail," he said dejectedly.

"That sounds like a good start, Archie," Maguire replied. "So here is what we are going to do. You are going to put an end to the protests. We will continue to investigate the death. If there are any mitigating racial factors uncovered, we will credit you with being the *voice of reason* that helped heal the city. In the meantime, you will meet with Agent Baxter. You will provide him with any and all information regarding the monetary offer you were given. I'd also suggest you make a plan to get your arrears taken care of while you are at it. Understood?"

Jennings nodded his head passively.

Maguire reached into his pocket and removed a pen, writing on the paper in front of him and slid it across the desk to Jennings.

"Just so that we understand what my next course of action will be if you try and double cross me," Maguire said.

The man reached out and took it, reading what Maguire had written on it. He swallowed hard and put the paper into his pocket.

"I guess we are through here, folks. If you don't mind, I have a homicide investigation to deal with. I hope you all have a wonderful day."

The four men stood up and Jennings immediately turned and headed for the door without saying a word.

"What the fuck was on the paper, Paddy?" Baxter asked.

"Private cell phone number for Elijah Chapman," Maguire replied.

"The man is that afraid of a *politician*?"

"Elijah Chapman isn't your ordinary politician, Bubbles. Back in the 70's he was a vocal proponent of the Black Panther party. Even back then he had higher politically aspirations. So, while he wasn't *actively* involved in the membership, per se, he steered and directed a lot of activity. Let's just say that not all of it involved promoting social programs, alleviating poverty or feeding the children. They could never establish a link, but he was figured to be involved in at least four, probably five, retaliation murders. His Intel file is three inches thick. I think it is safe to say that I don't think he'd be exactly *forgiving* if he found out old Archie was playing the part of the canary."

"That's cold man," Baxter replied with a smile. "But I can't think of anyone better, than that pompous ass, to play that hand on."

"I thought it was a nice touch."

"I hate to bring this up," Silverman chimed in. "But we still have a mole somewhere dishing out secrets and we don't know why."

"That's why we get paid the big bucks," Maguire replied, picking up the folder. "Let me know if Archie fails to get in touch with you, Bubbles."

"What about lunch?" Baxter asked.

"Gonna have to take a rain check, my man," Maguire replied with a laugh. "Besides, it doesn't look like you have missed too many meals."

"That's wrong," the man replied.

"National security issues don't wait till after dessert is served."

"You see," Baxter said, clearly agitated. "That's that bullshit Mothers always talking about."

"You know what they say," Maguire replied. "Mothers are always right."

Maguire left the men at the elevator bank and made his way to the private elevator with Torres.

"So how'd it go, Boss?"

"Like I expected," Maguire replied. "Jennings is the class clown. He has a big mouth, but when it comes down to it, he'll tuck tail and choose self-preservation every time."

"He's going to call an end to the demonstrations then?"

"Yeah," Maguire said, as they stepped into the elevator. "But that just means we have to get back to figuring out how our victim ended up dead on the Belt Parkway and why."

"Hey, we've got the greatest detectives in the world working for us. It shouldn't take too long."

"You're one helluva optimist, Mike."

The two men exited the elevator and headed back to the office. As Maguire passed Liam Martin's office, he heard the man call out.

"Commissioner?"

Maguire peeked his head inside the office.

"Yes, Liam, what do you need?"

"Captain Johnson called, she said to have you call her back ASAP."

"Did she say what it was about?"

"She said something about a burglary at the Medical Examiner's Office."

Maguire shook his head.

Could things get any weirder? he wondered.

"Thanks, Liam."

He walked back to his office and sat down at the desk. He reached over, picking up the phone, and dialed the number for Johnson.

"Ann, it's Commissioner Maguire," he said when she answered. "What have you got?"

"Sorry to bother you, Commissioner," she replied. "I thought you'd want to know about this. I got a call from Bill Hennessey, seems that when the Chief Medical Examiner went to retrieve some records from Dr. Miller's office, they found it ransacked."

"They know if anything was taken?"

"Her computer hard drive is missing, other than that it is hard to tell. The place was a real mess. It might take some time to piece together all the paper work that was strewn about."

"We need to send someone over to her residence," Maguire said.

"Already did," Johnson replied.

Maguire could hear the tone in her voice. He knew he wasn't going to like what came next.

"And?"

"It's apparent that someone is looking for *something*," she replied. "Her apartment is even worse than the office."

Maguire chided himself for asking if things could get weirder. Clearly he had his answer.

"Crime Scene?"

"I had them come out," she said. "They are already done at the M.E.'s Office, and are over at the apartment now."

"It'll be a miracle if they pull anything," Maguire said. "We're not dealing with common thieves."

"No, but we have gotten lucky before."

Maguire knew that she was right. Great police work was often anchored in luck. In August of 1977, David Berkowitz, the notorious *Son of Sam* killer, who had terrorized New York City for over a year, was brought down due to a parking ticket. Berkowitz had illegally parked his car on a fire hydrant near the scene of his last murder. A witness came forward several days after the shooting to say she had seen a suspicious man in the area after the police had left.

"You're right, Ann," he replied. "Stay on top of this and let me know if they come up with anything."

"Will do, Sir," she said.

Maguire hung up the phone and rubbed the palms of his hands over his eyes. He felt tired.

"Coffee, Boss?"

Maguire looked up to see Amanda Massi standing in the doorway holding up a mug. He smiled and waved her in. She walked in and set it on the desk in front of him.

"Thanks, Amanda."

"No problem," she replied. "It looked like it was shaping up to be one of those days."

"That's an understatement," Maguire said, taking a sip. "I feel like I'm on the bow of a ship, holding on tightly, as the wave's crash over me and wondering if the next one will get me before we can make port."

"Maybe you just need to get some rest. Come back to it with a fresh mind."

She was right, he thought. He looked up at the clock on the wall.

"Gather Mike up," he said. "I'm going to make one phone call and then we can get out of here."

BISHOP'S GATE

"Sounds like a plan," Amanda said and walked out of the office."

Maguire picked up the phone and placed the call. A moment later he heard the gravelly sound of the man's voice.

"Monahan."

"Dennis, you really need to get a secretary," Maguire said.

"I'm lucky I have a desk to sit at," he replied. "Haven't you heard the State's broke?"

"Sure they are," Maguire replied. "Until they need to fund a politically expedient project in a district they need to win in November."

"Politics, it's not for the faint of heart," Monahan replied. "But I don't think you called to give me pointers on scoring political favor."

"No, unfortunately I need to bore you with more mundane things, like crime."

"I could use the break. What do you need?"

"You hear about a *hit and run* down in Lake George?"

"Yeah, I did," Monahan replied. "Doctor from the city got taken out in a restaurant parking lot. It happened on the southern end though, so Troop G Investigations picked it up."

"Yeah, she was a medical examiner here. Funny thing is someone ransacked her office and residence *after* she was run over."

"You think they are related?"

"You believe in coincidence?" Maguire asked.

He could almost see the man's face contorting into a grimace. Neither of them were big fans.

"What do you need me to do?"

"Scrounge up the report and see what the witnesses had to say. I'm looking for something that might help me figure out what is at play here."

"Ok, let me make some calls and see what I can do."

"I appreciate it, Dennis. I'm heading out the door for the day, but you can get me on my cell anytime."

"It's only noon for Christ's sake," Monahan said. "It must be nice being at the top of the food chain."

"It doesn't suck," Maguire said with a laugh. "Call me when you've got something."

"Will do."

Maguire hung up the phone and grabbed his coat as he headed for the door.

CHAPTER THIRTY-NINE

Southampton, Suffolk County, N.Y.
Monday, February 25th, 2013 – 2:43 p.m.

"*Wilson Pope*?" Melody said. "Are you sure?"

Genevieve sat on the sofa across from her, staring up at the ceiling.

"His number, his file, Mel," she replied, her voice filled with a mixture of sadness and anger.

"Holy shit, this is a fucking nightmare," Melody replied. "Where is he?"

"I don't know. I tried to reach him several times by cell, but it kept going directly to voicemail. I finally gave up and I called down to Maryland. I spoke to Pamela Hayes, but she hadn't seen him, so I asked her to look into it. It seems he called up earlier and told his secretary that he was taking a few days off."

"What did you do?" Melody asked.

"I had security lock down his office and had IT cancel all his access," she replied. "What else could I do?"

"No, you did right, Gen," Melody said. "I know you had a good working relationship with him, but we need to protect the company. Hopefully there is a good explanation to all of this and not just piss poor timing on his part."

Gen smiled and nodded her head. Neither woman believed it.

"Are you going to tell James now?"

"No, he's on his way home," Melody replied. "I just figured I would wait till he got here."

"What do you think is going to happen?" Gen asked.

"I honestly don't know. James said that the FBI will be investigating this; it is after all a national security issue. If those files had gotten into the wrong hands, it would have been a disaster."

"I don't want to sound cold, but what would have happened to GDL if that had occurred?" Gen asked. "I mean it's going to be a publicity nightmare as it is, but if a foreign nation had gotten hold of the data and found a way to hack into the system. Could you imagine the fallout, if we shot our own planes out of the sky?"

"I need you to take the lead on this, Gen," Melody said. "I can barely handle going to the bathroom by myself, let alone cooperate in an investigation. I want us to be as transparent as we can with the investigators, and by that I mean not what supposedly passes for *transparent* at 1600 Pennsylvania Avenue these days. I also want you to ride the computer geeks like rented mules. I want redundant safeguards to the redundant safeguards, so that we never have to worry about a scenario like the one you imagined. I won't have innocent blood on our hands."

"I understand," Gen replied. "I've already set-up a conference call tomorrow afternoon with all the department heads."

"Good thinking."

"Originally I was going to head out to Montana, but I figured I should stay local in case you needed me."

"I imagine that they are going to want access to Pope's records as soon as possible. I'll let James talk to them first and you can coordinate with them."

"I'm sorry, Mel," Gen said. "I feel like I let you down."

"Gen, no, you didn't. You have never let me down. If Pope is involved, there is no way either of us could have known. Besides, we don't know that he was. Right now we are just speculating. Let's allow the professionals do the investigation. Pope liaised with a lot of people, including those in the Pentagon and across the river. So we wait for the experts to let us know what really happened and then we respond."

Melody looked up as she heard the front door open and watched as James walked into the room.

"Who died?" he asked, as he looked back and forth between the two women.

"Gen figured out who the file belongs to," Melody said.

"Please just tell me it *wasn't* either of you?" he said.

"No," Melody said.

"Thank God," he replied, taking the seat next to her. "The way this day has been going, nothing would have come as shock. Although I am extremely gratified that it didn't belong to either of you."

"It belonged to Wilson Pope," Gen said. "He's one of the main players in GDL, so it's almost as bad."

"For what it's worth, I'd much rather see him led away in handcuffs then either of you," James replied. "Do you have any idea where he might be now?"

"Supposedly took a few days off," Melody said. "Gen had his office locked down and his computer access is revoked."

"That at least minimizes the damage to what has been done already," he said. "You up to talking to the feds now, Gen?"

"I know it has to be done, might as well get it out of the way."

"Atta girl," Maguire said.

He reached into his pocket and removed his cellphone, placing the call.

"Kurt, it's James. They found out who the file belonged to. I'm going to let you speak to Genevieve Gordon; she can fill you in on the particulars."

Maguire handed the phone to Gen who walked away as she began to speak with Silverman.

"It's killing her," Melody said. "She feels betrayed. Gen dealt with Wilson Pope on almost a daily basis."

"You think you know people, until you realize you don't," Maguire replied. "No one really knows what is in the hearts and minds of other people."

"Ok, *Mister Heartless*," Melody said, rolling her eyes.

"Hey, I'm *just* saying."

"Well, *don't* say anything," Melody scolded him. "She feels bad enough, and she's pregnant. She might have a crying jag that ends with her killing you in your sleep with a letter opener."

"It sounds like you may have given that idea some thought."

"I may have *thought* about it, but I never sharpened it," Melody replied with a mischievous grin. "So tell me about your crazy day."

"First, I need a glass of wine," he said, getting up from the couch. "Want some?"

"Sure," Melody said. "Is everything all right?"

"No, not really," Maguire replied. "I keep hitting more brick walls."

He walked over and removed a bottle from the wine chiller. He uncorked it, filling two of the glasses and returned to the couch.

"Cheers," he said, lightly tapping her glass.

"So, what's got my highly trained detective so frustrated?"

"This Belt Parkway investigation is turning into quiet a mystery. What started out as a potential hate crime is now spiraling into something out of a *Clancy* novel."

"How so?"

"First the body gets hijacked by the State Department; but not before the medical examiner removes the microchip, containing the GDL file, from the victim's body. Then the M.E. ends up dead in a hit and run upstate. Now her home and office have been ransacked. Add to that the original victim is a known spy and that the guy involved in removing the body was also involved in the release of our former terror ringleader. I think you can understand why I'm considering buying stock in Advil."

"Yeah, it would be giving me headaches as well," Melody said, taking a sip of wine.

"Enough of this shop talk, angel," he replied. "Tell me how you are feeling."

"Getting stronger every day," she said. "It won't be too long before I'm back in the gym."

"Yes, it will," he said with a laugh.

"I know," she said. "I keep lying to myself, hoping that I'll begin to believe it."

"You'll get there, just don't try to over-do it, or you'll only make it worse."

"Yes, sir, *Dr. Dudley Do-Good*," Melody replied, snapping a jaunty salute at him. "Whatever you say, sir."

"Oh, you're funny," Maguire said. "I'm glad to see your sense of humor wasn't affected by all this."

"Well, I could always lie to you," she said. "Tell you what want to hear and then do what I wanted to do in the first place."

"Yeah, you could," he said, his voice trailing off.

Melody heard the change in his voice and looked over at him. He was staring blankly at the fireplace. She could immediately tell that something wasn't right.

"James, what's wrong?"

Maguire shook his head, as if willing himself back to their conversation.

"Nothing, it's just……," he let the words trail off and then turned to look at her. "What did you just say?"

"I said I could lie to you, and then just do what I want."

"*Sonofabitch*," he said, getting up from the couch.

"What did I say?" Melody asked.

"Nothing wrong, babe," he replied, "but you just might have knocked down one of those brick walls for me. I'll be right back."

Maguire tracked down Gen and retrieved his cell phone.

"Kurt, she'll call you right back," he said, hanging up the phone. He jotted the number down and handed it to her.

"Sorry, Gen. This is really important."

He selected the number from the contacts and waited.

"Johnson."

"Ann, this is Commissioner Maguire. I need you to do me a favor."

"Sure, what do you need?"

"Head over to the limousine service and track down the driver who reported the vehicle stolen."

"Ok, but we have his statement. You want him re-interviewed?"

"No, I want to know who he is, where he is from. Photos, the whole works."

"You think he is involved?"

"I think the vehicle theft is convenient," Maguire replied, "maybe a little too convenient. What if he just told us what we wanted to hear?"

"I'm just finishing up at Dr. Miller's place. CSU didn't find anything. I'll head over to the livery place personally," she said. "As soon as I get something I'll give you a call back."

"Thanks," Maguire said, ending the call and walking back over to the couch.

"You really think that the driver was involved?" Melody asked.

"It wouldn't be the first case of *hiding in plain sight*," he replied. "The real question is will he still be around?"

CHAPTER FORTY

Upper West Side, Manhattan, N.Y.
Monday, February 25th, 2013 – 5:23 p.m.

Ann Johnson sat in her unmarked Chevy Impala, outside the V&R Limousine Service on 11th Avenue, staring down at the photocopies of the documents she had just obtained. She had her cell phone propped up on the steering wheel and set to speaker.

"Driver's name is Dov Horowitz," she said. "His address is a location in Forest Hills. One of my teams was in Long Island City so I sent them over to take a look at the place."

"How long has he worked for the company?" Maguire asked.

"It says on the employee sheet that he started at the beginning of the month."

"Outstanding. When did he work last?"

"According to the time sheet, his last day was Wednesday, February 20th. Same day our victim died."

"I'm pretty sure I've had my fill of coincidences in this investigation," Maguire said. "Do we have a photo of our mystery man?"

"Yeah, hold on for a minute. I'll take a photo and send it to you."

Maguire waited.

"Ok, I sent it over to you," Johnson said. "Try to remember my photographic skills are not the greatest."

"I've probably seen worse," he replied.

A moment later he heard the alert for the incoming message.

"Got it, let me take a look."

He scrolled through the apps, selecting the messaging one and waited for the image to appear. When the image appeared on the screen, all the imaginary brick walls, which had been blocking the investigation, collapsed and he felt a cold chill run down his neck.

"Can you see it okay?"

"Yeah, it came through clear," he said.

In the background, Maguire could hear radio traffic.

"Castle Leader, on the air?"

"Castle Leader, go with message," Johnson replied.

Castle Leader, this is Castle Four, we're 10-84 at the location you gave us. It's an empty lot, ma'am."

"10-4," Johnson said. "Did you hear that, Commissioner?"

"Yeah, no surprise there," Maguire replied. "I want you to grab some people and head over to the Sudanese Consulate. Scour the area around it and see if you can spot any surveillance cameras. There are a bunch of high-end stores on the corner, if memory serves me correctly, and probably a bunch of residential ones as well. See if anyone has any recordings from the night Morgan was picked up. If anyone asks, make-up some bullshit story about a missing child. Tug at their heartstrings."

"You think Horowitz was involved?"

"Oh, I *know* he was involved," Maguire said. "I'm just looking for the cherry to stick on top of the shit cake that I'm about to serve on someone. Just for the record, this conversation stays between us."

"Yes, sir."

"Seal up the documents, along with any video you come up with, and bring them to me tomorrow. I'll advise Commissioner Stargold of what has transpired."

"Okay, Commissioner," Johnson said. "I'll see you tomorrow."

Maguire ended the call and immediately called Rich.

"So the stress of working Jennings over was too much for you and you had to go home?" Rich said jokingly, when he answered the phone. "And here I thought you Navy guys were tougher than that?"

"I hope you're sitting down, smartass," Maguire replied.

"What now?"

"I'm ninety-nine percent certain the limo Morgan was in, the night he was killed, was being driven by Alon Ben Simon."

"Are you fucking shitting me?" Rich replied, all trace of the levity in his voice now gone.

"I'm looking at his photo right now. No one's that ugly to have a twin."

Both men were well acquainted with Alon Ben Simon from their days in protection. Ben Simon had been a member of the Israeli security agency, *Shabak*, also known as *Shin Bet*. Prior to his assignment on the prime minister's security detail, he had been a member of *Yamas*, their special operations unit. It was unclear what actions Ben Simon had participated in, since the very existence of Yamas is denied, but whatever he had been involved in, it had clearly affected him. While he was an extremely professional security specialist, most folks in the protection community steered a wide berth around him, simply referring to him as *shell-shocked*.

"Now it makes more sense why State is involved," Rich replied.

"Maybe," Maguire said, "maybe not. I'm still not sure who the players are or, for that matter, what sides they are playing for."

"How did you come up with Ben Simon?"

"I had Captain Johnson, from Major Case, pull the employee folder from the livery company, which the car was *stolen* from. His photo was in their file, along with a bogus address in Queens that turned out to be a vacant lot. I have her over by the consulate pulling surveillance videos as we speak."

"What's your next move?" Rich asked.

"Wait to see if they can pull up any video showing him at the scene. I don't want to give them any wiggle room. If there is *any* crack, you and I both know they will figure out a way to slip through it."

"And if you come up with Alon on video?"

"Either way, I'm going to be paying a visit to Yoni soon."

CHAPTER FORTY-ONE

Upper West Side, Manhattan, N.Y.
Monday, February 25th, 2013 – 9:41 p.m.

Special Agent Dean Oliver sat behind the wheel of the black Chevrolet Suburban, which was parked on the street, just beneath the massive fantail of the U.S.S. Intrepid. He gazed up at the grey behemoth as the person on the other end of the phone droned on.

"Yes, I do understand the serious implications," he said, in a firm and measured voice. "Unfortunately, what I don't think you understand is that I cannot simply make the chip appear out of thin air. Wherever that chip currently is, it is not in her office or in her apartment."

His comment elicited another salvo of angry words.

"Perhaps that was something you should have considered *before* you told me to eliminate her."

Snow was beginning to fall and he watched as the flakes melted on the windshield, refracting the light from the street light up above, like a prism. Outside a couple walked hand-in-hand along the pedestrian footpath.

There was a time when this area was a *no-man's land* in New York City. Where a simple left turn at the bus terminal, over on 42nd Street, meant that you were taking your life into your own hands. How the times had changed. Now families walked along the streets as if they were strolling down the thoroughfare at Disney.

A jogger ran past the vehicle, his hand slapping the front fender of the truck in disgust as if to say 'you're blocking my path'.

Oliver raised his left hand and casually flipped the man off.

He much rather preferred the *old days*.

Of course he was much too young to actually remember those days, but he had heard the tales recounted by some of the senior agents earlier in his career. At thirty-seven he was one of the youngest special agents in charge, especially considering his current posting was to the prestigious New York Field Office. Although with his blonde hair, blue eyes and deep tan, he seemed more likely to be at home on a beach in California, with surfboard in hand, or on a movie set.

He'd parlayed his looks and charm into a series of high profile protection assignments. The fact that he was smart and extremely good at what he did was an added benefit. It didn't take long for the right people to notice. He'd served on a series of important details before being parachuted into his current slot.

"If the chip is gone, then you have to consider that it has fallen into the *wrong* hands," Oliver said. "I would advise you to get rid of any other loose ends now; before whoever has the chip has the opportunity to put the pieces of the puzzle together."

He knew what was coming next and it didn't bother him. Long ago he made the decision to do whatever it took to further himself and his career. A conscience only got in the way of things.

"Understood," he replied and ended the call.

He pulled the car away from the curb and made a u-turn, heading back up the West Side Highway toward the George Washington Bridge.

Why the hell do they call it the New York Field Office when it's in New Jersey? he wondered.

CHAPTER FORTY-TWO

1 Police Plaza, Manhattan, N.Y.
Tuesday, February 26th, 2013 – 8:20 a.m.

Maguire stared at the series of grainy photographs that the computer guys had pulled from the surveillance cameras of an upscale clothing boutique, several doors away from the Sudanese Consulate. Despite the quality, the image of the man in the dark suit, holding open the car door for Charles Morgan, was unmistakable. It was Alon Ben Simon.

He slid them back into the folder and laid it on the desk before reaching over for the ringing cell phone.

"Hey, cowboy," Melody said. "How's your morning going?"

"Plugging along," he replied. "How are things on you end?"

"Quiet, at least for me. Gen is heading down to Maryland in a little while to meet up with the feds. We are giving them access to everything in the hopes that we can minimize the potential damage to the company and the program."

"How bad do you think it will be?" Maguire asked.

"Hard to tell" she said. "I expect that my cell will be burning up soon as word leaks out. I still hold a few good cards and several well placed friends up on the *Hill*. I also have Gen working with the programmers to change the computer protocols."

"I'll pretend I know what you are talking about it," he said with a laugh.

"Well, if the damage is limited to Pope just being the leak, then we don't have to worry, since the data apparently never made it to its destination. However, since we know that something went wrong, we are going to ensure that the basic component of the programming is double and triple locked, so no one will be able to hijack it."

"Good luck. Speaking of Pope, any news yet?"

"No," Melody replied. "No one has heard from him yet. It's hard for me to imagine a worse scenario. I don't want to believe that he is the leak, but right now it doesn't look good."

Maguire understood. It was difficult to believe that those closest to you betrayed you. Yet it happened all the time in both the government and private sector. Secrets were a commodity, just like every other thing. As long as there were buyers, there would always be sellers. The only question that remained was the price. Most did it for money, others for revenge, and even a few for principle, even misguided ones.

Still, nothing could really prepare you for duplicity's sting when it came at the hand of someone close.

"Maybe this will have a happy ending," Maguire said. "Maybe he's just as much a victim."

"Yeah," Melody replied sarcastically, "and he just had *bad timing* in choosing to get away. Not to mention the fact that his chosen vacation spot apparently has piss poor phone and internet reception."

"Well, I was just trying to be optimistic."

"I appreciate it, babe, really I do. But sugarcoating a shit sandwich doesn't change that it is still a shit sandwich."

"God, you're starting to sound like me," Maguire said.

"Aren't you glad I called?"

"Actually, I was just getting ready to call you," he replied. "I have to head out of the office this morning and you won't be able to reach me."

"Oh, that sounds *mysterious*."

"Actually, I have to go see an *old* friend and no cell phones are permitted."

"What is he in jail?" Melody asked.

"Almost, but his prison cell is a government cubicle."

"That sounds like fun, enjoy yourself."

"I'll work on that," Maguire replied. "Call you when I'm done. Love ya."

"Love ya too, cowboy."

Maguire ended the call and got up, grabbing the folder from the desk, before he headed to the door.

"Are we going somewhere, Commissioner?" Amanda Massi asked.

"Not *we* this time, Amanda, just me. I need the keys to the truck."

Massi looked at him hesitantly, not exactly sure what to do.

"It's okay, Amanda," he said with a smile. "I really do have my driver's license."

Massi reluctantly handed the keys to Maguire.

"I'll be back in a little while," he said. "If anyone is looking for me take a message. If the world starts to collapse, go see Commissioner Stargold, he'll know how to reach me."

Yes, sir," she replied.

Maguire grabbed his coat and made his way to the elevator.

It felt a bit odd as he slid into the driver's seat. It was the first time in two months that he was driving out of the headquarters parking garage without his security detail.

Two months, he thought. *Is that how short it's been?*

It seemed like forever since he'd been sworn-in. So much had happened in that brief period of time. First the thwarted terrorist attack, then Melody being shot, and now this, whatever *this* actually was.

He pulled the truck out of the underground garage and through the checkpoint, smiling at the astonished look the officer at the security post gave him when the cop realized that he was *behind* the wheel.

Never forget where you came from, he remembered one old timer tell him.

He piloted the vehicle through the side streets until he hit South Street and then headed north, where he got onto the FDR Drive. Morning traffic had begun to subside and the other cars around him moved at a steady pace. He got off at the 42nd Street exit and then turned right, onto 1st Avenue, where he headed north, past the United Nations complex.

Maguire gazed over at the squat, curved, concrete building that housed the general assembly. Its drab exterior contrasted sharply with its designer interior.

Maybe that was the look they were going for, he thought. *Make the world think your serious, when inside it's just one big party.*

He'd spent so much of his career here, watching motorcades pull in and out, ferrying one diplomat or another to meetings, dinner, and other activities, which were general frowned upon in their home country. Nothing was ever really resolved here because no one had the clout. They were just titled minions, who would have to run for the phone and call home to make sure they got the green light before they agreed to anything. Politics was the same; the only thing that ever changed was the flag.

If this was normal business, he would have turned on 43rd Street and headed over to the consulate on 2nd Avenue. But this wasn't normal and the person he needed to see wouldn't be there, unless something was going on at the UN. No, the person he was calling upon was in a satellite location, off the beaten path, yet still close enough, should the need arise.

He continued north on 1st Avenue for several more blocks, then turned right onto a side street that dead-ended in a little promenade, overlooking the East River. Maguire pulled the truck into a parking spot across from the location. He removed both cell phones, along with his gun and shield, and placed them in the center console. When he was done, he grabbed the folder and got out of the truck.

The building was as nondescript as you could get. A narrow, four-story, grey stone structure with a utilitarian, brushed chrome trim around the frosted glass doors and windows. But just like the U.N. building, which Maguire had passed on the way up, this one was also deceiving. He walked up to the door and picked up the handset for the intercom. Maguire smiled for the unseen camera, as he waited for the voice to come on the line.

"Yes," said the metallic sounding voice over the intercom.

"James Maguire to see Mr. Hamilton."

"Sorry, he's not in today."

"Then can I speak to his partner, Mr. Meadows? I'm catching a flight this afternoon and won't be back until next week."

"One moment please."

The conversation was a ruse. Neither man existed, but was simply a cryptic chat. Hamilton was never around, and Meadow's would only see you if you were catching a flight. He'd always wondered if there were other scripts that got you access to others, but his only reason for ever coming here was to see one person.

At least *officially*.

He heard the door buzz and he opened it up. He stepped inside and closed the door behind him. The interior was a small, enclosed foyer, with frosted glass panels and another locked door in front of him. The glass matched the ones on the exterior, which most passer-bys just assumed was privacy glass. However, these doors and windows also featured a level eight ballistic rating, meaning they would stop calibers up to, and including, the 7.62.

Maguire stood waiting for it to buzz open, knowing that as he waited; someone on the other side of the wall was operating the full body scanner.

He heard the click and watched as the door swung open. Standing on the other side was Yonatan 'Yoni' Ashkenazi.

"*Shalom*, James," the man said, before wrapping his arms around Maguire and kissing his cheek.

"*Shalom*, Yoni," Maguire said, returning the embrace.

Had he brought his weapon in, he would have been greeted by another party, and it would not have been as cordial. In the intelligence world, you learned to play by the *house* rules.

"I didn't expect to see you," the man said, as he ushered Maguire down the hall. "I assumed you would still be tied up with the attack on your lady friend. Did you get the flowers?"

"Yes, I did. They were very thoughtful, thank you."

As they walked down the hallway, Maguire glanced over toward a small vacant office, and then quickly turned away as they approached the man's office.

Please, have a seat," Ashkenazi said, gesturing toward a chair and closing the door.

Like Alon Ben Simon, Yonatan Ashkenazi was also a member of the Israeli intelligence community, but his assignment was with Mossad, the foreign service branch for Israeli intelligence.

The Mossad were responsible for intelligence collection, covert operations, counterterrorism, as well protecting Jewish communities. Prior to his assignment with the Mossad Ashkenazi had served in the *Shayetet-13*, the maritime unit of the Israeli Special Forces. He and Maguire were around the same age and they had shared many of the same military experiences. As a result, the two men had become good friends outside of work. Maguire even had Yoni's S'13 'bat wings' badge hanging on his wall back at the boat.

"So what brings you here today?" Yoni asked. "I don't see any beer, so I assume it's not a social call."

Maguire opened the folder and slid one of the photos across the desk.

"Thought you might want to share with me the reason why Alon Ben Simon is operating in my city."

Yoni picked up the photo and stared at it, his frown growing longer with each passing moment. He laid the photo on the desk and stared at Maguire.

Even in February the man looked like he had just stepped off the plane from some tropical resort. He had a swarthy complexion, which only served to highlight his rugged good looks. However, at times like this, it also served as a warning that he was an incredibly dangerous person, one not to be trifled with.

"Where did you get this?" he asked.

"From a surveillance camera, just down the block from the Sudanese consulate."

"Fucking idiot," Ashkenazi said, leaning back in his chair.

"Can't argue that point," Maguire replied. "But I'm going to go out on a limb here and say that there is more to the story."

"Alon screwed up back home. He was a little too *aggressive,* with the wrong person who is close to the prime minister."

"Wow, there's a surprise. So they shipped him here?"

"He wasn't my choice," Yoni replied, holding his hands up in mock surrender. "Like you have said, it was *above my pay grade.* His father thought a little time away, in the field, might do him good."

"Father must have had some major clout," Maguire said.

"The old man is a colonel, old school. He was a member of the *Kidon*, the *tip of the spear*. He was part of *Operation Wrath of*

God, the group that hunted down the terrorists responsible for the Munich Olympic attacks. He is also a friend of the PM, who did him a favor and shipped Alon here."

"He's a fucking psychopath," Maguire replied angrily.

Yoni shrugged his shoulders.

"So you wanna tell me why he was driving around a guy who, a short time later, ends up as road kill on the Belt Parkway?"

"No. Not really," Ashkenazi replied. "You know it's not personal, I can't."

"Fine," Maguire said, getting up from the chair and heading toward the door. "You can keep that photo, I have more. Oh, and let *Tel Aviv* know I said 'it's nothing personal'."

"What are you going to do, James?" the man asked, his voice sounding very tired.

"By six o'clock his name, along with his photo, will be on every newscast and paper in the tri-state area."

"You can't be serious?"

"Like a heart attack," Maguire replied. "You and I both know Alon wasn't working a part time gig as a limo driver and I sure as hell know, that you know, that passenger wasn't a tourist. So you tell me why Mossad is targeting a Sudanese Intelligence officer or I plaster his face all over the media. Won't help Mossad, but at the very least it'll get him kicked out of the country and out of your hair."

"Sit down," Yoni said, reaching for the phone.

Maguire sat down.

"How's your Hebrew?"

"Please," Maguire said with a sarcastic laugh. "I have a hard enough time understanding North *Brooklynese*."

As he listened, Ashkenazi carried on a rapid fire conversation with the person on the other end of the call. Maguire may not have understood everything that was being said, but he *understood* what was being said. Yoni was a straight shooter, and he didn't like being put in the middle of a screwed up operation. Especially when it seemed that he wasn't exactly thrilled with the person who had been foisted upon him by the powers that be.

Maguire casually turned in his seat and looked out the glass panel wall, toward the office he had glanced at earlier.

He heard the handset slam into the cradle.

"I get the impression that they aren't happy."

"More fucking idiots," he replied. "Everyone thinks *they* know better, and then, when it fails, all they want to know is *who else* is going to take the blame."

"Let me guess, tag you're it?"

"My office, my op…" Ashkenazi replied.

"So, what's it going to be?" Maguire asked.

"They have given me their *blessing* to speak with you," Yoni said. "They were also kind enough to inform me that if it comes back to bite them, I will take the fall for an *unsanctioned* op."

"Politicians," Maguire said. "They're all the same."

"Mossad had an op going in Sudan. Nothing major really, more of a test program, than anything else. Anyway, we got some video feed on a U.S. State Department official, a guy named G. Prescott Linehan. He was meeting with some people from Sudanese Intel in Darfur."

"You get ID's on any of the others?"

"No, they caught the bird before we could," Ashkenazi said. "We just got a plate number, which we tracked back to NISS."

"Caught the bird?" Maguire asked.

"You didn't hear about that one?" Yoni said with a laugh.

"If you haven't noticed, I've been a little bit busy these days."

"The techno-wonks in Tel Aviv came up with an *interesting* new method of static surveillance. They outfitted a vulture with GPS and solar-powered equipment capable of broadcasting images via satellite. That's how we caught the meeting. Unfortunately, for us, one of the natives caught the damn thing. I guess he figured he had an easy meal. We only found out when the signals started indicating it wasn't flying anymore."

"You're not serious," Maguire replied.

"Hand to God," Yoni said. "Once the story broke in the Arab world, the Israel Nature and Parks Authority came out and said it was their bird. They explained how it was one of a hundred vultures fitted with a system equipped to take distance and altitude readings to study migration patterns. Which was actually true, to a certain extent, they just neglected to mention the surveillance component."

"And they bought that?"

Yoni rolled his eyes.

"They're not *that* stupid, James, but they couldn't *disapprove* it either. Everyone else thought the allegations were preposterous and that the Sudanese government was just putting up a stink because of the munitions depot bombing in Khartoum."

"I heard about that one," Maguire said. "They said that they had their radar defenses jammed right before the attack. I imagine that Hamas is pissed about losing their weapons as well."

"Sucks to be them," Yoni replied. "Anyway, it turns out that this same official also served in Syria years ago, so our interest was certainly piqued. When we got alerted that Yusif Dawai had flown the coop and had been sent to D.C., we knew something was going on. Everyone put on their headphones and began listening. They started monitoring the calls going in and out of D.C. and New York. Then chatter picked up between New York and Khartoum. When we saw the one way flight we knew we had him and started up Operation Bishop's Gate."

"Bishop's Gate?"

"Inside joke," Yoni said. "Linehan has been very vocal, in certain circles, about his support for the Assad regime in their civil war. He claims that Assad is the only protection for Christians in Syria, and he's right, to a certain extent. So they gave him the call sign Bishop. We decided to call the operation Bishop's Gate. We figured if anyone heard about it, they would be scouring London looking for clues."

"Why were you guys so quick to key up on Linehan?"

"He's got some sheltered *rainy day* accounts, in countries with some rather loose banking standards. One of those accounts just got a whole lot wetter recently. We assume that it was some type of a payoff. If he isn't involved, he's the unluckiest bastard I have ever met."

"You guys all need a vacation really bad," Maguire said, shaking his head. "So what happened with Dawai?"

"When he showed up in New York, we figured he had made a pick-up or spoke to someone. The Sudanese consulate always uses the same car service, so we routinely have people *working* there. You'd be surprised what those idiots talk about while they are being driven around town. Alon had the rotation so he picked up Dawai. It was supposed to be a simple snatch and grab, that wasn't. The officer that was supposed to take him out of the vehicle lost his grip and Dawai bolted, before anyone knew it, he was running through traffic and got whacked."

"What were you going to do with him?"

"He was still going on a one way trip, but the final destination was off by a little bit. We had an *El Al* flight waiting. Interrogate him in the air find out what was happening, and then have enough time to decide what to do with him afterward. Dawai has spent a lot of time in the west and word is he wasn't exactly enamored with the pension plan offered by the NISS."

"So you were going to turn him?"

"That was the plan, at least on paper."

"So where are Alon and the others now?"

"On *vacation*," Yoni said. "Like you said, we need it really bad."

"So what happened with the investigation?"

"I thought I just gave it to you."

"That's pretty funny, Maguire said, picking the photo up from the desk and sliding it back into the folder. "So, do you plan on running any more ops in my city?"

Yoni smiled.

"We never had this conversation, James."

"How could we? I was never here," Maguire said. "But I expect that if any of the birds you have sitting on wires hear anything….."

"We'll do lunch," Yoni said, as he got up from his chair. "It was good to see you again, we shouldn't let as much time go by. Life's too short."

"I agree, brother," Maguire said. "We're holding a Passover celebration at 1PP in March, would be nice for you to stop by."

"I look forward to it."

The two men embraced and Ashkenazi led him out the door. As they walked down the hallway Maguire glanced over at the still vacant office.

"Tzviya's not here, James."

"Oh," Maguire said curiously, "is she on *vacation* to?"

"Yes," Yoni replied, "but not for the reason you think. She went back to *Be'er Sheva* for a few weeks."

"Is everything alright?"

"No, it's *complicated*," he said, as the two men reached the door.

Maguire could see that Yoni was struggling with the words that would come next.

"Let's just say that the news about your lady friend surviving the attack was not met with the same level of *joy* that the rest of us felt."

Maguire shook his head understandingly.

"*Shalom*, my friend," Yoni said.

"*Shalom*," Maguire replied, shaking the man's hand and walking out the door.

Once back in the truck he removed his shield and gun from the compartment, followed by the cell phones, checking them before putting them away. For a moment he sat staring back at the building thinking back to the last time he had seen her.

It was in late November, 2009, on a cold and dreary, rain soaked day. *Fitting in a way*, he thought. He'd been at the houseboat when he heard the knock on the cabin door. When he opened it she was standing there on the back deck. He knew she wasn't alone, he could see the windshield wipers of the company car trying to keep up with the rain. Her wet, raven black hair lay matted against her face; and her normally bright green eyes were tinged with redness from the tears that they had recently shed. Still, nothing could take away from her beauty, not even that hellish day.

This did nothing to soothe the blow that he instinctively knew was coming.

They'd managed to keep their nearly yearlong relationship secret, or at least they thought they had. For two people who had spent so much time dealing with covert assignments, they had forgotten a cardinal rule of the game: no secret lasts forever.

Time had made them reckless and, in a moment of passion, they had stolen a brief kiss in what they believed to be an empty hallway. It wasn't, and the person who witnessed the lovers embrace made quick use of the information, contacting the woman's father, Shay Harel, a brigadier general in the IDF. She was immediately summoned back to *Tel Aviv* and ordered to end the relationship which she dutifully did, even though it broke her heart.

No, that wasn't true, he thought. *He'd 'seen' her one more time, after he had been shot.*

It had been after hospital visiting hours had ended. Monsignor O'Connor and his flask had stopped by earlier, so by the time the nurses came in with his evening pain medication he was already feeling *no pain*. They had turned down the lights in the room and he began feeling the effects of the medication. At first he thought it was a nurse, but the figure moved only in the shadows. Even with the effects of the medication, he began to react, but then all at once he felt a calming *presence*. While he never actually saw her face, instinctively he knew it had been her.

Maguire had known that her *choice* hadn't been hers, that someone else was pulling the strings. The shooting had made him realize that time was much too short for them to live their lives by someone else's rules. He'd tried to call her when he got out of the hospital, but her cell phone was no longer in service. Once he was mobile again, he drove by the apartment, but it was vacant. The super told him that the woman hadn't left a forwarding address.

Grudgingly, he resigned himself to the fact that she had purposely shut down that part of her life. He thought about calling Yoni, but he didn't want to put the man into a position where he would have to choose between lying to him and breaking a secret.

In the end, he had no alternative but to accept the decision she had made and move on with his life. Still, he didn't have to like it.

Maguire snapped himself out of his memories of the past and started up the truck. He pulled away from the curb and headed back to 1PP.

CHAPTER FORTY-THREE

"So what did you find out?" Rich asked as Maguire sat down in the chair across from him.

"It was a sanctioned op," James replied.

"Fuck," Rich replied. "What else *didn't* they say?"

"There might be more of a State Department involvement here than we think," Maguire said. "They ID'd a guy in a surveillance photo shot in Sudan. Does the name G. Prescott Linehan ring a bell?"

"Linehan? Yeah, he's the Deputy Secretary of State," Rich replied. "Are they saying he's involved?"

"Right now it's still a very cloudy pool, but I think it certainly bears a closer look."

"I take it you're not thinking about a friendly *how do you do* call," Rich said

"No, between the terrorist snatch, the body grab and now this, I'm not really sure which side they are working for."

"You still have any contacts down there that might be able to shed some light on the topic?"

"Yeah," Maguire replied. "But when this is all said and done, the Department is going to be paying the tab for all the meals I owe to people."

"Done," Rich said. "Whatever it takes, just get some answers before this city finds itself back in some psychopath's crosshairs again."

"Then I'm outta here," Maguire said. "Call me if you need anything and I will let you know whatever I find out."

"Good luck," Rich said.

On the way out the door, Maguire sent a text message to Mother: *Everything on G. Prescott Linehan ASAP*

CHAPTER FORTY-FOUR

Southampton, Suffolk County, N.Y.
Tuesday, February 26th, 2013 – 5:53 p.m.

"Hey, Dennis," Maguire said, as he answered the phone. "How are things going?"

"Overworked and underpaid," the man replied gruffly. "But I got that information you were asking about."

"Anything about it setting off bells?"

"I'll email you copies of the report, but the short version is that only real witness was the guy she was hooking up with."

"Hooking up with?"

"Yeah, turns out your M.E. was having a little thing on the side," Monahan replied.

"What did he say?"

"Said they were just going into the restaurant when he stopped to tie his shoe, he looked up just as she got hit. He said the vehicle just kept going."

"Did he say what kind of car?" Maguire asked.

"He said it happened too fast, he couldn't tell what it was, except a big black SUV."

"An SUV?"

"Yeah, there was another witness, not to the accident, but who was driving on the road when he saw the truck come flying out of the parking lot. That witness said it was a Suburban."

"They didn't get a chance to see who was driving, did they?"

"Nope, said the windows were backed out."

"Fantastic," Maguire replied.

"There really isn't that much to go on," Monahan said. "They got an image from a gas station but there are no plates visible."

"Yeah, and a Suburban isn't an uncommon vehicle."

"No, not up here it isn't," Monahan replied.

"Just another piece of the puzzle, I guess."

"Eventually all the pieces fit, you just have to be patient."

"Yeah," Maguire said. "And pray no more bodies pop-up in the meantime."

"If it was easy, everyone could do it."

"True," Maguire replied.

"Sorry I couldn't help more," Monahan said. "If anything new comes up I will let you know."

"Thanks, Dennis. I really appreciate it. Stay safe."

Maguire ended the call and laid the phone on the table. He let what Monahan had just told him sink in.

It was true that Suburban's were common civilian vehicles, but it was also true that a number of government agencies, including the State Department, used them as well.

"I think, that from now on, we should leave the cell phones in the salon," Melody said, as she looked at Maguire.

"I think you right," Maguire replied. "We should leave them in the house, then you and I can go to the boat and really be alone."

"That actually sounds like a wonderful idea."

"It certainly does, angel," Maguire said, as he finished off the last of the wine in his glass.

"One day, things will get back to normal," she said.

"My little optimist," he said with a smile.

Suddenly he felt the vibration of the other cell phone in his jacket pocket.

He reached inside and pulled it out, looking down at the screen.

"I have to take this one, Mel," he said.

"I know," she said. "It's the life of a cop."

"What do you have for me?" he asked.

"Where are you at?" Mother asked on the other end of the phone.

"Just getting done with dinner," Maguire replied.

"Put on your coat and go for a walk along the beach, it's a beautiful night. Good for the digestion."

"I'll do that," Maguire said. "I'll let you know how it works out."

Maguire got up from the table and kissed Melody.

"Duty calls, angel," he said.

"Don't let it call too long," she replied with a smile. "I'd like at least one night where we can shut the world outside."

"I'll be really quick," Maguire said.

"I'll be watching the clock, cowboy."

He grabbed his overcoat, buttoning it up, and walked out the back door, heading down toward the beach. He passed one of the security patrols on his way, and, once he was sure he was out of earshot, he called Mother back.

"What do you have for me?" Maguire said.

"You want the boiler plate or the juicy stuff?"

"Is this ala carte or a buffet package?"

"You're paying either way," Mother said.

"Then give it all to me," Maguire replied.

"Deputy Secretary of State G. Prescott Linehan is a career diplo-dweeb," Mother said. "He has spent much of his career dealing with Africa and the Middle East. He was born in Taylorville, Illinois in 1959. Father was a farmer during the week and a Baptist preacher on Sunday. Mother was a school teacher. Has one sister who's married to a college professor and lives in Chicago. He speaks Arabic, French and Turkish. He received his undergraduate degree in history and fine arts from University of Illinois in 1980 and his Master's degree in Law and Diplomacy from the Fletcher School of Law and Diplomacy at Tufts University in 1982. Along the way he married his college sweetheart, Anne Dunston"

"Busy little guy, isn't he?"

"Indeed," Mother replied. "When he was done fucking around on his parent's dime, he joined the U.S. Foreign Service in 1986 where he served his first tour as consular officer in Khartoum, Sudan. From 1988 to 1991 he was the economic officer at the U.S. Embassy in Turkey. He then got shipped back to Africa as a special assistant concentrating on the coordination of U.S. assistance. In 1995 they uprooted him, shipping him to the U.S. Embassy in Tel Aviv where he covered economic issues in the Gaza Strip until 1998."

"You should have told me to bring a cup of coffee along with a pad and paper," Maguire said.

"This will be in the biography I send you, but it bears hearing out."

"Pardon my interruption, please continue."

"In 1998 they sent him to serve as the chief of the Political and Economic Section at the U.S. Embassy in Riyadh, Saudi Arabia. He remained there until 2001 when he went back to the Embassy in Tel Aviv as the ambassador's special assistant on peace process issues and then later became the deputy principal officer at the U.S. Consulate General in Jerusalem."

"He certainly gets around, doesn't he?" Maguire asked.

"Clearly he was being groomed for bigger and better things," Mother replied. "He volunteered to serve at the Coalition Provisional Authority office in Iraq and was later appointed as the Assistant Secretary of State for Near Eastern Affairs. Not long afterward he was confirmed as the United States Ambassador to Syria. Prior to the last administration change he was brought back in as deputy secretary of state. Then, when the secretary stepped down, they made him acting. It lasted into the new administration, so he must have thought he had a good shot at staying on, but that was when the cookie finally crumbled. In June 2009 Eliza Cook was appointed secretary and she opted to retain him as her deputy, probably because of his history and connections in the region."

"I'd say that had to be a blow to his ego," Maguire said.

"Now I told you that story, to tell you this one," Mother replied. "My source over at the *Agency* said Linehan had been tasked as the go between on an arms deal that hadn't worked out as planned."

"Now that's a shock. CIA and guns, what could possibly go wrong?"

"Now, now, let's not disparage our misguided brethren. Besides, word is that it was the administration that was behind the fuck-up. Apparently, after the debacle in Benghazi, they were looking for a new route for weapons shipments into Syria. Somewhere along the way, the folks over in Saudi Arabia decided that they would be willing to be the *port in the storm* for the arms supply. It seems that King Abdullah isn't a big fan of Assad so he saw it as a win/win."

"But I take it that things didn't work out exactly as planned?"

"That's one way of putting it," Mother replied. "Reports say that the shipment arrived in Jeddah as scheduled. From there it was supposed to make its way up the Mediterranean through Turkey."

"I thought Turkey was staying out of the Syrian fight?"

"*Enemy of my enemy*," Mother said. "Officially, Turkey wasn't picking sides, aside from complaining about the humanitarian crisis. Then Syria started lobbing ordinance over their boarders and shooting down their planes. That's usually a game changer. Like the Turkish President said, '*We are not interested in war, but we're not far from it either*'. Unfortunately, after it left Jeddah, it apparently went west instead of north, ending up across the Red Sea in Sudan. No one seems to know what went wrong."

"That place seems to be popping up a lot lately."

"Regardless, I don't expect it to be added to the Travel Channel's top ten destinations anytime soon."

"It does however seem like our little globe-trotting diplomat has logged in a bunch of visits to these little foreign gems," Maguire said.

"Seems to be the reason he was selected," Mother replied. "I guess Eliza Cook wasn't the only one who wanted to make use of his contacts."

"Who ran the operation on the receiving end?"

"A guy named Omar bin Salam was running the program for Saudi's. He was vetted by the agency. Bin Salam is a mid-level royal, with solid connections. Word is that he was sent to Jeddah to oversee things after the flood in 2011. Apparently the King didn't think that the local administration acted quickly enough in responding. Bin Salam did such a good job that the King kept him there as his point man, to make sure there were no more problems. It was a big promo for the guy. Jeddah's the biggest port on the Red Sea and the gateway to Mecca and Medina."

"You think he turned?" Maguire asked.

"Hard to tell," Mother replied. "Everyone has their price, although I can't imagine what his would be. He seems to have the world by the balls."

"True believer?"

Maguire could hear Mother laughing on the other end.

"Should I take that as a no?"

"You know better, my son," Mother said. "The true believers scratch out a hand to mouth existence, praying for the opportunity to strap a bomb to their chest and blow their miserable asses out of this existence. They whack-off to some screwy dream of having seventy-two virgins, sans burkhas, to spend eternity with. With his money, this bin Salam fucker could pay to have seventy-two virgins shipped in every night for the next ten years and not even put a dent in the interest he accrues. No, he may say all the right words, but I guarantee you he ain't gonna sacrifice anything for the *cause*."

"So that leads us back to Linehan."

"More or less," Mother replied. "At least you have a starting point, but tread carefully, tadpole. You're dealing with some major league folks. You make even the slightest fuck up, not even that shiny new badge of yours will save you."

"Nice to know you care, mom," Maguire said with a laugh.

"Care my ass, that list of dinners you owe me is growing longer by the day. I just don't want to miss out on any meals, before I get a chance to collect."

"I'll let you know what I find out," Maguire said. "If you hear of anything else, keep me in the loop."

"Will do," Mother said. "Enjoy the rest of the evening."

"Oh, I certainly intend to do just that," Maguire said with a laugh.

CHAPTER FORTY-FIVE

Southampton, Suffolk County, N.Y.
Wednesday, February 27th, 2013 – 5:11 a.m.

Maguire sat in his office on the houseboat, drinking a cup of coffee, as he watched the laptop in front of him power up. Outside, darkness still held onto its grip and a cold wind was blowing in off the sound. He checked his watch, then picked up his cell phone and placed a call.

While sunrise was still more than an hour away here, it was just after one o'clock in Riyadh, Saudi Arabia. After a few rings, he heard a voice on the other end.

"Al Reshedi," the man said sternly.

"Casper, how the fuck are you?" Maguire said.

"Paddy, I'm doing well," Al Reshedi replied, his tone changing drastically. "How are you?"

"Eh, you know me, wine, women and song."

Maguire had first met Saqr Al Reshedi when he was deployed as a Naval Special Warfare training advisor to the Saudi Royal Navy. His team had spent several months training them in tactical ship boarding operations.

Back then the man had been a *wet behind the ears* ensign who'd get lost going to the head. Over copious amounts of beer, he'd made the alcohol fueled mistake of standing up and proudly informing the SEAL's that his name stood for *Falcon*. He then proceeded to turn as white as a ghost and passed out on the floor. Once they realized that he wasn't dead, he was officially dubbed *Casper*. Months after the SEAL's left, Al Reshedi was still being

307

inundated with care packages containing photos, stickers, and other mementos of the *friendly ghost*.

It was highly unlikely that anyone used that nickname anymore. He had left the navy and now served in a high ranking position in the *Al Mukhabarat Al A'amah*, the Saudi General Intelligence Presidency.

"It's been a long time, my friend."

"Too long," Maguire said. "I miss those days, but now they went and made me legitimate."

"Not you?" the man replied incredulously. "Say it isn't so."

"It is," Maguire said. "I'm the number two at the NYPD now. They gave me a shiny gold badge and everything?"

"Next you'll be telling me you gave up booze and are getting married."

"Let's not get crazy," Maguire replied, "although there is someone now."

"Well if you have no further use of that famous black book…."

"I'll leave that to you in my will," Maguire said with a laugh.

Al Reshedi looked up at the clock on his wall.

"Judging from the time back in the U.S.; if you're not in bed, then this must not be a social call."

Spooks were all the same, they lived for the minutiae.

"Are we alone?" Maguire asked, making sure the phone line was secure.

"Yes," Al Reshedi said. "My end is clean."

"Does the name Qaseem bin Khalid ring a bell?"

Maguire could hear the man chuckle on the other end of the phone. He wasn't sure if that was a good omen.

"What has *sweet-cheeks* gotten himself into this time?"

Sweet cheeks? Maguire thought. *I can't wait to hear this one.*

"He was part of a terror cell we broke up here a few weeks back. We hit them before they were able to put their plan in motion."

"Bin Khalid? That's Impossible," Al Reshedi said. "He was on a government sponsored trip to northern Syria."

"He upgraded," Maguire said. "I was in the middle of watching the folks from Langley introduce him to the finer points of enhanced interview techniques when he was *rescued* by our very own State Department."

"And you wonder why the situation here is getting worse? Your own agencies don't even work together in the U.S. let alone in the Middle East."

"You're preaching to the choir, brother," Maguire replied. "So what's the story on this little shit bird?"

"He's a rich kid with some *higher* end connections on his father's side. He got hooked up with some other kids who liked the western lifestyle a bit too much. They started partying with some of the western contractors doing business here. Normally they are hands off, but apparently the *Mutaween*, the religious police, had been given information about a party. When they raided the place, they found booze, narcotics and sex."

"The unholy trifecta of the *hudud*!" Maguire said.

"That's one way of putting it," said Al Reshedi. "According to the reports, when they found bin Khalid he was in the middle of a threesome."

"Isn't that every boys dream?" Maguire replied.

"No, you didn't hear me correctly. He was in the *middle* of a threesome."

"Ah, *sweet cheeks*. Got ya!"

"Anyway, he was facing the executioner's sword, but an influential member of his family intervened on his behalf so he was given an out. He would be allowed to cross over into Syria and fight for the rebels, in order to restore his family honor. If he survived, he might even be allowed to come home."

"Well, I hate to break the bad news to you, but he found an option number three. When he hit Syria he hooked up with the village idiot, another disgruntled jihadist named Ramzi Sharif. The two of them, along with three others, came here to do a series of car bombings."

"Where is he now?"

"That, my friend is the million dollar question," Maguire replied. "Like I said, he was just being taught that cooperation was in his best interests, when the kind folks over at the State Department burst in, claiming diplomatic immunity, and hauled him out."

"Diplomatic immunity," Al Reshedi said with a laugh. "That kid's probably never even been within a hundred miles of a diplomat. What did this Sharif tell you?"

"Nothing," Maguire said. "He had a premature ejection,"

"You mean premature ejaculation?"

"No, ejection," Maguire corrected. "He set off his explosives early and pieces of him were *ejected* in every direction."

"Sounds like a fitting end."

"It would have been, but he took out two of my cops when he did it."

"I'm sorry to hear that, Paddy."

"Thank you," Maguire said. "There's no love over at State Department, so I can't even make inquiries without setting off a ton of bells and whistles. I was hoping you might be able to shed more light on the matter."

"I wish I could, but like I said, he was presumed to be in Syria."

"Can you check to see if he ever arrived back home?" Maguire asked. "Maybe he had a sick pet he had to nurse back to health."

"Yes, let me run a name check for him," Al Reshedi said.

Maguire could hear the sound of keys clicking away.

"I've got nothing, Paddy," the man said a moment later. "If your State Department shipped him back home, it wasn't under his own name."

"Eh, it was worth a shot," Maguire said.

"So when are you coming back to the Kingdom?" Al Reshedi asked.

"I'm not marrying your sister, Casper."

"Her herd is up to six hundred head now, prime animals. You would be a Bedouin king," the man said with a laugh.

Neither man could even remember the origins of the joke, but they had laughed about it for years, with the size of the herd growing with each retelling.

"No, thanks," Maguire replied. "I'm done picking sand out of my mess kit."

"You American's have no sense of adventure," Al Reshedi said.

"Hey, before I hang the phone up on you, do you remember the name of the family member who got bin Khalid sprung?"

"Eh, I'm getting older, the name escapes me. Hold on and let me go pull the folder."

A few moments later he heard Al Reshedi pick the phone back up, and could hear the man flipping through papers.

"Here it is, Omar bin Salman."

"What did you say?"

"Omar bin Salman," Al Reshedi said. "Is there a problem?"

"No," Maguire lied. "Bad connection, couldn't hear the name the first time. What's the uncle's story?"

"That's why we were plugged into the case. He's the King's man in Jeddah. He's a pretty stand-up guy, solid family except for the idiot nephew."

"Ok, Casper, I appreciate the info," Maguire said.

"If you hear anything more about the kid, let me know. I doubt he gets a second chance this time, regardless of who his uncle is."

"Will do. I'll be in touch."

Maguire hung up the phone and stared at the name he had written down on the pad in front of him.

The coincidences were starting to pile up at an alarming rate.

He picked up the cell phone and placed another call.

"Has it even been twelve hours?" Mother said.

"Remember that guy named Omar bin Salman, the mid-level royal, with solid connections, who was the go-to guy on the arms shipment?"

"Yeah, what about him?"

"Guess who's uncle he is."

"It's too early in the morning for pop quizzes, junior."

"Qaseem bin Khalid, my little fucking jihadi that State stole."

"Where did you get that little gem?"

"Casper, I just got off the phone with him," Maguire replied. "He says junior was playing *bottom bitch* in a drunken orgy when the religion *po-po* kicked down the door. Uncle Omar bought him safe passage to fight in Syria, to atone for his sins."

"I fucking hate politicians," Mother said.

"You and me both," Maguire replied. "This shit's cloudier than a southern gene pool."

"Go over what you know for certain."

"Starting in order? First was State stealing bin Khalid. Second was the same guy from State stealing the body of Dawai, who was heading back to the Sudan with military secrets and being chased by Mossad. I have my suspicions that State might be involved in some other activities, but nothing I can confirm at the moment. Then we have Linehan, also State, who acts as the intermediary on the arms shipment. The Saudi point guy, bin Salman, who is supposed to make the shipment go north, sends it west, to the Sudan. The same guy, who's nephew was snatched at the beginning of our story."

"One big happy fucking circle-jerk," Mother said.

"What I can't figure out is, why would bin Salman fuck over the same people that saved his nephew?"

For a moment there was dead silence on the phone as the two men let the statement play over in their heads.

"Well, what if bin Salman didn't actually fuck them over?" Mother asked.

"What do you mean?"

"What if he redirected the shipment as payment for the save?"

"You know what you're suggesting?"

"I do," Mother replied. "Some nefarious shit, tadpole, but we don't live in paradise do we?"

"Yeah, but I'm going to need more than murky connections, and disjointed coincidences, to make a case against a deputy secretary of state."

"Who else knows about this?"

"Right now? Just you and I," Maguire said. "And, in about a half hour, my boss."

"You trust him?" Mother asked.

"Rich? Yeah, with my life. We both have a dog in the fight, we lost two cops and I damn near lost Melody to these fuckers. I wanna see that little pricks head on a pike and any of those other treasonous fuckers as well."

"I need to make a few phone calls," Mother replied. "Keep everything close to the vest and I will call you back."

"I'll be waiting."

"Trust no one, Paddy, and watch your back."

"Hooyah," Maguire replied.

CHAPTER FORTY-SIX

National Mall, Washington, D.C.
Thursday, February 28th, 2013 – 8:23 a.m.

Maguire watched as the tall figure, clad in a dark gray overcoat, approached him with a stride more accustomed to a military parade ground then out for a casual walk. The man's close cropped hair might have been a bit grayer, but the steely blue eyes and chiseled jaw, gave warning that he was one *senior* that should not be trifled with.

"Glad you could make it," Maguire said. "I was beginning to think you overslept. Doesn't the nursing home have alarm clocks?"

"Nope, just helped myself to an extra serving at breakfast," Mother replied. "I figured you'd find a way to weasel out of buying lunch so I had better be prepared."

"After I just sat on this park bench, freezing my *cojones* off, drinking a cup of cold coffee and a protein bar, I'd say that's a safe bet."

Maguire got up from the park bench and embraced the man. Senior Chief Petty Officer (SEAL) Roy K. Gentry, US Navy – *Retired*, had been like a second father to him. But unlike his biological father, who had taught him an appreciation for art and chess; this man had taught him the art of war and tactics. Ironically, in spite of being a father figure to many of the SEAL's who worked for him; he'd been given the nickname *Mother*, for keeping after them and being protective, like a mother hen.

"What, they don't serve breakfast on your girlfriend's helicopter?"

"Where do you think I got the coffee and the protein bar?"

"Tough lady," Mother replied. "So where did you park that thing?"

"South Capitol Street Heliport," Maguire said. "The MPD chief was kind enough to hook me up with a landing pad and a ride over here."

"I guess that badge is good for something," Mother said. "It's good to see you again, Paddy. It doesn't look like the civilian life has made you go *too* soft."

"It's nice to see you as well. Glad to see you're getting around without the walker."

"Walker, my ass, tadpole," Mother replied. "By the way, you need a haircut or are you going for the hippie look now?"

The two men began to walk east, along the National Mall, toward the Capitol building.

"I thought you said that you hated politicians?" Maguire said sarcastically.

"I do," Mother replied. "Under normal conditions I try to steer clear of the bottom dwellers. These however aren't normal conditions."

"So what's this guy's story?" Maguire asked.

"Senator Mays?" Mother asked. "He's the ranking member of the Senate Intelligence Committee. I spoke to him about your *problems* and he was eager to have a chat with you, *mano y mano*. Seems, like you, that he has some reservations about the folks over at Foggy Bottom. I told him that you would be happy to ruin your morning for him."

"Do you trust him?"

"He's a politician, Paddy. I trust them about as far as I can throw them. But he's also Navy, so I'm trying to give him the benefit of the doubt."

"The Navy's a big place, Mother. What was his pay grade?"

"He got out as an O-6, rear admiral, lower half," Mother replied.

"Great," Maguire replied. "That instills a lot of confidence. A Bureaucrat in the Navy isn't much different than a bureaucrat in government."

"True, but he also worked for a living at one time. He flew an *aluminum cloud* back in the day," said Mother, referring to the nickname given to the Grumman F-14 Tomcat fighter jet. "But what is more important to me is that his father was old school UDT, a plank owner in Team 14."

The UDT was the Navy's Underwater Demolition Teams, the forerunners of today's SEAL's. They were created back in World War II and were used to reconnoiter and destroy enemy defensive obstacles on beaches prior to amphibious landings. As the Navy's elite combat swimmers, they were used to breach enemy harbors, plant limpet mines on enemy ships, as well as locate and mark mines for clearing by minesweepers. They also used explosives to demolish underwater obstacles planted by the enemy. In later years they were also tasked with retrieving astronauts after splashdown in the Mercury through Apollo manned space flights.

Being a 'plank owner' in any Navy unit meant that you were one of the original members. A plank owner of UDT 14 meant that he had been there at *Iwo Jima*, clearing the way for the invasion force.

"Hopefully the old man taught the son right," Maguire replied.

The two men crossed 3rd Street SW, and made their way toward the Ulysses S. Grant Memorial, in front of the Capitol building. They turned north, passing the Peace Circle, and then walked along the outer edge of the grounds. They crossed Constitution St NW, and headed toward the Russell Senate Office Building.

"Are you *packing*?" Mother asked.

"You told me that this was a *covert* visit," Maguire replied.

"Just wanted to make sure that we didn't set off any alarms, and then have to explain to the nice Capitol cops why you were here."

"Nope, I'm traveling *light*," Maguire said.

The two men looked at each other for a moment before breaking out in a laugh. Traveling 'light' meant something entirely different to them. Just because Maguire was not carrying his gun, didn't exactly mean that he was unarmed. It just meant that the items he carried on his person were not going to be picked up by the magnetometers that they were about to pass through. Not that either man actually required a weapon to be deadly.

They walked up the steps and entered the cold, marble and limestone building. After passing through the magnetometers, they made their way upstairs and located Senator Mays' office. They stepped into the office, closing the door behind them.

For as cold and foreboding as the exterior of the building was, the interior was equally opulent. Clearly those who called the Russell building 'home' were accustomed to the finer things.

Our tax money, hard at work, Maguire thought.

"May I help you?" asked a young, blond haired woman who sat behind the desk.

"Mr. Gentry to see Senator Mays," Mother replied. "He's expecting us."

"Please have a seat," she said, pointing to a leather couch that sat against the wall. "I'll let him know you're here."

Maguire watched her get up, and head toward the door opposite them. The woman was probably in her late twenties, with long legs and was endowed with quite a large chest.

"I'm sure she has a great *GPA*," Maguire said softly.

"I doubt it," Mother replied.

A moment later Senator Vernon Mays stepped out of the office, a huge smile on his face, and approached the two men, who stood up.

"I'm delighted to meet you gentlemen," Mays said, shaking their hands. "Can I get you something to drink?"

"Coffee would be great," Gentry said. "Black is fine."

"Make it two," Maguire added.

Mays smiled and turned to look at the woman.

"Mindy, can you get us three coffees please; two black and you know how I like mine," the man said. "Please follow me."

The three men walked into the well-appointed office. Photos adorned the walls, showing Mays with prominent politicians, including the last three presidents. There were also a number of Navy memorabilia, including a fighter pilot's helmet that sat on top of a book case.

"Have a seat," he said, gesturing to the two leather chairs in front of the desk.

Mays closed the door behind him, and then walked around to take his seat at the desk.

"Seems like a nice, young lady," Mother said.

Suddenly Mays entire face changed, from jovial politician to one that seemed weathered and tired.

"She's a fucking idiot, to be honest," Mays replied. "Like everything around this place, it's either fake or incompetent. She's the state party chairman's daughter and he wanted her to come to D.C. to get her feet wet. That's like sending your virgin daughter to *Sodom and Gomorrah*. It has almost become a full time job trying to keep her from being bent over the desk of one of my *esteemed* and *honorable* colleagues. This place is a goddamn cesspool, Chief."

"You're shattering my illusions of our fine political system, Senator," Mother replied.

"I've been here for two terms now, just started my third, and each one was going to be my last," Mays said, his voice sounding weary. "Believe it or not my wife talked me into running again. She said if the good people ever abandoned politics, imagine how much worse it would be."

"She does have a point, Senator."

"She does, Chief, but my fear is that if I stay here any longer I might stop being one of those *good* people. This place eats at you, like a cancer. I've seen the same good people come here and it's not too long before they become victims. They get elected to this *lofty* position and soon fall to the vices that inhabit these *hallowed halls*: avarice, debauchery, ambition, flattery, and power. It consumes them."

"It has to change somewhere," Mother replied.

"That's the problem, Chief. I've come to learn that nothing ever changes. Me, the guy or gal down the hall, we just occupy the seat for a finite period of time. We might try to improve things, but it is like shoveling shit into the wind."

"So what's the problem?" Maguire asked.

Mays looked over at Maguire. James could see the pensive look, as if the man was genuinely trying to come up with an answer.

"In short, the parties are the problem. They are the ones that control the purse strings. Many of us get into politics because we think we can help fix the problem, but we need the parties to get elected. Once we get elected, most of us want to get re-elected, so we have to do the parties bidding, even when we may not agree. If we don't, there goes the money and any shot at keeping the seat."

"What about the voters? Don't they count?"

"Not really," Mays said, sounding a bit melancholy. "Most of them are good natured folks, but they have gotten caught up in the party nonsense as well. Rather than judge the candidates on who they are and what they stand for, they go down the ballot and ignorantly check the box with their parties letter next to their name. You could elect a dead guy as long as he had the party's endorsement. Which would be ironic considering, that in certain states, the dead actually vote."

"You're painting a chilling picture, sir," Maguire said.

"Son," Mays said. "We elected a community organizer who had no substantive voting record to his name, but he promised to *change* things. Well, he did that. Now, we have a foreign policy that crossed the border into insanity. One in which we are talking to our enemies, sending them money that we don't have, and rebuking or flat-out ignoring our friends. He said that adding to the debt was *unpatriotic,* but he then he added nearly seven trillion dollars to that, and it continues to go up. Now, the government, that seems to be incompetent on the best of days, is set to take over our healthcare system. Is there anything really rosy in that picture to get excited about?"

"Well, when you put it that way," Maguire said with a half-hearted laugh.

"The problem is, he's from *my* party, and I am supposed to support him. How the hell can I do that with a clear conscience? He pisses in the other party's drinks, and then publicly chastises them when they won't *toast* him. I've been trying to warn my friends that when the pendulum finally swings away from us, it's not going to be pretty. Which brings us right back to square one, the party controls everything. Common sense goes right out the window with those folks. It's all about *us versus them.* They could care less about the country and the folks who elected us. There are times when I feel like a band member on the Titanic. Playing soothing music, saying the right words, and knowing in my heart we're all about to go for one helluva long, cold, miserable swim."

Just then, there was a knock on the door, followed by Mindy walking in with a tray holding three mugs of coffee. She set it down on the edge of the desk and handed a mug to each of them.

"Will that be all, sir?"

"Yes, Mindy. Thank you so much," Mays said, his face radiating that charming politician's smile. "Please hold all my calls; we don't want to be interrupted."

Yes, sir," the woman replied, as she picked up the tray and exited the room, closing the door behind her.

"And that brings us back to here, gentlemen," Mays replied, his voice sounding weary again. "I'm glad you could make it on such short notice, Commissioner Maguire. Chief Gentry was explaining your *concerns* to me last night. I think you and I share the same views."

"Well, since you know what I'm dealing with, sir. What can you tell me about Deputy Secretary of State Linehan?"

"He's your typical diplomat, sees the world through his rose colored glasses, thinking that all the ills can be solved through talking *nicely* to people that want to kill us."

"I take it you don't share that philosophy?"

"I prefer Theodore Roosevelt's ideology of 'speak softly and carry a big stick'. I know that may seem a bit *Machiavellian* to a lot of my colleagues, but most of them never went into harm's way either. I understand that our enemies want to kill us, and, while I am not opposed to trying to talk them out of it, I want the biggest, baddest military I can have behind me when those negotiations inevitably break down. More importantly, I want them to know the ramifications for screwing with us."

"And you don't think Linehan embraces that position?" Maguire asked.

"No, but that doesn't necessarily mean that he wouldn't bend things to fit his needs," Mays replied.

"How so?"

"I had a chance to talk to Linehan on several occasions. Sitting on the Intel Committee gives me a lot of face time with folks. At one time Linehan believed that he might have a shot at becoming secretary of state. I didn't want to break it to him that he had a snowball's chance in hell, figured that was something that would be done far above my pay grade. When POTUS nominated my *esteemed* colleague, Eliza Cook, for the seat, let's just say that Mr. Linehan took the news rather personal."

"I guess that means he wasn't exactly happy?"

"The boy was so distraught I think it was the first time I ever saw him *not* look at Mindy's tits. He came here to talk about some problem in Kandahar and just about balled his eyes out."

"But he stayed," Maguire replied. "It couldn't have been too traumatic for him."

"Like I said before, Linehan is your typical diplomat, narcissistic and self-important. Ultimately, he convinced himself that he had to stay, because the secretary of state *needed* his knowledge and experience. I think he also believes that if he can just wait her out, she'll be gone and he will be considered a loyal team player to be rewarded accordingly."

"You don't think so?"

"Cook got the slot because she is a political animal. She's a visionary, plays all four quarters. Linehan is a worker bee," Mays said. "He doesn't have the deep pockets or the backing of an influential donor, nor does he present a political threat to be neutralized with a high profile position."

"So, if you don't mind me asking, why exactly is he on your radar?"

"He and Secretary Cook have *philosophical* differences when it comes to our present situation in Syria. Cook has publicly denounced the Assad regime and supports providing aid to the rebels. Not a stretch, since that is the marching order that is coming out of the West Wing."

"You don't agree?" Maguire asked.

"That's like asking which end of a shit sandwich is my favorite. Don't get me wrong, Assad is a prick that should have been dealt with a long time ago. But he's only one guy, on a long list of people who shouldn't be running a country. We kinda, sorta, helped get rid of Gaddafi and Mubarak and how exactly has that worked out for us?"

"You do have a point there," Gentry said.

"To be honest, the more important issue is that, when we should have backed the rebels, when they were an honest, homogenous, grass roots effort, we didn't. We allowed outsiders to come and infiltrate them. Now the weapons we are sending are falling into the hands of terror groups, like Ansar al-Islam and Al Nusra Front. I'm just an old salty dog, but I have a feeling that might not be the brightest thing to do. You know, before World War Two we used to send a lot of metal to Japan, and they returned a lot of it back to us on December 7th, 1941. What's going on in Syria is only the tip of the iceberg. I'm afraid that we are seeing a wave that is only going to spread out."

"So you agree with Linehan that our current role in Syria is misguided?" Maguire asked.

"Linehan feels as if Cook is pacifying the rebels for a political agenda and that she doesn't see the full ramifications of this folly. I tend to agree with that assessment. I can't get into certain specifics, but we are getting disturbing reports about our new *friends* in the Free Syrian Army and their *lethal* intolerance for other religions in Syria."

"Religion of peace," Gentry replied matter-of-factly.

"If you say so, Chief," Mays replied. "Right now, our choice is between supporting the rebels, whose ranks are filled with terrorist organizations that are killing religious minorities at will, and the Assad government, which is a state sponsor of terrorism, but protects the religious minorities. What end of that sandwich do you like best, gentleman?"

"I say we sell tickets and watch from the sideline, sir," Gentry said.

"Not a bad idea, Chief. The good Lord knows we don't have a good track record of picking winners and losers lately," Mays said.

Maguire took a sip of coffee and stared out the window.

"You alright, Paddy?"

Maguire set his mug down on the desk and looked back over at Mother, then at Mays.

"What if that's what Linehan is doing?"

"Doing what?" Mays asked.

"Picking winners and loser," Maguire replied. "You said it before, Cook is going to go. I still know a few people in this town as well. Word is that things aren't going so well between her and the other folks over at 1600 Pennsylvania Avenue. Supposedly she's tired of being the cheering squad for ill-advised policies and positions that continue to blow-up in the administrations face. She has greater aspirations and doesn't want to get caught without a chair when the music eventually stops. What if Linehan's philosophical differences stem from the fact that he knows what's going on in Syria with the rebels? He figures that Cook is going and saw this as an opportunity to have a substantive impact on the conflict?"

"So you think Linehan orchestrated this?"

"Maybe we are looking at this from the wrong direction. We assumed that the Saudi's redirected the arms shipment over to the Sudan as repayment for saving the nephew. But what if they handled the shipment exactly as Linehan told them to?"

"Go on, Commissioner," Mays said, his voice clearly expressing concern.

"When did the shipment go missing?" Maguire asked.

Mays opened a folder on his desk and flipped through the papers till he found the one he was looking for.

"It says here that they disappeared sometime between January 7th and the 15th."

"*Sonofabitch*," Maguire said, pounding his fist into his thigh.

"What's wrong?" Mays asked.

"Linehan directed the weapons to go to the Sudan *before* the kid got picked up."

"How do you know that?" Mays asked.

"The nephew was never part of the equation," he replied. "He wasn't in our custody till the end of January. The weapons were already gone long before he was on our radar."

"So you think Linehan wasn't getting a payback for a favor, but that he called in a favor to have the weapons rerouted?" Mays said.

"That's the only thing that makes sense," Maguire said. "The question now is *why* did he redirect the weapons shipment over to the Sudan? I need more background on him; I need to take a peek inside his personnel folder."

Mays stared at Maguire for a moment, and then looked over at Gentry, who just nodded. The man reached down and opened one of the desk drawers. He reached inside and removed a thick manila folder. He set it down on the desk and then slid it over toward Maguire.

"I'm going to take Chief Gentry over to the cafeteria for a real cup of coffee," Mays said. "You can't take this with you, but feel free to sit back and take any notes you might think are relevant. I'll make sure Mindy knows you're not to be bothered."

Mays and Gentry walked out of the room as Maguire opened the folder and began to sort through the papers.

CHAPTER FORTY-SEVEN

Penobscot, New Hampshire
Thursday, February 28th, 2013 – 12:32 p.m.

Alex took a final drag on her cigarette and then crushed it out in the ashtray. She picked up the coffee mug and headed out into the squad room to get a refill.

"Hey, Chief," Officer Abby Simpson called out.

"Yeah, Abs?" Alex replied, as she began to refill the mug.

"Just got a possible hit on our missing sociopath," Simpson said.

"Where?"

"A place called Flowery Branch in Georgia."

"What did they tell us?"

"They had a drive-off from a gas station down there. When they pulled the video surveillance tape they came up with a silver Mercedes with New Hampshire tags. The tags came back to a green Volvo in Laconia. Then one of their officers remembered the APB we'd put out on Susan Waltham. Checked the description of the driver and they thought it was a close enough match to alert us."

"So where the hell is Flowery Branch?" Alex asked.

"Tell you in a second," she said, as she tapped a few keys on the computer.

"According to this map it looks like it is just north-east of Atlanta," Simpson replied.

"Great," Alex replied. "That narrows it down."

"What do you mean, Boss?"

"Think of Atlanta as being the hub on a bike wheel," Alex explained. "From there you head out, up the spokes. You can go east to South Carolina, west to Alabama, south to Florida, and even back north to Tennessee."

"So it's useless?" Abby said.

"No, not entirely," Alex replied. "It does tell us where she isn't, and that's here. Did it mention if there was anyone with her?"

"According to what they sent, no."

"Ok, well contact the PD down there and thank them, ask if they can send us out whatever information and photos they pulled from the tape. Then amend our APB to include the information as a possible sighting. List the plate, but indicate that it may already have been changed."

"Will do," Simpson replied. "Why do you think she drove off?"

"She might be getting desperate. It's been six months, so I'm sure that whatever money she managed to get her hands on has got to be dwindling down. If she's on her own, then she is going to have limited resources, which works to our advantage. She'll begin to make mistakes, like the drive-off."

"It would be nice to close the book on this case."

"It certainly would, Abs."

Alex walked back into her office and sat down. She reached into her pocket, pulling out the pack of cigarettes and lit one. Then she reached down into the bottom drawer and removed a folder.

She sorted through the papers until she found the one with Susan Waltham's photo. She stared down at the high school photo. To the rest of the world it would look like any other happy-go-lucky, seventeen year old girl, but behind the vibrant smile and pretty eyes was something different, something sinister.

Suddenly, the cell phone on the desk began to vibrate, startling Alex.

She laid the photo down and took a drag on the cigarette, as she answered the phone.

"Hello?" she said.

"Alex?" a woman's voice said on the other end. "Hi, it's Melody Anderson."

"Melody, hi, how are you feeling?"

"Oh, just plugging along," she replied.

"I'm glad to hear that," Alex said. "What can I do for you?"

"Well, I just wanted to reach out to you and say thank you again, for all you did."

"Oh, it was nothing."

"No, it was something," Melody said. "You put yourself out to help James; you even put your own life at risk for someone you didn't know."

"James would have done the same for me, if the tables were reversed," Alex replied.

"I know, and I also know the two of you have a bond from being partners, but that doesn't mean that you don't deserve to be recognized for all that you did."

"Well, thank you, Melody. That means a lot."

"I just wanted to let you know that you are welcome here anytime you care to visit. In fact, that's the reason I called. I'm planning on having a party at the end of March, to welcome in Spring, and I would be honored if you could come."

"That's very sweet of you," Alex said.

"I wanted to make sure I gave you ample notice," Melody said. "Plus, I know that James would really love to see you, without the world imploding for a change."

"He is certainly a little trouble magnet."

"So, will you come?"

"Sure, I'd love to."

"I'll text you over the information. If you can let me know what airport you're near, I'll provide the transportation."

"How could I say no to that?" Alex said. "But honestly, you don't have to go to all that trouble for little ole' me."

"Listen, anyone who can keep up with James is someone I definitely want to know more about."

"He certainly has his moments," Alex said, taking a drag on the cigarette. "How's he doing?"

"He flew down to D.C. this morning; they have some sensitive case they are dealing with."

"Yeah, I saw something about that on the news," Alex replied. "Is it as bad as they are making it out to be?"

"Honestly, it is bad, but not in the way it is being reported," Melody said. "I really can't say much about it."

"Trust me, I understand."

"That's a relief," Melody said. "I'm new at this whole cop's girlfriend thing. I never know what I should or shouldn't talk about."

Alex's jaw clenched tightly and she crushed the cigarette out in the ashtray.

"Hey, Melody," Alex said. "I hate to cut this short but I have a one o'clock meeting with the Mayor, who wants to chew my butt off about something."

"Oh, sure," Melody replied. "I didn't mean to keep you. I'll text you over the information. Can't wait to see you again."

"Same here," Alex replied. "Talk to you soon."

She hit the end button and tossed the phone on the desk.

"*I'm new at this whole cop's girlfriend thing*, my ass," she said out loud, as she lit another cigarette.

"You say something, Chief?" Abby called out from the squad room.

"No, Abs," she replied. "I'm gonna exercise my fifth amendment right against self-incrimination."

A moment later Simpson appeared in the doorway.

"You plan on killing someone?"

"Let's just say that I'm leaving my options open for the moment," she said with a mischievous grin.

"Save that anger for the gym tonight," Abby replied. "It's leg day!"

"Seems like my list of potential victims just doubled," Alex replied.

"Trust me; you'll love me come the summer."

Alex rested her chin on her hand as she thought about what Simpson had said.

"You know what, Abs, how about we shoot for spring?"

"Now that's the spirit, Chief!"

CHAPTER FORTY-EIGHT

Russell Senate Office Building, Washington, D.C.
Thursday, February 28th, 2013 – 2:57 p.m.

"So what do we know, Paddy?" Mother asked, as Mays closed the door behind them.

"Glad you two could make it back," Maguire said, looking up from the papers scattered on the table in front of him.

"Someone was kind enough to buy me a *real* lunch," Mother replied, nodding to Mays. "Besides, I figured you'd be busy with the paperwork anyway."

He laid a paper bag on the table.

"What's that?" Maguire asked.

"Something slightly better than an MRE," Mother replied, sitting down in the chair.

"Thanks."

"So have you figured anything out yet?"

"Linehan has his fingers plugged into so many global hotspots, he looks like the *goddamn* Dutch Boy," Maguire replied.

"Do any of those fingers point to something useful?" Mays asked.

"It's sorta like a spider web," Maguire replied. "You just have to know where to look. Bear with me while I make sense out of my notes. I'm piecing together a lot of source material."

Maguire flipped through the legal pad, locating the material he had highlighted.

"Linehan first went to the Sudan in 1986, remaining there for two years. There's nothing significant in that period, other than I assume he became familiarized with the players. Then in 1991 they brought him back to Khartoum, but this time he was the special assistant coordinating U.S. assistance."

"That's not too uncommon," Mays replied. "That's just an over-glorified bean counter position."

"The posting may not be significant, but who he got cozy with is. When he returned to Khartoum he worked side by side with Mustapha Taban, of the Ministry of Federal Affairs. The very same MFA which is headed by Abdel Al-Mahdi. Al-Mahdi is close counsel to Musa Ali Dawai, the uncle of Yusif Tahir Dawai, who was killed on my highway. That's coincidence *number one*."

"Go on," Mays said.

"In 1996, there was a bombing of a military base in Dharan, Saudi Arabia. The U.S. believed Iran was responsible for the attack, but the charges never stuck. In 1997 there was a meeting in Iran of the Organization of the Islamic Conference. It brought about a shift in the attitudes of Arabs toward Iran. Iran had always criticized Saudi Arabia because of its control of the holy cities of Mecca and Medina, as well as its relationship with the United States regarding security. During the summit meeting, Saudi Arabia was represented by then Crown Prince Abdullah and the Minister of Foreign Affairs, Saud Al Faisal. Apparently some sort of circle jerk went on, because Saudi participation proved helpful in the process of further reconciliation between Iran and Saudi Arabia. After that relations between the two began to warm up. As a result, a Saudi ministerial delegation visited Iran and later on, in February 1998, the official visit of President Mohammad Khattami to Saudi Arabia took place."

"Seeing the *change* on the horizon, the U.S. sent Linehan to serve as the chief of the Political and Economic Section at the

U.S. Embassy in Riyadh, Saudi Arabia. Basically he was trying to counter Iran's influence. During his time there he worked closely with several representatives in the Ministry of Foreign Affairs, including an aide to the minister, namely one Omar bin Salman, who we now know is the uncle of our recently sprung terrorist, Qaseem bin Khalid. That's coincidence *number two*."

"Starting to sound like one too many," Mays said.

"That's the end of the direct links for right now, but here is where it gets really murky. His cables back to the U.S. indicate that he had met with several delegates from Iran. He alluded to the possibility of a potential for normalized relations and suggested that we pursue it. Not sure what happened, as the cables seem to have come to an abrupt end around 2000. In 2001 he went back to the Embassy in Tel Aviv as the ambassador's special assistant on peace process issues. Something *definitely* happened there, because the tone of these cables took on a much different demeanor. This was at the height of the suicide bombings. Almost from the very beginning he seemed to believe that Israel had some higher moral obligation to stand down from it retaliatory response. He claimed that their constant reprisals to Palestinian attacks was just fanning the flames of war and preventing peace from being achieved. There is a three page tirade accusing Israel of instigating the siege at the Church of the Nativity when they occupied Bethlehem. It wasn't long after that, that President Bush called for an independent Palestinian state."

"You think that religion has something to do with this?" Mays asked.

"Like I told you, this is like a spider's web," Maguire replied. "It's just a matter of connecting all the strands back to Linehan. However, it has been my experience that religion, or at least man's interpretation of it, does seem to fuel a lot of the world's *issues*. It was after that when Linehan volunteered to serve at the Coalition Provisional Authority office in Iraq. Again, he sent several cables regarding Iranian influence in the region, claiming that if we didn't attempt to work with them now, we would lose an opportunity down the road. I guess there was push back by the Shiite's, who saw the Iranians as supporters of the Sunni population, and that derailed that. Not long after, he was confirmed as the Ambassador to Syria. Despite the government's outward stance against Bashar al Assad, he had at least one fan in Linehan. Cables show that Linehan continually praised Assad for his work in protecting the Christian minority and warned that growing dissension in the northern areas of Syria would split the country into sectarian violence."

"Well, in light of what is going on in that region, it seems quite *prescient* now," Mays said.

"Linehan believed that the U.S. would benefit through direct talks with the Assad regime. He said that Assad and his wife were quite *charming* and were open to a dialogue with the west. Not sure how well that went over down the street, but judging from the current state of affairs in Syria, I don't think it was met with much success."

"So you think Linehan spent too much time in-country and went rogue?" Mother asked.

"I believe Linehan came to the job with certain *personal* views," Maguire replied. "I think he may have drunk the local Kool-Aid as far as it pertains to who the good guys and bad guys are. Hell, for all I know, maybe he believes that, because of his relationship with some of these nut jobs, that he can influence things and win himself a Nobel Peace Prize."

"And you don't think this is all just coincidence and conjecture?" Mays asked.

"This is what pushed it over the top for me," Maguire said, pulling out a press photo and sliding it across the desk to Mays.

The man picked it up and looked it over. It was a photo taken during a tour of Baghdad. The caption identified Linehan and several other members of the new Iraqi government. On the periphery were several members of the security detail.

"What's this?"

"See those guys with the M-4's, walking behind Linehan?"

"Yeah," Mays replied.

"Those are members of the State Department's, Diplomatic Security Service."

"Yeah, so what?" Mays asked. "That was protocol for our people over there. Baghdad wasn't exactly a safe haven back then."

"You're right about that," Maguire said. "But it's not the whole security detail that interests me, just one of its members. You see that guy directly behind Linehan? That is Special Agent Dean Oliver. He is the same agent who is responsible for taking custody of our terrorist, along with removing the body of our dead spy. That would be coincidence *number three*, and I don't know about you, but I'm pretty sure they aren't."

"Fuck!" Mays exclaimed. "What the hell is this guy up to?"

"I don't know, but I'm planning on finding out," Maguire replied. "How are your relationships with the folks over at NSA?"

"We still exchange Christmas cards," Mother replied. "What do you need?"

"I'd like them to run some numbers through MYSTIC and see what they may have on file."

"What are you thinking about doing?" Mother asked.

"I'm going to take a trip," Maguire said. "I think it's time me and old Uncle Omar bin Salman have us a little chat."

CHAPTER FORTY-NINE

Jeddah, Saudi Arabia
Friday, March 1ˢᵗ, 2013 – 1:23 p.m. (*Eastern Standard Time +7 hrs*)

Maguire gazed out the window of the Gulfstream G550, watching as the sun baked runway rippled like a mirage. Off in the distance he could see the main terminal of the King Abdulaziz International Airport, but this was as close to the terminal as he would get.

The sleek jet continued its meandering journey through the airport complex and finally taxied over toward a non-descript hanger, on the south eastern edge of the airport boundary. As it came to a stop, he could see a small convoy of three Mercedes Benz, G550 SUV's, parked in front of it.

He closed the folder he had been reading, and placed it back inside the black leather portfolio.

By this time the pilot, Captain Katrina Mann, was already opening the door.

"Show time," Maguire said, getting up from his seat and taking the portfolio with him.

"Happy hunting, sir," she replied.

"Keep the engines warm and the doors locked, Hurricane," Maguire said, using her old Air Force *call sign*. "I'll call you when I'm on my way back."

"Roger that," Mann replied.

Maguire stepped out the door, into the sweltering midday heat, and made his way down the steps. As he approached the vehicles, he observed the front passenger door of the middle SUV open. A tall, dark haired man in a suit, who was clearly a security officer, stepped out and opened the rear door for the passenger. As Maguire approached, Saqr Al Reshedi exited from the vehicle and walked toward him.

"Casper, you old goat fucker," Maguire said, extending his arms wide and embracing the man in a hug.

"Paddy, it is good to see you again," the man replied. "I hope that your trip was good."

"I've flown in worse," Maguire said, as he looked the man over. "You don't look as if government work has made you soft."

"Still hit the gym every day," the man replied. "Just in case I fuck with the wrong *relative* and I have to start working for a living."

"Smart man," Maguire replied. "I hope that I am not putting you in a bad position with the *wrong* relative."

"Not at all," Casper said, as he led Maguire toward the waiting car. "In fact, I had a call from the King himself this morning."

"No shit," Maguire said.

"No shit," Casper replied. "After we spoke last night, I had a conversation with the Director General of Intelligence, Faisal Aziz. As you are aware of, he and the King are related. The King was very displeased to hear about the actions of Omar bin Salman. He has personally sanctioned the investigation. He has authorized the Director General, and by extension us, to use any means necessary to determine the reasons why bin Salman acted as he did. He wants to identify any risks to the Kingdom or the United States."

"Do we know where he is?"

"He's on *ice*," Casper said with a laugh. "As soon as the King gave his consent, we had him notified that he was being summoned to an emergency meeting. When he left his house this morning we picked him up halfway to the airport. No one will question his whereabouts for a while."

"Sucks to be him," Maguire said.

"True, although I think this interview will be the least of his worries. The King does not deal with disloyalty issues very well."

"I would imagine not."

Treason was a capital offense crime in Saudi Arabia, and their method of carrying out the sentence was generally enough to keep people from considering it. Whether it came from being stoned to death, or by the executioner's sword, it was a particularly brutal way to go.

"The King also said to tell you that he understands that you are on a very tight schedule, but he wanted me to extend his most sincere thanks to you for bringing this *sensitive* issue to our attention. He also says that he wishes that you might be able to return back with Ms. Anderson and that he might be able to extend the same hospitality that you did when he visited New York City a few years ago."

Maguire reached his arm out and stopped the man, before they reached the cars. He turned and looked at Al Reshedi.

"He said all that, Casper?" Maguire asked.

"Yes," the man replied. "He most certainly did."

"Fucking politicians," Maguire said. "They're the same all over, aren't they?"

"They're all charming," Casper said with a laugh. "As long as they think you can help them."

Yeah, and he is letting me know, in a friendly way, that he is plugged-in and knows about my private life, Maguire thought.

James walked around to the other side of the Mercedes and got in. The three vehicles pulled away, heading toward the airport exit.

"Hey, have you got any friends left over at the Royal Air Force?" Maguire asked, pointing a finger back in the direction of the base.

"Yes, a good friend of mine is a colonel over there, why?"

"You mind giving him a call and seeing if he wouldn't mind sending over some chow to my pilots? I don't need them getting lost looking for take-out."

"No problem, I will make sure they are treated as guests of the King," Casper replied.

"I appreciate that," Maguire replied. "So how is old Omar doing?"

"The usual, kicking and screaming at first, then it was all a big misunderstanding and he wants to help clear things up," Casper replied, looking down at his watch. "By now he probably realizes how bad it is and is crying for his mama."

"Good, that saves me from having to warm him up."

It was about a twenty minute drive to the white washed warehouse on the edge of town, near the port. To the casual observer it looked like any of the multitude of similar warehouses, that dotted this part of the landscape, but to the trained observer, the tell-tale signs began to add up quickly.

The building was about three stories in height and was ringed by a security fence that was topped with concertina wire. Large concrete flower pots dotted the perimeter. They added a certain charm to the place, along with providing protection against vehicle borne threats. Inside the warehouse grounds security cameras maintained their watchful vigil. These were positioned on poles, spaced at regular intervals, which allowed one to observe both the grounds as well as the roadways leading up to the building. These were supplemented by back-up cameras mounted on the building itself, which provided an increased field of vision. There were no windows on the lower two-thirds of the building, nor were there any visible doors.

As the motorcade pulled up to the location, the officer inside the armored security booth lowered the hydraulic powered, steel anti-ram bollards, positioned in the middle of the roadway, allowing the cars to pass through. The motorcade then made its way down the length of the building and pulled into an open loading bay.

As Maguire got out, the steel reinforced security door was closing behind them.

"Nice place you got here," he said.

"It's off the radar," Casper said. "And the neighbors are *really* quite."

"I get the funny feeling that no one wants an invitation to one of your parties."

Once the door was closed, they walked up the stairs to a solid steel door with a camera perched above it. Casper stepped up to a small computer screen that was adjacent to the door, and leaned down. Maguire watched as the screen came to life and began scanning. The red light changed to yellow and the man punched a code into the keyboard. When the light hanged green, there was an audible click and the door unlocked.

"Welcome to warehouse five," Casper said, as he motioned James inside.

While the exterior gave the impression of a rundown warehouse, the interior looked more like something out of Silicon Valley. Numerous work stations dotted the main room and a dozen large screen televisions were mounted on the far wall.

"This is our intelligence operations center," Casper said. "We can monitor everything in the region from here."

"You said this was warehouse *five*," Maguire replied. "I assume there are others."

"Yes, we have about a half dozen other similar facilities scattered throughout the Kingdom. It might seem redundant, until something catastrophic happens."

"You're preaching to the choir, Casper. I remember when I first heard that they were going to set-up the new Emergency Operations Center, for New York City, inside 7 World Trade Center. All the folks on the ground said it was a dumb idea, especially after the first attack back in 1993, but the powers that be thought they knew better. Besides, it was a more *prestigious* address, than some out of the way place."

"The politicians, who make the *decisions* about such things, rarely ask the people who actually *know* about these things."

"I'd like to think they learned the folly of that mistake on 9/11," Maguire replied. "There is nothing like putting all your eggs in one basket, and then hiding that basket *inside* a target."

They made their way through the operations center to an elevator, riding it three floors down. When the doors opened, there was a decidedly chilly quality to the air.

"Nice A/C," Maguire said. "I would have brought a coat."

"I told you we had him on *ice*," Casper replied. "We found that it heightens the level of discomfort."

"How long has he been inside?"

"About six hours, give or take."

"Be careful, before you know it, the human rights groups will start to accuse you of inhumane treatment."

"If they *know* about this place, Paddy, then they should probably be more concerned about *their* treatment."

They walked into a dimly lit observation room, peering at the man sitting on the other side of the glass.

Omar bin Salman sat shivering behind a metal table. Maguire had read the file on the way over, but the man on the other side bore no resemblance to the one he had read about. He appeared much older than the age of fifty-six, which the file had listed him as being. He had a *haggard* look to him, as if he was a man already resigned to the fate which lay ahead of him.

"Has anyone spoken to him yet?" Maguire asked.

"No, we didn't want to tip your hand," Casper replied.

"Thanks. Hey do me a favor," Maguire replied, reaching into his pocket and withdrawing a USB drive. Play that file when I give you a thumbs-up signal, and raise the heat up as well. Bring it up to about seventy-five."

Casper nodded to the man sitting at the terminal, who took the USB drive from Maguire. He then brought up a program on the computer and began making the temperature adjustments. After a few minutes, the temperature passed the seventy degree mark.

"OK, take me inside."

The two men walked out of the room and down the hall, stopping at another door. Casper punched a code into the terminal and the door unlocked.

"Good luck, Paddy."

Bin Salman looked up, as Maguire strode into the room, taking the seat across from the man and laying the leather portfolio on the desk.

"Who are you?"

"Who I am is not important," Maguire said. "But what I know is."

"What do you know?"

"I know who you are, I know who you know, I know that you have had favors done for you, and I know that you have done favors for others."

"So," the man said. "Everyone does favors."

"True," Maguire replied. "Except for when those favors cross the line into *treason*."

"Treason?" the man exclaimed, his eyes going wide in terror. "I haven't done anything treasonous."

The man looked past Maguire; to the unseen persons he knew watched him from behind the mirrored glass panel, an angry expression contorting his face.

"The King will hear about my treatment!" he shouted out. "How an infidel was allowed to question my loyalty."

Maguire quietly unzipped the portfolio and opened it up, then began leafing through the papers inside.

"Do you hear me?" bin Salman cried out. "I demand to be released immediately! I will see to it that your necks will all fall to the executioner's sword!"

Maguire picked up a photo from the file and slid it across the desk toward the man. Bin Salman gazed down at it, the color draining from his face.

The photo, courtesy of one of Mother's contacts at the CIA, showed Linehan shaking hands with Omar bin Salman down at the docks.

"If I were you, I'd start worrying about my own neck a little more," Maguire said stoically. "I don't think King Abdullah will be too happy to hear about some of the *favors* you have done, Omar."

"Where did you get this?"

"Does it really matter?" Maguire said, holding his clenched fist down low and raising his thumb up.

From an unseen speaker, the room was suddenly filled with the sound of voices.

"*Ahlan*?"

"*Assalamu alaykum*, my friend," a voice replied.

"*Walaykum salaam*, it is good to hear from you, my friend."

"Yes, but I am afraid I must discuss something with you that may be a problem. I am sure you will understand that it is best for all concerned if we are discrete in our conversation."

"Of course, please what is troubling you?"

"You remember your nephew, the one you said you were having problems with?"

"Yes, the one I sent to live with friends across town."

"Well, he ran away from home, and got hooked up with a bad crowd. Now he is in trouble and I don't know what to do with him."

"How much trouble?"

"The worst kind."

"Can you help him?"

"I can give him a ride to the bus station, but I don't know which one is the best. If I send him home, I think it will only make things worse."

"I will make arrangements with his other uncle, Qassem. He lives far to the east. It will be a much tougher life, but perhaps it will be better for him and the rest of the family. I will make the arrangements and have someone meet you at the bus station."

"He will be there shortly."

"*Shukran*, thank you, my friend."

"What are friends for, if not to help in times of distress, as you have done for me?"

"You are too kind; I take it that all has worked out well for the package I sent for you?"

"Yes, it will be useful for the protection of the poor, *Insha'Allah*, God willing."

"*Insha'Allah*, and thank you for watching over my family."

The call went dead.

"Where did you get this?"

"It's 2013 Omar; did you really think that your phone calls were still private?" Maguire asked. "All that matters is that I have it, and, more importantly, I know who and what the two of you are talking about."

"What is it that you want?" bin Salman asked.

"Answers," Maguire replied. "Just answers."

CHAPTER FIFTY

Southampton, Suffolk County, N.Y.
Friday, March 1st, 2013 – 7:46 a.m.

"Hello?" Melody said groggily into the cell phone.

"*Wakey, wakey*," Gen's cheery voice said on the other end of the phone.

"What time is it?"

"It's almost eight, time to drag your sorry butt out of bed."

"I *was* enjoying a pest free morning."

"Eh, they're highly overrated," Gen replied. "Besides, you need to start getting yourself back to work, slacker."

"Can't I start on Monday?"

"Look at it this way, you work one day and then you have the weekend off."

"Well aren't you the eternal pessimist this morning?"

"Just another service I cheerfully provide. Speaking of pest two, where is old hot stuff?"

"Right now? Probably somewhere in the Middle East."

"Aw, did you two love birds have a fight?" Gen asked.

"No, you *dork*; he flew over last night to do an interview. He's working, unlike *pest one*."

"Oh, and you think playing babysitter for some overzealous FBI agents isn't work?"

"How's that going?" Melody asked.

"Fine, now," Gen replied. "But I think they took everything that wasn't nailed down in Pope's office. God only knows what they took from his house."

"Anything critical to our operation?"

"Not that I know of," Gen said. "We had a bit of a go round over some files and such, but I reached out to your old friend at the Attorney General's Office. They graciously allowed us to copy our own paperwork before they took the originals. However, they did confiscate Pope's computer. They said that they would return it, after they had done a forensic audit of the files."

"Do we know anything more about what Pope may have been doing?" Melody asked.

"Not really. I mean there really wasn't anything that I would have deemed to be red flags. He attended all his usual meetings and met with several people regarding projects, but that was it. At least up until he took off."

"And he didn't talk to anyone about that beforehand?"

"No, that was completely out of the blue."

"Has there been any activity on his phone?"

"Nope," Gen replied. "According to what I was able to get from Tom Fitzsimmons, he's the FBI agent running things, the Bureau IT geeks say his cell phone went dark almost immediately after he took off."

"This is so crazy," Melody said. "It's like we were dealing with two different people."

"According to Fitzsimmons, it actually fits. People involved in this type of activity often live two different lives. This accounts for why people always seem so shocked when they hear about it. His secretary, Virginia, has really taken it hard."

"I would imagine. Was she able to add anything?"

"Not really," Gen replied. "I went over Pope's schedule with her for the last few months. She didn't see anything unusual. In fact the only thing she could not explain was an entry Pope had made on his personal day planner for Friday, February 15th. It just read *Eagle Diner 1:15 p.m.*"

"Well, I guess everyone needs to eat."

"Yeah, but you see, we checked and there is no listing for a diner named *Eagle* anywhere near here."

"Ah, so the plot thickens," Melody replied. "It makes me wonder what else he might have been involved in. I think we need to have the security folks launch an internal investigation into his activities going back, see if there may have been any other programs which might have been breached."

"I've already spoken to them about it. I know they have been assisting the Bureau people, but once there isn't a threat to that aspect of the investigation, I will have them go over all our programs to make sure they have not been compromised."

"That's my girl, always thinking."

"So when is James coming back?"

"Not sure, he said that he didn't know how long it would take. He promised to call when he was on his way back. All I know is that I am starting to go stir crazy in this house."

"Sounds like we need a girl's night out," Gen said.

"You know, that doesn't sound half bad," Melody replied. "What are you thinking?"

"Nothing extravagant, how about you, me and Mary go out for dinner and a few drinks tonight? Just get out of the house and *stretch our legs* a bit. I can call and see if Mary will be free. I should be back this afternoon."

"Oh, and you think James will go for that?"

"Does he have to know?" Gen asked. "Besides, it's not like we *won't* be surrounded by a ring of friggin' security. I figured we fly in, meet Mary, and then we come back home, long before he even knows we were gone."

"I don't know," Melody replied. "Let me think about it."

On the other end of the phone, she heard the distinctive sound of a chicken clucking.

"Oh, you're so mature," Melody said sarcastically.

"So what are you going to do now?" Gen asked.

"Well, I guess I'm going to have to get my sorry butt out of bed, now that you woke me up."

"I bet you can't wait to get back in the gym," Gen said.

"Don't even remind me about that," Melody replied. "I'll tell you what I am going to do first though. You mentioning that diner made me hungry for comfort food."

"That's a great plan," Gen replied. "No gym and bad food. I'm sure James will love going shopping with you, when you can't fit into anything."

"Ha, remind me just how funny that sounded when you hit your third trimester and you're craving junk food."

"Uh oh, bad connection gotta go, love ya....."

"Love ya too, chicky" Melody said with a laugh. "I'll make sure the kitchen stocks up on pork rinds and cupcakes."

CHAPTER FIFTY-ONE

Jeddah, Saudi Arabia
Friday, March 1st, 2013 – 3:17p.m. (*Eastern Standard Time +7 hrs*)

"You're not helping your cause here, Omar," Maguire said.

The two men had been playing verbal ping-pong for an hour, each trying to gauge what exactly the other one knew, suspected, or was unaware of.

"Please, I'm telling you everything that I know," bin Salman said. "I just did what was asked of me, I was following orders."

"Bullshit!" Maguire exploded. "You're fucking lying to me, you little shit and I have about had it up to here with your fucking excuses."

Maguire stood up, and began gathering the papers that were on the table, slowly placing them back into the portfolio.

"You know, maybe they were right," Maguire said. "Maybe you're just too fucking stupid to realize that you're out of your league here. Maybe you just need a wake-up call. Well congratulations, you just joined the major leagues, Omar."

"What do you mean?" the man said, panic creeping into his voice.

"Saudi Arabia and the United States have been friends for almost as long as Saudi Arabia has existed. That friendship goes all the way back to Ibn Saud himself. Do you honestly think that the King is going to allow *you* to come between that relationship? I've been given *carte blanche* to resolve this matter by the King himself, so that's what I'm going to do."

Maguire turned to look back in the direction of the mirrored window. He twirled his finger in a circular motion.

"Hook him up boys," Maguire said.

"What?" bin Salman cried out. "What do you mean?"

Immediately the door opened and two burly, uniformed men came in and seized bin Salman roughly.

"What's going on?" the man said, as he struggled in vain against the two officers.

"What's going on is that you've gotten on my last fucking nerve, you dumb shit. What you did in helping Linehan redirect that shipment was an act of providing *material support of terrorism*. You honestly think that Linehan is going to risk his life to save yours? Let me tell you how this works. Only one person gets the *get-out-of-jail-free* card, everyone else just gets screwed. You were just too dumb to realize that."

"I was just following orders!" bin Salman exclaimed.

"Yeah, you go ahead and stick with that answer," Maguire replied sarcastically. "Because it worked so well in Nuremberg, back in 1946."

The two men began to escort bin Salman out of the room.

"Wait, where are you taking me?"

"Right now?" Maguire asked. "You're going on a little cruise, courtesy of the USS Bataan. You'll probably *not* enjoy a few weeks sailing around the Mediterranean Sea, before they transfer you to your new living accommodation, and I use that term *very* loosely, at this wonderful little scenic resort called Camp Eagle in Tuszla, Bosnia."

"Wait, I'll tell you everything you want to know," bin Salman said pleadingly.

"Oh, I know you will, Omar," Maguire replied, as he led the way out of the room. "It just won't be too me."

"Please, I beg you, in the name of Allah. I can tell you everything about Linehan."

Maguire turned sharply.

"Fuck you, Omar, you had your chance and you wanted to play tough guy. So be a tough fucking guy. You won't last two fucking days on that ship before they have you pissing your pants and crying for your mommy, who'd probably come running, if she knew where the hell you were. The only problem is that, when we leave this room, you become a ghost, Omar. Someone who existed once, but doesn't anymore. Welcome to your new life."

"He's working with the Iranians," the man said and began sobbing.

Maguire paused in the doorway and slowly turned around to face bin Salman.

"What did you say?" he asked.

"The Iranians," Omar replied, his voice breaking. "Linehan is working with the Iranians."

Maguire motioned for the men to return bin Salman to the table and he sat back down across from him.

"I swear, Omar. If I even think that you're *thinking* about holding out on me, I'll start the interrogations myself, and, when I'm done with you, that ship will look like a fucking fantasy cruise. Do I make myself clear?"

Bin Salman hung his head and nodded somberly.

"From the beginning, and I mean first date beginning."

"I first met Linehan when he was assigned here back in 1998," bin Salman explained. "We worked on several projects together. He was a very nice man, but he held very deeply religious convictions which didn't make him too popular. But I got along with him and so I was often chosen to work with him."

"What kind of religious beliefs?"

"He is a devout Christian, and it sometimes clouds his thinking."

"How so?"

"He sees things differently, from religious points of view. He is not opposed to working with others to improve the lives of Christians in this area."

"Like the Iranians?" Maguire asked.

"Yes," bin Salman replied. "Like the Iranians, the Syrians, and whoever else he feels will help shield Christians in this region. Linehan sees things on a much deeper level. Theology drives much of what he does and says. He isn't above brokering deals with people he might not agree with, in the hope that his God will use it to His advantage."

"And you don't have a problem with that?"

"There is only one Allah to me," bin Salman said cautiously. "How He uses others is a mystery that I don't claim to understand."

"How did Linehan meet the Iranians?"

"Here," bin Salman replied. "He met them when he worked here. There was a warming up of relationships between the Kingdom and Iran. A *normalizing* of relationships if you will. A number of them were also involved in projects that included Linehan and me."

"What projects?"

"Nothing important really," bin Salman replied. "What was important was that Linehan engaged the Iranians in discussions which led to a *friendly* relationship between them. I thought they were playing with him, but he seemed to enjoy the discussions they had, whether it was politics, socio-economic issues, or religion."

"Then what happened?"

"After he left here, he went to Israel. We stayed in touch and he would often complain about the situation between the Israelis and Palestinians. I do not pretend to know what goes on there, it is much too difficult to understand all the political and religious differences. So I would just let him talk."

"What did he talk about?"

"Mostly he would complain that the Israelis needed to just pull-out and allow the Palestinians to live their lives without being occupied. He complained that the Jews had already caused so many problems in the world, and that it was no wonder why no one really liked them. In fact, he blamed all the suicide bombings in Jerusalem on the Jews, because they were an *occupying force* and that the suicide bombers were patriots, sending a message. Then, I remember one day, in 2002, when the Israeli Defense Force went into Bethlehem. He called me enraged; I had never heard him use such language before."

"What did he say?"

"He accused the Jews of being nothing more that war mongering savages, who were determined to crush out Christianity and its holiest places. He accused them of laying siege to the Church of the Nativity and using the Palestinians, who he claimed had sought sanctuary in a holy place, as an excuse to destroy it. I recall that we spoke several times during this period, and he was particularly upset by what he thought was the IDF's assassination of religious leaders and the mentally impaired."

Maguire remembered the incident very well, although his take on it was significantly different from Linehan's.

Operation Defensive Shield was a massive military operation in 2002 that was conducted by the IDF, during the course of the *Second Intifada*, the Palestinian uprising against Israeli occupation. It was the largest military operation in the West Bank since 1967 and was an attempt by the Israeli Army to stop the increasing deaths from terrorist attacks, especially by suicide bombings, by groups such as *Hamas* and the *Al-Aqsa Martyrs' Brigade*. The incident that had sparked the military operation was a suicide attack that occurred during the Passover Seder on March 27th at a hotel in the city of Netanya; when a Palestinian suicide bomber killed thirty.

On April 3rd, IDF forces entered Bethlehem. A special forces unit targeted the Church of the Nativity to deny it as a place of refuge, as it had been in the past. However, the unit arrived a half hour too late. Dozens of militants; members of the Fatah, Hamas, Palestinian Islamic Jihad and Palestinian Security Forces, had fled into the church and fortified it. Some 200 monks and other Palestinians, including Bethlehem's Governor, arrived at the site for different reasons. In response, the Vatican warned Israel not to damage the church, which marks the site of the birth of Jesus.

Israel claimed that those being held by the gunmen were hostages, but the monks claimed that they were *voluntary* hostages and had chosen to stay to express solidarity with the

Palestinians. Those seeking refuge at the church claimed that they had done so in order to flee the IDF. However, a senior Palestinian militant commander later said that "*the idea was to enter the church in order to create international pressure on Israel....We knew beforehand that there was two years' worth of food for 50 monks. Oil, beans, rice, olives. Good bathrooms and the largest wells in old Bethlehem.*"

The paratrooper brigade that laid siege to the church specialized in sniper operations. They were given the order to shoot anyone in the church carrying a gun, which resulted in several armed militants being killed by IDF personnel. In addition, the church bell-ringer was killed and an Armenian monk, who the IDF said looked armed, was seriously wounded. On May 10th the siege ended, with a deal seeing some militants deported to the Gaza Strip, and the rest exiled to Cyprus. Inside the church, the IDF discovered forty explosive devices, including some that had been booby trapped.

Once again, the criminals had perfectly orchestrated a plan that made the good guys look bad.

"Not long after that," bin Salman continued, "I remember him calling me and saying that he could not work there any longer. He left Tel Aviv and took a posting, working for the Coalition Provisional Authority Office, in Iraq."

"Do you recall any conversations with him during this time?" Maguire asked.

"Yes, he called me once and said that he had run into our old friend, Qassem."

"Who's Qassem?" Maguire asked.

"Qassem Husseini," bin Salman replied.

Maguire fought to control his response, taking a slow, deep breath. In the blink of an eye, this investigation had suddenly taken on an element with sinister implications.

"Major General Qassem Husseini?"

"Yes," the man replied.

Maguire felt a coldness grip his body and fought the instinct to shudder.

Major General Qassem Husseini was the commander of the Iranian Qods (Jerusalem) Force, a special forces unit of Iran's Revolutionary Guards that reported directly to the countries supreme leader, the Ayatollah. Qods was responsible for *extraterritorial* operations, which was a nice way of saying that they trained and maintained contact with fundamentalist terrorist groups through the Islamic world.

The Qods force was organized into eight different directorates based on geographic location. These oversaw operations around the globe, from North America to Russia and every region in between, including Iraq, an area that they had been particularly active in over the years. In fact, the origins of the unit could be traced back to the early 1980's, during the Iran-Iraq War. Back then, it provided support to the Kurd's fighting against Saddam Hussein.

Like all things in the Middle East, at the very heart was religion. Iran was a predominantly Shia religious country, as was Iraq. However, under Saddam Hussein, Iraq was controlled with an iron fist by the Sunni minority. The Iranians were certainly not above picking sides, when it behooved them, from a religious position.

After the attacks of September 11th, 2001 the United States sent a senior State Department official to Geneva to meet with

Iranian diplomats, acting under the direction of the Qods commander. The purpose was to establish a way for the two countries to collaborate on destroying the Taliban, which had targeted Shia Afghanis. This was instrumental in identifying and capturing high value Al Qaeda targets, as well as targeted bomb operations in Afghanistan. However, this period of cooperation came to an abrupt end in January, 2002, when then President, George W Bush, named Iran as part of the "Axis of evil" in his State of the Union address.

With the outbreak of the Iraq war, in 2003, the Qods Force was deployed to challenge the United State military presence in Iraq, which put 165,000 American troops along Iran's western border. They were also accused of flooding Iraq with EFP's, explosive formed projectiles, which fired a molten copper slug able to penetrate U.S. armor. It is estimated that this particular type of ordnance accounted for nearly twenty percent of American combat deaths in Iraq.

They remained an active participant in the Iraqi political scene, and were believed to have been instrumental in engineering the Iraqi coalition government, supporting the election of Iraqi Prime Minister Nuri Al-Maliki, who was a Shia. In 2008 they also mediated the ceasefire between the Iraqi Army and the Mahdi Army.   The activity in Iraq also earned the Qods commander a designation as a terrorist by the U.S. Government.

What was significantly more interesting to Maguire was the fact that, in recent years, they had been particularly active in Syria. Qassem Husseini was considered to be a brilliant tactician and had recently been sent to Syria, when the Assad regime was seen as losing control of the civil war against the rebels. The Qods force was deployed, along with elements of Hezbollah and militiamen from Iraq to reinforce the Syrian Army. Judging from reports coming out of that country, it appeared that they were having an effect.

"How does Linehan know Husseini?"

"They first met here. Qassem was a member of a delegation that the Iranians sent over. He is a very charming man," bin Salman said. "That is, once you get past the *ruthless* part."

"What did they discuss?"

"Mostly religion, as I recall. "Despite their differences, they had, what I would call, a mutual respect for one another. In fact, I know that he was deeply troubled the U.S. labeled Qassem as a terrorist. He'd been part of the Geneva delegation and believed that the U.S. had not only lost an opportunity to normalize relations with Iran, but had stabbed them in the back after getting what they wanted."

"Did they have any other dealings?"

"Not *officially*," bin Salah said. "I know that when he was in Iraq, there were several meetings that *didn't* occur. The Iranians exerted tremendous influence in Iraq, and the two of them met on several occasions to try and work things out. He always complained that he felt like he was being used by the government, but then they did whatever they wanted."

"That was it?"

"No, they met again when he was in Syria. Qassem has very close ties to Assad."

"The same Assad your nephew was sent to fight against?"

Bin Salman looked up at Maguire, but was met with a cold, impassive gaze, as if he was staring into the unblinking eyes of a statue. Maguire could see the struggle going on in the man's head, as he battled with the truth and his inherent need for self-preservation.

Maguire decided to make the choice easier. He reached down, grabbing the portfolio and began to get up.

"Yes," the man cried out. "I reached out to Prescott and asked if anything could be done to protect him. I know my nephew, he is not a fighter. He would have been killed as soon as he stepped foot onto the battlefield."

"And then what happened?"

"Honestly, I don't know. I told him what happened and he said that he would reach out to Qassem. He would see if they could locate him and get him out of harm's way, but he said that it would probably be expensive. A short time later he contacted me and said that it could be done. He gave me an amount and a bank account number."

"That's the last you heard about it?" Maguire asked.

"Yes, I swear," the man replied. "That was until he called me and told me that my nephew was in the United States."

"So why did Linehan ask you to redirect that arms shipment?"

"He believes that Assad is the only real safety for Christians in Syria. He knows what is going on there, knows that the rebel fighters have been infiltrated by Islamic terrorists. He knew what they were doing to the Christian minorities in Syria. When they approached him about setting up the deal, he reached out to Qassem and struck another deal."

"What kind of deal?"

"Qassem would make sure the arms didn't arrive in Syria. The Iranians and the Sudanese have a military cooperation pact. The Iranians are using the Sudan as a terror training site. They've even been smuggling weapons out of Libya and into Sudan. From what I know Qassem's Qods Force brought in a lot of old Russian equipment, including SA-24, surface-to-air missiles, and RPG-7, rocket propelled grenade launchers, from Libya and into Northern Darfur where they have a Revolutionary Guard facility."

"Small arms don't really seem to be that much of a deal to me, nor would I think they would be that big of an issue to the Iranians," Maguire replied.

"No, but Prescott believed they would be to the Sudanese. In return for the arms shipment, the Iranians would ensure that the Janjaweed would not only stop harassing the Christian missionaries, but would provide protection to them as well."

"So he had you send the shipment west instead of east."

"I was in charge of overseeing things, but the Iranians actually did the transport. The Red Sea has become a *dangerous* place in recent years. The Israelis know the Iranians are trying to establish control and they aren't happy about it. They have been conducting a lot of intelligence gathering in the area, and have thrown their support behind South Sudan. When South Sudan broke away in 2011 and established their own country, they claimed much of Sudan's oil reserves. This undermined the Sudanese government, and almost led to a coup, which the government believes Israel orchestrated. So they are happy to have the Iranians there, and have provided access to port facilities. This now gives the Iranians access to the backdoor of Lebanon, Palestine and Syria."

"Not to mention Israel," Maguire replied. "So what did you get out of it?"

"I got a *handling fee* from the Iranians for my trouble."

"How?" Maguire asked.

"They wired it into a Swiss bank account," Omar replied.

"So what was in it for the Iranians?"

"One thing that Prescott and Qassem agreed on was that a nuclear Israel was too powerful. Prescott believed that the United States had been providing material help for too long and that it needed to end. The Iranians were worried about the increasing number of air strikes, in Syria and Palestine. They know that their own weapons program is at risk, especially since Israel has been so vocal about striking Iran before they can obtain the capacity to build a nuclear weapon. The 2007 bombing of the Syrian reactor at *Deir ez-Zor* was a wake-up call for them. They even lost one of their Sudanese missile production sites to an air strike in 2012. On top of that, I know Qassem has a very personal ax to grind with Israel."

"What makes you say that?" Maguire asked.

"Did you hear about the assignation of Hassan Shateri?" bin Salman asked.

"Yeah, he was killed in Syria by the rebels."

"He was Qassem's 2nd in command and he doesn't believe that the rebels pulled this off by themselves. He believes that Israel was behind it. It seems that Shateri was killed in a targeted assassination somewhere between Damascus and Beirut."

"Someone got lucky," Maguire replied.

"Yes, but word is that Qassem was supposed to be the one traveling. He was going to Aleppo to get a first-hand look when he was summoned back to Iran at the last minute. Shateri went on his behalf."

"So someone has an inside track regarding the goings-on at Husseini's shop."

"It would seem so. Anyway, he is supposed to be enraged and looking for revenge."

"So how was Linehan going to help?"

"I'm not sure, he didn't get into details," bin Salman said. "I'm being honest. All I know is that the Iranians were extremely frustrated with Israel's *Iron Dome* missile defense system. He said that he could give them what he called a *game changer,* something that would level the playing field. Prescott believed that it would bring an end to the Israeli military domination in the region."

Dragons Breath, Maguire thought. *So that was what he was up to.*

"Where was that exchange supposed to take place?"

"I don't know," the man replied. "That was something he apparently had worked out with Qassem."

"So after the arms shipment you heard nothing else?"

"No, not until the call about my nephew," bin Salman replied. "Please, what is going to happen to me? I have told you everything I know."

"For now, nothing," Maguire said. "You are going to pretend as if nothing ever happened; we never had this little chat. If anyone asks, you went to attend a meeting. But remember this, the men who brought you here will be watching every move you make, monitoring every conversation you have, and tracking every call you place. When you are out to eat, they'll know what you're going to have, even before you place your order. If at any moment you deviate from the norm, if you try to contact anyone involved to warn them, your family will be told of your tragic, *accidental* death. The only thing is Omar, you *won't* be dead. Although after several days, you will wish you were. Do you understand?"

The color was gone from the man's face and he gulped hard before answering.

"Yes," was all he said when he found his voice.

"Good," Maguire replied. "Then my work is done here. Although your *meeting* will continue for a bit longer, as I am sure my colleagues from the *Al Mukhabarat* have their own questions to ask of you. I remind you, that it would be in your best interests to maintain the same level of transparency with them. Since my country and yours has such a long standing relationship, they have the same options available to them should they sense that you are withholding any information from them."

"I understand," bin Salman replied.

"Smart man, Omar," Maguire said, as he picked up the portfolio. "We'll be in touch."

Maguire walked out of the room, as two men in suits entered. Omar's day was about to become a whole lot more unhappier.

"What do you think?" Casper said, as he met Maguire in the hallway.

"I think it *really* sucks to be him," Maguire replied, "but he told us what he knows. I didn't see any deception."

"What do you think Linehan promised the Iranians?"

"That, my friend, is the *million dollar question*," Maguire said.

It wasn't that he was trying to deceive his friend, but the balance of power in the Middle East was a very *delicate* thing. Dragon's Breath was a program that was designed to protect the lives of U.S. military personnel. If it became known, all of America's close *friends,* as well as the acquaintances, would be beating down the door to try and get access to it. The more people who knew about it, the more there was a chance that someone would engineer a way to defeat it.

"So what will you guys do with him now?" Maguire asked, trying to deflect the conversation into a new area.

"Well, he is a member of the royal family, even if distant. The King does still believe in loyalty, to a degree. Besides, it would not be the first time a member of the royal family engaged in *inappropriate* behavior. Once your government no longer has a need for him, he will be given the option of *retiring* quietly. What happens after that...?" Casper said, the words trailing off.

Maguire nodded his head; he understood what the man was implying. The harsh reality was that the world was a dangerous place and accidents happened all the time.

"Can you stay for dinner?" Casper asked.

"Depends on just how good the *Al Mukhabarat* expense account is," Maguire replied.

"It's nice to know that, in a world where chaos reigns, some things never change, Paddy."

CHAPTER FIFTY-TWO

Jeddah, Saudi Arabia
Saturday, March 2nd, 2013 – 1:03 a.m. (*Eastern Standard Time +7 hrs*)

"Hey, ladies," Maguire said, as he peaked into the cockpit. "I'm so sorry to have kept you waiting."

"No problem, sir," Mann replied from the pilots seat. "It actually worked out pretty good; we were both able to get some sleep. Then someone sent us over a catering truck from the air force base, didn't they, Rene?"

"You don't say," Maguire replied with a smile.

"At first I thought Kat and I were in deep shit," co-pilot Rene Ashcroft said, as she finished securing the bulkhead door. "They pulled up in a motorcade. But then they started unloading trays of food, you'd think they were feeding the damn King."

"They must have gotten word that the best looking pilots in all of Saudi Arabia were camped out at their back door."

"Roger that," Kat replied. "Where too, sir?"

"Time to go home, Hurricane," Maguire replied.

"You heard the man, Rene," Mann said, as she began flipping switches on the instrument panel. "Grab your gun and bring in the cat."

Maguire made his way to the back, and took a seat in one of the leather recliners.

The Gulfstream engines came to life and the plane slowly made its way along the tarmac. A few moments later it made the turn onto the runway, where it paused a moment, waiting for clearance from the tower. Then the engines came up to full thrust and the jet began racing forward.

Maguire glanced out the window, watching the runway lights flash by. Then the nose lifted up effortlessly and the jet hurtled into the night sky. Below him he heard the sound of the landing gear retracting into the belly of the jet.

He glanced down at his watch and did the math. It was just after six o'clock back on the east coast. Maguire picked up the satellite phone and placed a call. He waited as he listened for the phone to connect.

"Hello," Mother said.

"I just got done," Maguire replied.

"That was a late one. Hope Uncle Omar's still in one piece."

"Casper wanted to play catch-up over a bottle of thirty year old whiskey, who was I to say no."

"Every cause has to have a martyr, huh?" Mother replied. "Did you learn anything useful?"

"Linehan is in bed with the Iranians."

"The Iranians? Are you sure?"

"Yep. According to bin Salman, Linehan is good friends with Qassem Husseini."

"Are you shitting me?"

"No, and I was right, this is about religion. At least it is from Linehan's perspective. I'm sure the Iranian's could give a rat's ass about it, they're just using *helping him* as a pretext for getting something in return."

"Dragon's Breath?"

"Apparently so," Maguire replied.

"What insight did he share on our *misguided* deputy secretary of state?"

"From what Omar said, Linehan thinks that U.S. policy in the Middle East is screwed up. He is seeing things through his own rose colored glasses. In his world, Israel is the big threat and U.S. aid is what is causing the rise in tensions. He sees the rebels in Syria as a threat to Christians, and he's right. The only problem is that he seems to ignore the problems on the other side."

"The enemy of my enemy is my friend," Mother said, quoting an old Arab proverb.

"Precisely," Maguire replied. "Linehan sees things in a skewed sense of black and white. The rebels pose a threat to Christians, so we should back Assad. There is some merit to his position on the rebels, but I'd be disinclined to give old Assad a pass on his atrocities."

"So what was up with the arms shipment?"

"It's sort of circuitous, but the bumper sticker version is that Linehan arranged for bin Salman's nephew to get plucked out of Syria by the Iranians. Then, when the arms shipment transfer came up, he and the Iranians made a pact. The Iranians would pick-up the weapons and transport them across the Red Sea to their port in the Sudan. They would go to the Janjaweed and the Iranians would ensure, as a way of thanks, that the Janjaweed would not only cease their attacks, but would actually provide protection to the Christians working in the Sudan.

"And for their diligent *humanitarian* work, the Iranians would get our latest military technology," Mother said. "That seems like an awfully high price to me."

"Depends on what your motivation is," Maguire replied. "Linehan seems to have deep seeded resentment to the Israelis. He blames them for a lot of the troubles in the region. So maybe giving Dragon's Breath to the Iranians, who support Assad, was his way of evening things out."

"So why not just give it to them direct, why use a courier like Dawai?"

"I gotta believe that with all the saber rattling Mahmoud Ahmadinejad has been doing lately, the Iranians, especially the Qods Force commander, are under an intense microscope."

"I guess it sort of makes sense in the *big picture* scheme of things," Mother said. "Take a low level ghost like Yusef Dawai, who is used to coming and going on assumed identities, let him do the pick-up, while everyone's attention is diverted someplace else."

"Exactly," Maguire replied. "Then Dawai flies back to the Sudan and he meets up with the Iranians, back at one of the training camps, to make the delivery."

"I imagine the Iranians are not going to be overly pleased to come out on the short end of this deal."

"No, I would think that they will probably *insist* on Linehan delivering what he promised. That is, if they haven't done so already."

"Which means we need to locate your girlfriend's missing executive and make sure he doesn't have a back-up."

"I'd also suggest that you get in contact with your friends over at the NSA and have them pay particular interest in any Iranian signals traffic," Maguire said. "If they think they have been screwed over by Linehan, they'll want to exact their pound of flesh."

"I'll make some calls when we get off the phone."

"While you're at it, I'd have them start monitoring the Israelis as well."

"You think they know something is going on with the Iranians?"

"I *know* they know something is going on. Whether they know what that something is, I'm not sure. But if they figure it out, we might have a blood bath on our soil and that won't bode well for anyone."

"*Jesus H. Christ*," Mother said. "That's all we need is a shooting war between those two."

"Ahmadinejad's always talking about the return of the 12th Iman, the Mahdi, and how he believes that it is his duty to hasten his return."

"That's that *end time's* bullshit, isn't it?"

"You really should have paid more attention to those briefing reports," Maguire said.

"Why? I had bright, young tadpoles like you to do that for me."

"Yeah, it's that end times shit. Anyway, President *Warm & Fuzzy* has repeatedly stated Israel should be wiped off the map. I remember when he spoke to the United Nations at the General Assembly in 2005. He claimed that during his speech he was in an 'aura of light' and 'felt a change in the atmosphere during which time no one present could blink their eyes'."

"He always has been a bit of a goofy little fucker," Mother replied. "We should have taken him out when we had the chance back in 1980."

"Yeah, be that as it may, he seems to enjoy talking in these apocalyptic terms and portraying the West as the Great Satan. But at the end of the day, this goofy *sonofabitch* truly believes that it is his duty to prepare the world for the coming Mahdi, by way of a world totally under Muslim control."

"That's a serene little picture your painting."

"And his term ends in August, think he might enjoy being the spark that plunges the world into chaos? Cause I bet that is exactly what the Israelis are thinking right now."

"I'll have them monitor both sides," Mother replied. "I'll let you know if they pick-up any chatter. I'll also fill Mays in on what you have found out."

"Sounds like a plan," Maguire said.

"What are you going to do now?"

"Sleep. I think I've earned it."

"You young kids," Mother replied. "You've got no stamina."

"Goodnight, Mom," Maguire said and ended the call.

He looked out the window. Below him, the moon reflected off the waters of Red Sea. It was such a beautiful sight; in such a deadly place.

He rubbed his eyes and picked the phone back up. He punched the number for Melody's cell and waited for it to connect. It rang several times before going to the voicemail.

"Hey, angel, it's me. I'm done and on my way back. It's about six thirty your time. I probably won't be home until sometime tomorrow morning. If you get this in the next thirty minutes, give me a call back. Otherwise, I'm probably going to try and get some sleep. Love ya."

Maguire ended the call.

CHAPTER FIFTY-THREE

Southampton, Suffolk County, N.Y.
Saturday, March 2nd, 2013 – 11:43 a.m.

"Welcome home, cowboy," Melody said, as she looked up from the magazine she had been reading.

"You don't know how glad I am to be home," he replied, dropping the bag he was carrying and taking the seat next to her on the couch.

"Did you have a rough trip?"

"Let's just say that it reminded me of the old days, and showed me just how *not* young I am anymore."

"Oh, I wouldn't exactly say that," Melody replied.

She leaned over, wrapping her arms around him and gave him a kiss.

"Mmmm, someone's frisky," he replied.

"I never stopped being frisky," Melody said, as she climbed up onto his lap.

"When is your follow-up with Dr. Rothman?"

"Next Wednesday," Melody said. "Why?"

"Because we're not doing anything till you get cleared, that's why."

"Seriously?"

"Do I look like I'm joking?"

Melody rolled her eyes, and climbed off of him. She sat back down and picked up the magazine she had discarded.

"Seriously?" he replied.

Melody glanced over at him and stuck her tongue out.

"Oh that's very mature," he replied. "I wonder who you learned that from?"

"Aw look, mommy and daddy are fighting," Gen said, as she jumped into the chair across from them.

"Wanna be sent to your room, little girl?" Melody asked.

"In fifteen minutes," Gen replied.

"Why fifteen minutes?" Melody asked.

"Cause that's when my little *Teutonic* knight is coming back," she replied with a mischievous smile. "He had to run over to Peter's to get some paperwork."

"At least *someone* in this house will be having fun," Melody replied, shooting an angry look over at Maguire.

Maguire wrapped his arm around Melody and pulled her next to him.

"Listen up, goofy. I almost lost you once. I'm not going to do anything that might jeopardize your health. If that makes me the bad guy, so be it."

Melody folded her arms across her chest and scrunched up her lips.

"The pouty brat look is so unbecoming," he replied.

"I miss you," she said.

"I miss you too," he replied. "But I also love you and don't want anything to happen to you."

"I know," Melody said dejectedly.

"I'll tell you what, as soon as Dr. Rothman clears you, you and I will fly to Paris for more than a quick weekend."

Melody's eyes went wide in surprise.

"Really?" she asked.

"Really," he replied.

"Oh, James, thank you," she said excitedly, climbing back up on his lap and wrapping her arms around his neck.

Across from him, Gen smiled and gave him a thumbs-up.

"By the way," Maguire said. "Where were you last night? I tried to call."

"Well," Melody said hesitantly. "We, uh."

"Oops, look at the time," Gen said, as she began to get up from the chair. "Gotta run."

"Sit back down," Maguire said. "I'm getting the impression that one of you was the others *accomplice*."

"We got hungry," Melody said.

"Who's *we*?" he asked.

"Me, Gen and Mary," she replied, smiling nervously.

"You've got to be kidding me," Maguire said.

"We had the *men in black* with us," Gen protested. "Besides that, Mary had her security detail as well."

"It really wasn't as bad as you think, cowboy," Melody, taking his hand in hers. "We flew in, met Mary, had dinner, and came right home. It wasn't as if we were out alone."

"Mel,…"

She held her finger up to his lips.

"Shhh! Look at me, I'm fine. I'm not some delicate China doll you put up on a shelf to gather dust. I'm not going to do anything dumb. I promise."

"The two of you are going to be the death of me," Maguire said.

Suddenly the phone in his pocket began to ring.

Maguire reached in and removed it from his pocket then checked the number.

"Damn, I have to take this," he said.

"Saved by the phone," Gen said with a giggle.

Melody slid off his lap and began talking to Gen as Maguire got up and walked over to the window.

"Hey, Kurt, what's going on?"

"Sorry to disturb you, Commissioner," Silverman said. "But I thought you'd want to know this."

"What have you got?"

"I just spoke to my buddy, Tom Fitzsimmons, down in the D.C. field office. He says that Wilson Pope's body was found."

"Where?" Maguire asked.

"Patuxent Research Refuge," Silverman replied. "It's just south of Fort Meade."

"Who found him?"

"Supposedly a Fish and Wildlife Officer, who was on patrol at some place called Hobbs Pond. She spotted a car that was parked back in the woods, off an access road, and she found him a short distance later, floating in the water."

"Fuck me," Maguire replied. "They have a cause of death?"

"Nothing official, but the exit wound would indicate that it is fairly unlikely that it was natural causes."

"Suicide?"

"Doubtful," Silverman replied. "Entry wound was to the *back* of the head. No weapon was recovered."

"A hit?"

"That's the premise they're operating under. It seems as if someone didn't want him talking."

"Two can keep a secret, if one is dead."

"Exactly."

"Any chance someone might have seen or heard something?"

"From the way he was talking, I doubt it. It's about twelve thousand acres of woods, rivers and streams. The fact that he was even found is amazing. Realistically, the *diligent* officer was probably looking for a place to catch a nap and stumbled upon it by accident."

"What a fucking mess," Maguire replied.

"It does make you wonder," Silverman replied.

"I'm in no short supply of wonder at the moment, Kurt. What I need are answers."

"Sorry, can't help you there."

"I know," Maguire said.

"Oh, there is at least one glimmer of good news," Silverman replied. "My buddy said that when the techies went through that microchip they discovered that there were a number of pages that were corrupted."

"What do you mean?"

"Well, according to them, when they decoded everything there were some portions of the data that were unreadable. They think that something screwed up during the upload. Chances are, even if they had been able to access it, the data would have been rendered useless."

"You don't think that could have happened in the accident?" Maguire asked.

"No," Silverman replied. "Those things are pretty robust. I'd say the tech gremlin got to it long before the car did."

'Unbelievable," Maguire said, shaking his head. "I appreciate the call, Kurt. Let me know if you hear anything else."

"Will do, Commissioner."

Maguire ended the call. His mind was racing as he tried to digest the information that he'd just been told.

Gregor had arrived and was now sitting next to Gen. The three of them were having a conversation about baby furniture as Maguire walked back over to the couch and sat down. He didn't relish the thought of having to share the news he had just learned. Immediately, Melody sensed that something was right.

"What's wrong, James?" Melody asked.

He looked at her, then over at Genevieve. There was no easy way to say it.

"Wilson Pope is dead."

"What?" Melody exclaimed, as Gen let out a gasp.

"That was Kurt Silverman from the FBI, he spoke to one of the agent's in D.C.," Maguire replied. "They found Pope's body in Maryland; someplace called the Patuxent Research Refuge."

Gen began to cry as Gregor wrapped his arm around her shoulders.

"Who found him?" Gregor asked.

"Some Fish & Wildlife officer," Maguire said. "During a patrol."

"What do they think caused it?" Melody asked, even though she instinctively knew what was coming.

"Well, it wasn't old age, angel."

"Dragon's Breath?"

Maguire nodded his head somberly.

"Shit," she exclaimed, lowering her head into her hands.

Maguire gently rubbed her back, letting her come to terms with the news. Across from him, Gregor was trying to provide the same support to Gen.

"Does this mean it's over?" Melody asked.

"I don't know, babe," Maguire said. "I assume that whoever did this, knew that if Pope was caught he would talk and I don't think that was a risk they were willing to take."

"All this over a file," Melody said.

"Well the good news is that the file was apparently corrupted."

"What do you mean?" Gen asked.

"According to Kurt, when the techs downloaded the program, they found several areas where the data wasn't accessible."

"All of these deaths, for a program that could never have even been used," Melody said.

"It appears that way, angel," Maguire replied. "The only question that remains is what happened to the original file?"

"It wasn't at GDL," Gen said, dabbing at her eye with a tissue. "I was there when they went through the place. There was no hard printout. I guess he could have had it at home and they didn't tell me."

"How good was Pope with computers?" James asked. "I mean could he have actually scanned the hard copy and then uploaded it himself?"

"I doubt it," Gen replied. "He was adequate with computers, but he never struck me as an IT geek."

"Which means that someone had to help him," Melody said.

"Yeah, but not just anyone," Gen said. "Whoever did this, the copying and uploading unto the microchip, had access to someone with serious computer skills."

"Could the GDL IT department do it?"

"Sure," Gen replied. "But they didn't."

"How can you be so sure?"

"First, it would have broken security protocols," she said. "There's a reason that all the files are personally encoded. They cannot be duplicated without approval."

"Who's approval?"

Melody raised her hand.

"Any request for the duplication of *any* encoded materials must be first submitted to, and approved by, the head of the IT department," Melody replied. "Then it is sent to me, and I have to sign off on it."

"What would they do in your absence?" James asked.

"Gen would be authorized for the period of my absence."

"What if Pope tried to circumvent it? I mean he does pull a lot of weight, doesn't he?"

"The head of IT reports directly to me," Gen said. "Besides, the Bureau guys put everyone in the IT department through a lie detector test."

"So he would have had to have gone outside GDL?"

"Yeah," Gen replied.

"What about any disgruntled former IT people?"

"None," she replied. "You should take a look at their salary and benefits package. I think over the last ten years we have lost less than a handful of people, and most of them went to either the National Security Agency or the Department of Defense."

Maguire leaned back against the couch and rubbed his eyes. This case had taken so many twists and turns, yet he still didn't have that last piece of evidence that he needed to go after Linehan, something which would directly link the man to Dragon's Breath.

Will I get it? he wondered.

The body count currently stood at three, and the last man standing was G. Prescott Linehan.

"I've got to call Rich," Maguire said.

He leaned over and kissed Melody. Then he got up and walked into the small study that sat off the salon. He pulled out his cell phone and made the call.

"Feel good to be home?" Rich said when he answered the phone.

"Yes and no," Maguire replied. "I liked seeing Melody's face, but I'm going to have to see yours again."

"That hurts," Rich said. "And after all I've done for you."

"That's the problem. You did this to me. I was happy being retired."

"You'd have just grown old and fat living in comfort. Think of this as me prolonging your life by giving it purpose."

"Another few months of this *purpose* and I'll have to start buying my aspirin by the case load."

"Geez, and here I thought you SEAL's were supposed to be tough," Rich replied. "How did your interview go?"

"It was enlightening, to say the least."

"I hate when you use that word," Rich replied. "Nothing good ever comes out of you being *enlightened*."

"Now who's whining?" Maguire asked, and then proceeded without giving Rich a chance to respond. "It seems as if our friend, G. Prescott Linehan, has his fingers in a lot of proverbial dams."

"The uncle implicated him?"

"Yes and no," Maguire replied. "The uncle gave him up as the one who boosted our terrorist. He also said that he had reached out to Linehan to see if he could use his contacts to get the little shit-head out of Syria when he first got sent there."

"So we at least have that."

Yeah, but it gets a lot more complicated, from the national security standpoint. There are a couple of tiny problems."

"I can't wait to hear this."

"Linehan is hooked up with the Iranians," Maguire said. "It seems that his friend is the Qods Force commander, Qassem Husseini."

"You're shitting me?" Rich said.

"Nope, he met him when he was assigned in Saudi Arabia. Anyway, it seems as if they share some common views when it comes to the political situation in the Middle East."

"Such as?"

"Neither of them are apparently big fans of Israel. Linehan apparently drank the Kool-Aid. Now he sees Israel as the big bad bully in the region. Husseini has a more personal vendetta. He believes they are behind the rebels in Syria and that they popped his number two guy on the road to Damascus. A high explosive *conversion*, if you will."

"So how is he tied up with the microchip?"

"Linehan didn't want the weapons shipment going to the rebels in Syria, because of what they are doing to the Christian minority there. His old buddy Qassem had them re-routed to the Sudan, where he promised they would be used to protect the local missionaries. The microchip was apparently going to be Linehan's thank you. Our dead Sudanese guy was supposed to play the part of the messenger service."

"The uncle admitted that?"

"Not in so many words," Maguire replied. "And that's where the problems begin. All Linehan referred to was something he called a *game changer*, but he never got into any specifics. You and I both know a decent legal aid attorney could drive a truck through that. His contact with Husseini may seem suspect to us, but at least at some point, it appears to have been sanctioned by the higher ups in the government."

"So we need to find someone to tie it directly to Linehan."

"That would be problem number two," Maguire said. "I just got a call from Kurt Silverman. It seems as if our missing GDL exec went for a face down swim in a wildlife refuge in Maryland, courtesy of a well-placed shot."

"Oh for crying out loud," Rich replied, his voice filled with frustration.

"That about sums it up."

"So now what?" Rich asked.

"Unless he has a come to Jesus moment and falls on the sword, I don't see Linehan admitting to the microchip. That leaves us with the providing material aid to a terrorist and that we do have him on. I suggest we get in contact with the U.S. Attorney on Monday and present them with what we have. Let them go after him."

"Makes sense," Rich replied. "There's only one problem."

"What's that?" Maguire asked.

"Linehan is coming here tomorrow. He's attending a *Friends of Israel* fundraiser in Manhattan with McMasters and the Israeli Foreign Minister, Levi Abram."

"I thought the Secretary of State was supposed to be attending that," Maguire said.

"She was, until the Israeli prime minister flew into *Andrews* at the last minute," Rich said, referring to the Air Force Base in Maryland that serves as home to Air Force One. "They're sharing a weekend *retreat* with POTUS. The three of them are up at Camp David, so I guess Linehan was tagged."

"Jesus, Rich, if the Iranians think Linehan screwed them over, they might be inclined to settle the score."

"You're talking about a potential blood bath," Rich replied.

"Can you think of a better place? They can get both the guy that stiffed them and the Israeli foreign minister."

"I need to call the C.O. of Intel," Rich replied. "They are going to have to redo the site survey and increase the security posts."

"I'll get in touch with my source and see if they have picked up any chatter. I'm also going to go have myself another chat with Yoni and see if there was anything he *omitted* the last time around."

"You know where to find him?"

"Oh yeah, if the foreign minister is in town, I know where he'll be."

"Be careful, I don't know how many more diplomatic *incidents* I can handle."

"Hey, it's only the beginning of month number three," Maguire said. "We still have nine more to go in your freshman year."

"I hate you."

"Yeah I know, but Mary loves me, and that's all that counts. Gotta go, talk to you later."

CHAPTER FIFTY-FOUR

Water Mill, Suffolk County, N.Y.
Saturday, March 2nd, 2013 – 7:11 p.m.

Maguire pulled the Mustang out onto Meadow Lane making a right turn. It felt odd to be heading there again after all this time.

It's been almost five years, he thought.

He turned left onto Halsey Neck and began navigating the back roads of Southampton, until he reached Montauk Highway where he turned left, heading east. The ride itself was only about ten miles, but it gave him just enough time to reflect on the past, on her.

He'd first seen her at the Park Lane Hotel. She was standing post outside the suite that the prime minister was staying in and looked like she had a broom handle firmly stuck up her ass. He'd even commented to Yoni about her, who simply shrugged his shoulders and declared "she's new." The next morning, when the prime minister went for a jog in Central Park, she still had the broom handle, although Maguire couldn't imagine how she had managed to hide it in the form fitting running outfit. For the next several days their paths would cross, and he found himself drawn to her, like a moth to the proverbial flame.

When the UN General Assembly session came to a close, Yoni invited him out for their annual *Wheel's-Up* bash. It was an annual party they threw for themselves after the prime minister's plane had departed JFK Airport. He'd been the only non-Israeli to ever be invited, which miffed some people, but no one was about to argue when Yonatan Ashkenazi invited someone.

Maguire had been assigned as the Intelligence Division's *number one* for the prime minister, meaning that he was never more than a few feet away. It was not always an easy assignment and involved finding a delicate balance with the visiting countries security apparatus. The two men's mutual special ops backgrounds helped to quickly erase any problems.

As Yoni and Maguire sat having a beer next to the pool, he watched her *unwinding* with the other members of the security detail on the other side. Occasionally he would catch her glancing over in his direction, but she would quickly turn away. He, on the other hand, could not help but stare at her. The bikini she was wearing seemed to light up next to her tanned, olive skin, accentuating every curve and her long black hair was draped playfully over her shoulders. Her stride was measured, purposeful, with no wasted movement. She prowled along the edge of the pool like a wild cat, graceful and yet very much lethal.

As Maguire watched, she glanced over at him, but this time, instead of turning away, she smiled. She was absolutely beautiful and he was hooked.

"Be careful, Paddy," Yoni said cautiously. "That one could kill you with just a word."

"Yeah, but what a way to go," Maguire said, raising his beer in a mock toast.

I guess in a way she had, he thought, as his mind raced back to that moment at the houseboat.

No other word has quite the same sting as *goodbye*, when it comes from the lips of someone you love.

Maguire was pulled back from his thoughts as the car came to a stop just outside the gate of the house on Mohawk Ave.

"Can I help you?" a voice demanded from the small speaker.

"Tell Yoni that Paddy is here to see him," Maguire replied.

Maguire gazed up in the direction of the house, where he knew the unseen snipers already had him in their crosshairs. A moment later the gate in front of him slowly began to open and the three massive bollards, just behind the gate, began to retract into the ground.

"Proceed slowly up the driveway on the left," the voice replied.

When the gate opened fully, he headed up the drive, bearing to the left, on the road that took him away from the main house and toward where the security personnel stayed. As Maguire pulled up to the building he saw Ashkenazi step outside. He parked the car and got out, walking over to the man.

"Paddy," he said. "What a surprise. You should have called."

"This conversation wasn't suitable for a phone call, Yoni," Maguire replied.

"I see, shall we sit or walk?"

"I could use a nice walk. I've spent entirely too much time in the air lately."

"Really? Well I hope that it was somewhere nice and warm."

"Oh, it was warm alright," Maguire said tersely. "But your definition of nice might be a bit different than mine."

When they were beyond earshot range Maguire turned to face the man.

"So you want to tell me what the fuck you really know, or we going to play this bullshit about vultures with video cameras?"

Yoni stared at Maguire, gauging what he had just said, trying to figure out how to play this.

"Where did you fly to?" Ashkenazi asked.

"Let me save us a whole bunch of pissing on each other's backs and calling it rain. Does the name Qassem Husseini ring any fucking bells, or is that above your pay grade too, buddy?"

Yoni turned and began slowly walking along the path.

"I'll tell you what, why don't I just play this game of *guess what I think*. If you think I'm full of shit, you turn and walk back to the house, then I'll go home. But if I'm not full of shit, you better be fucking honest with me or we are going to have a problem that Tel Aviv and D.C. are *not* going to be able to handle."

Yoni nodded and continued walking toward the edge of the property, which overlooked Mecox Bay. He sat down on a bench near the dock and stared out over the water, watching the lights from houses flicker in the distance. Maguire took the seat next to him.

"I think you guys have been monitoring the Sudanese and Iranians for some time. You both want the same thing, control of the Red Sea. I think someone put two and two together when you saw Linehan meeting with the same people and I think you figured out that he was in bed with them. So you started monitoring him and one of his accounts gets a healthy infusion of funds, but then there is a transfer of some of it into a known Qods account. So now you know you are onto something. So you pull out all the stops and begin aggressively monitoring him, which is how I think you learned that he and Husseini were close. It's also how I think you learned that Husseini was going to Aleppo. Only surprise, he zagged instead of zigged, and you ended up capping his number two. How am I doing so far?"

Yoni reached into his pocket and removed a pack of *Noblesse* cigarettes. He lit one and inhaled deeply.

"So now you have Husseini even more pissed off at Israel then he was before, if that was possible, and now he is clamoring for revenge. For his part, Linehan promised to deliver a *game changer*. So when our Sudanese spy suddenly appears on the scene in D.C., you know something is definitely in the works. But your snatch and grab goes south and your target ends up *DOA* in public. Now you're lost, no one to interrogate and no idea what Linehan is supposed to be passing along to the Iranians."

"For what it's worth, we had our own mole in Damascus feeding us information about Husseini's movements," Yoni said, taking a drag on the cigarette. "But everything went silent about ten days ago, after the op went south. If they are still communicating, then they have figured out something new."

"*For what it's worth*, the money transfer was to get one of Linehan's Saudi friend's nephew a pass out of harm's way. The little shit got banished to Syria to fight for the rebels. Linehan's offer came *after* you guys blew Shateri to hell. Then you go and get Dawai killed."

Yoni took another drag on the cigarette and flicked it into the air, watching as it sailed through the air and landed in the water with a hiss.

"First the failed assassination attempt, then the death of the courier. Have you ever thought that maybe, on one of those sleepless nights that come after a near death experience, Husseini thinks it was actually Linehan that double crossed him? I would even surmise that he might just want to exact a little revenge," Maguire asked.

"That would be *really* bad news for Linehan," Yoni replied with a chuckle.

"That would be a gross fucking *understatement*," Maguire said, as he stood up and faced the man. "But I'm not sure just how flippant I would be about it. Oh, by the way, in case you *didn't* hear, the secretary of state cancelled on tomorrow's dinner, but don't worry, everything's all good, she's sending her deputy in her place instead."

"Linehan?" Yoni exclaimed.

"You can almost cut the irony with a knife, can't you?" Maguire asked. "You guys put Linehan in the cross hairs, and now he's going to be sitting inches away from your protectee tomorrow night."

"My God," Yoni replied, as the significance of what Maguire had just told him sunk in.

"You might want to head back inside now," Maguire said casually. "Probably rethink that whole security threat assessment for tomorrow night's event."

"Will you increase your protective detail?"

"I've already spoken to Rich; he was calling the C.O. of Intel. We will bring in extra post standers and I'll make sure ESU doubles up on their personnel as well."

"Thank you, Paddy," Yoni replied.

"Don't thank me till everyone is back in their limo's tomorrow night," Maguire replied. "And just for the record, next time, I would appreciate the full story up front."

Yoni nodded in agreement.

"Otherwise, I'm sending Tel Aviv the bill for the jet fuel."

"Understood," Yoni said, as he stood up. "Now I have to go re-write everything. *Shalom*, Paddy."

"*Shalom*, Yoni," Maguire said, as he headed back to the car. "You're going to need it."

Maguire walked up the pathway as Yoni cut across the backyard, sprinting toward the main house. As he opened the Mustang's door, he paused and glanced up at a window on the second floor, watching as the curtains quickly closed. He climbed in and pulled away.

Once he was back on Montauk Highway, he removed his cell phone and placed a call to Mother.

"What do you have for me?" Maguire asked when the man answered.

"Nothing," Mother replied. "There's been zero chatter relative to our issue. I don't know if that is good or bad."

"Well, I just pissed in the Israeli's cereal," Maguire replied. "I told them that Linehan was being dispatched to have dinner with the FM tomorrow night. With the possibility that Husseini might target him, they are in a panic."

"That would be a helluva mess," Mother replied.

"Oh, and I got some even better news today. Our missing GDL exec isn't missing anymore."

"Why don't I get the feeling that it was a joyous reunion?"

"That's because he was found *swimming with the fishes* in Maryland."

"It sounds like someone is getting rid of their baggage."

"That's what I'm thinking. Without anyone to tie him to the file, we've got nothing. You might want to reach out to Mays and let him know that we are going to the U.S. Attorney on Monday morning. We'll present him with what we do know about his involvement with freeing our terrorist. We can't afford to leave him in play any longer."

"I'll call him after we get off the phone and give him the heads up," Mother said. "What are you going to do now?"

"Try to figure out how to keep him alive until the feds take over."

"Good luck, my son. Call me if you need anything."

"Will do," Maguire said and ended the call.

CHAPTER FIFTY-FIVE

LaGuardia Airport, Call Sign: *Baker*, Queens, N.Y.
Sunday, March 3rd, 2013 – 6:27 p.m.

The landing gear of the United States Air Force C-37B made contact with runway 22, and the plane immediately began to decelerate. Three-quarters of the way down it hooked a right turn and began taxiing over to the non-descript building on the western side of the airport, where the motorcade was staged.

Over the radio earpiece Maguire heard one of the Intel detectives mark Linehan's arrival.

"Falcon Twenty-Two to Falcon Base, we have wheels down at Baker."

Maguire stood next to the Suburban, watching as the aircraft slowly approached them, coming to a stop about fifty feet away from the main body of the motorcade. The aircraft was impressive, with the fuselage painted white on top and a powder blue on the bottom. The words *United States of America* were stenciled along the body and an American flag painted on the tail. The casual observer might easily confuse it for a *miniature* version of the President's plane, Air Force One. In fact, the C-37B was sometimes used by the President, when runways at certain locations did not allow for the use of the larger VC-25.

As Maguire watched, a portable ladder was positioned next to the plane. Two black Suburbans from the Diplomatic Security Service then pulled alongside the plane. Moments later the cabin door opened and Deputy Secretary of State G. Prescott Linehan emerged. He walked down the stairs where he was greeted by several diplomats, including the U.S. Ambassador to the United Nations. After several brief conversations and some hand shaking, he watched Linehan make his way toward one of the Suburbans.

"Showtime, folks," he said, as he climbed up into his vehicle.

Initially, the special agent in charge of Linehan's security detail was taken aback by the increase in the size of the motorcade. Maguire had managed to assuage his fears by explaining that the Department was now taking a more proactive approach to protection. Under the prior administration, manpower for the units that handled protection had been cut so severely, that many details were being staffed by detectives from the Detective Bureau, who had received only the minimum level of training in dignitary protection. Maguire explained that the new administration was changing that, part of which meant more secure motorcade packages.

The lead car from the Port Authority Police began to move out, followed by several motorcycles, a marked Highway Patrol car, an unmarked car from the Intelligence Division and then the two Suburbans from the State Department.

The first Suburban held Linehan and the agents from his security detail. In the second vehicle were members of the State Department's Tactical Support Team. Immediately behind them was an ESU Counter Assault Team, followed by the vehicle Maguire was riding in. Two marked Highway Patrol units brought up the rear.

The motorcade snaked its way through the back roads of LaGuardia until it reached the end of the airport property. When they turned onto Ditmars Boulevard, the PAPD car pulled over and Highway took the lead. Traffic was being held up by motorcycle units, which allowed the motorcade to proceed along Astoria Boulevard until it merged onto the Grand Central Parkway.

From there the motorcade made its way west along the GCP, taking the RFK Triborough Bridge over the East River, as it headed toward midtown Manhattan. Once it cleared the bridge, they headed south along the FDR Drive, exiting at the East 49th Street exit and making its way westbound. A minute later the motorcade turned right onto Park Avenue, then left onto East 50th Street, and pulled into the arrival well at the Waldorf Astoria Hotel, where the *Friends of Israel* banquet was being held.

Mike Torres pulled the Suburban to the sidewalk, adjacent to the side entrance for the hotel.

"C'mon Amanda," Maguire said, opening the SUV's door. "Let's go see how the other half lives."

Outside, it was well choreographed chaos. At the corners, uniformed cops held back gawkers who had gathered for a moment to gaze *into* the *fish bowl*. They craned their necks to catch a glimpse of whoever might have been inside the vehicles. Was it the President or perhaps a celebrity? As soon as they were told it was neither, most simply scoffed and moved along. On the other side of the street, protestors, both for and against, had gathered on the sidewalk. Cops tried to not only contain them within the protest area, but also from getting into confrontations with one another. The media dutifully set-up their cameras to cover them, hoping for *something* to happen. Many a news career was made by simply being in the right place at the right time and recording the *inhumanity* of an event for the voyeuristic public.

One group held up signs decrying the United States involvement in the Middle East. Some even named the countries that the protestors were interested in, such as Afghanistan, Egypt, Iraq, and Syria, to name a few. Vocal protestors called for the end of the Israel occupation of Gaza, and for the lifting of all embargos. Some went so far as to chant slogans such as "Death to Israel" and a few other *colorful* ones that *wouldn't* make the ten o'clock news. On another corner, a much smaller pro U.S. / Israel contingent was staged, but no one in the media seemed interested in them.

Inside the fish bowl, it was a different story. At the arrival site, the officers assigned to the security detail moved into pre-designated positions. They didn't care who was arriving, what they were interested in were the people gathered around. They watched the crowd, looking for the one person who could potentially pose a threat to the protectee.

The TST and ESU officers dismounted from their vehicles, clad in tactical uniforms and carrying M-4 assault weapons. They provided a visible deterrent to those considering mounting an attack against the protectee. Should one occur, the ESU officers would be responsible for providing the counter attack, while the TST officers would provide immediate close support as the detail agents removed the protectee out of harm's way.

As Maguire and Massi approached the side entrance, a detective from the Intelligence Division gave them a quick once over; identifying the security pin that each was wearing on their lapels, and stood to the side. The pins they were wearing provided full access for the event, while other pins only allow designated access for specific areas. Designs and colors were changed by venue, to provide enhanced security, yet easy identification. The wrong pin at the wrong place could potentially have dire consequences for the wearer.

"Evening, sir," the detective said, as he stepped aside, allowing them access to the hotel door.

"Evening, detective," Maguire replied. "Has everything been running smooth so far?"

"Yes, sir," the man replied. "No problems on the perimeter."

"Good to know," Maguire said, as they went through the door.

A few steps inside and they met up with Linehan's detail, which had just entered through the well entrance. They joined up, following them as they made their way through the hotel to the holding room for the event. When they arrived there, James spotted Rich talking to Yoni.

"Is there anything going on?" Maguire asked as he joined the two men.

"No," Rich replied. "Everything seems to be quiet. I had the C.O. of Intel double up on all the security postings. They also did background checks on everyone working the event tonight. Everything came up clean."

He handed Maguire several sheets of paper containing the names of the hotel employees working tonight along with a seating chart of attendees. Maguire glanced at them and handed them off to Massi.

"What about the State guys? Any questions about the increased security?"

"No," Rich replied. "I just told them that with everything going on in the world, I decided to increase the protection levels just for my peace of mind."

"How about things on your end, Yoni?" Maguire asked.

"Nothing," the man replied. "No chatter at all."

"So I guess we just wait and pray," Maguire replied.

"Not like we haven't been there before," Rich said.

The men just nodded their heads; they knew exactly what Rich meant.

Dignitary protection was a nasty business. You trained for every possible scenario, because you never knew what could happen. You had to be right one hundred percent of the time. If you did your job, everyone, including the protectee, went home at the end of the day. The protectee would go on to their next event, while those who had been in attendance would go home and tell everyone about how they met *so-and-so*. But for those who did security, it was finally a time to breath. To be thankful that it didn't happen on *your* watch.

Ninety-nine percent of the time most protection details went off without a hitch. Not that the threat *wasn't* present, but the would-be attackers had decided that either security was just too tight, or that it wasn't worth the risk of getting caught. Not everyone was so committed to their cause that they would risk arrest or worse.

Unfortunately, there was that one percent who were. It was that person who gave those who did protection sleepless nights. The one person who didn't set off any bells or whistles in the Intel community, the so-called *lone wolf* threat. Someone who decides one day, that they will kill another person.

A prime example of such a person would be John Hinckley Jr. who, on March 30th, 1981, attempted to assassinate President Ronald Reagan. Hinckley was motivated by an unrequited love with movie actress Jodie Foster. He even went so far as to move to New Haven, Connecticut while she was attending Yale University. When it became evident that his stalking was ineffectual, Hinckley formulated a plan that he felt would impress her. He would assassinate the president. He believed that by doing this he would become a *historical figure* himself and he would then be her *equal*. Hinckley began trailing President Jimmy Carter from state to state, managing to get within feet of the President at one event.

However, Hinckley was arrested at an airport in Nashville, Tennessee, on a firearms charge before he could act. After Carter left office, he then directed his attention to President Reagan.

After the shooting Hinckley wrote that what he did was "the greatest love offering in the history of the world" and was upset that Foster did not reciprocate his love.

On the day of the shooting, Hinckley stood outside the Washington Hilton Hotel among a group of bystanders. In what has been called a "colossal mistake" the Secret Service allowed this unscreened group to get within fifteen feet of the President's limousine. Hinckley hadn't crossed any intelligence *radars*, so he wasn't one of the known threats that the Secret Service routinely monitors. Every officer that does dignitary protection scans the crowd before them, hoping that there isn't another Hinckley among them.

Rich looked down at his watch and checked the time.

"Hey, look at the bright side," he said. "In an hour, we can all breath again."

"Well, it's about time for the guests of honor to go onstage with one another," Yoni said. "Hopefully they will play nice until this is all over."

"You have fun with that," Maguire said with a laugh. "My post standing days are long over."

"Alright, well I'm going to head inside with McMasters," Rich replied.

"Ok, I'm going down to the cafeteria and grab something to eat," Maguire said. "Call me if you need anything."

Maguire and Massi headed off toward the elevator and took it down to the basement.

"You ever eat here, Amanda?"

"No, Commissioner, first time," she replied.

"Nice place and top notch food."

The two of them walked inside the cafeteria and got their food. As they headed over to a table toward the back, two uniformed officers got up and began gathering their trays.

"At ease, gentlemen," Maguire said, setting his tray down on the table. "Even a commissioner needs to eat once in a while, but that doesn't mean that you have to stop."

The two cops smiled nervously and sat back down. Even so, they finished their meal rather quickly and took their leave. Maguire watched as they headed for the exit.

"That's the thing I don't get, Amanda. It wasn't so long ago that I was just another *flat-foot* cop down here, eating my meal like the rest. Now, I feel as if I'm a pariah when I walk into a place."

"No, Commissioner, you're not a *pariah*," Massi said. "I know it's sometimes easy to feel that way, but don't. There is a lot of respect for you out there. They know who you are, what you have done. I think that, for some of them at least, that itself can be a little bit intimidating."

"Ya think so?" Maguire asked as he stabbed at a piece of steak with his fork.

"I've talked to a lot of people and I haven't heard anyone say a bad thing about you or Commissioner Stargold. In fact, everyone I've spoken to says that they are excited about the changes you have begun to implement. The problem is that, for too many years, a majority of the department hierarchy treated the rank and file cops like they were *beneath* them. Give them some time, they'll come around."

"You're starting to sound like my press agent now, Amanda."

"Boss, if I didn't respect you, I would have put in for a transfer back in January. I know Mike and the rest of the detail feel the same way."

"Then I better keep you guys on my good side," Maguire replied with a smile. "Speaking of which, you might want to text him and see if he wants something to eat."

"When doesn't Mike like to eat?"

"That's true," Maguire said.

As Maguire ate his dinner, Amanda sent Torres a text message. A minute later she received a reply.

"Anything, what the hell is that supposed to mean?" she replied. "Why is it that men can never answer a simple question?"

"Because," Maguire said, looking up from his plate.

"Because, why?"

"Just, because, Amanda. Don't over think it."

"Sheesh, now you sound like my dad."

"Must be a wise man," Maguire said with a smile.

"I'm going to take Mr. *Anything* a salad and a bottle of water. I'm sure that next time, he'll tell me what he really wants. You want me to wait till you're finished?"

"Nah, I'm reasonably sure I'll be safe here," Maguire said. "Hey, before you go, let me see those papers I gave you earlier. I need something to do when I eat. I'll meet you upstairs in a few minutes."

Massi handed him the papers and then went to select the blandest food she could possibly find, for her recalcitrant partner.

As Maguire ate, he began scanning the lists. The first was an event staff listing. It covered everyone from cooks in the kitchen to the waiters and waitresses who would be working the banquet room, along with everyone in between. Most of them were long time employees of the hotel and were veterans of the background check process. There were a few new ones listed, but everyone had passed. Next he turned his attention to the attendee seating chart list.

The banquet was a screened event, meaning everyone had gone through a magnetometer. He looked over the table, reading off the names of everyone that was close to the dais. The protectees this evening had been seated last, and they came from a holding room behind the dais. This meant that their interaction with the majority of the room would be limited. They would also leave before everyone else, allowing them time to gather together for handshakes and photo ops with some of the big money donors. For some it would be a chance to pitch an idea, share their concerns about a topic, or just get a photo to hang on their office wall.

The list was a veritable *who's who* of the rich and famous. The odds were pretty slim that an attempt would be made by a Hollywood film producer, or a Fortune 500 CEO.

Slim, Maguire thought, *but not necessarily impossible*.

That was the thing about protection, *no one* was above suspicion. Protectees were human beings and as such were prone to crossing paths with the wrong person. Business deals went bad, politics could be cutthroat, blackmail was a hug motivator and sometimes it just came down to sex with the wrong person. At the end of the day you just ever knew who to trust, and that sometimes even included the protectee's own spouse.

Still, the notables were usually classified as a low threat. That being said, Maguire began scanning the unknowns, those who had *purchased* their seats because of fund raising efforts in support of a particular person or their cause. On this night there were a lot of them. You had those who had been part of McMasters' campaign, not to mention those who were staunch supporters of Israel.

Most of the names were unknown to Maguire, but what mattered to him was their proximity to the dais. Of those listed, several had red check marks next to their names indicating that they were part of the VIP pool who would be participating in the backstage *meet and greet* afterward. He began reading off their names.

Bruce Engeling

Stewart Hamby

Amy Frye

Dave Maasea

Tami Preston

Larry Wilson

Jodee Culberson

Brenda Melodia

"Hey, Commissioner," a female voice called out.

Maguire looked up to see Nikki Ryan approaching him.

"And here I thought I had a good hiding spot," Maguire said with a laugh. "Pull up a chair, Nikki."

"I ran into Amanda Massi and she said you were down here."

"I didn't know that you two knew each other?"

"Yeah, we worked together in the four-five," Ryan replied. "She was in my squad."

"Small world," he replied. "So what brings you out here?"

"The commissioner wanted CTB to be present, just in case. I had the rotation."

"Are you alone?"

"Nah, I got a dozen detectives with me," she replied. "Six inside and six outside."

"I guess it's always better to have them available and hope you don't need them," Maguire said.

"I didn't mean to interrupt your dinner."

"No," he replied. "I'm actually done. I'm going to head upstairs."

Maguire folded the papers and placed them into his jacket pocket. He then grabbed the tray, emptying it in the trash and the two of them headed outside.

"So anything going on in the wonderful world of counter-terrorism?"

"Not locally, thank God," she replied. "Most of our focus has been on monitoring overseas stuff. There's more than enough to worry about over there."

"The level of ignorance toward the conflicts in the Middle East has always amazed me," Maguire replied.

"How so?" Ryan asked.

"Most folks you talk to have no clue about what is going on over there. In a country that is a little more than two hundred years old, they have a difficult time understanding that conflict has been raging in that part of the world for more than three millennia."

"History is not a subject that most people willingly embrace," Ryan replied.

"True, but that is the very reason for the old saying 'Those who fail to learn from history are doomed to repeat it'. Too often politicians think that these issues can be resolved, without ever really knowing what those *issues* are in the first place."

"You and I both know politicians rarely ever solve anything," she said. "Look at the League of Nations."

"It's like everything else," he replied "Theoretically it works, up until you add-in the human component. Then greed, power and national interests take over, and theory goes right out the window."

"So how do you fix it?"

"Honestly, Nikki, I don't think we do. Call me a jaded old cynic, but I think we just keep repeating the cycle until we lack the capacity to fight anymore or God comes back. I think this penchant for self-destruction runs too deep in us to change."

"Wow, remind me never to come to you for a pick-me-up," Ryan said with a laugh.

"I've seen too much in my life to be overly optimistic about the human condition," he said, as they stepped outside.

It had begun to rain, and they stood under the awning listening to it bounce off the metal.

"Oh, I almost forgot the reason I came looking for you," Ryan said. "You asked me to look into any chatter coming from the Sudanese."

"Did you hear something?"

"I don't know," she replied. "There has been almost no traffic at all, aside from the usual 'hi dear mom, hi my sweet son' stuff. Then one of my guys handed me this. I almost lumped it in with the other stuff, but I figured I should run it by you just in case."

She held out a piece of paper on which a sentence was written in ink. Maguire took it and read it.

(Ibrahim) - can you host a friend of mine, (Esma Dava)? - He will be coming in for the feast and leaving immediately after.

"What do you think?"

"Hard to say," Maguire replied. "Sometimes you can have an invitation and it's a code for something evil; and other times the *invitation* is really just an invitation. The trick is trying to put all the clues together in time."

"My analyst tried to cross check, but he didn't find anything pertaining to a feast. Not officially or locally, so whatever it is remains unclear."

"What about the name?" Maguire asked.

"Nothing concrete," Ryan replied. "It's phonetic spelling. Not much to go on as far as Ibrahim. Esma might be Turkish, but there is nothing in the database, either with that spelling or anything close."

"It sounds vaguely familiar to me, but I'm drawing a blank as to why."

Maguire looked down at his watch, things were about to wrap up inside.

"Another fifteen minutes and we won't have to worry," he said.

"I better go catch up with my people," Ryan said.

"Mind if I keep this?" Maguire asked, holding up the paper.

"Not at all.

Thanks, Nikki. I'll catch up with you later."

Maguire made his way over to the Suburban as Ryan headed up the block, toward Park Avenue.

"Everything alright, Boss?" Torres asked.

"Yeah, you enjoy your salad?"

"You know she didn't even bring me dressing?" the man replied.

"I'd file that away for the next time she asks," Maguire said. "Always have an answer."

"Women," Torres said.

"Hell hath no fury," Maguire said, as he turned on the interior light.

Something didn't feel right, but he couldn't put a finger on it. It wasn't anything tangible, just a nagging feeling he couldn't seem to shake. He pulled the papers from his pocket and began going through them again. He read the top of the page: *Friends of Israel Banquet Seating Chart*.

Banquet, he thought. *A banquet can be a feast.*

He removed the piece of paper Ryan had given him. Esma Dava.

He pulled out his cell phone and did an internet search.

Esma Dava – No Record Found. Did you mean: *Esma Data, Esma Dado, Aesma Daeva?*

He clicked on the latter and waited for the results to come. As he waited, he scrolled through the seating chart again.

Suddenly the phone chirped and he glanced down at the results. Most of the search results were for a music group, except for one. This search indicated a hit for mythology. He clicked on it as he began reading the chart again. A moment later he spotted the name: Dave Maasea, table four.

He began marking off the letters on Ryan's paper.

Sonofabitch, he thought. *It's an anagram.*

Just then the phone chirped again and he looked down at the results.

In the Persian mythology, Aesma Daeva, also known as madness and fury, is the demon of lust and anger, wrath and revenge. He is the personification of violence, a lover of conflict and war.

Maguire looked at the name and spotted the red check mark.

"Falcon Two to all Falcon units," Maguire said into the radio transmitter. "Code red at David, table four. Lock down the hall."

"Let's go," he shouted to Torres and Massi, as he bolted from the Suburban.

CHAPTER FIFTY-SIX

Waldorf Astoria Hotel, Call Sign: *David*, Manhattan, N.Y.
Sunday, March 3rd, 2013 – 7:53 p.m.

The man known as Dave Maasea sat at the table, playing with the cake on the plate in front of him, with his fork. In his lap sat the white cloth napkin, underneath which he had slipped the steak knife that his dinner had been served with.

He stared at the man seated on the dais with a mixture of anger and loathing. It was because of *him* that he was here tonight and, *Allah* willing, neither would leave the room alive.

The man's real name was Farrokh Abbasi. His family linage could be traced back to the *Abbasid Caliphate*, the third of the Islamic caliphates. The Abbasid Caliphate was founded by the descendants of *Muhammad's* youngest uncle in 750 a.d. They ruled until 1519, when power was formally transferred to the Ottoman Empire.

Farrokh had grown up in the northern Iranian city of Qarchak, a suburb of Tehran. He came from a prominent academic family. His father, whom he idolized, was a noted PhD in nuclear physics and his mother was a professor of Iranian studies. Farrokh had decided to follow in his father's footsteps and in 1998 he attended Tehran's Imam Hussein University. It was there that he was first approached by a member of the Iranian Revolutionary Guard and recruited. At the time he didn't think much of it, until he was offered a new career in the United States. He would be set up as a businessman, with all the appropriate creature comforts. His sole responsibility was to assimilate into the western culture and wait for further direction. A *sleeper*, as they benignly put it.

Abbasi had acclimated himself well in his new homeland. While he was attending the university, he had changed his major from physics to engineering. After he had graduated, they relocated him and provided enough funding to start an engineering firm specializing in capital improvements and design optimization. After a few years he had grown the firm into a highly successful business. In doing so, he had grown to enjoy the trappings of his new life.

Then, in November 2010, he received word that his father and mother had been injured in an apparent assassination attempt. This occurred on the same day that another nuclear scientist was killed in a separate assassination attempt. The attacks were the most recent on scientists who were identified as being part of Iran's nuclear weapons program. While no one claimed responsibility, all indications were that Israel's Mossad had carried out the attacks.

Farrokh was enraged, but he was instructed to remain in place until further directed. Then about a week ago there was a knock on the door of his Central Park West apartment. The agent who contacted him advised him that his father's health had begun to deteriorate. While nothing was being said publicly, the doctors in Tehran believed it to be the lingering effects of the attempt on his life two years earlier. The prognosis was said to be terminal, a few months at the best.

The agent removed a folder, inside of which was a photograph showing several men.

"This is Moshe Erdan," the agent replied. "He was the Israeli Defense Minister, and the one who our intelligence believes gave Mossad the orders to assassinate your father."

"Where is he now?" Farrokh asked.

"He is coming here. We've gotten word that he will be attending an event at the Waldorf Astoria. Nothing can change your father's condition, but you may obtain justice for him."

"What do you want me to do?"

"Get close to him and kill him," the agent replied.

"How?"

"He will be attending a benefit, you are a businessman. You will contact the hosts and make a large donation. Say that you want to do your part to aid Israel. They will be ecstatic to have you as a benefactor and will of course want to introduce you to the foreign minister during a photo op. At dinner, you'll take the knife they bring you and hide it. Then, when it is time for the meeting, you'll plunge it into his chest and kill the vile creature."

"What about security? How will I get away?"

"Jihad is not an easy path, but the *Qur'an* makes it clear: '*You who believe, shall I show you a bargain that will save you from painful punishment? Have faith in God and His Messenger and struggle jihad for His cause with your possessions and your persons that is better for you, if only you knew and He will forgive your sins, admit you into Gardens graced with flowing streams, into pleasant dwellings in the Gardens of Eternity. That is the supreme triumph*'."

Farrokh was pulled back from his thoughts as a sudden flurry of activity gripped the room. Instinctively he knew what was occurring. Somehow, despite all the planning, someone had figured out what was happening. He quickly glanced around the room, watching as security personnel began to flood through the doors. In front of him, more security began to descend upon the dais.

He knew in his head that in a moment they would be coming for him. He owed it to his father to act. Allah willing, he would triumph.

The man jumped from his seat, the steak knife gripped in his right hand, and rushed toward the stage.

"*Allahu Akbar!*" he screamed. "*Death to Zion!*"

The fourth table sat to the immediate left of the dais, in the same path the security personnel had to use to remove their respective protectees. Mayor McMaster had been seated in the center with Deputy Secretary of State Linehan to his immediate right and Israeli Foreign Minister Moshe Erdan to his left.

DSS agents had already succeeded in removing Linehan and the Intel detectives assigned to the Mayor's Detail were just clearing the dais when Abbasi had lunged from his seat. Seeing that they were caught out in the open, one of the members of the Israeli security detail drew his gun as the wild eyed man rushed toward them. Immediately behind him, the others threw the FM to the ground, using their own bodies as a protective shield.

The security officer caught a reflection from the blade of the steak knife and opened fired at near point blank range. The first round struck Abbasi between the 2nd and 3rd ribs, the .40 caliber bullet shattering the sternum and sending bone shards tearing through the man's heart and perforating the left pulmonary artery. Immediately his blood pressure began to drop. The second shot struck the man in the zygomatic bone, just below the left eye. This bullet deflected off the bone, traveling under the skin till it exited at the temple with a devastating exit wound.

While the second bullet caused a tremendous amount of cosmetic damage to the man's face, it was the first that would prove to be lethal. Unfortunately for the security officer, that lethality would come about a half dozen seconds too late.

Even as the life drained from him, his adrenaline fueled momentum carried him forward. At the last moment he brought the knife down, plunging it into the officer's chest, twisting it violently. The two men crashed into the table and then slid to the floor.

Seizing the moment, the remaining members of the security detail scrambled to their feet and physically dragged the FM out of harm's way. All to a cacophony of screaming and crying coming from the shocked attendees, who had just witnessed the brutal attack.

CHAPTER FIFTY-SEVEN

Waldorf Astoria Hotel, Call Sign: *David*, Manhattan, N.Y.
Sunday, March 3rd, 2013 – 7:59 p.m.

Maguire and his security detail rushed into the banquet room with guns drawn as the room erupted into screams.

Immediately ahead of him he glimpsed movement along the dais, watching as several people hurried along the wall in the direction of the holding room. In an instant he recognized the agent bringing up rear security.

Zee!

He forced his eyes away from the woman, fighting the urge to go after her. Instead, he moved forward cautiously, scanning the room for any additional threats. Then he spotted the two bodies that lay crumbled on the floor in front of the dais. As they drew closer, Maguire could see one man lying on top of another. Maguire motioned for Massi and Torres to take up flanking positions as they approached the motionless bodies.

"Handcuffs," Maguire shouted.

Massi reached around to her back, removing the pair she was carrying, and then tossed them to Maguire. He holstered his weapon and grabbed the man's arms. He quickly snapped the handcuffs on, securing his wrists. He pulled the body away, revealing the extent of the damage. Then he looked down and stared into the glassy eyes of Alon Ben Simon, the handle of a knife embedded in his chest.

"Oh fuck," Maguire shouted. "Falcon Two, I have a man down. Get me EMS to the Banquet Room at David, forthwith."

He leaned down to check the man's vitals, but could not feel a pulse.

"*Sonofabitch*," he muttered.

Almost immediately, two FDNY paramedics appeared with a stretcher.

"Make way," one of them shouted as they made their way toward the dais.

Maguire stood up, allowing them to begin treatment.

"He's one of the good guys," Maguire replied. "He doesn't die *here*."

One of them looked up to argue that it appeared that the man was already dead, and then realized who was giving the order.

"Yes, sir."

They hoisted the limp body onto the gurney. One began working on him, while the other strapped him in for transport.

Plainclothes detectives and uniformed officers began to swarm into the room, and outside Maguire could hear the sound of sirens as the respective motorcades screamed away from the location.

An Intel detective approached Maguire.

"You with the hotel detail?" Maguire asked.

"Yes, Commissioner," the man replied. "Falcon Twelve."

"This guy is from the Israeli security detail, ride with him to the hospital. It doesn't look good. Don't let him out of your sight until we can get a hold of one of their people to relieve you. Notify Falcon base that you're acting on my orders and have them reach out to the Israelis."

"Yes, sir."

He saw a uniformed sergeant approaching the dais and waived him over.

"Sarge, grab some guys and establish a perimeter. Secure this until the detectives and Crime Scene Unit get done. The guy EMS is treating is an Israeli security officer from the detail; they're taking him to Bellevue. Secure his weapon. The cuffs on this guy are mine, have someone verify that he is in fact the perp. If anyone gives you any shit, refer them to me."

"Yes, sir," the sergeant replied and radioed for some cops to join him.

In his ear piece Maguire could hear the chaotic radio calls going out as the motorcades raced away from the scene.

"Falcon Two to Falcon One, on the air?"

"Falcon One," he heard Rich reply. "What's your location?"

"Falcon One, I'm in the Banquet Room. We have a problem."

"I'm with Osprey," he said, referring to Linehan's call sign. "We're heading to Baker, call my cell."

Maguire reached into his pocket and grabbed the phone as he made his way toward the holding room.

"Amanda, come with me. Mike, stay here and be my rep. I want the C.O. of Manhattan South Detectives here *yesterday*. I want to know who this guy was ASAP, and whether we have to worry about any other secondary threats."

"I'll take care of it, Boss," Torres said.

Maguire and Massi made their way to the empty holding room behind the banquet hall. Maguire pulled out the cell phone and called Rich.

"What the fuck happened back there?" Rich said when he answered.

"Looks like the perp jumped the gun, and rushed the stage. He's dead and, barring a miracle, so is one of the Israeli's."

"Oh shit," Rich replied. "Do we know who?"

"Alon Ben Simon," Maguire said solemnly. "Judging from the scene he stepped out in front to cover the team while they removed the FM and shot the perp, but the guy ended up stabbing him in the chest. He had no vitals that I could find."

"How did you know something was wrong?"

"Bumper sticker version is I ran into Nikki Ryan and she got some vague Sudanese electronic traffic. A name popped and when I was going down the table list I realized that it was an anagram for one of the VIP table holders. I figured the attack was planned for the photo op."

"You think the attack was directed at the FM?"

"At this point it is hard to tell," Maguire said. "But if I had to fathom a guess I would have to say yes."

"Handle things for me on that end," Rich replied. "Let me know as soon as you know something definitive. Everyone's going to want to know what the hell is going on."

"Will do," Maguire said and ended the call.

"Amanda, get Operations on the phone. Tell them I'm here supervising the scene and using the holding room as the Temporary Headquarters. Also tell them I want DCPI here forthwith, to handle the press."

"You got it, Boss."

"Commissioner!"

Maguire turned around to see Torres rush into the room.

"What do you have Mike?"

Torres approached him holding a pair of latex gloves and a clear plastic security envelope with piece of paper inside.

"Squad guys are here, they found this in the guy's pocket."

"What's that?"

"They say it's a confession. I didn't read it; I figured you would want to."

Torres handed him the gloves, and set the envelope down on one of the tables. Maguire put on the gloves and removed the paper. He opened it up and set it on the table, then began reading.

To the infidels: I am Farrokh Abbasi, although you will know me as Dave Maasea. By this time I will be dead, but so will the Zionist pig that has brought so much death and destruction to my country. I do this to avenge my father, a scientist, who this filthy Jew tried to have murdered in cold blood. The seed of Muhammad will never rest until the entire world is cleansed of the non-believers. Allah willing, I will feast tonight in paradise, for such is the reward for the martyr, while Satan will rejoice for the new arrival I will send to him.

Also, several people said that this was the guy that rushed the stage yelling "Allahu Akbar!" and "Death to Zion!"

"*Sonofabitch*," Maguire said. He pulled out a pen and piece of paper and copied the man's name on it along with a phone number. Then he put the letter back into the envelope.

"Mike give them back the letter and then get Inspector Ryan from CTB on the line at this number. Tell her I want to know who this Farrokh Abbasi is and who the hell he claims the FM tried to kill. Tell her to meet me up here when she gets it."

"You got it," Torres replied and headed back to the main room.

"Ops is notified, Boss. DCPI is already on their way."

"Thanks, Amanda," Maguire said, picking up one of the water bottles that had been staged on the VIP table and taking a drink. "What a cluster fuck, huh?"

"Commissioner Black Cloud has a nice ring to it, wouldn't you say?"

Maguire smiled and raised the bottle in a mock toast.

He reached into his pocket, retrieving the cell phone and called Rich back.

"What do you have?"

"Looks like the hit was on Erdan," Maguire said. "They found a handwritten confession on the guy. Still trying to figure out who he is, but he said his name was Farrokh Abbasi and that he claims Erdan was responsible for an attempt on his father's life."

"Holy shit," Rich replied. "Okay, I'll let DSS know; can you reach out to Yoni and pass that information along to the Israeli's?"

"Calling him next," Maguire replied. "As soon as I know more I will give you a call back."

"Thanks."

Maguire ended the call and immediately dialed Yoni's cell number.

"Paddy?" the man said when he answered.

"Yoni, it looks like the attack was directed at Erdan. Does the name Farrokh Abbasi mean anything to you?"

Maguire heard the man fire off something in rapid fire Hebrew.

"Not Farrokh, but he knows the name Abbasi. He was one of the Iranian scientists working on their nuclear weapons program."

"Well, apparently Farrokh is the son and he blames Erdan for trying to murder his father."

"Shit," Yoni replied. "Where is he now?"

"Dead," Maguire replied. "That's not the only problem."

"What else?"

"Yoni, Alon is dead as well."

"How?"

"Looks like he stepped up to cover the escape route and he shot the guy, but he also took a knife to the chest. They've taken him to Bellevue, but I couldn't find a pulse. I've got an Intel guy with him."

"Thank you, Paddy. I'll have one of my people go there immediately."

"If I hear anything else, I'll let you know," Maguire said. "Watch your six."

"You too, my friend," Yoni replied.

"That goes for Zee as well."

"I'll let her know your concern," he said and hung up the phone."

CHAPTER FIFTY-EIGHT

U.S.A.F. 89th Air Wing C-37B, Call Sign: *SAM60500*
Sunday, March 3rd, 2013 – 9:23 p.m.

"Yes, I understand. Thanks for the information."

"What did they say?" Linehan said to the man seated across from him.

Special Agent in Charge Steve Geske, the head of Linehan's security detail, hung up the phone and turned toward his boss.

"All indications are that it was an attack on Erdan," the man replied.

Linehan stared out the window, gazing down at the lights of Wilmington, Delaware far below them. He breathed a sigh of relief at the news.

"Did they say why?" Linehan asked.

"Revenge, apparently. It seems that Erdan was the one who authorized the Israeli ops, which targeted the Iranian nuclear scientists. One of them turned out to be this man's father."

"The Israelis," Linehan scoffed. "They can never just leave well enough alone, can they? And they wonder why so much of the world deplores them."

"They are an island," Geske replied.

"Yes, they are," he said sarcastically. "However, most of that is of their own choosing. They act as *de facto* masters of the Palestinian population, telling them what they can and cannot do, even going so far as to illegally blockade their ports and borders."

432

"But, sir," Geske said. "Didn't Egypt close their border as well, after Hamas came into power in Palestine?"

Linehan turned to face the man, a look of contempt on his face.

"I wonder," Linehan said with an edge to his voice. "What prestigious school did you attend, that you've mastered the intricacies of Middle Eastern diplomacy?"

"I just meant that…"

"Here is an idea," Linehan said, cutting the man off in mid-sentence. "I'll avoid telling you how to open car doors, and you leave the international diplomacy to the adults? How's that sound?"

"Very well, *sir*," the man said, adding extra emphasis on the latter. "Now, if you'll excuse me, I have to plan for our arrival."

"No, by all means, you're excused," Linehan said with a dismissive waive of his hand.

Geske got up and moved toward the back of the plane where the other members of the security detail were seated. He'd speak with the director of Diplomatic Security tomorrow. He'd been on the detail long enough and he had grown increasingly tired of his pompous ass of a *boss*.

It was one thing to constantly put yourself in harm's way for someone you respected; it was quite another to do it for someone you secretly loathed. He had heard enough grumbling from the other members of the team, who *believed* that Linehan viewed them as nothing more than over glorified door openers, but to hear the words come straight from the jackass's mouth was too much for the man to stomach. He'd prefer a posting back in Pretoria, as opposed to opening the door one more time for this narcissistic little prick.

Linehan leaned over in his seat, glancing back out the window. He felt the subtle change in the plane as it began to descend. He couldn't wait to get home, the strain of recent events were beginning to take its toll on him, both physically as well as mentally.

He needed to reestablish contact with Qassem. He understood the man's desire to keep their contact to a minimum, but he wanted to make sure their relationship was as solid as it had been before. The future appeared to be very bright for him. He believed that he could finally change the course of policy in the Middle East, once and for all.

His recent conversation with that prissy little bitch, *Queen Eliza*, had instilled in him the belief that she would back him for the top seat, once she stepped down. It was clear that she didn't feel as if the administration's foreign policies were being very effective. However, she still possessed enough political clout to make him her anointed replacement. She came from a very well connected political family. No one would dare cross her, for fear of losing their money and their influential votes.

So Linehan had nodded appropriately as she had voiced her *concerns*, even saying the words he knew that she wanted to hear.

That was what diplomacy was about, right? he thought. *Saying what the other side wanted you to say, and then doing what needed to be done behind the scenes*?

He recalled sitting across from her in her office, with all its trappings and finery. She was a pretentious thing, but he also had to admit that she was also politically savvy.

"I can use you, Gideon," she said, using his first name. She knew he didn't like being called by that, and used it anyway. It was how she asserted her authority. "People know you. You're an open book. They know what you think and where you stand. I want to be able to use those ideas and opinions when the time comes."

Linehan just smiled and thanked her for her kind words. The truth was, he would say and do anything to get the top spot. Then he would do what needed to be done to fix the problems in the Middle East once and for all. There was certainly enough time left between elections that he could begin to sway things. Once the momentum was in play, there would be little anyone could do to change it, especially after they saw the success.

Israel was a thorn in the side of American diplomacy. It was eight thousand square miles of problems and heartache. If they didn't have the Jewish problem to contend with, they could focus their attention were it really mattered, on rebuilding American / Arab relations.

It made sense of course. We were losing so much influence in that region, while others were eagerly exploiting it. The United States had become the enemy, only because of her ill-fated decision to support Israel. What did Israel bring to the table? Nothing! We gave her money, weapons, intelligence and what did we get? Headaches!

The current occupant of 1600 Pennsylvania area was a nice enough person, but he was clueless when it came to foreign policy. He allowed others to back him into a corner, supporting this *faux* relationship. The country was in real danger, but it wasn't from the Middle East. No, the threat was much further east, in Russia and China.

Russia and China produced nearly fifteen million barrels of oil a day, yet consumed only about thirteen million, providing them with an oil surplus. In contrast, the United States produced eight million barrels a day, yet consumed eighteen million, leaving us with a deficit of ten million barrels a day.

There was no way that the people's president was going to alienate his tree hugging base, and alternative fuels where proving to be an increasingly bad idea, propped up only by the money that the government seemed willing to spend endlessly on, like a down on his luck Vegas gambler hoping against hope for one more win.

It didn't take a visionary to realize that we needed to pick and choose our friends a bit better. Israel produced less oil than the tiny island nation of Belize. They gave us nothing, except for international pressure and scorn.

Maybe it did take a visionary. Maybe Washington needed someone to show them the cold hard facts. Do we isolate the Middle East, with its collective twenty-five billion barrels of oil production a day, for an impudent friend who makes war with its neighbors and account for just less than four thousand barrels a day? Surely reason must prevail.

Iran produced over four billion barrels of oil a day, yet used less than half of that. If he could convince the administration to set aside their outdated ideology, he could pave the way for a relationship that could open their oil fields. Once the rest of the Arab world saw that the U.S. was being an honest broker in the region, it would alter the course of history. It would be a game changer in American / Arab relationship. Even Israel could benefit, once they were put in their place and not allowed to act like the bully in the sandbox.

Linehan leaned back against the seat, a smug smile growing on his face.

Yes, that's what I am, a visionary, he thought. *History will preserve my actions for all posterity. I will be known as the man who changed how the game was played and brought peace to the Middle East.*

His revelry was cut short as a sharp *bing* filled the cabin, signaling that they were beginning their descent. He was happy that this farce of a trip was over. It was almost annoying that she would send him to a reception for the Israeli's, but sometimes in politics you just had to hold your nose. He'd make a point to reach out to Qassem tomorrow.

A few moments later, the landing gear of the C-37B touched down at Joint Base Andrews, and taxied along to the hanger where the cars waited for them.

As Linehan made his way over to the waiting Suburban, he stopped and turned toward Geske.

"Steve, listen, I'm sorry for that scene up there," he said. "The last minute trip, that incident back in New York, just has my nerves fried. I shouldn't have snapped like that."

"Completely understandable, sir," Geske replied.

"It's late, we're all tired, and missing our families. Why don't you cut the detail in half? You and the others go home early get some rest."

"No, it's alright," Geske replied.

"It's nearly two hours to the house and back," Linehan said with a frown. "Then everyone has to go back to their homes. Let them go early, it's an order."

"Yes, sir" Geske said.

As Linehan headed to the waiting vehicle, Geske circled his finger and gathered up the detail to inform them as to what was going on.

Linehan was reading a briefing that had been delivered to him when Geske got into the front passenger seat of the Suburban.

"What happened?" Linehan asked.

"I gave one of the other agents my seat," Geske replied. "I wouldn't have felt right. Lead from the front."

"Suit yourself," Linehan replied, then went back to his reading.

Geske nodded to the driver and the Suburban pulled away. As they cleared the main gate, the driver looked over at Geske.

"Echo," Geske replied.

The driver went straight as the follow-up Suburban turned right, heading for Pennsylvania Avenue.

They had six, pre-designated routes they would choose from. Whoever was in charge of the detail would make the call. It threw an element of surprise into the mix and would force anyone who was watching to either guess as to which one they were taking or cover all six. In addition, if at any point Geske felt the need, he could call out a new route and they would redirect the motorcade.

Being that it was Sunday evening and they were traveling solo, he selected the longer and more commercial route. It would add another twenty minutes to the trip, but Geske felt that it warranted it. Still, the vehicle blended in nicely with the rest of the traffic, so it made him feel a bit better in regards to traveling light. They made their way south along Route 5, through Camp Springs and Clinton.

The cell phone on the seat next to Linehan began chirping and he leaned over and picked it up.

"Yes, madam Secretary," he said when he answered.

"Gideon, are you alright?" Eliza Cook asked.

"Yes, I am," he replied. "But thank you for asking."

"It's been pandemonium here as they have sorted through it all," she said. "What can you tell me?"

"Not much I am afraid," Linehan replied. "All I recall is that we were just about to head to the room set-up for the meet and greet, when I was suddenly ushered out rather alarmingly by my security detail. Then I heard screams from behind me and then they raced me back to the motorcade and took off."

"How dreadful," she replied.

"Yes," Linehan said. "While we were in-flight I was informed that they apparently believe that it was directed against Erdan."

"Yes, that's what my security people informed me as well."

"Once again this reiterates the need for Israel to scale back their aggression toward their neighbors. You can't operate in a vacuum. If they believed that they could just assassinate Iranian scientists and that there would be no retribution, well it speaks volumes as to the level of their naiveté."

"We can discuss this later," Cook said. "I just wanted to make sure you were alright."

"Positively fine," he said. "Just looking forward to a good night's sleep."

"I would imagine so. I'll see you in the office tomorrow. We can talk about it then. Good night, Gideon."

"Good night, madam Secretary," he said and ended the call.

He closed the briefing folder and turned off the interior light. He felt very tired, as if the weight of everything that had transpired had suddenly come crashing down upon him.

What you need is a nice glass of wine and a good night's sleep, he thought.

A short time later the Suburban turned off onto Accokeek Road and headed west. The topography quickly changed, from commercial businesses to residential homes that dotted the lush wooded landscape.

Linehan had maintained a home in this rural section of Maryland for the last fifteen years. His wife, Anne, was not as fond of public service as he was, nor did she share his penchant for foreign travel. Which was just as well, he didn't need her sticking her nose into his affairs.

Once they had passed Indian Head Highway, the driver began navigating the back roads as they made their way to the house that sat on five acres of isolated land on the banks of the Potomac River.

As the vehicle came around a particularly sharp bend in the road, the driver suddenly slammed on the breaks.

"What the hell?" Linehan called out. "What's going on?"

"Threat!" Geske called out.

The SUV began going in reverse as Linehan looked out the windshield. He could make out a car, off the side of the road, and the body of a woman lay sprawled in the street.

"Wait, stop," Linehan said.

"No," Geske replied.

"That's an order," Linehan said angrily. "That woman needs help."

"It could be a trap," Geske said, turning in his seat to face Linehan.

"And she could be dead," Linehan replied. "Stop this car immediately. We are not savages, Mr. Geske."

The driver looked at Geske who nodded. The vehicle came to a stop.

"Go back and check on her," Linehan instructed.

The vehicle moved forward cautiously, stopping thirty feet away.

"Wait here," Geske said. "Lock the doors. The first sign something doesn't look right, you get the hell out of here."

"Yes, sir" the driver said nervously.

Geske removed the MP-5 machine gun from the floor mounted cradle and exited the vehicle. He scanned the area for any threats as he cautiously approached the motionless body. As he drew closer he could see that there was a large amount of blood pooling on the road beneath the woman. He reached down; brushing away the woman's long brown hair, then pressed his fingers to her neck and felt for a pulse.

There was none.

He moved forward, toward the car, checking to see if there was anyone else inside. The small green sedan was half in the road and half off. One headlight was still operating, and it lit up the scene in, highlighting the vehicles crumpled engine compartment that was resting against a large tree. The driver's side door was ajar and he peaked inside.

ANDREW G. NELSON

It was empty.

Geske turned around and headed back toward the woman. He made a slicing motion across his neck indicating she was dead, and then held his hand to his ear so that the driver would know to call it in.

He stared down at the pool of blood that was beginning to coagulate beneath the woman's head.

Sad, he thought. *Someone's wife, girlfriend or daughter was never coming home.*

He looked back at the car, then back at the woman. The engine compartment was mangled, but the windshield was still intact.

How'd she sustain that much blood loss? he wondered.

Geske reached down and gently rolled her to the side. Most of the right side of the woman's face was missing. Geske looked at the back of her head and now saw the entry wound. She'd been shot.

He stood up, panic gripping his body as he began to frantically wave at the driver who was too busy trying to find a radio channel he could transmit on. Suddenly a shot rang out and he felt a burning sensation in his chest as his body began to fall forward.

The driver keyed on the shot and glanced up. As he watched Geske's body falling forward, immediately his instincts kicked in. He dropped the shifter into reverse and slammed on the gas.

While the response time, for the man to *see* the threat and take action, was only a fraction of a second, their fate had been sealed minutes before when the vehicle had first come to a stop.

442

A dark figure emerged from the other side of the road and raised the RPG-7 into a firing position and pulled the trigger. At only fifty meters away, it took the anti-armor warhead less than one third of a second to cover the distance. Far more quickly than the vehicle itself could actually accelerate.

The PG-7VR HEAT warhead easily penetrated the front passenger door. It was a tandem charge explosive designed to take out vehicles with reactive armor. It had seen use in the Iraq war where it had been successfully used against the M-1 Abrams tank. In this case it was clearly overkill, but the person firing the weapon was not about to take any chances.

The small precursor charge at the tip of the rocket detonated as it entered the vehicle, taking out the armor. With the armor in this particular section of the vehicle now rendered useless, it was no longer able to protect the occupants against the much larger, and more powerful, shaped charge, which followed immediately behind. The main charge then detonated in the unprotected part of the SUV as it vainly tried to retreat. The vehicle exploded in a brilliant explosion, its momentum helping to lift it up off the pavement and sent it hurtling back into the tree line. By the time it landed, the two occupants of the vehicle had been completely incinerated.

Special Agent in Charge Steve Geske lay on the cold, damp roadway, and stared at the burning hulk of the Suburban. He tried to move, to get to his feet, in some vain attempt to rescue the men, whom he knew were already dead, but he couldn't.

It had been chilly when they landed at Andrews, but it didn't seem so bad now. Aside from the burning vehicle at the edge of the roadway, it was actually pretty serene. He gazed up into the night sky, at the billions of stars that cut a swath across the darkness of space, like diamonds sprinkled along a black sand beach. It seemed so peaceful. If he listened closely, he could almost hear the rush of the waves along the shoreline.

It occurred to him that his body was already beginning to shut down, as the blood continued to stream out of the exit wound in his chest.

It was such a pity that this sense of serenity would come at the end of his life, he thought.

Suddenly his view was blocked by a dark shadow. He fought to focus his eyes on it, to make out who this person was. Were they friend or foe?

As the coldness gripped his body, the futility of it all struck him and he smiled, just as the .40 caliber bullet tore through his skull, bringing his life to an end.

CHAPTER FIFTY-NINE

Falls Church City, Loudon County, Virginia
Sunday, March 3rd, 2013 – 11:13 p.m.

Eliza Cook sat up in bed, reading the notes she had taken earlier, during her meeting up at Camp David. It had been an emotionally draining day for her.

In her younger days she would have enjoyed the verbal jousting that had taken place. Back then she had the ability to end most arguments with just her pretty smile, or a tantalizing peak of exposed skin. Neither of which she had ever been hesitant to use, even now, if the conditions merited it. However, there were moments when she just wished that she could be in the company of mature adults from time to time.

All too often, she felt almost like a referee in the middle of some heavyweight fight. At times it seemed as if the Israeli prime minister was going to go ballistic, while the president appeared almost bored, glancing at his watch as if he had some other pressing matter to handle or another place to be.

The prime minister had originally requested the meeting months earlier, but each time the president had canceled due to an unforeseen scheduling conflict. Finally, he had forced the president's hand by arranging to meet with a bipartisan group of senators and congressmen in order to advise them on the deteriorating conditions in Syria.

Now that the two men were together in the same room, it appeared as if the unrest in the Middle East wasn't the only thing about to explode.

The situation in Syria was worsening by the day, with all-out war ravaging the cities of Aleppo, in the north, and Damascus, in the south. A fact which caused a lot of distress in Israel, due to the latter's proximity to the Israeli territory in the Golan Heights.

The prime minister warned that the rebellion was being hijacked by *outsiders*, which threatened to change the dynamics of the civil war being fought. He claimed that a new threat was emerging within the ranks of the Free Syrian Army, one with direct ties to global terrorism. The president argued that the Israelis were notorious at finding monsters hiding behind every door and that they often caused more problems, by overreacting, then they ever solved.

While the battle of wills raged on, each of their respective security details exchanged nervous glances as they wondered if they would have to separate the two men.

Cook laid the papers in her lap and removed her reading glasses. She closed her eyes, as she recalled the most heated exchange between them.

"*Abu Bakr al-Baghdadi!*" the Prime Minister screamed at one point. "Surely you know his name."

"Please, don't start on the whole Islamic State of Iraq nonsense again," the President replied. "I thought we were long past that nonsense. They're decimated and fleeing."

"I'm not sure what those sycophants, that you surround yourself with, are telling you, but I assure you they are not decimated. In fact, they are gaining momentum under al-Baghdadi and the ISI is moving into Syria."

"Of course they are," the President replied sarcastically. "Let's be honest, isn't this just another *bogeyman* for you to chase, Ben? I mean, when does it end?"

"You might have gotten elected by people who were willing to believe that you would 'heal the planet,' but the truth is you have no clue as to what you are doing. You think that by smiling that charming smile of yours, and making dismissive statements, that the whole problem in the Middle East will just fade away. You think you understand it better than those of us who have lived through it, because you read about it in one of your books."

"*Ayman al-Zawahiri* is running things for Al Qaeda. If there was going to be a push into Syria, we would have known about it."

"Are you a serious? Al-Baghdadi does not care what al-Zawahiri says," the Prime Minister replied. His tone had taken on one of exasperation, like a parent trying to explain to their child that something was bad for them, for the hundredth time.

"He is moving beyond ISI, he has much greater aspirations that include spreading his version of Islam. Our intelligence indicates that he is forming a new group. Al-Baghdadi wants to take over Iraq and the Levant."

"The what?" the President asked.

"The Levant, the Eastern Mediterranean. It's the area that comprises Syria, Lebanon, Jordan, Cyprus, Southern Turkey, Palestine, and Israel."

The President let out a laugh.

"Why am I not surprised? *Another* threat to Israel," the President said, pulling out his wallet. "Hey, Ben, why don't I just give you my nuclear code card here? Then you can just wipe out everyone that you think is a *threat* to you."

"Go ahead and make jokes, but mark my words. If the United States does not take action to keep terrorist organizations from joining up with the Free Syrian Army, the consequences will be dire."

"And where is this ragtag group going to get the ability to do this?"

"He is already receiving financial backing from Saudi Arabia and Qatar," the Prime Minister replied. "There are also large numbers of fighters that are joining him each day, including many Sunni's in Iraq who are disenfranchised with the government in Baghdad."

"That's not my fault," the President replied defensively. "I didn't even want to be in Iraq."

"You do realize that you are the President of the United States, don't you? No one forced you to take this job and you don't get to whine about things not being your fault. If you think something is broken, you fix it; you don't talk about how you didn't break it."

Just then there was a knock at the door and a woman peeked inside.

"Mr. President, your party is waiting for you down at the helipad."

"Oh, thanks, Julie," he said, standing up. "Hey, Ben, I hate to cut this short, but something's come up and I have to fly back down to D.C. Secretary Cook will be happy to discuss your concerns and what's happening in Syria. I am sure that between the three of us we can figure out a solution to this vexing problem."

And with that he was gone.

"Where is he going?" the Prime Minister asked with a surprised look, as he stared at the door the president had just left through.

"With the warm weather today, I would think that he decided to go down and play a round of golf at Andrews."

"Is he kidding?"

"Oh, trust me, he never kids about golf," Cook replied, sounding a bit exasperated.

"Eliza, this is serious, I don't think he realizes what is happening in Syria."

"No, I don't either," Cook replied. "The sad thing is that nothing you or I say is going to change that."

The Prime Minister stood up and walked over to the window, staring out at the Marine Corps helicopter that was waiting to whisk the president away for an afternoon of golf.

"The people he believes are his friends," the man said, "are the very ones that are supplying al-Baghdadi with money and recruits. They shake his hand and then stab him in the back when he turns around. He is either too stupid or incompetent to realize what is going on."

"He has a different world view then we do," Cook said.

"Different world view? He has *no* world view! You and I understand that the world can be a vile and reprehensible place. He thinks he can charm people into seeing things his way. It's going to blow up on him, and when it does, I'm not sure *we* will be able to undo the damage."

"What are you proposing?"

"I'm not proposing anything, Eliza. When he returns from his *play date*, let him know that Israel *will* protect itself, with or without backing from the United States."

449

"You know that the United States has always supported Israel, Mr. Prime Minister."

"Yes, I do," the man replied. "*Has always* does not mean the same as *will always*. I don't trust him, and I cannot count on him to be proactive, so we will."

"What does that mean?"

"Eliza, you and I both know that Assad has chemical weapons and, if he feels that he is being backed into a wall, he *will* use them. He is also getting help from the Iranians. If we don't do something soon, we will miss out on an opportunity to get rid of him. I also will not allow those chemical weapons to get in the hands of Hezbollah."

"What will you do?" Cook asked.

"We will back the rebels, and we will strike at Assad whenever our security demands it. But you have to make him realize that if the United States does not act soon, there will be an influx of radical foreign fighters joining the rebels. The rebels will use them, because they need to, but as their numbers grow, they will hijack the rebellion. Then your disengaged president will have to decide whether to back a rebellion, filled with radical jihadists who hate the United States, or a dictator with chemical weapons, who is a state sponsor of terrorism."

Cook rubbed at her weary eyes. The Israeli prime minister had been right. The *Presidential Daily Briefing* reports were filled with the same information, yet he seemed unable, or unwilling, to accept it.

He'd run his last campaign on slogans, successfully promoting how he had decimated the enemy. Yet now, all indications pointed to the fact that they were not only *not decimated*, but actually stronger and more active than before. The problem was that his ego would not allow him to admit when he was wrong.

She knew that something had to change. She felt like she was trapped on a sinking ship. Her adult life had been spent pursuing politics in one form or another. Each position she held was successively more important, grooming her for the future. Even her marriage was by design, allowing Cook to gain influence and notoriety in the *right circles*.

She would be damned if she was going to allow someone as completely unqualified as *him* to derail her future. It had taken some time, but she had been able to plant her *seed's* in all the right places. Whispers had been growing about her leaving, and, while she had vehemently denied them publicly, privately she lamented that she was growing tired of having to be the face of the president's foreign policy, spinning it when it inevitably failed.

It had been a lot of work, but she had gained the sympathy of the necessary people. They viewed her as a faithful member, putting the party above her personal needs. Each had promised her their support, when the time came.

Now there was only one thing that remained.

She put her glasses back on and continued reading her notes. She made an entry in the column to schedule a private meeting with the director of the Central Intelligence Agency. She wanted a briefing on al-Baghdadi and the CIA's assessment as to the long term threat he may pose.

The phone on the night table began to vibrate. She reached over, picking it up and answered it.

"Hello?"

"It's done," the man replied.

"Excellent," she replied. "Enjoy your trip back to New York. I'll be in touch soon."

Cook ended the call and laid the phone back down on the night table.

The sleeping figure beside her began to stir.

"Who was that?" the man said groggily.

"No one you know, darling," she replied. "Just business."

"For crying out loud, Eliza, can't they call during *normal* business hours?"

Cook laid the papers down on her lap and glared at her husband.

"You had better learn to deal with it, Harry, or you'll find yourself sleeping on the couch in the White House. So let me get back to work, or you can start getting used to that new sleeping arrangement *now*."

Harry rolled over with a huff.

Men, she thought. *They were quite the pain at times, but they all had their role to play, even those like Gideon Prescott Linehan.*

CHAPTER SIXTY

1 Police Plaza, Manhattan, N.Y.
Monday, March 4th, 2013 – 7:04 a.m.

"Morning," Maguire said, as he walked into Rich's office and took a seat.

"Hey, did you hear about Linehan?" Rich asked.

"Yeah, I got a call from Silverman on the way in," he replied. "I guess they had a plan 'B'."

"You don't think we missed anything, do you?"

"No," James replied. "We did everything we could. It was a perfectly executed bait and switch. You feint in one direction, then, while everyone is rushing that way, you cut back and hit where you intended."

"Man that had to be a mess," Rich said. "They said that the vehicle was blown off the road."

"It had to be something heavy duty. My guess is an RPG. Apparently the Iranians have a ton of that stuff, and it wouldn't have been hard to get it into the country."

"Makes you feel all secure, doesn't it?" Rich asked.

"It's harder for us to cross the border into another country, then it is for them to cross over the border into ours. There is no point in denying the facts."

"So now what?"

"Now, nothing," Maguire replied. "Unless we can resurrect some bodies, we've hit the proverbial dead end."

"Doesn't that strike you as being extremely convenient?"

"You know full well my rocky relationship with coincidence," Maguire replied. "However, unless Qassem Husseini suddenly has a *come to Jesus moment*, I'm pretty much out of folks to interrogate."

"You hear anything back from the Bureau guys about Pope?"

"Silverman heard back from his contact," Maguire said. "It looks like everything at Pope's place was professionally scrubbed."

"You think they were looking for the original?"

"Either that or someone was making sure there was nothing linking this back to them."

"I take it you don't think this was the Iranians?" Rich asked getting up from his seat. "Coffee?"

"No and yes," Maguire said.

Rich walked over to the credenza and poured two cups of coffee. He returned back to the desk, handing Maguire one of the cups.

"Thanks," James said, taking a sip.

"I'm almost afraid to ask, but who's at the top of your list?"

"I think this all originates out of Foggy Bottom, with Linehan. I don't think he was actually involved in the dirty work. He didn't strike me as the *super-secret squirrel* type, so I have to assume that he had someone working for him."

"Someone inside State?"

"That would be my guess," Maguire replied. "And if I am right, they've gone way beyond stealing national secrets, all the way up to murder."

"You mean Pope?"

"I'd say Pope at the minimum and most likely the medical examiner."

"You think Dean Oliver is involved?"

"I *know* Dean Oliver is involved," Maguire replied. "The only question that remains is to what extent."

"So now what?"

"Like I said, there's no one left for us to interrogate. Like it or not, this investigative train left our station. I say we call up the head of the Bureau; tell him we need to have a chat. We give him what we know and let them run with it. It's their bailiwick now."

"I never thought I would ever hear you recommend giving up a case," Rich said. "Let alone giving it up to the feds."

"You know I don't like the idea, but I'll be the first one to admit when something is above my pay grade. That doesn't mean I have to like it."

"I guess that means we are maturing?"

"Speak for yourself," Maguire said with a laugh. "Besides, it's not like we are going to be able to access any State Department records.

"What do you think is going to happen to Omar bin Salman?"

"I think the Vegas odds on him aren't too good right now," Maguire replied. "I certainly wouldn't be taking any car rides with him."

"It's a helluva world we live in, isn't it?" Rich asked.

"You know, I'd like to say that this is something that is unique to this time and this generation, but it's not," Maguire replied. "History is littered with examples of man's inhumanity to man. Whether it is driven by lust, money, power or religion, we are not above taking the life of another person, in order to succeed."

"You know what I have to say to that, don't you?" Rich asked.

"Here's to job security," Maguire said, holding up his coffee mug in a mock toast.

"Amen to that, brother!"

CHAPTER SIXTY-ONE

The White House, Washington, D.C.
Monday, March 4th, 2013 – 9:01 a.m.

The President and Secretary of State Cook walked along the portico that led from the Oval Office and stepped out into the Rose Garden, where a podium had been set-up.

The dark mood of the hastily called press conference was in stark contrast to the bright sunlit day. The President strode up to the microphone, while Eliza Cook stood off to his left, a somber look on her face.

As she listened, the President went on about the tragedy that had occurred the night before. He referred to those who had killed Deputy Secretary of State G. Prescott Linehan, as cold and ruthless criminals, who had the blood of an honest, and true, patriot on their hands. He also spoke about how he had tasked the attorney general with tracking down and prosecuting those individuals who were behind the cowardly attack. He said that every American could count on the unrelenting and tireless efforts of the Department of Justice in seeking to bring those responsible before a court of law.

She had to hand it to him, he was an eloquent speaker. It was one of the skills that he had used so effectively when he had run for office. That was, as long as he had something to read the equally eloquent words from. Eliza wondered just how far he would have come without the aid of his beloved teleprompter.

Sadly, the words spewing forth from his mouth held little meaning. His Justice Department would vigorously investigate, *ad nauseam*, until the matter either fell off the collective radar of the media or the administration got lucky and they could drop a hellfire missile on a convoy in the middle of the desert. Either way it was viewed as a win/win. The President liked it that way. It wasn't as complicated as actually doing something.

In a way it made sense. He'd never actually accomplished anything substantive in his career. She'd watched him time and again piss away opportunities to take meaningful action on matters. If he had simply not done it because of political pressure, or a desire to not offend his supporters, she could have appreciated it. But it wasn't a matter of simply being wishy-washy; he just didn't seem to care.

Everything about him was about achieving bigger and better things, and once he had obtained it, he moved on to the next. The only problem with being the President of the United States was that there wasn't anything *after* that. He seemed to have figured that out and just put himself on cruise control.

Eliza had been called many things in her career, but *disconnected* was never one of them. She was feared and admired by those of both parties, which said a lot. Secretary of State had been her consolation prize, for throwing her backing to the president after he had won the party nod. At the time she had been a governor, and many had thought that she should run for office. But Eliza Cook was a very savvy politician. She knew that the momentum was on his side, and opted to take a step back. If he succeeded, she'd be praised for putting the party's needs ahead of her own; if he failed, they'd turn to her for salvation. The way things looked now, it was most likely going to be the latter.

The President concluded his speech and turned toward her. Eliza stepped up to the microphone, and stared out at the media that had assembled before them. As they waited patiently for her to speak, she kept her silence. She was a master of the art of public speaking, knowing the exact moment that she had her audience's undivided attention. The fact that the cameras absolutely adored her certainly didn't hurt.

At forty-eight she wasn't the youngest secretary of state, that distinction belonged to Edmund Randolph, who was forty when he served under President George Washington. But even in the drab business suit she had selected for the occasion, she was sure she had much better curves and assets then Mr. Randolph every enjoyed. Cook had the good looks to go along with her keen intellect and she had learned very early on that in politics, you used everything at your disposal to get ahead. She had, and, God willing, she would continue to do so.

Behind her, the President looked at his Chief of Staff, Ron Bellamy, who grimaced and shrugged his shoulders. They were beginning to wonder what they should do when, much to their relief, Eliza began speaking. Unfortunately for them, what came next was much worse than the silence.

"My fellow Americans," she began. "Today I gather with you to mourn the loss of four brave Americans, including my dear friend, Gideon Prescott Linehan, who were assassinated in cold blood."

She paused again, letting the words hang in the air.

"To be sure, the attack on my deputy was an act of terrorism, but it was also an attack on the heart of America."

"This country has long stood as a protector of the weak and a champion for the oppressed. Sadly, there are many around the world who would like to see us fall, so that they might pray on the poor souls we have always protected. That is what I was taught, and that is what I have always believed."

She stared out at the throng of reporters. They were hanging on each and every word, their cameras and microphones recording every second for future posterity. They thought they were summoned to cover just another speech about another tragedy. Little did they know they were about to cover history.

"For much too long this great nation has sacrificed our best and brightest, whether in the battlefields of the Middle East, or on some rural country road in Maryland. For each one of them, the price was too high, but it is a price we as American's are willing to pay, in order to see liberty and justice go forth throughout the world."

"Last night was a reminder that the war is not *over there*, that our enemies are not relegated to some dark cave, in some cold mountain, half a world away. No, our enemies are here, and they are bringing with them a war that we must fight. We must fight it for ourselves, for our children, but most important for those who have already laid down their lives for us, so that their deaths must never be in vain."

She paused for a moment, allowing a spontaneous round of clapping to emanate from the gallery.

The President's chief of staff walked over to him, whispering in his ear about what was happening. Clearly this was an unscripted moment and no one knew what to do.

Eliza smiled inwardly, she had them now and she knew it.

"Last night America was attacked. It was an attack that saw an innocent young woman brutally gunned down, in order to ambush and assassinated three members of the United States Government. It was a heinous and brutal act that will forever be etched in our history. It is during times like this when American's, young and old, turn to the Nation's Capital looking for answers, and what do we get? The *promise* of a vigorous *investigation*."

The stinging rebuke hung silently in the air for the briefest of time, and was then engulfed in a clamor of cameras clicking, as still photographers all fought to capture the moment.

"Mr. President, this country demands action, not investigations," Cook said, glancing back at the President, who seemed horrified by the sudden outburst directed at him, then back toward the cameras.

"Last night, an act of war was committed against this great nation. The President believes that he can soothe us with yet another promise of a criminal investigation, designed to bring these barbarians to *justice*. I think he has greatly misjudged the American people's idea of justice, as well as my own. For too long I have publicly championed this administrations misguided foreign policy, all while trying to work behind the scenes to improve it. I am sad to admit that I have failed. This administration would rather bury its collective head in the sand and ride out the rest of its days on the golf course. I can no longer accept that. I owe it to you, the American people, to the memory of my late deputy, to all those around the world that look to the United States for leadership and protection, to take a stand for what I believe in."

"This administration, by virtue of their inaction and incompetence, has alienated our friends and emboldened our enemies. They have brought the fight to our doorstep, and all our President can do is talk about bringing them to *court*. This country needs better leadership, but more importantly, this country deserves better leadership. I cannot in good conscience, be a part of the problem that is plaguing this great nation. Therefore, I am tendering my resignation as the Secretary of State, effective at the close of business today."

The crowd of reporters erupted in a hail of questions as Eliza Cook turned and approached the President, who was fighting a losing battle at disguising the anger that now gripped him.

"Do you have any idea as to what you have just done?" the man asked his voice low and seething with rage.

"Yes, I do," Eliza said in a cool and defiant tone. "I've told the world that you were an impotent coward, who has no stomach for a fight."

"I'll..... I'll....." the man stammered, barely containing the fury inside him, which threatened to boil over.

"You'll what? Prove me wrong?" Eliza asked. "We both know that I have bigger balls then you do."

"You are a fucking bitch," he said.

"You're right, I am," she replied. "And I have worked very hard to hone that particular skill."

Ron Bellamy whispered in the President's ear, reminding him that the cameras were still rolling and that maybe they should take this discussion inside.

"You've been outplayed, deal with it," she said. "You spent much too long reading the press clippings about how you were going to win the game, when you should have been actually *playing the game*. Anything you do now will be viewed as weak. If you act aggressively, you'll be universally condemned for having to prove your manhood, but if you don't act, you'll be exactly who I said you were, weak and feckless."

"I'll destroy you."

"You?" Eliza asked incredulously. "My dear, I was playing political hardball while you were a simple rabble rouser, appealing to the weak minded and uneducated of society. If you think I'm intimidated by your threats, you are sadly mistaken. If you think I won't destroy you politically, then you are sadly naïve."

The three of them stood there staring back at one another, only Cook appeared calm and relaxed. She reached into her pocket, removing an envelope, then turned and looked at Bellamy, handing it to him.

"My formal resignation," she replied. "If I were you, Ron, I'd take him inside before the *peanut gallery* behind us starts asking the really tough questions."

Eliza Cook marched off, with her security detail in tow. She headed back into the White House, passing by the Cabinet Room one last time, before she made her way out through the lobby and toward the motorcade that was parked on Executive Avenue, in front of the Old Eisenhower Executive Office Building. As she climbed into the motorcade, she paused for a moment, staring back at the White House, and smiled.

Someday, she thought. *Someday soon.*

As the head of her detail closed the door to the Suburban, he lifted his hand up and spoke into the mic he held discretely in his left hand.

"Eagle is departing Castle, en route to Birds-Eye."

CHAPTER SIXTY-TWO

1 Police Plaza, Manhattan, N.Y.
Monday, March 4th, 2013 – 9:33 a.m.

"Yes, I just saw it," Maguire said.

"What do you make of it?" Melody asked

"Damned if I know," Maguire replied. "I can't remember if there was ever a public *smack down* of the president like this before."

"She's right though."

"Oh, I'm not saying that she is wrong. I just think that we haven't seen the other shoe drop yet."

"You think she's setting herself up for a run?"

"Oh, yeah, without a doubt," Maguire replied. "Eliza Cook has been in politics so long she doesn't know anything else. You don't throw away a cabinet secretary position unless you 'A', plan on actually retiring, or 'B', plan on advancing up the ladder. I don't see her as being the *Heidi Homemaker* type."

"Where do you go from Secretary of State?" Melody asked.

"For her, there is only one spot. If she wanted VP, she could have had that by being a loyal soldier and carrying the party banner. No, I would imagine that she'll parlay this into an all-out run for the presidency."

"You think she can pull it off?"

"It's a gutsy move," Maguire said. "She is going to alienate a segment of her party, but I have to believe the lion's share of them already have buyer's remorse. She could be counting on picking up votes from the other side, by showing that she stood up against the president when it mattered. They might even be willing to overlook some of her *perceived* past indiscretions."

"Well, it certainly was dramatic," Melody replied. "I can't say when the last time a political speech made my jaw drop."

"Sadly, I don't see anything changing in the short term. Cook was right; this administration sees things from a much different position. They think that you can talk to these folks who hate us. It's been my experience that the only thing that talking does is to give them a chance to reload their weapons. Unfortunately, they seem stuck on doing it their way, regardless of whether it is wrong or not. During one of their *talks*, the other side might just manage to get a lucky shot in."

"You mean another 9/11?"

"Yes," Maguire said somberly. "As much as this administration wants to make us believe that we are disliked because of our past politics, the truth is that those who hate us are driven by an ideology that melds religion with a warped world view. It makes no difference to them who sits in the White House; they hate us on a much deeper level, for who we are. Unfortunately, while they target us, our politicians try to blame one another so they can get elected or reelected."

"Politics," Melody said with disgust.

"Oh, it takes a very special breed, my dear."

"On that note, I'm going to delve back into my world. Gen is being a task master as she gets me caught up on all the wonderful things I have missed during my convalescence."

"You go have fun, I'll call you later."

"Ok, are you going to be home on time tonight?"

"Yep, I've got nothing on my plate so I should be home early."

"Ok, cowboy," Melody said. "I love ya."

"Love you too, angel."

Maguire ended the call and laid the cell phone down on the desk. He powered up his laptop and, while it was starting, he got up to refill his coffee mug. For the first time in weeks he actually had a quiet morning ahead of him and decided to play catch-up with all the little things that had been left unattended.

He sat down and typed in his password, watching as the desktop icons appeared. He selected the one for his private email, something he had been remiss in checking lately. Under the circumstances, that was to be expected. He took a sip of coffee and began scanning through them. Most of the early ones were from folks who had heard about Melody and sent their wishes for a speedy recovery. Of course, once the immediate danger to Melody had passed, the usual jokes and banter began anew with some of his former teammates.

There was also an email from Alex who said she was just touching base to see how things were going, and that she thought Melody was a really nice woman and wished the two of them the best. He made a mental note to call her tonight and see how things were going up in Penobscot. It had been good seeing her again; he hadn't realized just how much he had missed her. She was the only partner he had ever felt that he could share everything with and, she always seemed to find a way to make him laugh. He'd always wondered if they could have had more, but he'd never quite gotten that feeling from her.

In the end, he never wanted to risk ruining what they had. Girlfriends were easy to find, a partner like Alex was rare.

Thirty minutes later he had managed to make his way through most of the emails. Finally he got to one from a sender, Kevin Bernard, whom he didn't recognize. It wasn't unusual. Even after leaving the private security field, the news hadn't filtered out to all his old clients and he was still getting referrals.

He clicked on the email and began reading it.

Hi James,

I hope this email finds you well. How is your girlfriend doing?

Sorry that it has taken me so long to contact you, but things have been a bit busy on my end. Then again, from what I have read in the paper, and watched on the television, I am sure you can understand.

I just wanted to let you know that I was doing well. After our last conversation, I decided that I needed a change of scenery. I think for too long I just got in a rut. Once you break outside the box, you can be amazed at what opens up for you.

Take for instance this email. Of course, you don't know anyone named Kevin Bernard. Or maybe you do, I hadn't actually thought about that. If you do, then I am sorry and send you my sincere condolences.

Sadly, Kevin is no longer among the living, so I figured I would avail myself of his computer and send you this little email to bring you up to date. Actually we had a wonderful first dinner together, and he was amazed when I agreed to go home with him. It had been a while, so I figured what the hell. At least he went out with a bang, before he went out for good.

You'd have loved the restaurant I selected. It was one of those upscale places that I guess you frequent now. It's a far cry from your roots, isn't it? I mean, do you ever get tired of the 'pretend' life? Don't you just miss the simple things in life, like picnics out on the bluffs overlooking Corlaer Bay? I know I do.

Oh well, as much as I would like, I guess too much has happened for us to ever go back. It's ironic isn't it, James? What started out as love has ended in this struggle? I have to warn you, Keith was right, one day you'll have to make a choice. It would have been easier for you if it was just him, but will you be able to do it when our time comes?

Don't worry, that's down the road. I'm taking full advantage of my new found freedom. Not that everyone will be thrilled. I imagine Kevin here would have a dissenting opinion. I'll try and keep you updated from time to time on my exploits and adventures. Not enough to hinder my fun, but just enough to keep you intrigued. For now I think I have had enough of the snow and might head out west for some much needed sunshine and a new view of life.

By the way, say hello to your girlfriend for me. I was going to the other night at the restaurant, but I saw that Genevieve was with her and I didn't think that it was the right time. However, I thought you'd appreciate this photo.

Love and kisses, T

Maguire clicked on the file and watched as the image appeared on his screen. It was a blurry cell phone photo of the woman he had once known as Trisha, but he could also make out Melody in the background, sitting at a table. She was laughing, and he could also make out Gen, who was sitting with her back to the camera.

"Jesus Christ," he said, his jaw clinching tightly in anger."

EPILOGUE

Key West, Florida
Saturday, March 9th, 2013 – 5:16 p.m.

Tatiana sat on the small, concrete seat, smoking a cigarette and staring at the large, painted buoy that indicated that it was the southernmost point in the continental United States.

It wasn't actually true.

Florida's official southernmost point was a place known as Ballast Key, which was a privately owned island southwest of Key West. In fact, if she just looked to her right, she could see land that extended much further south. But since this was strictly a photo op for tourists, no one ever bothered with little details like that.

Still, it was a very relaxing place.

She took a drag on the cigarette as she watched the ocean waves come rolling in. She closed her eyes and listened to the sound of the water breaking on the rocks below. In a way it reminded her of her childhood growing up on Lake Champlain. They were good memories, but they were just that, memories.

Times had changed, she had changed.

Tatiana took a final drag and then flicked the cigarette into the air. She watched as it arched upward, passing through the wrought iron gate, just beyond the buoy, and onto the rocks below. She got up, making her way past the tourists, who were lined up to take a photo at the landmark, and headed down South Street. When she reached Duval, she turned and then walked back in the direction of the beach. There was a restaurant on the water that she had taken a particular liking to. With all the hotels in the area, there was always an *interesting* clientele to be found hanging around.

She took a seat on the back deck and ordered a *mojito*, watching as the tourists casually strolled along the sandy beach in front of her.

Tatiana didn't consider herself a tourist. She wasn't here to see the sites. She imagined herself as being like one of the sharks swimming out in the ocean; a tireless predator who was just waiting for the right *bait* to come along.

She reached into her pocket and removed the license she had taken from Kevin Bernard. She hadn't had time to mail it to the mailbox service that she had set-up, in the next town over from the safe house she was using to store her stuff. Keith Banning had a series of them scattered throughout the northeast, each stocked with supplies and money.

He looked much younger in the photo then he had appeared sitting at the restaurant's bar. It hadn't taken much work on her part to get him to buy her drinks and then dinner. She'd told him she was on vacation in New York City, celebrating her divorce. Her friend was supposed to come with her, but had canceled at the last moment. She asked him to take a photo with his cell phone. She said that she wanted to share it on Facebook to show everyone what a great time she was having and what her friend was missing out on.

Once she was sure she had the photo she needed, she suggested that they go someplace quieter to talk. The poor bastard nearly fell out of the chair trying to get up. They went back to his place, and had several more drinks. She played the part of *grateful guest* and let him have his way with her.

It had been awhile since she had been with a man, and she was actually looking forward to it. Unfortunately for her, the man didn't exactly excel in the stamina department. It was over before it ever really started. Between the physical exertion and the copious amounts of alcohol that he had consumed, the man rolled off of her and passed out almost immediately. It was a sleep that he would never awake from. Lying next to the sleeping man, she simply finished what he had begun.

When she was done, she got up and went to the kitchen. She searched the drawers until she found just the right knife, and went back to the bedroom where she slit his throat nearly ear to ear. She drove the knife in, cutting through both the carotid artery and jugular vein that ran along the right side of the man's neck.

She stood back, watching as the torrent of blood quickly saturated the sheets. There was a brief few seconds of gurgling, as the man seemed to struggle, but it subsided very quickly. It had been an incredible rush.

Tatiana had wondered how it would be, her first *anonymous* kill. She wondered if she would hesitate at all, but she hadn't. It didn't help his cause that he had *left her hanging*, so to speak. In a way she felt extremely powerful. She had come into the house holding his fate in her hand. If he had been an amazing lover, there was a chance, slim as it might have been, that he would still be alive.

It was as if she had half the power of God and it made her feel so alive, so powerful. Her victims would never know what awaited them, until she decided their fate.

Would any live? She wondered.

It would certainly be an interesting game.

She thought about leaving a calling card, but dismissed the idea. The way to avoid being caught was to not get cocky. Careless criminals created patterns that could be tracked and analyzed. Then they became prisoners of the state. Smart criminals traveled the country at will, because there was never a pattern to predict where they would strike next.

Anyone who managed to survive their encounter with her wouldn't need to know how close to death they had come. It would suffice enough for her to know that she had seen fit to *spare* them.

Once she was done, she showered and then went out to the couch. It was just after 4:00 a.m. when she awoke. She made herself breakfast and then turned on the man's laptop computer. As she ate, she scrolled through the folders; taking a quick glimpse into the man's life. When she was finished playing the part of *voyeur*, she downloaded the photo from his phone and sent the email to Maguire. She gathered up her stuff, and left the house before the sun came up, disappearing like a ghost into the fog drenched, sleepy suburban street.

Tatiana had watched the news, waiting to see how long it took them to find Bernard. It was Wednesday before she'd heard anything about the man's death. She rightly assumed that they'd tracked down his address through the man's internet provider. Unfortunately for them, it would always be too late. By using that particular method of communication with James, she would always remain one step ahead.

Don't get cocky, she chided herself.

She might have had the upper hand with James, but that didn't mean that there were no risks. He had managed to find her much earlier than she had anticipated. He wasn't a fool and she'd learned a valuable lesson.

When her drink arrived, Tatiana paid the bill and made her way out onto the beach, taking a seat in one of the vacant lounge chairs that sat along the shoreline. She lit up a cigarette and took a drag. It was nearly sunset and the restaurant had turned on the lights, which were strung between the palm trees, creating a festive feel. Despite many of the locals walking around in jackets, she found the evening temps thoroughly delightful. Then again, anything beat the downright frigid temperatures of Maine.

Tatiana took a sip of the mojito, and glanced around, spying a young, dark haired girl checking her out, a few chairs over. She smiled, raising her glass to the girl in a mock toast, and then turned her attention back to the waves that were lapping at the shoreline.

A few moments later, the girl took a seat in the lounge chair next to her.

"Excuse me," the girl said. "Do you have a light?"

Tatiana set the drink down on the small table next to her chair and removed the lighter from her pocket. She leaned over with a smile and lit the girl's cigarette.

"Thank you,....." the girl said.

"Tatiana."

"That's a lovely name."

"Well, thank you," Tatiana replied. "Now you have me at the disadvantage."

"Oh, I'm Hannah, Hannah Kurtz."

"Well, Hannah, I'm very pleased to meet you," Tatiana said.

The girl smiled, then took a drag on the cigarette.

"What brings you to Key West?" Tatiana asked. "Business or pleasure?"

"Both," Hannah replied. "Mostly a change of scenery."

"Ah, I so understand. I came out here for the same reason. I couldn't stand the snow anymore."

"Really? Are you from up north?"

"Yeah, I grew up in the Adirondack Mountains," Tatiana replied. "Most recently I'm from Maine."

"No kidding," Hannah replied. "We're neighbors. I grew up in New Hampshire, on the border of Maine."

"Small world," Tatiana replied, as she eyed the girl up.

She looked young, maybe in her late teens, but she was very pretty. She was wearing an overly tight tee shirt that left very little to the imagination, and a pair of faded denim shorts that could have passed for being painted on.

"Are you old enough to drink, Hannah?"

"Yes I am, Tatiana," Hannah replied with a smile. "I'm also old enough to do a lot of other things as well."

"I doubt that," Tatiana said. "But I'd be a hypocrite if I said I didn't break the rules myself."

Tatiana raised her hand, catching the attention of the waiter.

"Two mojitos, please."

"Yes, ma'am, I'll be right back," the waiter replied, as he turned and walked away.

"Are you by yourself or is someone missing you right now?" Tatiana asked.

"Nope, I'm all by my lonesome," Hannah replied. "I needed a break from home, from love. I figured that this was about as far away as I could get."

"I completely understand," Tatiana replied, taking a drag on her cigarette as she gazed out toward the ocean.

"So what brought you down here?"

"Death," Tatiana said casually. "Of my heart."

"Guy or gal?"

"Both, to be honest."

"Bummer," Hannah said, intrigued by the woman's answer.

"Not really, I prefer to focus on the positives. If that hadn't happened, I wouldn't be sitting here with you, now would I?"

Just then the waiter returned, handing each of the women a glass. Tatiana slipped a twenty to the man with a wink.

Hannah leaned over and tapped her glass against Tatiana's.

"To new *friends*."

"New friends," said Tatiana.

The two women spent the next two hours drinking, while talking about everything and nothing. They laughed and joked like two long lost friends. Finally it was Hannah that broke the proverbial ice.

"You know, Tatiana, you're not my type."

"Really?" she replied. "And what exactly is your *normal* type, Hannah?"

The girl stared out into the blackness of the ocean, pondering the question for the first time. It had been several long months since her life had been thrown into turmoil.

"I don't know," she said, looking back at Tatiana. "I thought I did, but that all changed. Now I look back and I realize that they were nothing. They had no meaning, I had no meaning. We were all just sort of *existing*, I guess. Then something changed, and I realized I was no longer a part of that world anymore."

Tatiana sat up, swinging her legs over the side of the chair, and looked at Hannah.

"You feel as if you're in a foreign country, and you're just a visitor, right? You're watching everyone going about their daily routine like mindless sheep, and all you can do is stare at their apathetic existence."

"Exactly," Hannah replied, sitting up and facing Tatiana. "I have nothing in common with any of them."

"I understand," Tatiana replied. "I feel the same way. I've learned how to deal with it."

"Have you?" Hannah asked. "I want to feel something again. Can you give me that?"

Tatiana leaned over, putting her hand on the back of Hannah's head and pulling her close to her. Their lips met in a soft, gentle kiss, which quickly consumed by a dark, passionate desire that engulfed them.

Tatiana pulled back, staring into the smoldering eyes of the young woman in front of her. She stood up and held out her hand.

"You can come with me, and never feel alone again."

Hannah reached out, taking her hand. She held onto it tightly as she stared at Tatiana.

"Can I trust you?" Hannah asked.

"Yes," Tatiana replied.

"With everything?"

"Yes."

"I have demons," Hannah said.

"We all have demons, Hannah," Tatiana replied.

"But do you ever feel like you're on the verge of going crazy?"

"I was locked away," Tatiana replied. "Left alone for so long, that I had to create the sound of madness in my mind. Just so that I would have something to listen to, other than my own screams."

"I've hurt people."

Tatiana gently pulled at Hannah's hand until she stood up, staring into one another's eyes. The girl was young enough to be her daughter, but that wasn't what she was feeling at that moment. There was a passion inside her that had been awakened, but there was something else, a feeling of a kindred spirit. Something had happened to this girl, and she felt the need to protect her, to take her under her wing.

"Some people need to be hurt."

"You won't hurt me will you, Tatiana?"

"Never."

"I trust you," Hannah said. "Can you teach me to be like you? To be strong?"

"Yes."

Tatiana held her hand and led her down the beach, toward the hotel where she was staying at.

Tomorrow the world would change for the two of them, but tonight they would find solace in each other's arms.

About the Author

Andrew Nelson is a twenty-two year law enforcement veteran and a graduate of the State University of New York. He served twenty years with the New York City Police Department, achieving the rank of sergeant before retiring in 2005. He and his wife have four children and currently reside with their Irish Wolfhound in central Illinois.

He is the author of the James Maguire and Alex Taylor book series'.

For more information please visit:

http://andrewgnelson.blogspot.com/

Like us on Facebook:

https://www.facebook.com/pages/Andrew-Nelson/168310343376572

21663714R00279

Made in the USA
Middletown, DE
07 July 2015